"B[...]nd c[...]
ple[...]ok . . . if you lost
your heart to *The Last of the Mohicans*, then you'll love
Somewhere to Dream."
— Susanna Kearsley, *New York Times* bestselling author

"With fearless realism and flawless prose, Graham reaches
into the minds of her characters and the hearts of her readers
to create one unforgettable story."
—Kaki Warner, national bestselling author

Sound of the Heart

"Captivating and heroic . . . An amazing tale of adventure
and the power of true love." —*Fresh Fiction*

"Beautifully written. The characters had depth, passion, and
they made the tale feel genuine." —*Caffeinated Book Reviewer*

"Sweeping and epic." —*Truly Bookish*

"Another well-crafted, historically accurate novel that is as
much historical fiction as sizzling romance."
—*RT Book Reviews*

"With a rich flair of history and a great deal of romance, readers
will fall in love with Genevieve Graham's second novel, *Sound
of the Heart*. I am definitely looking forward to reading more
from this fantastic author." —*Moonlight Gleam's Bookshelf*

"A gem that really can't be missed." —*Turning The Pages*

continued . . .

Under the Same Sky

"...autiful**l**y written, riveting novel that had me hooked ...n the ope**n**ing sentence. Genevieve Graham is a remark-...ble talent."
—Ma**d**eline Hunter, *New York Times* bestselling author of
The Counterfeit Mistress

"*Under the Same Sky* weaves together the lives of its two pro-tagonists with such skill and poetry it's like entering a dream, one that will leave you both marveling and richly sated."
—Shana Abé, *New York Times* bestselling author of
The Deepest Night

"The type of book that you can get lost in . . . A story that will hold on to you until the last page (and beyond)."
—*A Bookish Affair*

"Absolutely rapturous, full of lush imagery and a quiet, con-fident voice . . . Graham is one to watch for historical romance readers."   —*Historical Novel Review*

"I felt like I was right there, inside the book for every moment from the very first sentence . . . Outstanding work by Genevieve Graham. Stunning, beautiful, *epic*."
—*Bookworm2Bookworm*

"A uniquely crafted love story . . . Readers will wait with bated breath for the sequel."   —*RT Book Reviews*

Somewhere to Dream

GENEVIEVE GRAHAM

B

BERKLEY SENSATION, NEW YORK

THE BERKLEY PUBLISHING GROUP
Published by the Penguin Group
Penguin Group (USA) LLC
375 Hudson Street, New York, New York 10014

USA • Canada • UK • Ireland • Australia • New Zealand • India • South Africa • China

penguin.com

A Penguin Random House Company

SOMEWHERE TO DREAM

A Berkley Sensation Book / published by arrangement with the author

Berkley Sensation Books are published by The Berkley Publishing Group.
BERKLEY SENSATION® is a registered trademark of Penguin Group (USA) LLC.
The "B" design is a trademark of Penguin Group (USA) LLC.

For information, address: The Berkley Publishing Group,
a division of Penguin Group (USA), LLC,
375 Hudson Street, New York, New York 10014.

ISBN: 978-0-425-26557-4

PUBLISHING HISTORY
Berkley Sensation mass-market edition / November 2013

PRINTED IN THE UNITED STATES OF AMERICA

10 9 8 7 6 5 4 3 2 1

Cover art by Gregg Gulbronson.
Cover design by George Long.
Hand lettering by Ron Zinn.
Interior text design by Laura K. Corless.

*To my real life hero, Dwayne,
and our incredible daughters, Emily and Piper*

ACKNOWLEDGEMENTS

When Adelaide Johnson woke me from a sound sleep and whispered that she had her own story to tell, I was as surprised as anyone. In a good way. I'm glad that after everything she'd been through she still wanted to step out of the shadows to share her adventure. Thank you to my editors, Wendy McCurdy and Katherine Pelz, for giving me the opportunity to tell Adelaide's story.

An ongoing thank-you to my literary champion, my agent Jacques de Spoelberch, for being the voice of reason when he's bombarded by my emails, and the velvet hammer when it comes to plot ideas. He's the consummate professional and a legend in the field, and I'm extremely fortunate to be represented by him.

I humbly thank my readers, who surprise me constantly with their enthusiastic support and encouragement. Just knowing that the stories in my head and heart touch yours as well means so much. Yes, I will keep writing. I promise.

Thank you to Ironhead Vann at www.CherokeeByBlood.com for generously sharing his expert knowledge. Any errors in the book regarding the mighty Cherokee are mine, not his.

Thank you to my medical expert—and the woman who literally saved my life—Dr. Terri Staniland, for helping me diagnose the ruptured spleen at the end of the story.

To my long distance mentor and friend, Kaki Warner, for always being there to listen and cheerlead.

And speaking of cheerleading, my mom leads them all,

and has for my whole life. She brought me up with the belief that I could capture that brass ring, and now I'm holding on tight! My friends and family have been amazing, spreading the word, helping a new author succeed in this crazy world of publishing. I wouldn't be here without you all.

When I was thinking about writing this—incredibly, my third novel's acknowledgements!—my husband told me I shouldn't dedicate this book to him. What a sweet but silly thing to suggest. I dedicated the first two books to him because he's my soul mate, the reason I'm able to write what I write, the inspiration for the unshakable, eternal love running through my stories. Nothing has changed about that, so of course this book is dedicated to him. I love you, Dwayne, and I will always be grateful for the support, encouragement, cups of tea, impulsive lunches, and unconditional love you give me. You're my everything.

But I did take his suggestion to heart, and I have decided to include our team of beautiful and brilliant daughters, Emily and Piper, in the dedication. The two of them are growing at an alarming rate, despite the fact that their mother is perpetually locked in her office, tapping on her computer. I love you both so much, and I'm incredibly proud of the compassionate, honourable, loving young women you have become.

Thank you Adelaide and Jesse, Maggie and Andrew, Dougal and Glenna, Janet, Wahyaw, Soquili, and everyone else I've met along this journey. I know you have more adventures to share, and I can hardly wait to write them.

PART 1

Adelaide

CHAPTER 1

The Colour of Dreams

My mother's hair was blond, but it never attained the near snowy white my hair turns in the summertime. Hers was the colour of straw. Like tattered wisps of grass after the autumn chill had stripped the land of any green. And though she loved to comb my hair until it shone, humming songs without words, hers was rarely tended. Like the grass again, dry and brittle, as if it might splinter at the slightest wind. In that way, strange as it might sound, my mother was much like her hair.

On the other extreme, little Ruth's curls bounced with shiny abandon, a perfectly blended white and gold, as if the sun had painted the strands one by one, taking time to choose the exact gold, the exact white. Everything about Ruth bounced and glowed. Ever since that cloudless day of her birth in the summer of 1736, the most difficult thing about Ruth was getting her to sit long enough so mother could comb the tangles from her lively tresses. Even then, her rosebud lips constantly moved, telling stories, singing songs she made up herself, filling the stale air of the room with a light warmer and more illuminating than any candle.

The last time I saw my mother's hair, it blew in a moth-eaten veil over her eyes, their fading blue locked forever open and sightless under a neat black hole. Blood the shade of crimson maple leaves trickled in a thick path down the side of her face, sticking wisps against her cheek and turning them a dark chestnut, more like Maggie's hair.

And when I last saw Ruth, there was no more bouncing. The joy that had lit every part of her had been snuffed out, the soft white curls knotted around eyes red and swollen from tears. She looked like a doll that had been left in the dirt, and I imagine that's how they saw her as they tore her to bits. Nothing but a sweet, helpless rag doll with which they could play then discard.

When the wind brings them back, I blame myself. It can be almost anything—the sharp smell of charred meat over a fire, an evergreen's fragrant cloak. Even the sound of running water can call to mind the voices and smells and sights little girls should never imagine. So I built myself a wall. It is thick and sturdy, able to hold back all the pictures, the sounds, the smells, the pain I can't bear to relive. If thoughts seep through, threatening to weaken my wall's resistance, I immediately plug any holes. I refuse to see any of it ever again.

But the wall itself will always be a reminder of that day. Though I no longer see the evil, I know very well it lurks there, just beyond. I am often left empty while my entire soul is taken up by fighting. And when I lose myself in the pain of it all over again, I know I should have tried harder.

I should have practised. Even in secret, like Maggie did. After all, I always knew the power was there. If I hadn't always been so scared of what might happen, who might find out, what I might do, maybe I could have done something.

But I didn't. I spent my childhood watching Maggie, seeing what her dreams did to her, and vowing never to wake my own hidden secret. It was enough that I knew it was there.

My secret wasn't exactly like my sister's. Our messages

came in dreams, but unlike Maggie, I could walk away from them when I was awake, ignore their existence. I had that choice, and I took it because I was too afraid.

When they came as nightmares, I fled. From an early age, I taught myself to burst from the monstrous images when they became too real. A useful skill for me, without question. A selfish one, perhaps. Because by doing this, I never saw the endings to my dreams. And by missing that elemental part of them, I didn't know the inevitable conclusion.

But that was the dilemma. Were the endings inevitable? If so, was it worth forcing myself to stand up to the images, daring to push past the invisible wall that sent me screaming to the surface? If I had seen the ending, could I have changed it, or had that been the only possible outcome anyway?

So I chose to block them out entirely. I avoided the question, as well as any answers that might follow.

Other than that, my life was straightforward. We lived simply, surrounded by little that should frighten a child, yet stepping outside my regular routine—testing the water, so to speak, doing anything I didn't understand—sent me skittering back into the shadows. That fear was intimidating in itself. Simply put, I was afraid of fear. I never understood how Maggie—or, for that matter, how little Ruth—could run into the unknown and embrace it. I ran the opposite way and never let it touch me.

Everything in my life changed that day in the forest. Everything except my fear. That only got worse. So, like I have always done with my nightmares, I blocked it all out. The images, the pain, the knowledge that day had wrought on us was gone for me. Never happened. Because admitting it had happened was too terrifying to consider.

CHAPTER 2

Tsalagi

I do recall waking up at the end of it. The voices of the people around me came and went in confusing melodies, most of them round and reassuring, cut occasionally by clipped guttural syllables. The words meant nothing. I needed to see what was happening; I couldn't stay in the dark, much as it beckoned. The process of opening my eyes was torturous, but I fought my heavy lids until I could make out the shapes and colours looming around me. Forced to keep still by the bruised proof of our nightmare stomped into my face, I said nothing and moved only my eyes.

The light was dim, gold, soothing, and the air was still, whisked occasionally by the passing of a blurred figure. I was indoors, lying beneath a ceiling of smoke-darkened thatch, my aching body cradled by something soft. Faces visited me, peering into my line of sight, dark eyes deep with concern, brows angled with curiosity. I felt tentatively safe, bundled in my cocoon. They hadn't killed us yet, after all. But that could change as quickly as a leaf overturning in a breeze. Because I knew who these people were, these saviours who had flown from the trees, arrows singing.

These soft-spoken people who had tended us, encouraged us to sleep, carried us home.

Tsalagi. My defences were down, crumbled to useless mounds of rock in the back of my mind, so I didn't know if the word had come from that forbidden voice inside me, or if it had been spoken by one of the dark-skinned people gathered around me.

Tsalagi. I knew that word. Our father had used it, spitting it out with disgust.

Tsalagi. Cherokee. People who ate their victims' hearts while they still beat, who peeled back the scalps of white people as easily as if they peeled a pear.

But not us. Not Maggie and me. The Cherokee had leapt to our rescue as if they'd been called, appearing out of nowhere with an obvious goal: to bring us back alive.

I lost track of time in that long, low house. I slept with the aid of their teas, gave in to their healing touch. Growing up, I had learned the healing arts from my mother, but these people knew so much more. If I had been thinking more clearly, I would have learned a lot.

I based the passing of hours, of days, on the coming and going of visitors. Some became familiar, like the girl who seemed the same age as we were, and the two healing women who had first arrived along with the rain of arrows. I began to relax, which was an alien feeling for me. The Cherokee were taking care of Maggie and me as if we were special guests, and it made no sense to fear them. Not yet, anyway.

Fear had served as a useful tool for every one of my sixteen years. No one ever expected poor, timid Adelaide to step out on her own, to venture into the unknown. But the Cherokee didn't know that. As our health improved, they gathered around Maggie and me, chattering, staring, and pointing, occasionally prodding with a curious finger. But though they might have been invasive, not one touch, not one glance was done out of malevolence. Their earth-brown eyes were filled with a childlike fascination at seeing something new and different, and yet their guileless interest seemed tempered, merged with the wisdom of the ancients.

They tended us with the utmost care, healing as much as they could of both our bodies and our hearts.

I was shocked when Maggie revealed her secret to them, and I told her so. Before then, we had never told anyone outside of our family about Maggie's dreams. Our grandmother, who had been burned at the stake for speaking of her own dreams, had passed the gift to Maggie from beyond the grave. So we'd always kept quiet about what Maggie could do with her mind. Selfishly, I feared not only that Maggie would be put to death if she were discovered, but that her persecutors would kill her family as well. Or worse, they might discover Maggie's quiet sister, Adelaide, had her own secrets. The image of flames snapping in a pile of tinder at my feet, crawling up my body with a broiling hunger, kept me quiet. I'd told no one of my selfish fear, but Maggie knew.

"Why would you do that?" I demanded. "Telling them only puts us in danger."

Maggie shook her head. "I don't think so. The feeling here is . . . I don't know." She looked at me, her eyes lit with that strange, dreamy look she sometimes carried. She knew I understood some of what she lived with, though she didn't know how deeply. No one did. Not even me. But she knew she could talk to me about it, if no one else. "Can you hear it, Addy? The wind? How it flows through everyone here, connects them all?"

I shook my head and looked away. I didn't even try to listen. If I'd opened myself up to it, I would have sensed the messages in the breeze. My gift was strong enough for that. But I didn't want to know the messages. My life was complicated enough without throwing in more threats.

"Well, I do," she insisted. "It feels as if someone holds my hands here. As if they believe in me—in *us*, Addy."

Lying in the quiet dimness of the council house those first few days, I had time to think. I came to the conclusion that Maggie's gift had somehow sounded the call that had brought them to our rescue in the woods. These people heard more than just sounds, and I believe they sensed her plea for help. From the beginning, they accepted us as part of the village, teaching us their language and lessons as we became more comfortable with this new world. The women came to Maggie in the mornings, asking about her dreams, wondering how what she'd seen might affect them or their families. I stayed silent in the corner of our house, or in my bed, listening.

Then Grandmother Wah-Li took Maggie under her aged wing. She had been taken to the old woman's house after two days, leaving me to sleep and mend. When she returned to our house, she glowed. She sat with me and held my hands, beaming like the sun.

"It's all right, Addy. We're meant to be here."

"Oh? What does that mean?" The words came out shorter than I'd intended, but she made me nervous with her grand words.

"Addy, don't be angry. And I'm not crazy. But being here means so much. We belong with these people. They'll take care of us. Oh, Addy. I wish I could tell you how wonderful I feel. I met Grandmother Wah-Li, and she is . . ." She hesitated, her sparkling eyes looking skyward as she searched her thoughts. She grinned, then flinched as one of the cuts on her lip split. "She is a magical being. It's as if her spirit is tied to mine. Addy, *I felt her inside my head.*"

I stared at her, lost for words. What did that mean? When I didn't speak, she did, waving her bandaged hands and pacing the room while she talked about what had happened.

"And Addy," she said, coming back to sit in front of me. "She gave me a gift."

"What? Where is it?"

Maggie pointed to her head and grinned. "I can understand their language. She did something to me when she was inside my mind, and now I understand what the people are saying. I'll teach you, and we'll be fine here."

Just like that, Maggie practically became *Tsalagi*.

The Cherokee girl who had visited us throughout the first few days became Maggie's closest friend. I watched in agony as I was replaced. But I couldn't hate the girl, no matter how I tried. She said her name was Kokila, and she was sweet and kind. To be fair, Kokila spent hours with both of us, watching, learning, teaching, chattering in her foreign words. But because of Wah-Li's gift to Maggie, my sister shared her jokes, laughed when she did, followed along, translating as if she'd always known the words. And I watched.

Two days after Maggie met Grandmother Wah-Li, it appeared the old woman decided I'd had enough rest. Kokila told Maggie, "Grandmother Wah-Li wishes to see your sister." And Maggie translated smoothly, but I shook my head. Kokila, her smile warm and friendly, tugged my arm and led me toward the outside. She seemed not to notice my panic. I glanced over my shoulder at my sister, who had turned toward the other women already, not bothered for me at all. Had she forgotten? This would mean stepping into a dark place with strangers. This was something I simply couldn't do.

"Come with me, Maggie," I begged.

"I can't," she told me, and the calm in her voice smoothed her face into a soft smile. "It's you she wants to see."

At her refusal, I felt suddenly exposed. As if someone had peeled off my clothing and stood me in front of a crowd. I was very alone, and I wasn't used to being alone. The one time I had been separated from my sisters—but no. I couldn't think of that. This was nothing like that. Besides, those memories were safely hidden away behind the wall in my mind. Still, my voice shook.

"Please, Maggie? I can't go in there alone."

"Kokila will be with you. You'll be fine." Finally her eyes filled with a familiar reassurance, and she pressed my hand between hers, trying to share her strength. If only she could have. "Go on. Then come back and tell me what happened. I promise you'll feel good about her. It's a new beginning for us, Addy. Don't be afraid."

Ducking reluctantly out of our stuffy house, I followed Kokila across an open space to the council house and stooped through the low door. It was darker inside than where we were living, the space lit only by a pile of glowing embers in the centre of the room. Four women sat by the fire, their faces flickering orange, the shadows of their features giving me an eerie, skull-like impression of vacant spaces. Kokila nodded at me, smiling, then gestured toward the women. But I didn't want to go. It wasn't so much the fear of the unknown that paralyzed me. It was something deeper. Maggie had told them her secret, opened her mind and heart to total strangers. That had been her decision to make, I supposed, but I didn't want to reveal any secrets to these women. My heart raced, and I fought the urge to shove Kokila aside so I could flee into the sunshine.

One of the women muttered something and pointed her crooked finger accusingly at me.

"I'm sorry?" I said. She repeated the odd syllables and her finger drifted, suggesting an empty place on the floor.

Kokila patted my hand as if I were a little girl and gently forced me down. "Sit."

When I was seated, Kokila smiled again, then turned and left without a sound. My ability to breathe went with her. From deep within me rolled a series of tremors, forcing fear through my chest, through my throat, finally through my eyes, where it escaped and slid down my cheeks in hot, revealing tears. It was as if my bones wanted to shake me hard enough so my mind could escape whatever had me frightened.

I stared at the women through the dim light of the house, but the one who had spoken before only smiled. Finally, when no one moved, I took a deep breath of the sage-scented air. My damp hands pressed against my lap as I tried to control the shaking, and I stared down at where they linked. It was the only place I could look, unwilling as I was to meet the intense stares of the women. My heart beat so quickly that I feared it might burst into flames.

As I sat curled into myself, I felt a heavy breath of warm air waft over me, redolent with herbs, tickling like a summer breeze at the top of my head. Except there was no breeze in the stifling building, and I knew that. Regardless, I closed my eyes, feeling soothed, relieved to disappear in the growing warmth. The sensation embraced me, melting into what felt like a whisper-thin vapour on my cheeks, my chin, my neck.

And the air had a voice. Its strange, floating melody caressed my nerves, softening their tension, and though the notes and words seemed familiar, they came from somewhere I'd never been. A sensation of half-remembered lullabies cascaded over me, rolling in waves over my eyelids, my lips, tumbling over my shoulders and settling like an embrace in my chest. My heart slowed. I opened my eyes and stared at my hands. They were still.

I felt no fear.

I looked at the women but only truly saw one of them. She was ancient, with wrinkles crisscrossing deeper wrinkles, her lips folded under where teeth should have been. What was left of her silver hair was only strands, and those were as fine as a baby's. But her eyes were alive, twinkling with youth and wisdom. They questioned, answered, offered, demanded, but expected nothing. She kept her gaze on mine, and I became aware of her actual voice. It was more of a croak than a normal voice, but I listened as she muttered words not meant for me. The other women made small sounds of assent, then, with some effort, roused themselves and followed Kokila's silent exit.

I was alone with Grandmother Wah-Li, except I had never felt less alone. In truth, I felt as if I would never again be alone as long as she existed.

"I am Wah-Li," I heard, and remembered Maggie's stories. *The old woman was inside my head!* Now she was in mine, talking and listening at the same time. "You have nothing to fear from me."

I believed her. My body felt light, almost fluid with relief. I felt absolutely no fear. I didn't remember having ever, in my entire life, experienced that kind of freeing sensation.

"U li helisdi, Oohdeeyuhlee Ageyujah," she said, but her eyes spoke in a language I somehow understood. "Welcome, Shadow Girl. I see you as I saw your sister. You and she are new to our family but have been in my heart for many lifetimes. You do not wish it, but I see your Hidden Power, your *Guhsgaluh Ulaniguhguh*. You and I, we will find it together. It will not be the ugliness you fear."

CHAPTER 3

Moving Onward

I didn't have much choice but to move on, move ahead. The world around me showed no signs of slowing. Maggie stepped right into the Cherokee world without a backward glance, which was how she always did things. I didn't think there'd ever be much to add to my life, since it no longer got either bright or dark after that one eternal day I refused to remember. But I did what I could. I let the Cherokee voices and songs, the smells and sounds of the village, soothe my pains and bind a tentative wrapping over my wounds. I tried to be happy. I tried to understand them and my place among them.

The Cherokee were a generous, loving people. Their world was all about family. The entire tribe was one big family, and now Maggie and I were a part of it. The People lived at peace with Mother Earth, offering prayers of thanks before hunting, before eating, offering songs of praise for just about any event. Their closeness was almost smothering at times, their connections to each other unquestionable and impossible to break, should anyone ever wish to try. Their bond seemed even stronger than familial love. It went blood deep, as if being connected to each other was vital to their existence. Their children laughed together, cried with whichever parents they chose. They were all one.

But they were also a cruel, vicious people. Any hint of threat to their families or to their pride was punished without mercy. When white settlers began multiplying, their farms spreading like a stain across the Keowee Valley, the Cherokee wanted them to go back to their homelands. Of course, the settlers had no intention of leaving. They had discovered a harsh but fertile land where, given a lot of hard work, they might someday prosper. They spoke of sharing with the native people, of staying separate from the Indians yet still reaping the benefits of the land, but it was not to be. The two worlds could never coincide in a state of peace. The white folks considered the Cherokee to be little more than barbarians and treated them as such. The Cherokee saw the settlers as unwanted vermin who showed no respect for Mother Earth and had to be exterminated.

Among the men in the tribe, there were constant grumblings about the whites, complaints hissed through bared teeth as they worked themselves into a froth. The elders held out hope of living in peace with these strange pale people, but the warriors saw the truth. They were adamant: get rid of them before they get rid of us.

They sent out scouts, who studied the timber homes from a distance, watching the comings and goings, learning what they could about the enemy. Every day they crept closer, surrounding the oblivious settlers like coyotes around a dog. Eventually they were spotted, and the white men gathered, raising hysteria levels and planning their defence. When the first rifle shot cracked through the air, it echoed for miles. It also killed a careless Cherokee youth who had been keen on getting as close as he could, answering a dare from his friends. That was when it started, the back-and-forth killings. The Cherokee, given a perfect excuse to release their fury, did exactly that, enthusiastically burning and slaughtering. Once the bloodletting began, the frenzy spread, and fighting wasn't reserved for white people. The strange-looking Choctaw, with their flattened brows, were always spoiling for a fight. They attacked our village frequently, and as a result they were punished accordingly, again and again.

Neither Maggie nor I ever went on any of the raids. Few of the women did. But I saw the warriors return, blood-streaked and burned by gunpowder, eyes gleaming with ghoulish delight as they described the battles. I watched the warriors march captive men back to the village one day after a raid, and I asked Kokila what had become of their families. She told me the women and children were usually left behind in their still-smoking homes, believing their menfolk were as good as dead. The thought reminded me of when my father had died. My mother and sisters and I had been left on our own, faced with the daunting prospect of living without a male provider. I pitied the widows and wondered if their fates might be worse than those of the men. That was my initial thought.

I had been wrong. Had there been any sort of competition regarding who would suffer more, the prize went to the captive men. Some were kept as slaves, treated little better than dogs, but some were doomed to another fate. Sickly green with terror, drenched in sweat and fear, the prisoners were led into the centre of the village. There they were surrounded by shrieking dancers whose painted faces only added to the confusion.

For a few days after that, captives were kept in solitary confinement, fed small bits of food, and ignored, for the most part, by everyone. I understood and hated the reason for this confinement. They wanted their victims to be paralyzed with fear by the time they were punished for their pale-skinned existence. The Cherokees' skill at instilling terror was unmatched. If the captives fell into an uneasy sleep, one of the women dashed in, screeching unintelligible threats, poking their wounded bodies with sticks or slapping their faces with open hands. If anyone dared attempt an escape, they were stripped naked, bound to a pole in the centre of the village, and flogged to the bone for the crime of fearing for their lives.

After the first time, I could never again be witness to the Cherokees' idea of destroying their enemies. The man I saw tortured was old enough to be my father. After two days of near starvation, he was forced to run between two lines of tribespeople, all of whom swung their weapons of choice. They beat him mercilessly, slamming his head with clubs, whipping the backs of his knees so he fell and had to struggle back to his feet. He ran desperately, stumbling toward what he would have prayed was a safe haven.

He survived, but only because it was part of the ritual. The Cherokee believed the greater the torture they inflicted, the greater the honour to their ancestors. They needed their victim to be alive when they tied him to a stake and danced around him, hurling obscenities he couldn't understand, whipping him with branches, using tomahawks to shear skin off his legs and stomach.

The tribe, the people I knew as caring, loving individuals, who had nursed me back to health with the same care a mother would use tending an infant, cheered and sang as the man's fingernails were torn off. When the screams weakened, the warriors were handed long splinters of pine about a foot and a half long. One end was sharpened. The warriors used what was left of the man's tortured body as a target, and when the pieces of wood stuck out of him like quills on all sides, they lit them. The man still breathed as his flesh roasted, his heart still beat as they hacked into him with tomahawks, sliced off his fingers, and held the stumps to the growing flames.

I raced from the village, running as far as I could, afraid to let any of the others witness my reaction. What if they saw my horror? What if they knew my heart bled with the poor soul whose body now spattered and sizzled within the flames? Would I, too, be strapped up and torn to shreds for their entertainment?

Their depravity disgusted me. And through the systematic torture and killing of my own people, the Cherokee proved the white men correct. These kind, loving, healing people were barbarians who revelled in the agony of others.

My white-blond hair and blue eyes tied me to the wretches on the stakes. My new home and friends rooted me here. In truth, I belonged to neither, and that knowledge sharpened my loneliness to a dangerous edge.

And yet when the excitement died down, the dead cut loose and disposed of, life in the village continued as if nothing had happened. The women taught me basket weaving and put me to work sewing. We gathered at the stream for bathing and cleaning clothes, giggling with gossip as we worked. I was treated like a friend, a sister, a daughter. My closest friend was an older woman named Nechama, the village healer. She worked with both Maggie and me, teaching us how to mend the warriors when they returned from raids, how to help a sick child, how to welcome a babe into the world.

She did what she could to ease the agony raging within me, the ache I refused to acknowledge. But that kind of vacant pain could never completely disappear, nor could it be filled, because the missing part of me was my lost sister, little Ruth. Her dancing blue eyes still watched me, like corn cockles bobbing in the breeze. She was there when I fell asleep at night, waiting beyond the council house door, hoping to entice me to play. She watched me eat, stared over my shoulder as I sewed. She possessed every moment of my days, and her absence sucked any hope of happiness from my heart.

I cried every day. Every single day. I cried in the morning, when I remembered her sunrise smile, and every twilight when the sun set on those memories.

I visited Wah-Li every few days. I was no longer afraid of her but still wasn't as enthusiastic about our meetings as Maggie was. Maggie seemed to float when she came from Wah-Li's house. I, on the other hand, went to see her out of duty, not desire. She and I spent hours in the quiet, eyes closed, thinking of nothing. Her mind probed mine, eased open the door I had so tightly locked. I fought back, all the while telling her I was willing to learn. No one argued with the Grandmother. Who was I to refuse her?

But I feared what she said existed within me. No one was supposed to know about what I could do within my mind. I hadn't even let myself understand it. But she had seen it that first day in her council house, within just a few seconds, and she had let me know she believed it was my responsibility to learn and appreciate what I had been given. I had spent my entire sixteen years ignoring whatever my mind wanted to show me, but Wah-Li had spent an eternity learning about the thoughts of others. She worked and worked on me, like a fire under a pot refusing to boil. That was what it felt like. As if all my life my body had simmered with something, pressing against my skin, demanding to be set free. After a while, the flames persist too long, and the bubbles cannot resist rising to the surface.

It took a few weeks of sitting, breathing, opening my mind, and spending hours in pure nothingness with her before anything happened. The only sensation I felt was a strange pressing and kneading as Wah-Li's thoughts massaged mine. Suddenly, everything released; my willpower disintegrated and strengthened at the same moment.

Pictures began to come, their images rippling like water at first, their edges blurred. Nothing like what Maggie had described to me, of course, but perhaps that was because she had always used her gift, and had honed its powers. This was new to me, and completely intimidating. It was as if I had sprouted wings, but I didn't trust them enough to step off the ledge. I clung to Wah-Li's ancient strength as she taught me to chase away the rest of the world and disappear with her. In the darkness where Wah-Li led, when all was quiet, I began to choose my own paths, following images that presented themselves to me like offerings.

But I stepped carefully. Often too carefully. And that was, as usual, my downfall. Every footfall brought terrifying images whose meanings could be unclear, and the sight of them sent panic shooting through my veins. Unable to deal with the terror in my head, I burst from the semi-slumber that I had welcomed in the visions, allowing any possibility of their completion to evaporate harmlessly into the air. If

I dreamed of a fire raging within a council house, I awoke in a sweat and raced to the house, only to discover the fire had been extinguished, the family returned to their meal. When I saw a cougar tracking one of the hunters, I paced the village continuously, dreading the news of his death, then saw the body of the cat hanging on a pole carried between two of the hunters. Apparently, they'd known about him as well. Had I waited, allowed my dreams to finish, I would have known I had nothing to fear. I was my own worst enemy.

In effect, while Maggie's dreams warned the Cherokee, told them everything from the impending weather to where the best hunting would be found, my dreams were mostly useless. Wah-Li continued to encourage me, to placate me when I admitted I believed my dreams were a curse, so I kept up my lessons.

When I was with her, quiet in the dark, my nostrils tingling with the smell of the smoke she constantly drew from her fire, I was braver. Wah-Li didn't see what I saw unless she had her fingers pressed to my temples, but she could sense my panic before it happened. Her ancient voice vibrated like a bowstring, urging me forward, assuring me I hadn't yet received the message and I should stay in the dream a little longer. But my fear ran too deep.

So I knew he was coming before she did, I think. Her seeking fingers were nowhere close when I saw the white warrior with the golden hair, his brown eyes so light they seemed almost yellow. Those eyes carried the piercing malevolence of a wildcat, both hunting and hunted. I sensed the rage in him, felt how his soul had hardened to rock. The white warrior began to take over my dreams almost every time I sat with Wah-Li, and when I followed the angry line of his thoughts, I touched on hate so deep, it burned. And seeing him, I became more afraid than ever.

CHAPTER 4

The Dark Side of Light

Though I averted my eyes from men, for the most part, even I could admit that Soquili was impressive-looking. He stood tall and noble, with strong Cherokee features and dark eyes intent on every word. And he loved Maggie. He loved her with an intensity everyone could see. At the Green Corn Ceremony, I watched from the doorway of my council house as he finally leaned in and she let him kiss her.

Oh, I had cried after that. Because when Maggie opened her heart to a man, any man, that left me alone in my pain. To me, men were still beasts to be feared, avoided whenever possible. After a few months, I could watch them, appreciate their existence, perhaps even speak with one, but to let a man touch me was inconceivable. The Cherokee seemed to understand this and didn't push me toward any contact I might have refused. Soquili spent every minute he could with my sister, right up until the day she left the village.

His brother, Wahyaw, stood by me. If Soquili was impressive, Wahyaw was magnificent. Both were tall, but Wahyaw looked down his straight nose three inches or so when he spoke with his brother. The corded muscles of his biceps were ringed by black tattoos of triangles and wolves, and the lower half of his face was permanently painted the red of poppies. A gold ring adorned his nose, passing straight through, and the lobes of his ears were stretched, dominated by black, cone-shaped earrings. He didn't often wear shirts, and breechclouts were his preferred trousers. Other than the red on his face, any other colour came from the two or three feathers that occasionally dangled from his tuft of spiked black hair. Like the other men, he had no facial hair, and the sides of his head had been plucked clean since childhood.

Wahyaw paced like a wolf. He often appeared unable to sit. If he did, it wasn't long before he lunged to his feet and hunted down whatever was bothering him. Wahyaw was my protector, but he never touched me. With my natural fear of men and his natural dislike of conversation, we didn't speak much. But he came to my side whenever possible, standing sentry if the least threat arose. I came to feel comfortable with him and nervous when I couldn't see his familiar profile. As a gift, I made him a pendant in the Cherokee style, using a beautiful abalone shell. On its surface I carved the triangular pattern of his tattoo. He wore the pendant all the time, occasionally stroking the back of it—though I'm sure he wasn't even aware he was doing it. He was my friend, and I missed him when he wasn't there. I believe it was the same for him.

After three months of this friendship, he stared at me with his usual, unsmiling expression and laid out his plans.

"We shall wed," he declared. "After the next moon."

I stared back, speechless. When I found my voice, it was stronger than I'd expected. "No, we won't."

His eyebrows shot up. He was unused to anyone disagreeing with him. But I shook my head. "I cannot marry anyone, Wahyaw."

He hesitated, showing the first glimmer of uncertainty I'd ever seen in him. "It—it is done. It has been blessed by the Grandmother and the council. After the next moon," he repeated. He turned, paused for a moment as if he wanted to add something, then changed his mind and walked away.

I stared at his back as he loped across the open space.

Marry him? Yes, he was a good man. And yes, he made me feel safe. But marry him? Live alone with a man? Engage . . . engage in the intimacies marriage entailed? Never.

As always, I hid from this new fear. As his words sank in, seeming more unavoidable with every one of my breaths, I fled to the council house and dove under the bearskins covering my sleeping pad. I didn't cry, but I shook so hard the blanket eventually slipped off me. The sun beamed through the hole in the roof, warming the room and bathing it in a warm golden hue, but my fingers were like ice.

It was late in the afternoon, and I was alone in the house. My eyes flicked from wall to wall, searching for something—escape. Then, as if I had called to it, my newfound confidence, so tenderly nurtured by Wah-Li, shoved through the fear. I felt its strength and clung to the possibility that I could deal with this. I would be all right. I would find a way.

Oh, Maggie. If only you were here. I tried to picture her face through my scattered thoughts, in search of her simple brown braids, her intelligent blue eyes, but couldn't find her.

Because Maggie was gone. Over the space of a few months, everything in the world had changed for us. The story is hers to tell, but what I will share here is that in the end it was not Soquili who filled her heart and took her away. At the time, I could have gone with her, started a life with her new family, but I chose instead to stay with Wah-Li, to continue my training. I wasn't ready for the white man's world. I didn't tell her I doubted I ever would be, but I suspect she knew anyway.

I roused myself from my sleeping pad and folded my legs neatly before the fire, sitting tall and dipping a branch of sage into the flames. It sizzled when it caught, and I waved the fragrant smoke around my head, filling the air with the scent of calm. The tip burned orange when I set it back down, and its thin line of smoke rose straight up, then curled and dissolved as the breeze caught it. I closed my eyes, and with each deep breath, I became more acutely aware of individual parts of my body. My mind eased my pains, softened my fears, focused my thoughts. This bringing of peace was what I had been taught over and over again, by the same woman who had just sentenced me to a marriage I couldn't even begin to contemplate.

I had never before tried to summon dreams without Wah-Li's help, and I wasn't sure I'd be able to sink low enough in my mind to reach the images I knew waited for me. If I could, I wasn't sure what I'd do with them once I'd found them. But in my desperate state of mind, diving into my dreams seemed the only distraction strong enough to help me through this.

At first I saw nothing in the silence. Then the nothing evolved, becoming the side of a house, cracked and weathered as our family's had been. At my feet, poking between my pale toes, quivered tickling blades of grass.

The silence rose, giving shape to raised voices: men in the heat of battle.

I followed the line of the wall until I reached the corner, then peered around the edge. Men ran, screamed, fought in faraway fury on the other side of a field. I could see no faces, but the colour of their skin and hair, the manner of their dress, was obvious. There were perhaps ten Cherokee, ten white men, all screaming like wild animals. Arms were raised, and I knew without seeing that the angry hands clutched tomahawks and knives.

A rifle went off, cracking a puff of white smoke into the air, shooting death into a man. I felt the impact in my own body, a solid punch I knew could only bring death. A warrior fell backward, clutching at his chest. The fallen was tall and young, but too far for me to distinguish much else. Except . . . something about the line of his body was so familiar. As he fell, I felt a sudden loss that left me aching and hollow. So he was someone I loved. I stared, waiting for an answer, aware of the tenuous pounding of his dying heartbeat. Then I knew. It had to be Soquili, his body torn and bleeding onto the rich green grass. Everything in me ached to go to him, to heal him, but I was trapped in my mind.

I had to get out. Had to stop this tragedy from happening. I forced myself from the trance, shooting upward until tiny stars spun in my vision. The ground rocked beneath my feet when I stood, and I stumbled toward the open doorway, needing to get to the Grandmother. She would know what to do. Maybe there was still time. Maybe I could save Soquili. I burst through the door, my arms held out as if I were trying to catch something, but was confused by the sunshine, dizzy with the effects of the vision. I collided with a body and a pair of solid arms closed around me.

Wahyaw. His fierce eyes glared down at me, the arch of his brow betraying a mixture of irritation and curiosity. "What is it?"

I struggled out of his embrace and grabbed his arms instead. "You have to go, Wahyaw. You have to save your brother."

The frown deepened. "What are you saying?"

A flush rose up my neck, burned in my cheeks, but I couldn't stop now. "I had a vision. Just now. Soquili—"

"He is not here."

"Did he go on a raid?"

Wahyaw narrowed his eyes, studying me. I know he saw confusion, but it was a confusion based on belief. "A vision?"

"A dream."

He took a step back, crossed solid arms over his chest, and eyed me speculatively. "You. Not Ma-kee, but you."

I straightened, slightly offended. "Yes, me. I have been working with the Grandmother, too, you know. Maggie's not the only one with gifts."

"I did not know—" He blinked, clearing whatever he'd been thinking from his mind, then nodded. "Soquili rode out. I will go, but I wanted to see you first. I felt bad for our last talk."

I shook my head, dismissing his worries. Mine were bigger. I pressed my hands against his arms, shoving gently at him. "Go. He's in terrible danger."

He nodded, then bit his lip. I hadn't seen that expression before. Almost apologetic. "I did not mean to frighten you, Ad-layd. We will marry. But I can wait for you to be ready. I understand."

To witness this warrior, this powerful, unshakable man, holding his heart in his hands before me in a poignant display was moving. Any other time, I would have treated his emotions with more care.

"Thank you," I said. "Now go."

He did, running toward the corral and swinging easily onto the back of a large spotted horse. He urged the animal toward the trees, and they disappeared within. I stood frozen, staring at the place where I had last seen his broad back. My thoughts weren't with him anymore, but with the question of what to do next. Should I go to the Grandmother? Tell her what I'd seen and done? What if she was angry? But how could she be? I had only done what she had always encouraged me to do. I had trusted my visions, let my mind sink into them until a message—an important message—had come to me. I had done everything she'd taught me to do, except for one thing: at the first hint of danger, I'd panicked, breaking out of the trance, determined to escape the threat.

Maybe I had saved Soquili's life. But what if . . .

I turned toward the seven-sided council house in the centre of the village and ducked inside. The Grandmother huddled by the stack of orange embers pulsing in the centre of the room, in quiet conversation with Nechama. Silver strands from both women's braids caught the sunlight when I entered, shimmered briefly, then dulled again as I lowered the flap of the doorway. The room was dark, providing only a vague outline of their profiles as I stepped in. The women turned, startled to see me standing in the doorway. I rarely visited Wah-Li without an invitation. No one did.

But she welcomed me in as if she had been waiting. "What is it, Shadow Girl?" she asked. "Come and sit with us."

Nechama cocked her head, intrigued. I took my place across the hearth from them, slightly out of breath from racing across the field to her home. Neither was used to seeing me in that condition. Usually I was so quiet they had to keep checking to make sure I was still breathing.

I told them what I had seen and what I had done. The women exchanged glances, then Wah-Li extended her hand to take mine. Hers was dry and wrinkled, but soft as a dove's wing. Her ancient eyes flickered with curiosity.

"And how did it feel, my girl, to open your wings on your own? Were you afraid? Or did you step into the unknown with feet ready to walk?"

"I . . . I felt . . ." I shrugged. "I don't know. I did it because something else had frightened me, and I thought if I tried, I might be able to find calm. I didn't expect to see anything."

"And Wahyaw? What did he do when you told him?"

I smiled, remembering. "I think he was surprised. He didn't know I could do that."

The women chuckled. My eyes had adjusted, and I could see Nechama flick one eyebrow. "I think you are right," she said.

"He went to save Soquili."

"Tell me," Wah-Li said. "Was it the end of the dream when you walked away?"

I flushed. "I don't think it was, Grandmother. I saw Soquili fall, and I couldn't wait to see anything more. I wanted to *do* something." She was quiet, and I bowed my head. "I should have waited. I understand that. But—"

Wah-Li still held my hand, but her eyes hardened into circles of black as I watched. Her voice hardened as well, though it wasn't accusatory. "You cannot always trust what your visions tell you. We do not know yet what you can do. It may be as you think, or it may be something different. You must be careful."

I frowned. "But I did right, didn't I? Sending Wahyaw to Soquili?"

"We will see," she said. Icy fingers of dread scratched at the base of my neck and flitted down my spine. "We will see. But we must always be careful when we speak of dreams."

CHAPTER 5

One Less

It was dusk when the war party returned. Their arrival was unusually subdued, the warriors hunched over their horses instead of rushing in with their usual confident gallop, whooping with victory. If it hadn't been for the shuffling of hooves on dirt and the objections of the captives staggering among them, all might have been silent.

The sun sent its final rays over the earth, and the shadows of trees reached like fingers, grasping for the past. Poor light kept me from seeing if blood coloured the men's faces and bodies, or if it was merely war paint. Behind the first riders slid two travois. One was completely covered by a heavy bearskin. I felt cold and my stomach churned with unease.

One of the horses broke away from the others and trotted in my direction. As he drew closer, I made out Soquili's profile. My heart leaped, and I raced toward him, grinning with relief.

"You're all right! Oh, Soquili! I thought—"

My smile faded, since his expression encouraged no celebration. I waited in silence as he slid off his horse and silently landed on the rough leather of his moccasins. He didn't look at me, instead kept his eyes on the ground as he walked. When he stood two paces away, he stopped and looked into my eyes. Grief pulled the skin tight across his cheeks.

He swallowed hard, his eyes dark with sorrow. So much sorrow. "I am sorry," he said.

I blinked. My heartbeat accelerated, and my breath was suddenly tight in my chest. "Why? What happened?"

"Wahyaw—" he said, then stopped to clear his throat. He swallowed, then gazed beyond me, into a coming night as dark as his eyes. "My brother is dead."

CHAPTER 6

Death and Rebirth

No one would ever speak Wahyaw's name again.

Behind us, a wailing rose up in the village, the sound of so many hearts twisted and bleeding with loss. Soquili, needing something to keep him upright, accepted my arms around his waist, then cried silently above me.

I didn't cry. I was empty, nerveless. *What had I done?*

When I managed to sleep that night, it was in brief snatches filled with dreams. I saw Wahyaw as he'd been when he'd come to me earlier that day, then I saw him again, dead. The dead man rose and walked toward me, the spectre's body the same as it had been in life, except his chest had been torn apart by a white-man's bullet. When the face of Wahyaw was a foot from my own, I stared into his familiar brown eyes, hard with ferocity even in death. Then they changed, transforming into the eyes I had dreamed. They sharpened, lightened, became an unblinking, furious yellow glare. The white warrior with the golden hair.

The following day, the house in which Wahyaw had lived, and where I would have gone as his wife, was visited by the village priests. I assumed their duties normally would have fallen to Wah-Li, but I doubted her ancient bones were up to the task. I also, somewhere in my heart, wondered if she was staying away from me, saving me the agony of seeing her eyes. She knew what I had done, though my intent had been nothing but good. Only she and Nechama knew.

The Cherokee always treated the deceased with the utmost respect, but they believed everything to do with the dead was unclean. Following tradition, the priest ordered everything within the walls—furniture, clothing, food—to be taken from the house and thrown into a bonfire near the new grave. Then he cleaned the hearth, the place where I had so often seen Wahyaw laugh with his brother and friends, and he lit a new fire.

I was included among Soquili's family when they were cleansed by the priest. He was a strange, one-eyed, silver-haired old man with a scar and a pronounced limp, probably twenty years younger than Wah-Li. I watched him hang a pot of water over the new fire, strongly scented by an herb I couldn't identify, then boil it into tea. Soquili, his parents, and I sipped from our cups, then washed our hands and faces with the hot liquid. Whatever remained in the pot was sprinkled around the inside of the house.

The cleansing continued as the strange little priest led us to the river. We waded into the freezing water until it licked at our waists, then turned to the east and the west, immersing ourselves completely seven times. When we were finished, we were given new clothes, and what we'd worn before was dumped into the fire along with everything else.

We didn't go back to Wahyaw's house afterward. Instead we went to his parents', where we waited in silence for the priest's messenger to finish the ritual. The man arrived bearing two gifts, then presented them to Soquili's stone-faced mother. The first was a piece of tobacco, which I was told would "enlighten our eyes" so we could bravely face the future. The second was a strand of beads meant to bring comfort.

Later that night, when we sat as honoured guests in the council house and received sympathies, I sank lower in my self-loathing, unable to stop blaming myself for sending Wahyaw to his death. If not for me, he might still be alive, thick arms crossed over his chest, scowling with warning at anyone approaching me. He would be staring eagle-eyed into the distance, constantly seeking out threat. Instead, his solid, vital strength was gone, his body cold and stiff, covered by layers of earth and rocks.

I didn't stay to watch the dance, and Soquili shot me an angry glance when I stood and left the gathering. I just couldn't.

Had I, as a child, accepted what I'd been given and learned about my powers, I believe I would have understood what to do. I would have read the dream more carefully and known not to send him after his brother. But I had been afraid as a child, and I was even more afraid now. I didn't know how to live the way Maggie did, trusting the dreams, and I never should have attempted it. I decided not to return to Wah-Li's house.

I did, however, go back to the house of Nechama, working harder than ever at learning the healing arts. Nechama asked no questions about my state of mind, for which I was grateful. Under her guidance, I settled into a more confident role as healer. My place was in helping others in the physical world, I decided. If they wanted to learn about the future, they should go and visit my sister in the mountains.

I often felt the urge to go to Maggie, to unload my secrets and my fears, but she had another life. One that revolved around her new family. I was on my own. And Soquili's smile was gone, replaced by an expression of such loneliness that I often looked away when he was near. Kokila came to sit with me occasionally, but we had little to talk about, and her visits became less frequent over time.

Raids continued, seeming to grow more ravenous as days and weeks passed. After Wahyaw's death, every Cherokee, even those curious about the white people's presence, wanted the settlers gone. I hid from returning war parties if they led prisoners, knowing the nightmare that was coming. But the sounds the captives made, the screaming and pleading, couldn't be shut out. The noise made me physically ill, as did witnessing my friends celebrate it. Sometimes I left the village entirely when the ceremonies took place. I know the People saw me as weak. They blamed every white person for Wahyaw's death, and I was, after all, white. And it wasn't just that. As his betrothed, they felt I should be celebrating the punishment of these people. But I couldn't. So I hid as I always had.

One afternoon, Soquili returned from a raid and came to my door. "Ad-layd," he said.

I had been beading, enjoying the solitude inside my shared council house. Hearing an unexpected lightness in his voice, I scrambled to my feet and went to him.

"I must speak with you, Ad-layd. It is about the raid today." He must have seen how I tensed, because he reached for my hand. He smiled, showing me the first true smile I had seen since Wahyaw's death, and its brightness took me by surprise. "It is a joyful day, Ad-layd."

His smile should have encouraged my own. But something inside me began to tremble.

"I have found a new brother," he said. "My brother's spirit is strong in him."

I was surprised to hear this, but I had seen it happen before. When a tribe member died, the Cherokee often sought to fill the empty places in their homes and hearts, finding some kind of spiritual connection—real or imagined—between themselves and the occasional enemy. Sometimes it worked out well for the prisoner, sometimes not, but when it did, at least it saved them from torture and burning. Usually the new tribesmen or women were from other tribes—the Tuscarora, the Catawba, the Creek—but there had been times when white people were discovered and dragged to their new life.

I could hear him yelling now, this new "brother," and thought Soquili was maybe right. The venom spitting from the man's mouth, as wild as a fire crackling through forests on a dry autumn night, could only have come from a warrior as proud as Wahyaw. The words, however, could only have come from a white man.

"Come, Ad-layd. You will see. It is him again. It is my brother."

I couldn't deny my curiosity. Obscenities the likes of which I had never imagined spewed across the yard, roared in explicit English.

"Do you know what he's saying, Soquili?" I asked, hiding a smile.

"No, but he is strong, is he not?"

"Oh yes, he is that."

Soquili's excitement was obvious, though I did notice his smile check once as we drew near. The captive had been walking ahead of one of the warriors, his face a mask, smeared with dirt and blood. He grimaced every time he was poked from behind with his own rifle, then suddenly spun and thumped his antagonist with his tethered fists. I recognised the warrior, Dustu, as he toppled backward, answering with his own expletives, and his friends laughed. To a Cherokee warrior, any laughter directed his way is a challenge. By the time Dustu had struggled to his feet, face tight with anger, the white man was already jeering at the others, wrestling the rope around his wrists and neck.

Dustu was shorter than the other warriors and used to being teased. Because of that, he had become a ruthless brawler. His fist struck the prisoner's lower back, just off his kidneys. It was a dare that spoke as clearly as any shouted curse. And it was easily translatable in any language.

I could have killed you easily. Now let me see what you have for me.

Soquili's new brother collapsed to his knees at the blow, but he shot a defiant glare over his shoulder at the warrior. *Oh yeah? You sure you're ready?*

We were about twenty feet away from the war party when Soquili called out. "Cut his ropes." He spat to the side, critical eyes narrowed at Dustu. "Only a coward would fight a bound man."

All heads turned at Soquili's voice, now they glanced

back at the prisoner. The white man had no idea what had been said, but he watched warily, sensing something was about to happen. His attention focused on one of the other men as he advanced, knife extended before him. I saw the whites of the captive's eyes, the flaring of his nostrils as he drew back, sensing approaching danger, but at the last minute the Indian stopped and laughed. He shook his head, still grinning, and muttered something I couldn't hear. He held up his own hands, which he'd connected at the wrists as if he were mimicking the prisoner, then made a sawing gesture with his knife. The white man glanced from him to Dustu, trying to read their thoughts, then held out his hands.

The captive kept his eyes trained on Dustu while the bindings were cut from his wrists. When they fell away, I saw the torn skin, bleeding where the rope had burned his flesh when he'd fought against it. He didn't touch his hands for comfort, as I surely would have, but dropped them to his sides, clenching and unclenching his fists to get the blood pumping through them again. He and Dustu began to circle one another, reading each other's body language, and I saw something white flash across the prisoner's dirty face. With shock, I realized the man was smiling. I would never understand men.

Dustu had it easy. Hidden under a mask of filth, the white man could have been any colour, had it not been for the light, mussed hair and the English curses shooting from his mouth. He had obviously fought hard before they'd arrived, and had a long cut down one thigh, which looked deep. His torn trousers were stained with blood, and though he tried to hide it, he limped slightly. Another slice cut across his chest, small and shallow, but nevertheless staining the worn fibres of his shirt around the edges. His face had received its own share of violence. One eye was swollen almost completely shut, the sneering upper lip split at one side.

Dustu planted his knife in his leg holster and held his hands open in front of him, making it clear he had no intention of using it. Then he grinned maniacally and opened his eyes wide, rocking back and forth in a hunched fighting stance. I was used to the warriors fighting among themselves.

It was practice for them, usually. But this was unfair. The prisoner was injured and obviously exhausted. The warriors formed a circle around the fighters, clapping and laughing, spitting at the white man's feet. While they clearly saw this as entertainment, I saw hate and intent in Dustu's eyes.

Soquili looked at me, sensing my discomfort. "This man is a warrior," he explained, "but he must be taught how to use this power. Today he will have his first lesson."

Dustu started it, lunging across the small space so he bowled the prisoner over, then loomed above the man on all fours. He grabbed the white man's throat, then pounded the back of his opponent's head against the ground, over and over, until I saw the eyelids of the prisoner flutter.

"Dustu's going to kill him. It's not a fair fight," I said.

"He will be fine," Soquili said, looking strangely confident. "Watch."

As if he'd heard, the white man suddenly grabbed Dustu's wrists and shoved them apart so Dustu collapsed flat on his chest and was flung aside. The prisoner got to his feet and bent over, breathing hard, fists at the ready.

"You call that a fight?" he said hoarsely. "You fight like one of your toothless squaws. That all you got?"

Dustu knew a fair amount of English, having visited trading posts and listened in on other people's conversations, but the prisoner spoke quickly. Dustu couldn't have understood what had been said, but he had to be completely aware of the tone being used. He jumped nimbly to his feet and charged, but the prisoner stepped to the side, sticking out his boot at the last moment so Dustu fell face-first into the dirt. The rest of the Cherokee roared with laughter, approving of the move, and Dustu got to his hands and knees, spitting mud. When he stood, his face was an angry purple, and I watched the white man narrow his distinctive, almost beautiful eyes.

Light-coloured, almost gold. I'd seen those eyes so often in my dreams, but in those dreams I'd run from them. Now they stared at Dustu, willing him to come. Answering the challenge, Dustu went for the man's face, catching him on the jaw. Blood spattered from the captive's torn face, but he snapped back and caught Dustu once, twice, hard in the gut. Dustu folded, groaning and drawing into a ball, despite his friends' heckling. The white man stood beside him, looking down his nose and waiting. He wiped an arm across his bleeding face, then looked around at the circle of jeering men.

"Who's next?" he demanded.

In the moment when the man looked away, Dustu reached into his holster and unsheathed his hunting knife. With all his strength, he slammed the handle into the prisoner's thigh wound, and I grabbed Soquili's arm.

"Make him stop!" I demanded. "Dustu is fighting unfairly."

"*Shh*, Ad-layd. My brother will take care of that."

I didn't see how. All the blood had drained from the man's dirt-encrusted face and seemed to be spilling from his thigh. Dustu, grinning madly, had gotten to his feet and now slammed his fist into the captive's stomach, catching his face when he curled reflexively in half. The prisoner staggered sideways before his injured leg finally gave in, and he fell.

"Soquili," I hissed, watching Dustu's determined expression as he circled the injured man. I had seen wolves surround an injured stag, tearing it to bits while the beast twisted and thrust uselessly with his antlers. I had seen cats play with mice, tossing them from paw to paw until the little creatures lay listlessly, wishing for the end. I had no desire to witness this. I stepped forward, wanting to put a stop to the violence, but Soquili grabbed my arm and jerked me back.

Dustu kicked the man's open thigh wound, then lifted his hands over his head, grinning and nodding at his tribe. *See? See who is the man here?* Dustu's enthusiasm was contagious. He returned to kick again, and the prisoner made a gurgling sound through clenched teeth. Before long, the others were cheering along with Dustu.

Soquili shifted beside me, the only indication of his concern a subtle clenching of his jaw. Dustu went back a third time, but before he could connect again, the prisoner grabbed Dustu's foot and yanked it in a savage twist. I heard the bone crack, Dustu shriek, and Soquili hoot with laughter, his voice rich with approval.

The man was forgotten as the others gathered around Dustu. The warrior rolled and howled, clutching at his broken leg. As I approached Dustu, keen on my duty as healer, I glanced down at the white man. He lay curled off to the side, much paler than before, with one hand pressed to his bleeding thigh. He blinked up at me through his swollen face, seeming confused at the sight of my blond hair. I met his golden eyes, those eyes I knew from my dreams, and my breath stopped for an instant. What did I see in them beside hatred? Violence, unquestionably. Intelligence was there as well, calculating all the time. And deeper within, even beyond the wounds of his body, I sensed pain. So much bitter pain, but not the kind that could be healed with salves or stitches. I fought the urge to drop to my knees beside him. I had to tend to the Cherokee first.

It was difficult to look away. I'd never met the man before, but I knew those eyes so well they might have been with me all my life. After he'd been cleaned a bit, I knew his hair would be golden, his body sleek and strong as a mountain cat's. I had spent my life running from my dreams. This man lying bleeding on the ground, blinking through the eyes that had haunted those dreams . . . he was as real as could be.

CHAPTER 7

Healing

"Ad-layd."

I stepped away with reluctance and crouched beside Dustu. I did a quick check of his injuries, called for what I needed, and two young boys ran to get it. I ran my fingers over the break gently, trying not to make Dustu yelp.

"You must be calm," I said to him. "Breathe through your nose."

"Ha!" he replied. His eyes shifted cruelly toward the prisoner. "He cannot breathe through his beak. I broke it."

I shook my head and lifted one eyebrow. "Sorry, Dustu. It was already broken before you hit him. You just got his lip going again."

"Quiet, woman," he grumbled, but Soquili chuckled beside me. He folded his arms over his chest and glared down at Dustu, pale and sweating into the dirt.

"I told you this man is mine," Soquili told him. "Why do this?"

"Soquili, you are a fool," Dustu spat through clenched teeth. "This is no man like your brother. This is a toad. He is not worthy of your family."

Soquili spoke briskly before turning away. "That is not for you to say. Especially now. You are a small man for fighting an injured man. I had thought you braver than that." Dustu made a furious noise, but Soquili shook his head with disgust and addressed me. "Fix the coward, Ad-layd, then go to your house. I will bring this man for you to heal."

Once the others dwindled and I had Dustu in place, he seemed to get over his initial agony and bite down on his sounds of pain. Dustu wasn't prone to sitting still for long. A broken bone would take a long time to heal with a man like this. I told him what I suggested he do, including rest, then said I would stop in at his house later to check on him. He frowned, then nodded once, dismissing me. I rose and collected my things, then left.

By the time I arrived at my house, Soquili had already brought the prisoner. He sat in a corner, glaring at us like a cornered bear. Except a bear would have had a thicker, more impressive coat. This man's torn clothing was a dull mud brown, patched with blackened blood.

"I need to clean you off so I can see to your wounds," I said.

It was an odd experience, speaking English after so many months. The prisoner looked slightly startled, but said nothing, only maintained his forbidding glare. I approached cautiously, thinking this would be like treating a wild animal. I half feared he might bite. I dipped a cloth into a wooden bowl set at his side, disturbing the still surface and inviting the aroma of sweet herbs into the air. I wrung out the cloth, watching the man closely, then held it out for him to assess. He seethed.

"It's only water," I assured him, then pressed the cloth against my cheek in illustration.

His chin lifted, seeing proof that whatever was in the bowl was safe, then he gave me a brief, almost imperceptible nod. I took his wrist between my fingers, feeling the rounded sharpness of his bones, then gently caressed his forearm with the cloth so he could feel the truth. He flinched at my touch, then slowly relaxed and let me cut through the dirt with the cloth.

From across the room, Soquili watched, then grunted as if he'd just remembered something. He came toward us and reached in the direction of the man's throat. The prisoner instantly jolted backward, pressing his back against the wall of the house, fists raised. I barely caught my bowl before it was kicked over.

"What are you—" I began, just as confused as the man.

"His shirt," Soquili explained.

I glanced at Soquili, then back to the man. "Of course," I said, then sighed. "But I think he can do that himself, don't you?"

The prisoner's gaze shifted from Soquili to me, and the slightest twinkle of hope shone in the back of those amber eyes as he waited for my explanation. I thought it likely that he saw me, my language, my blond hair, and my blue eyes as a sign that he might survive this.

"He didn't mean to frighten you. It's only you need to take off your shirt. Your chest is bleeding."

The man sniffed, studying both our faces. Soquili gave him a tentative smile and obligingly moved away. Keeping his eyes trained on Soquili, the man wriggled painfully out of his filthy shirt, yanked it over his head, then tossed it beside him.

I was used to men in various states of undress. After all, the Cherokee rarely wore much of anything during the summer months. But the lean lines of this man's muscles, stretched tight across his chest, drew my gaze. Under his shirt, the skin was almost clean, the colour of cream, making him somehow seem more vulnerable. I examined a deep gash on his arm, trying not to touch his chest, though I knew I would have to when I tended to his wounds. A thin line of blood snaked down from over his right breast, following the contours of his ribs and congealing on the pale blond hairs of his stomach.

"What? Never seen a white man before?" he muttered, lifting my eyes to his.

"I've seen plenty," I assured him, returning my attention to his arm. I decided the wound would heal without stitches, as would the one on his chest. They needed cleaning, though. Blood had trapped grime and pebbles on the shredded lips of the cuts.

Soquili sat quietly on the other side of the house, watching.

"Does he know why he is here?" I asked in Cherokee.

"How could he know?" Soquili asked, shrugging.

I nodded. Just as I thought. The man must be thoroughly confused, expecting to be killed, yet here he was being tended and healed. "Should I tell him?"

Soquili considered this. I looked over my shoulder at him, waiting for an answer. Finally, he shook his head. "Not yet."

"What's going on?" the man asked.

He hissed through his teeth when I dabbed at the cut on his chest. "I'll put balm on all of these. It'll help." He closed his eyes while I continued to clean him up and smear small patches of melted bear grease across the injuries. My patient wrinkled his nose, and I shrugged.

"It will help the healing."

It was like a map, this body, and my eyes followed roadways of past injuries marked by various lines and scars. It had seen a great deal of abuse. Four deep pink lines stretched across his belly. I touched them, and he jumped as if I'd tickled him.

"Cougar?" I asked gently.

He looked away, but nodded. "Why didn't they kill me?" His voice was hoarse, tired.

"I can't explain that to you yet."

"But why—"

"I can't. Just wait awhile, and you'll find out."

His glare returned. I could feel his eyes burning me, though I kept my attention on his wounds. "What's awhile?" he demanded. "An hour? A week? Give me something, girl. Am I just waiting to be tortured to death? Because if that's it, you might want to save your medicines for the next man."

"Sorry. I don't know the answer. You'll just have to bide your time."

"But—"

I turned toward Soquili and held out my hands in question. "He wants to know why he's not dead."

Soquili scowled, not changing his mind.

I studied the cuts I'd tended. The bear grease flickered slightly with the light of the hearth fire, and I tried not to shake my head with disgust. Such a waste of time. They'd let these injuries heal, then they'd tear them open again. I knew the Cherokee. This poor, bewildered man was only going to get more confused. I could tell him everything—Soquili would never know—but I wasn't sure that would help. The stranger still stared at me, waiting, though my focus was on his chest. His gaze was so intense, I felt I could be at the other side of the room and still feel the beam of those eyes. I looked up.

"I deserve to know," he said quietly, echoing my thoughts. I continued to look at him, saying nothing, and he took that as an invitation to explain more. "When I was a kid, these sons of bitches killed my mother, my sisters, and my brother. I ain't got no love for Injuns. But I ain't afraid, neither. I just wanna know what's going on."

I squeezed the cloth under the water and touched the side of his face, hiding my smile. Not afraid. He wasn't much of a liar. He winced but didn't pull away.

"And I have no love for white men," I said. He was silent, but I'd already said too much. What could have prompted me to share my secret with a stranger? I bit my lip.

Frustration creased his brow, but he didn't ask anything else about me. His immediate concern had to be for himself, and that was a relief.

"Are you gonna tell me what's going on?"

"I can't. I don't know exactly, to be honest."

I slid the cloth over his brow and felt him relax a little further. I knew my touch was soothing, the sweet-scented water refreshing. His hair was cut short so it curled behind his ears, tickled the bottom of his neck, and I knew once it was cleaned, it would be golden. Not white blond like mine, but gold. One stubborn curl in the middle of his forehead twisted away from the rest, and another flicked like a wave over one ear. His eyes watched me as I worked, a beast of prey scouting the territory, but he said nothing. When his face was clean, I leaned back and examined it.

"What you looking at?"

"Seeing if you have more damage," I lied.

In truth, I wanted to admire him. Now that most of his face was revealed, the pictures from my dreams were coming together, touching in his eyes, shaping around the strong set of his battered shoulders. He was about my age. And despite the swelling, he was undeniably handsome.

But he was a man. And a white man, at that. I shoved the traitorous thought out of my head.

"Well?"

I reached into a small cup by my knee and pulled out a leech, black and wriggling between my fingers. My patient was no stranger to the treatment, because he didn't object when I gently pressed three of the creatures to the swollen skin around his eye.

"You're not going to impress the ladies for a while, I'm afraid," I said with a vague smile.

"No?" A hint of humor curled in his voice. "Not even you?"

I was surprised to feel blood rush into my cheeks. "No. Not even me."

He was still pale, and I knew it had to do with his leg. I looked down at the tear in his trousers and saw the bleeding had stopped, but it was a long cut. It would need attention. When I glanced up at him, he was frowning.

"You ain't gonna need to see that, are you?"

"Of course I am."

"Well, I ain't gonna—"

From the other side of the room, Soquili chuckled. I glared at him. He got to his feet and went to the far end of the house, leaning down to reach for a blanket. He dropped it beside my patient.

"Look away, Shadow Girl," he said, grinning. "You will see all of him soon enough."

I stood and looked toward the open doorway, arms crossed over my chest. I knew I was blushing and hated myself for it. "Why would you say that, Soquili? I have no desire to see him."

The prisoner grunted with effort as he worked his way out of his trousers then hid under the blanket. When Soquili said it was safe, I turned back. My patient leaned against the wall, slightly paler than he had been, wearing nothing but a blanket from his waist to his knees. An unwelcome shiver passed down my spine and settled with heat in my belly. I fought the sensation, reminding myself that I knew well what was beneath that blanket. I knew what men could do with the weapons God had given them. No. I wouldn't allow myself to feel anything for this man. I knelt beside him and rolled the blanket up the side of his thigh so I could heal the ugly gash. It stretched almost all the way from hip to knee.

"Why did I say that?" Soquili chuckled. "I thought you would know that by now. This man carries the spirit of my brother. That means he is my brother, but he is also your betrothed."

CHAPTER 8

Introductions

I went about my daily routine, tending whoever needed me, doing chores with the women, sitting and talking with Nechama. My mind, however, dwelt in the small, silent tent near the centre of the village. They had tossed him in there with nothing but the blanket, and now took turns terrorizing him. I knew they hadn't allowed him more than a couple of hours sleep. He was going to have to prove himself, and he was going to have to do it with next to no strength. In my opinion, they'd planned a horrible welcome-home party for Soquili's so-called brother.

I stayed purposefully away from him, though it bothered me how much I wanted to peek into that tent. I fought my curiosity for as long as I could, but I was plagued at night when his yellow eyes glared into my dreams. After a day, I gave in. I lifted the edge of the tent's flap and squinted through the opening, relieved to see his eyes were closed. He sat straight, facing the tent's flap, ready to defend himself . . . except his head lolled over his shoulder, long lashes rested on his pale cheeks, and soft snores padded his breathing. The cut on his brow seemed, from where I stood, to be healing all right. The scab was dark, and the purple-black bruises around his eyes were beginning to melt into an ugly greenish tinge. The swelling was mostly down.

He looked younger when he slept, but then we all do. I wondered vaguely what his smile looked like. Then I sighed. Why bother wondering? Another day or so and his pretty face would be pounded to a pulp again. What a waste.

I heard a sound behind me and turned slowly, not wanting to wake him. It was Kokila, and I smiled to see her. She didn't have a mean bone in her body.

"Does he sleep?" she whispered. I nodded, and she pulled the flap farther, then squatted beside me. I felt exposed, as if we trespassed, but Kokila didn't seem bothered by it. She tilted her head, studying him, then smiled gently at me.

"Does he eat?"

I shook my head. An untouched bowl of corn and rice sat by him. It had been brought the night before. The water bowl, however, was empty.

Kokila's pretty mouth quirked up at one edge, and she nudged me with her elbow. "You could do worse," she whispered.

I looked away. Though I'd said nothing of it, Soquili's teasing hadn't left my mind since he'd uttered it. *He is your betrothed.* I refused to make any kind of comment, but what he'd said simply would not happen. Not in this lifetime. I wouldn't marry anyone. But to even consider pairing me with a white man? Did these people forget who I was? What I'd survived? This new approach was strange and confusing to me. They were usually so caring.

Kokila looked back into the dark tent. It was midday, and the air was still. Sweat trickled down the prisoner's chest and over the cougar scar while he slept.

"Tomorrow," she whispered. "He will run tomorrow."

A sadness swelled in my chest. Not for myself, surely, but for this brave young man who had done nothing but defend himself. I hadn't spoken with him since I'd cleaned his cuts, so he was completely in the dark about what was coming.

Sometimes I hated the Cherokee with every one of my breaths. I hated their sense of right and wrong, their demeaning perspective that everyone but them was an imbecile, and their brutal methods of declaring superiority.

Superiority. Hardly that. For them to beat an exhausted man almost to death so he could prove something of which he had no idea? How could that be superior? I tried not to dwell too much on this aspect of their society, because I could do nothing about it. They were what they were, and despite what they might believe, I knew they weren't better or worse than anyone else. They were human. But knowing what was coming for this man made me sick. My throat tightened as I stared at his sleeping form.

The Cherokee were human. White men were human. And yet they were so dramatically different. Their hatred was a living thing, and each wanted nothing less than to annihilate the other.

Somewhere in the middle was me. I straddled both races, terrified to plant one foot permanently in either camp. This man slumped before me was trapped between worlds as well, but he didn't have to choose one or the other. He knew he was white all the way through. He knew to hate the Cherokee.

I didn't know who I was anymore. I had once been a quiet middle sister with a skill at sewing. Nothing more than that. I thought of myself as Maggie and Ruth's sister, not my own person, and I was happy that way. I liked to hover behind others like a shadow, watching but silent. There was nothing special about me. Nothing except for the dreams I despised and ignored.

This man's presence reminded me that I was a part of two separate worlds, but a member of neither. I was alone. I used to want that. Then everything changed and being alone turned into being lost. Now I wanted, more than anything else, to be found.

Kokila's soft hand touched mine, and I turned toward her. Her eyes were dark, liquid with mirrored pain. She didn't have to say a word. Her gaze, deep with the gentle soul of the Cherokee, loving and loyal and beautiful, apologized on behalf of all of them. *It is something that must be done,* said her black eyes. I looked away and tried to remember the caring, healing hands, the songs the women had sung to rid my sleep of nightmares, the lessons Wah-Li had taught me that had come close to freeing me from myself. Remembering their generosity of spirit reminded me of the creatures from whom Maggie and I had been rescued. I had steadfastly refused to remember those monsters or that day again, but just the thought of them helped me to see the prisoner as a white man again. That made it much easier for me to nod and back away from the tent.

In the morning, excitement was as thick as the shrieks of cicadas in the air. Soquili and the others applied fresh war paint and bounced around one another, grinning with anticipation. The women were all outside, the children as well, and their laughter should have lightened my spirit.

Instead, I felt sick. While the preparations were getting under way, the guest of honour sat trembling in his tent, unaware he was the reason for all this noise. I couldn't stand it. I stomped back to his tent and stood face-to-face with the warrior on duty.

"I'm going in."

"You are not allowed."

I narrowed my eyes and tried to give my best impression of an angry Cherokee wife. "Do you have any idea of who I am to this man? It is not your place to keep me away."

Uncertainty flickered. "Only for a moment," he said, and I ducked inside.

The prisoner's eyes flew open, then narrowed with suspicion.

"I'm not allowed to be here," I said quickly. He didn't reply, only watched and waited. "But I thought you should know that you are to be tested this morning."

He closed his eyes and exhaled loudly through his nose, which was still slightly swollen. Something that might have been resignation sagged across his shoulders. I frowned, then knelt on the dirt across from him.

"That doesn't mean they'll kill you. In fact, they'll probably do just about everything *but* kill you."

He kept his eyes closed. "So I'll just wish I was dead," he muttered.

I couldn't argue with that. "Probably. You just have to get through them all. They won't let you die, I don't think. They definitely won't let you escape, though."

The golden eyes opened slightly and stared at me. His voice stayed low. "So what's the point? Why are you here? Just to bring me the good news?"

"All you have to do is make it to the council house. I brought you more water and some meat to help you stay strong." He didn't reach to take either from me, only sat in stoic silence. I set them beside him. "It's better to survive, in case you're wondering. They don't kill people nicely around here."

I sat back, feeling unusually conversational. "What's your name?"

"Why does that matter?"

"I want to know." I debated with myself, then said, "I'm Adelaide."

"Adelaide, huh?" He snorted and stared at his legs, stretched out in front of him. "Adelaide the Injun."

I ignored the intended barb, and his sneer relaxed. "All right. I'm Jesse. Black. Jesse Black."

"Nice to meet you," I said reflexively.

"Why ain't I dead?"

"They have something else in mind for you."

A dark flush rose up his neck. "I won't be a slave to these savages," he growled. "I won't do it. I'll kill myself before that happens."

Male voices came from outside, and I recognized Soquili's. I didn't have time to say anything more before the flap opened and Soquili stormed in.

"Why are you here?" he demanded. "You cannot speak with this man today."

I frowned at him, fighting the instinct to cower under

those eyes. "No? You'd have me marry a man I know nothing about?"

He jammed his hands on his hips and paced, though the tent was only two steps wide. "What did you say to him?"

"What I say isn't up to you, Soquili. You can't tell me what to do." That was true enough. They were a fierce, warlike tribe when they wanted to be, but the Cherokee were mostly ruled by their women. And I was one of Wah-Li's favourites, so he would have to check his tone. He did. He also gave me a cynical grin.

"It is an important day for this man. He needs his rest."

"Ha!" I said, shaking my head. "Rest? No one has left him alone for more than five minutes since he got here. The poor man is exhausted."

"What's going on?" Jesse drawled. He leaned his head back against the tent wall, trying to appear as if it didn't matter to him one way or the other. But the tight fists at his sides told a different story.

I looked from him to Soquili. "He deserves to know what's happening. He needs to understand why he has to go through today's torture, and why he hasn't been killed. Don't you think you should tell him he's your . . ." I struggled with the word, then finally blurted, "your brother?"

Soquili frowned, but it wasn't out of anger. The tightness at the corner of his lips gave me the impression that he was nervous.

"So can I tell him?" I asked.

"Hey, Adelaide," Jesse said. "I asked what you're talking about."

I lifted my eyebrows at Soquili, and eventually he shrugged. "Yes. Tell him."

"Adelaide?"

I turned back to Jesse, who leaned forward now, elbows on his knees.

"I need to tell you something. You're not going to like it, but it's better than the alternative." I gestured toward Soquili. "See this man behind me?"

"Hard to miss."

I smiled. "True enough. This is Soquili." I turned toward Soquili and said in Cherokee, "This is Jesse." The men nodded warily at each other, like big dogs unsure whether to sniff or growl. "Soquili's brother was killed a couple of weeks ago."

Jesse nodded, not even blinking at the news. Why should he? What did he care about a dead Indian?

"Soquili believes you are the spirit of his brother come back," I blurted, and Jesse's eyes widened. "Yes. He thinks you are his brother."

"I ain't no Injun!" Jesse exclaimed.

"Calm down," I suggested when Soquili tensed beside me. I gestured for Soquili to step outside, and, with a sigh, he did so, leaving me alone with Jesse. "Here's what you can do," I said simply. "You can choose to allow them to adopt you in this manner, see how that is, or you can burn on a stake. Soquili has chosen to let you live. Would you throw that away out of stupidity?"

Jesse stared at me, glanced over my shoulder, at the place where he'd last seen Soquili, then back at me. "What would I have to do?"

"You'd be like a brother. Just like that. You'll share food, friends, family—"

"Family?"

"His parents will be yours. He has no other brothers, no sisters."

The most exquisite look of repulsion crossed his face. "I ain't got Injun parents, no how."

"Maybe not," I said, trying not to laugh. "But if I were you, I'd pretend."

I neglected to mention that he was not only expected to be a brother and a son but a husband as well.

CHAPTER 9

The Gauntlet

Outside the tent, the drums began to pound. They were slow, muffled heartbeats, soon joined by warbling male voices. I shuddered, then regretted the movement when Jesse shot me a glance.

"That's for me, ain't it?"

I didn't want to look at him, see hate and fear glint in those beautiful eyes. "Yes."

"I will send for him," Soquili said, peeking through the tent flap.

We sat listening to the sounds for a moment. The singing grew louder, until the hair stood up on the back of my neck. The air in the tent felt suspended. Tight.

"So . . . this ain't gonna be good, huh?" Jesse's voice had lost its aggressive snarl. He was quiet now, trying to accept what was coming.

"No."

I looked back and took in whatever progress he'd made over the past couple of days. Other than the places I'd wiped clean, he was still filthy. His wounds were healing well, the long gash on his thigh still inflamed and black with bruising, but nothing oozed out of it. For now, it was all right. Except for his nose, his face had resumed its natural shape. The bruises and cuts were still ugly, and his lip was full but not swollen. But after today . . .

I looked away again. "I'll be waiting at the other end for you. I'll tend your wounds."

He snorted and gazed out through the open flap. "Great news."

Two warriors came for him, and I rose, backing toward the exit. He still hadn't touched the food I'd brought, but it was too late now. Anything he ate would only come back up.

"Run fast and fight back as long as you can, Jesse. They want to know that you deserve this honour."

He looked as if he wanted to spit with disgust. The idea of honour among the Indians was plainly ridiculous to him. But he said nothing, only clenched his jaw and gave me a short nod.

I went to the council house and waited for Wah-Li to invite me in. When she did, I knelt in front of her and bowed my head. I hadn't been able to meet her eyes since Wahyaw's death. She was quiet, and I wondered if she waited for me to look up. I didn't.

"It is good to see you again, Shadow Girl," she eventually said. "I have wondered at your absence. Was it shame? I asked myself, then thought that maybe yes, that was why you did not come to see me. Shame is a thick wall of smoke, Shadow Girl. The only way to see through it is to extinguish the source." I looked up and met her milky eyes. "You did nothing wrong. Who is to say the man would not have gone anyway?"

"Now this man will suffer," I said quietly.

She nodded slowly. "But I have seen he will be brave. And I will meet him when you have healed his physical body. I must see your mate for myself. I believe him to be a good man."

"He is not my mate," I snapped.

Her ancient head tilted slightly to the side. "Shadow Girl, you must not be afraid of everything. You must learn to take *ulanigvgv*—take your power into yourself. Not everything that is done comes from punishment or a desire to hurt you."

"I didn't say I was afraid. Just that he isn't my mate. Neither was—" I stopped, remembering. No one was ever to mention a dead man's name out loud. Never.

"You are not alone in this world."

"No, I know that," I replied shortly, knowing my words were more curt than they should have been. She was wrong, though. I was very alone. I shrugged, letting her have the argument. "I have Maggie, and you, and Kokila, and Nechama—"

"And the gods have given you a mate."

Voices rose outside, and I recognized one of them as Jesse's. He was spouting words I hadn't heard for a long time, threats and insults from another lifetime. One I'd hoped to forget. My throat felt thick, but I didn't want to cry. I clenched my jaw and swallowed.

"He is *not* a good man, and he is *not* my mate. And I do not believe he is Soquili's brother, either. He is too full of hate."

She chuckled. "Just so. Go now and send him the strength you carry, Shadow Girl. He needs you there." I shook my head, but she smiled her toothless smile. "Go now."

Voices had risen with anticipation, drowning out Jesse's curses. I stepped into the sunlight, my stomach queasy with dread. I wanted to flee, to hide in the trees and try to forget any of this was happening. A kind of connection already existed between me and Jesse, and I not only felt nauseated by the whole ceremony, I felt protective of the strange, coarse man. Our skin colour and our non-Cherokee upbringings were the most obvious ties. But more than that was the reality of his eyes in my dreams. I'd known the white warrior was coming; it appeared he had arrived.

I looked at the crowd reluctantly, and my eyes sought Jesse. He was easy to find—the source of the most movement in the group as he struggled, giving me the occasional flash of dirty-blond hair. He wrestled their grip, trying to yank his arms free, but they had him. He wasn't as tall as his captors, but though he limped and was gaunt from not eating recently, he looked as strong as they did. He was dressed in Cherokee clothing, which meant leggings and a breechclout but nothing more. I knew he hated that. Hated anything that hinted at his being a part of this despised society. But I also wondered if maybe, within that sculpted, pale chest, his heart beat with a little more strength now that he knew he was being considered worthy of joining them as a brother.

I wormed between some of the people, wanting suddenly to see, as if maybe my presence might offer a little strength. The crowd roared and my stomach sank when he was shoved into the midst of them. One minute I saw his blond head, and the next it had sunk into a sea of black hair and feathers. I knew he still moved forward with the flow of violence, because I could see arms and legs swinging at him, sticks and rocks pounding, though their quarry was buried beneath. He appeared now and then, bloodied face contorted with rage, teeth bared, eyes on fire. He was like a drowning man bobbing to the surface for air before being dragged under again, but he was determined to take them with him. There were yelps when he made contact, shouts of either rage or encouragement, laughter that didn't belong before they yanked him away again.

I didn't want to watch. I was so tired of blood and pain and anger. With a sigh, I turned away and faced the open expanse of the field, watched the lazily twitching tails of nearby horses. I was tempted to walk to them, to lay my palm on a velvety nose and feel warm, wet breath tickle my wrists, but I couldn't. I was needed here. I was responsible for this man's care, whether I wanted to be or not. I cursed Soquili for choosing him, for dragging him back here and dropping me in the middle of it all.

Send him the strength you carry, Shadow Girl, Wah-Li had said.

I turned back to the violence and closed my eyes, willing Jesse to survive.

A tingle flickered across my fingertips, like tiny

snowflakes dancing over my hand. I imagined Jesse's face, focused on his expression when a hint of trust had appeared there. I felt myself being sucked into the vision, and I rode its wave. The sensation grew stronger as it spread up my arms, through my chest, then swirled into my mind. It was similar to what I'd done with Wah-Li, except it was entirely different. I was not in the dark, in the quiet, trembling with anxiety. I was in the midst of chaos, yet my mind was calm. The shouts and shrieks grew muffled, losing their violent edge, but through the quiet din burst Jesse's furious voice, as clear to me as if he were the only one speaking. I hadn't expected anything like this—it had never happened before. But as much as I'd tried to ignore my gift, tried to force it from my mind, it was there all the same, just waiting for me to call it.

Soquili waited at the end of the gauntlet as they shoved and kicked his new brother toward him. He was grinning, cracking his knuckles in anticipation, something that filled me with an unreasonable rage. What was it that made me react this way, that made me defend a man I knew nothing about? But by now my mind was buzzing, demanding, *Don't you dare give up, Jesse. Be strong. Fight back.*

All at once, his eyes caught fire within my vision. Somehow I'd reached him. A roar came from deep within the mess of people. Jesse's roar. I opened my eyes, feeling calm.

Soquili glanced away from the scrum for a moment and caught my expression, reading my disapproval. His smile faltered, then bounced back as he turned toward the crowd. He called to someone, and I heard an answering laugh.

Then Jesse was through the gauntlet, standing two feet away from Soquili. Blood painted half his face like an eerie reminder of Wahyaw's tattoo. The eye that had just healed was back to the way I'd first seen it. He swayed unevenly on both feet, hunched slightly over a belly I imagined screamed with pain from the pummelling it had received. When he saw Soquili and sensed the easing of other men's fists around him, he tried to straighten. But I could tell from the twisted expression on his face that he knew the ordeal wasn't over. Soquili would get the final blow.

Jesse smiled at Soquili as if he were looking forward to this final confrontation. His teeth were gruesome, awash in a bright red stain. He spat to the side and swiped a filthy arm across bloody lips. His glare was completely focused on Soquili.

"All right, *brother*," he growled. "Let's see what you've got."

Soquili returned the smile, but his words were in Cherokee. "White brother, I hope you have saved some fight for me."

In response, Jesse surged forward, slamming the top of his head into Soquili's stomach. Soquili grunted and staggered back, then swung a fist under Jesse's bent form and hooked it upward, catching his face. Jesse stood and cupped his hands over his nose, holding back the gush of blood.

"Bastard," Jesse snarled, and Soquili laughed, though he was still short of breath.

Jesse let go of his face and staggered forward, swiping awkwardly at Soquili, who dodged the punches easily. Finally Jesse's fist connected with the side of Soquili's face, and it was a sound hit, one that knocked Soquili two steps sideways. Bellowing with challenge, the Cherokee jumped back, grabbed both of Jesse's ears and yanked them down so that Jesse's face connected with Soquili's knee.

I heard a sickening crunch, and Jesse crumpled. If his nose hadn't been broken before, it undoubtedly was now. Soquili raised his arms with victory, and the crowd cheered. Life was as it should be. Soquili had won, the challenger had survived and fought well. He had proven the Cherokee were still superior. All was good.

Not for Jesse. He had lost consciousness and lay sprawled flat on his face, blood staining the dirt around him in a rapidly growing puddle. No one went to help him. Instead, they stepped around him, moving to congratulate Soquili. The bloody body was left to the side like a piece of meat. Now that this part of the ceremony was over, the festivities could begin.

Soquili was one of the tallest men in the tribe. He shot

me a grin over the heads of the adoring people, and I shook my head with disgust. I would never understand these people.

While the others headed toward the next part of the celebration, I knelt beside Jesse. I pressed my fingers against the side of his neck, feeling for his heartbeat. It was strong, almost aggressive, as if it were angry at the rest of his body for giving in. Moving very slowly, I turned Jesse's face to the side to take the weight off his nose. Blood spurted, hot and sticky, into my hands. He moaned, keeping his eyes squeezed tight, then slowly cracked open one eye.

"Bad, huh?" he asked, his voice distinctly nasal. I nodded. "And him?"

"Not like you."

He closed his eye again and tried to frown, despite a deep cut on his brow. It was short and clean. Maybe sliced by an antler horn somewhere along the gauntlet.

"I'll get him next time," he mumbled and lost consciousness again.

CHAPTER 10

Family

On the day after the gauntlet, Jesse was summoned to Soquili's parents' house for a meal. I was curious, wanting to watch their reaction to this new son. I had expected suspicion, aloofness maybe, but I was perfectly wrong—at least, in Salali's case. We stepped inside, and she embraced me, then Soquili. He gestured toward Jesse, who followed us in and frowned mutely, glancing around the house with a critical eye.

He looked horrible. Most of his face was a dark mottled purple, swollen despite the leeches I'd reapplied. I'd set his broken nose, but for now he could only breathe through his mouth. He limped and held one arm against his stomach. He no longer wore a shirt, since his had been beyond saving after the gauntlet. The Cherokee didn't seem to notice.

Salali, her deep eyes liquid with something I couldn't imagine, held out her arms as if Jesse truly was a long-lost son, rather than a newly discovered white man. She grabbed his damaged hands before he had time to pull them away and gazed up at him with an expression of sheer joy.

"My son. My heart is full of happiness. Welcome home."

He stared at her, then glanced toward me for help. I smiled. "She just welcomed you. She believes you are her son, returned to her." I tilted my head and gave him a crooked smile. "Though, personally, I don't see the resemblance."

"Ha, ha," he said wryly, trying not to smile and split his lip in the doing of it. "So what do I do now?"

"I think you should say something nice to her."

"Like what?"

"I don't know. Think of something, and I'll tell her."

"Fine." He pointed at the pot over the hearth. "Tell her she ain't as ugly as some of the others here. Then tell her I ain't eatin' none of that. Far as I know, it's part of one of my friends she just cooked up."

Without batting an eye, I turned to Soquili and his mother. "Jesse says he is honoured to be with you and has missed your cooking greatly."

Soquili's eyes narrowed. He'd caught some of Jesse's words but wisely chose to keep quiet. Salali grinned and threw her arms around Jesse, then started crying. I hadn't expected that. Jesse looked entirely bewildered.

"Stand still," I said at his panicked expression.

Jesse was almost a foot taller than Salali, so when her tears calmed, she had to look up to study his face. Her tough copper hands caressed his tender, bristled cheeks, her gentle fingers floated over his bruises and cuts. She traced his eyebrows with her thumbs, then touched the soft spring of his hair with her palms.

"What—" he started.

"Hush," I said. "Be kind if you can. I told her you were happy to be here."

He arched one eyebrow at me. "You're a liar."

"No, I'm not," I replied, maintaining a cool smile. "I imagine you're happier to be here than you would be tied to a stake."

A movement caught my eye, and I spied Soquili's father, Ahtlee-Kwi-duhsgah, sitting cross-legged and silent at the back of the house. In his stillness he almost blended into the dark wood. Jesse followed my gaze.

"Your new father," I murmured. "Don't try his temper."

Jesse's eyes burned as he squinted at the older man, and I watched for Ahtlee's response. There was none. I hadn't expected one, really. The man was a sturdy, stubborn twin of his son Wahyaw, and one of the smartest people I'd ever met. He spoke little but knew much.

"Come," Salali said cheerfully in Cherokee, grabbing our attention again. "Please sit. Soquili?"

Soquili nodded, then went to the back of the house. Jesse and I sat with Salali, waiting in silence as she beamed at him. Soquili returned and handed Jesse a bundle wrapped in deerskin. Jesse stared at it, looking unsure.

"A gift," I said.

"Yeah. I can see that. What am I supposed to do with it?"

"Don't be an idiot, Jesse," I hissed. "Open it up and look at what they have given you."

He unfolded the deerskin, and his eyes widened at what he saw within. The first item was a shirt. His face reflected surprise, then appreciation.

"Tell her thanks," he said, managing a hint of a smile at Salali before he slid the shirt over his head. I passed along his message, then tried to help him with the sleeves, but he shrugged me off, stubborn despite his wounds. He returned to the bundle, pulling out a new blanket, a breechclout—which he immediately set aside with a scowl—a pair of buckskin leggings, and moccasins.

Salali handed him a bowl of stew, which he sniffed carefully. Since he was the guest of honour, he was to be the first to eat, so we all sat waiting. He glanced nervously at me, then finally spooned up some of the meat and started to chew, wincing as the bruises on his face made themselves felt. Salali watched his expression carefully, as if his judgement of her cooking was vastly important. In a silence that must have seemed huge to Jesse, we watched him swallow. He smiled vaguely at all of us, then dug back in, eating as if he hadn't seen food for days—which, of course, he hadn't. He even graced Salali with the occasional smile between bites.

We didn't speak much until afterward, then it was Salali who spoke, with me translating.

"It is good to have you among us, Jesse. You do not look like my son, but your spirit is his. Soquili brought you home, and I am grateful to him for that. You have made an old woman happy."

I turned to Salali. "You're not old."

"Ah, Ad-layd. But sometimes I feel older than the Grandmother."

I smiled at her. "This man is fortunate to have you for a mother."

"And I am fortunate to have you as a daughter," she teased, flicking one eyebrow.

"Oh, not you, too! You know I am not ready to marry, Salali."

"No, but you will someday."

"Perhaps."

"What's she saying?" Jesse demanded. "Is it about me?"

"No," I snapped. "It's about me."

Salali beamed at Jesse, and I continued to translate. "Soquili tells me you will not cut your hair. That is all right. My son wore feathers in his hair, and yours is already gold like the sunshine. We will cut your ears, though, and maybe give you paint."

"What?"

I nodded. "They want to pierce your ears and give you a tattoo, but she'll leave your hair as it is."

He looked as if I'd just suggested he leap off a cliff. "A tattoo? That's for savages."

"Like it or not, you are one of the Cherokee now. I suppose that makes you a savage." I tried to appear nonchalant. "Like me."

He frowned at me, opening his mouth slightly as if he weren't sure how to react. "You're no savage."

"Exactly," I replied, grinning. "Neither are they. You're the most savage creature here."

"Hey!" he objected, looking injured. "I've behaved."

I couldn't help smiling. "Yes, you have. You've done well."

Salali began speaking again. "We have more gifts for you, son."

A quiet shuffling came from the back of the house as Ahtlee rose, carrying with him another bundle, this one wrapped in a dark deerskin. There was something about just watching Ahtlee approach that made it feel like a ceremony. Soquili stood beside his father and glared down his nose at Jesse. Confused, Jesse struggled to his feet, wincing when his wounded thigh twisted. I stood up as well and tried to disappear beside the three of them, feeling strangely like an intruder, though the conversation couldn't have worked without my translations.

Soquili glanced at me, looking slightly self-conscious, then spoke in his choppy English.

"Jess-see. I welcome you. A white man killed my brother, but now a white man is my brother." He looked at me, shrugging slightly and looking adorably sheepish. I nodded. *You're doing well*. Reassured, he looked back at Jesse, frowning slightly. "You stand in his place. You and I have same friends and fight same enemies."

Jesse said nothing, but stood perfectly still, studying Soquili and his father with the unblinking stare of a cougar. The words Soquili had meant as a welcome had the opposite effect on Jesse. The atmosphere grew so taut between the three men that when I cleared my throat it seemed the air shuddered like a plucked bowstring. Rage crackled behind the golden eyes, but the others didn't seem to notice. Or if they did, they didn't react. Soquili turned toward Ahtlee, who held out the bundle, then folded back the deerskin cover and inspected the contents.

Jesse's eyes flickered in my direction. He glared at me and muttered, "I ain't no damn Injun."

"For you," Soquili said. With formal elegance, he handed Jesse the rifle that had originally been taken from him during his capture. He followed up with both powder and shot. Jesse stared at the weapon in his hands, frowning with disbelief. Then Soquili gave him a tomahawk and a knife, adding a leather leg holster as well. I studied Jesse's shocked expression, felt the rush of blood through his veins as if it were my own. I could practically see the thoughts spinning through his mind as he worked out a plan to use these very weapons to slaughter us all and take to the hills.

"Don't do it," I quietly advised.

He turned his swollen face slowly toward mine. The lines beside his eyes were tight with grief, anger, desperation, and his voice was low when he spoke through his teeth. "Why not? Why shouldn't I? They ruined my life years ago."

"These people aren't who killed your family. You described those warriors to me. They weren't Cherokee."

"They're all Injuns, Adelaide. You and me, we're white. We're not meant to mix. You know that."

I shook my head slowly. "I don't know that. These people treat me better than white people ever did."

"Ad-layd?" Soquili said, curious.

I held Jesse's gaze a moment longer, then I turned to Soquili and spoke in Cherokee. "He is not ready for this, Soquili. He does not understand and carries much hate for Indians who killed his other family. He is very angry. I fear his rage."

Soquili nodded, then examined Jesse closer, through narrowed eyes, considering the clenched jaw and hostile expression. "Then I will watch him, Ad-layd. But this is a good thing. An angry man is a strong man. My brother was the strongest of all."

"But he was not angry," I objected.

Soquili shrugged. "He could be angry. And if white people killed my family, I would be angry like this Jesse."

Why couldn't they see this was a mistake? "An angry man may be strong," I said, "but he is difficult to predict. He can be foolish and dangerous. Do you still want him?"

Soquili looked at his mother, who shut her eyes, leaving the decision to him. His gaze passed over me and rested on Jesse. He nodded. "I believe it is right. If I am wrong, he will not live. If he runs, he will not live. So he should make me right, and not run."

I smiled. "That makes sense."

"We shall see," Soquili said. He cocked his head to the side, eyes narrowed. "Do you see him as your husband?"

"Stop saying that," I hissed. "I don't want to talk about that."

Jesse's eyes snapped between Soquili and me, trying to follow our tone, if not our words. I glared at him. "Nothing for you to worry about."

"Tomorrow I shall take him hunting," Soquili declared, smiling broadly. "I will teach him."

I crossed my arms. "Could you perhaps wait until his leg heals a bit? He can barely walk."

He frowned, then shrugged. "Fine. Two days from now, we shall go."

I rolled my eyes. "Oh, sure. Two days, and he'll be good as new."

"What's he saying?" Jesse demanded. When I told him, the corners of Jesse's mouth curled in a derisive grin. "*He* wants to teach *me* how to hunt? That should be interesting. What are we hunting?"

By now I'd had enough of translating for two impossible men. "Something big and dangerous, no doubt." I rolled my eyes. "Something guaranteed to prove you both very manly, I'm sure."

After that, I did everything I could to stay away from Jesse. Maybe he'd escape. In fact, maybe I should help him escape. If he left the village, I wouldn't have to marry anyone.

PART 2

Jesse

CHAPTER 11

Daylight

Something soft hit his eyelid, and Jesse's eyes sprang open. "What the—"

A pair of light green eyes, pupils dilated with curiosity, stared down at him. Delicately bowed whiskers twitched on either side of a light brown nose. Seeing Jesse was awake, the triangular ears perked forward with anticipation.

Jesse shoved the cat away. "Get off," he snarled, then winced as his lip split. Again. He had just shut his eyes and started to doze again when two more lightning-fast whacks struck his eyelids. This time, the cat bounced out of reach when he grabbed for it. Growling, Jesse sat up, then immediately regretted moving.

Everything hurt. Someone was beating a hammer inside his head, hitting louder and harder with every strike. Both eyes throbbed and were swollen almost completely shut. He poked gingerly around his face, grimacing when he felt the extent of the swelling. That white girl—what was her name? Adelaide. Adelaide had set his nose—God, he remembered the grating agony as she'd worked it back into place. He still couldn't breathe through it. His thigh felt as if a hot poker had been shoved into it and was being slowly rotated. And his mouth . . . Lord, his mouth was dry as death. He tried to swallow but couldn't. The sensation was stifling, like he was suffocating. He turned in desperation, searching for something wet.

There. A small clay cup, filled to the brim with water. His hand shook as he reached for it, his stiff fingers closed around the vessel, and he cursed himself every time he spilled a drop. He used both hands, making sure he brought the water to his lips, then sucked it back. He tasted iron with the water and gulped more down. Blood from his lip. Didn't matter. When he finished, he hung his head over his bent knees and closed his eyes. Blindly, he set the cup back on the mat beside him, letting the time and place get a grip on his senses again. He was still here, with the damn Injuns. Cherokee, she'd called them.

And he was still alive. What would his father say to that? Probably call him a liar and club him over the head.

Sweet Jesus. That couldn't make him hurt more than he already did.

Jesse slowly turned his head, careful not to strain his injuries, and studied the room, taking in the details. The sweltering building was a welcome change from the tent where they'd first tossed him, though he'd never admit that out loud. Dried corn hung from the rafters, and baskets of food were set in neat rows against the dark wood walls of the house. In the centre of the room, a tiny circle of embers glowed, dining on sticks and twigs. The little fire provided the only sounds in the place, tiny sizzles and pops that were barely there. Any other noises came from outside.

If it had been raining, he would have heard drops pattering on the thatch overhead. As it was, the sun beamed across the floor with invitation. Three giggling little faces peered through the door, round cheeks flushed, then vanished with squeals of excitement when he glowered at them. The cat returned, this time soft with persuasion, pressing her nose with suggestion under his hand. Jesse absently stroked the tiger-striped fur while he watched the activity outside.

Where was the girl? Without her, he was lost. These people and their strange language scratched his ears, making no sense in his brain. What was he expected to do? Was anyone going to come and check on him?

He groaned and pushed tentatively to his feet, grasping at the wall for support. The cat twitched the long crook of her tail and, sensing the end of attentions, disappeared outside. Jesse hardly noticed her leaving. Willing his feet to step one in front of the other was a mental exercise. They hardly felt as if they belonged to him, the pain was so foreign. Sure, he'd been beat before, plenty of times. But he couldn't recall anything ever feeling quite this bad. He was amazed nothing besides his nose had been broken. At least nothing that he'd noticed. Maybe a rib or two, but Adelaide hadn't said anything about that. Sure could have used Doc right about now.

Lifting his arm as a shield from the blinding sun, Jesse stepped outside. The three children hadn't run far, and now shrieked again, seeming deliriously happy to see the monster on his feet and lurching in their direction. He looked beyond them, then across the expanse of open space between the houses. It was a busy place, with men and women passing through, stopping to speak with one another, doing whatever business they were required to do. Like anywhere else . . . only different, with all the naked skin and plucked heads, the women with long black hair in tails falling down their backs.

A corral of horses was at one end of the yard, filled with a variety of healthy-looking beasts in all different colours. Probably all stolen from white folks, Jesse figured. He didn't see any saddles, or even a barn where they'd store such things. The savages probably didn't use them. Why bother? These people were just like animals anyway.

He was almost bowled over when a large black-and-brown dog bounded toward him, tail curled into a loose coil, pointed ears alert. When Jesse didn't move, the dog dropped his chest to the ground so the wagging tail stuck up in the air, looking ridiculous. The damn dog wanted to play.

"Ain't no time for that, boy," he said. "I don't think I could throw a stick if my life depended on it, anyway."

"Dog," said a male voice, startling Jesse. He hadn't heard anyone approaching, which bothered him. Must be all the swelling in his head making him deaf. With a grunt, he tilted his head to one side and looked up into Soquili's calculating expression. The men frowned at each other for a moment, then Jesse nodded.

"Yeah. Dog."

"*Gitli*," Soquili said, pointing at the dog.

Jesse flashed a brief, cynical smile, though it hurt to do so. He shook his head the smallest bit, fearing the headache that would surely follow. "Dog."

One side of Soquili's mouth rose in a half smile. "Gitli."

Jesse sighed. "I ain't talking like that. I'm no Injun. It's a damn *dog*."

Soquili's hand flew out of nowhere, and his palm landed with a loud smack against Jesse's face. Jesse staggered back, tears springing reflexively to his eyes. "God*damn* it!" he exclaimed.

Soquili stepped close enough that he was only a few inches from Jesse's furious face. "Gi-tli," he pronounced carefully.

Jesse's voice came out hoarser than he intended. "Dog."

Soquili's hand seemed even faster this time. Jesse didn't move, but tears stung behind his lids. He breathed deeply, forcing them back. Damned if he was going to give in. "It's a goddamn *dog*."

This time Soquili's breath was on his face, the man had come so close. It made Jesse want to scream, having that stone-cold Indian right there, glaring down at him. Was it worth losing his scalp over this?

"Gitli," Soquili murmured. "Gitli, Jess-see."

A soft pressure wrapped around Jesse's ankles, and he recognized his visitor from earlier. He gave Soquili a cold sneer. "Cat," he said.

Soquili actually smiled. He nodded. "*Wes*," he said, then pointed at the dog again. "Gitli."

Jesse said nothing, just crossed his arms over his chest. This was never going to end. Soquili did the same thing, assuming a solid stance, feet planted like he planned on standing there all day.

The big Indian continued, pointing first at himself, then at Jesse. *"A-wi-na."*

He did the pointing thing again: his chest, Jesse's chest. "A-wi-na." Then he turned and pointed toward a pair of beautiful young women walking behind him. They giggled, and he wiggled his brow appreciatively. *"A-ta."*

Sucking up the courage he feared might slip away if he waited any longer, Jesse narrowed his eyes and jabbed his finger at his own chest. "A-wi-na," he said. Then he poked Soquili's chest, making sure Soquili understood what he was about to say. He smiled through the bruises and, voice twisted with sarcasm, muttered, "Gitli."

CHAPTER 12

Savages and Healers

The first days were the worst. Physically, Jesse was a mess, but he figured that was the least of his problems. In fact, when it came down to it, he didn't much mind the injuries, because that meant Adelaide had to come and tend to those. He looked forward to seeing her more than he'd ever admit.

His physical injuries were slowly healing, and his mind was clearing, which meant life with the Cherokee was no longer a blur. When they'd first brought him in, bound like a wild animal, Jesse had been a vibrating mass of fury, bent on destruction. He had welcomed the fight with Dustu and had almost looked forward to more of them challenging him after that, even after the bastard had opened up his damn leg again. The gauntlet had been fierce, a beating like none other he'd ever received. And yet he'd survived. And he'd apparently impressed them enough that no one led him to a burning stake. Not yet, anyway.

When he'd been entrusted with the same tools he'd intended to use on his captors, he had wanted to laugh. He'd wanted to strike out, shoot that damn "brother" of his in the face, then scalp him as his doting mother watched. It was inconceivable to Jesse that anyone could be that stupid. They couldn't possibly think he *wanted* to be there.

But Adelaide, that pretty little white mouse, had been there, whispering, reminding him of his limited options. He was divided about the girl. She was undeniably beautiful, and smart, though she said little when they were together. Her eyes jumped around a lot, dancing with a constant stream of nerves. Fear? Was it him she was afraid of, or just everything in general? He would have suspected the Cherokee of subjecting her to something horrible, but it was clear she was comfortable among these people. She'd *chosen* to be here. Well, that made him think twice. What kind of woman would do that? Maybe she was crazy. A looney like his great-aunt Bonnie. The Injuns had killed Bonnie, sliced her down when she ran screaming out to meet them. Their blades had cut that scream short.

Bonnie's murder was probably the first memory Jesse had. He'd been about four or five, he guessed. He and his father had gone off to check traps then come home to a smoking house with nobody left alive in it. His father had yanked him down behind a little hill, and they'd lain there on their bellies, watching the whole thing go down. He wanted to run, to stop the massacre, but his father shook his head.

"Nothin' you can do, boy."

So they'd lain unmoving, helpless, watching the monsters hack at Great-aunt Bonnie, then walk away carrying her braid of long, gray hair, still attached to the bloody skin of her scalp. They'd left with a lot of scalps that day. He hadn't seen them take his mother's or sisters', but fifteen years later, he could still remember burying their mangled bodies after they figured it was safe to come out. His brother had been slung over one of the horses, and Jesse remembered the crazy sight of his head bobbing and bouncing as the Indians galloped away. Jesse had never seen him again after that day, but a few days after he'd arrived here in the Cherokee village, Jesse saw how he'd probably died.

Since they wanted Jesse to be one of them, the savages had forced him to pay attention to this ritual. They'd squeezed his cheeks with iron fingers so he faced the fires, even pried his eyelids open so he couldn't blink. The heat on his skin was scalding, but that was only a breeze compared to what the others felt.

There were three of them. Men he'd known his entire life, friends of his father. Two of them were big men, the other wiry as a weasel. He'd always known them as tough scrappers, and unafraid. They all saw him, their captive audience, and their eyes had pleaded for help. *Jesse! Jesse!* But he couldn't do anything. The prisoners forgot about Jesse after a while, forgot about anything but the pain, the unthinkable, unbearable pain. They wept and screamed, begging for death as tomahawks sliced and flames crackled. Jesse breathed through his mouth, as he'd done every time he'd cleaned the chicken coop back home, and silent tears poured down his burning cheeks. And all around him the Cherokee had danced and sung, their strange painted faces alight with celebration.

Not Adelaide, though. When they'd finally released their hold on him, he'd sought her out, needing something familiar to lean on, even if it was just the colour of her skin. But the little mouse was nowhere to be seen.

He found her the next morning, down by the stream. As usual, Soquili was with him, but for some reason, when Adelaide was nearby, Soquili gave them space. It was the one thing for which Jesse was grateful.

She watched him come toward her, her expression curious but sad. She knew what he'd seen. "Still thinking of running?" she asked.

He twitched a half smile in her direction, then plunged headfirst into the cold stream. He didn't want to talk. The water dug into his thigh, attacking the open cut, flushing it clean, though Adelaide had already done a skillful job with that. He swam to the other side, deft as an otter, then popped up and carefully wiped the water from one eye, letting it stay and soothe the swollen one. The stream wasn't deep where he stood, and the slick pebbles underfoot were like velvet against the calluses on his feet. Soquili squatted on the shore, splashing water on his face, keeping a subtle but wary eye on his new brother.

What a strange, strange concept. Jesse scrubbed his fingers through his wet hair, scratching hard into his scalp. Yank an enemy off the field and decide, "Yeah. You'll do." What did the crazy savages expect? That his bone-deep hatred of Indians would just be washed away like the dirt that had masked the layers of bruises on his body? That he would forget everything his father had taught him? Walk away from his former life and just be *okay* with this idea? Made no sense at all, as far as Jesse could see. And yet it must happen occasionally, since Adelaide was here.

He glanced at her, trying not to be too obvious, but she wasn't looking at him. She was scrubbing something, working out a stain, sitting with her long legs mostly displayed in front of her. One thing you could say for these folks, their fillies sure wore enticing clothes, though most of the women he'd never even consider looking at. Adelaide's pale buckskin covered only halfway up her thigh, affording him a view of more soft white skin than he figured was proper. But he wasn't about to argue, or even ask her about that. He wasn't a fool, no matter what these people might think.

She was beautiful. No doubt about that. Like him, she was blond, a beacon among all the shining heads of black hair. This morning her waist-long hair was tied into one long, shiny braid down the centre of her back. He imagined tugging out the leather thong that held it in place, then fanning out her rippled locks. The sun had turned it almost pure white in places, and he imagined if he had her pinned beneath him, her hair threaded through his sun-browned fingers, it would be soft as the down on a dove. He backed up until the water licked the bottom of his chest, letting the sun warm his aching shoulders and back, then let her image wind its way through him.

As if he had said her name out loud, she looked up and stared directly at him, tilting her head slightly. Her nostrils flared briefly, like whiskers twitching on a mouse, and he had the eeriest sense that in that instant she had read his mind. He stared back, meeting blue, blue eyes before she looked away.

It was a shame he'd have to leave her behind when he left. But he obviously couldn't stay here, and having her along would only complicate matters. She might not even want to go, foreign as that idea was to him. He did. He wanted out of this place, and he wanted it done yesterday. But he'd bide his time. He'd wait for the right time, a safer time, then he'd be gone, disappearing into the welcoming coolness under the trees. It would have to be done when he was trusted, left on his own, and that wasn't about to happen anytime soon. Adelaide rarely came by to visit these days, but Soquili never left his side.

Didn't matter. He was getting out of here. Eventually.

CHAPTER 13

Doc

Jesse figured he might not know these woods as intimately as the Cherokee did, but he'd be fine once he escaped their piercing eyes. He was a survivor. He'd spent enough time lost in the woods as a boy, and he knew how to get himself found again. All those nights he'd fled the alcoholic fumes on his father's breath, knowing if he didn't, he'd be at the quick end of a switch for as long as the old man could hold out. Then there were those other nights, when Thomas Black had called on his crazy friends and they'd spent entire nights drinking and getting worked up, eventually going out and hunting down some poor Indian or girl of any colour and doing what their natures drove them to do.

Jesse'd watched his father and his gang beat and string up an Indian boy once. He didn't know what kind of Indian—back then, they didn't have names, they were just "Injuns." The boy had been young. Only about twelve or so. He'd been out with his friends when Thomas and the others had found him. The whole thing made Jesse sick just thinking of it. He'd wanted to stop what he saw, to try to speak reason to the men, but he was only a boy himself. As the men's enthusiasm grew, he feared they might turn on him as well. But he remembered the tear-tracked face of the boy—his small, trembling chin before it jerked out of reach—and he always would. The other boys had escaped, but the one ended up twitching at the end of a rope. Thomas Black had never been a gentle man. Jesse knew from personal experience that he was capable of inflicting damage that could go on for a long time. All things considered, at the time Jesse had thought the hanging a blessing for the poor boy.

They'd left the body dangling from a branch, but in the morning, it was gone. Claimed by the boy's family, he'd supposed. Jesse had always known his father was low, but that one time gave him a new word to use in his head whenever he addressed Thomas Black: coward. Who else but a coward could take pleasure in the murder of an innocent boy, no matter what colour he was?

Jesse didn't consider himself to be a coward. But sometimes, when he got really angry, he struck out, pounded his fist hard against a wall or a post. It was like the anger turned into a hot, hungry lava that thickened his blood, making it so he could barely see. When those times came over him, he couldn't help but wonder how much of Thomas ran through his veins. And when those thoughts came, he went off and sat by himself, trying to cool down.

There had been many other occasions when he could have witnessed his father's violence, but Jesse had turned away, run to safety and sanity. His father had jeered at his departing form, calling out, "Hey, boy. This could have been you. You ought to be glad!" He knew it bothered his father at first, not having his only remaining son at his side while he was torturing folks, but Thomas eventually got over that. He was having too much fun to worry about sharing.

Jesse had run and hid so many times in his life, it was second nature for him to dive into someplace he'd never been before and swim with the ease of a fish. He could climb like a snake and was willing to eat just about anything that crawled his way. He had an uncanny ability to see clearly in the dark and could run soundlessly through the forest. He'd had to admit that Soquili knew the forests well and had a lot to teach about hunting, but nobody could teach Jesse much about survival that he didn't already know.

To Jesse, the fabric of the forest was created to blanket him, to hide him when he needed to disappear. The water provided refuge as well, though he preferred the land, with its caves and trees and secret places. He'd taught himself to swim one dark night after his drunken father had thrown him into a lake and left him there.

Fortunately, just as Jesse had thought he couldn't keep his head up for another breath, he'd been fished out by Doc Allen, a gentle—if somewhat odd—old man. Doc lived on his own, in a tiny white house outside of town, and every time Jesse had appeared on his warped doorstep, a big grin had spread across Doc's craggy, bearded face.

"Come in, come in, my boy! How have you been? Ah, would you mind letting me take a look at your eye? Seems a bit puffy," he would say, referring to an eye swelled by Thomas's fist. Or, "I see your arm is paining you a bit. I have just the thing." That was when he'd broken his arm against something—he couldn't recall what now—and Thomas had threatened to break the other one if he didn't stop crying.

And always it was, "Come and settle here, boy. I've something you'll like." Jesse would be led into the kitchen where he'd feast on fresh biscuits and sweet things, occasionally warm milk, then be shown to a comfortable bed, its mattress stuffed, incredibly, by cotton. It didn't rustle when Jesse lay down, didn't smell at all. Like Doc himself, the bed welcomed him, and sometimes Jesse slept the night, and the entire following day, before waking to more careful tending by the infinitely patient Doc Allen.

Thomas glared at his son every time he returned home bandaged and cleaned up, but Jesse never told his father about Doc. He decided in the very beginning that Thomas could beat him black and blue, but he'd never give up his friend. No way on earth would he lead the devil to the saint in the little white house. He had no doubt Thomas would kill Doc for the crime of healing his son. Because although

Thomas seemed to enjoy punishing his son, he also wanted to be the only one to lay hands on him. Jesse was the only family Thomas had left, and that was his way of protecting his own.

And wasn't it ironic, Jesse thought, that folks called Doc "crazy."

Jesse didn't call him crazy. "Eccentric" was one of the words Doc had taught him, and Jesse thought that suited Doc perfectly. Sometimes Jesse sat in the main room of the house while Doc bustled around him, fiddling with this or that. The old man spoke to himself most of the time, when he wasn't speaking to Jesse, and from what Jesse could make out, it was a two-sided conversation within one man, a discussion that consisted entirely of unfinished sentences.

"But maybe the comfrey . . ."

"No, no. Remember the last . . ."

"Did I get enough willow . . ."

"Next time I must get more . . ."

Oddly shaped coloured bottles lined up like soldiers along the windowsills or in black boxes designed to keep out the light. Jesse liked the ones by the window, because on a sunny day the light flooded through them, spilling muted yellows, browns, and greens onto the sill and floorboards. Powders, liquids, leaves, even animal parts were filed neatly around the house, all a part of Doc's eternal quest to heal the world. Unfortunately, not many people gave him the opportunity to try. For some reason, they feared that Doc, with his wild hair and confused rantings, would do more harm than good, which was untrue. So when Jesse appeared—and kept appearing—with injuries, he was almost a gift for Doc.

Doc's one disappointment was that Jesse had no interest in learning the art of doctoring. His repeated pleas for "someone to carry on the knowledge" were consistently met with blank stares. Jesse couldn't keep one bottle separate from another in his mind, and he didn't care to anyhow. Eventually, Doc gave up trying, traded his frown for a good-natured shrug, and went on scribbling notes and fussing with his bottles.

Doc had a shaggy black dog who lived inside the house. She seemed to have the same even temperament as her owner. Gentle, welcoming in an unassuming way, tail always wagging. The mutt was named Chiron. Doc explained that she'd been named after an ancient Greek centaur who had apparently been credited for having invented medicine.

That was another thing Jesse loved about Doc Allen. The man was a walking encyclopedia, always teaching Jesse new words and amazing facts he'd never have learned otherwise. Every time Jesse visited, Doc slid heavy, leather-bound books from his ceiling-high shelves. He set them carefully on a worn but always clean table, declaring he had come across something fascinating that he wanted to teach Jesse on that particular day.

"So good of you to stop in today," he'd say, absently bandaging up one or another of Jesse's injuries. "I'd felt the urge for a celebration, so now we may share it. Did you know, Jesse," he'd ask, eyes bright with amazement, "that the planet Jupiter has four moons? Imagine that! Look here, Jesse, in my telescope."

Or he'd spin the large globe in the corner, indicating continents and oceans with one slightly crooked finger. "If it hadn't been for explorers over two hundred years ago, you and I might still be living somewhere across the sea . . ." Occasionally, Doc stuck a finger somewhere on the globe and declared himself determined to discover something about the place. Geography books filled with drawings and facts, both amazing and dull, found their way in front of Jesse.

On slower, more reflective days, when words seemed almost to weary him, Doc pulled out books of art, showing Jesse paintings from all over Europe, leading the boy through a maze of sculptures and architecture from ancient Egypt and Greece. On those days, he rhapsodized with a kind of wistfulness, marvelling at the greatness of the human spirit, the voice of the heart. Those were the days when he sat Jesse down afterward, looked into his eyes, and tried to convince him that he carried greatness within himself. He told Jesse he could be whatever he wanted to be, if he strove to live well and always worked toward that goal.

Jesse never fully bought into that particular lesson. While Doc might be able to lose himself in lessons and faraway stories, Jesse was stuck in his father's shabby house on a flat pile of nothing in the middle of the Carolinas. And as much as he'd love to discover something new in his life, he really didn't see a whole lot of options. But Doc had persevered, telling him that even if he did nothing but raise horses and marry a good woman someday, the way that he did it meant the most of all.

"Your time will come, Jesse. You are a great man, and you're here for a reason."

Jesse held his tongue. Despite everything Doc tried to tell him, there was always a part of Jesse—a small, scared part of him—that dreaded what he might become. He was Thomas Black's son, which made him the son of the devil.

Doc seemed oblivious to Jesse's worries. "A man such as you," he said, "is not one to fritter away his days on nothing at all. Remember the great Shakespeare, the poet and storyteller?"

Jesse nodded. "*Hamlet*," he said. "You read me that."

"And *Macbeth*?"

"The old man and all the blood. Yeah. I remember that one."

"Then remember this, my boy:

All the world's a stage,
And all the men and women merely players;
They have their exits and their entrances,
And one man in his time plays many parts . . ."

"Uh-huh," Jesse grunted.

Doc showed him books of the stars and showed him how to read them, how to use their light if he was ever lost in the wilderness. He taught him the origin of everyday things, told him stories about inventors and scientists, about explorers and adventurers who had made history. He expanded Jesse's vocabulary, teaching him words that made Jesse feel intelligent.

Most important of all, Doc taught Jesse to read. They laboured over books, with Doc demonstrating the different sounds each letter made and Jesse throwing regular tantrums when his brain reached its limit. But he kept coming back. When written words became familiar to Jesse, he had to be careful not to let his father know. Thomas couldn't read, and never even once suggested Jesse should learn. But because of Doc, he had. Jesse devoured books. One of Jesse's favourite pastimes was losing himself, and reading gave him a whole world to escape into. Though he politely refused to read Doc's library of philosophical, medical, or political books, he read other books for hours, ensconced among *Gulliver's Travels, Leonidas,* and the works of Daniel Defoe. He must have read *Robinson Crusoe* five times.

He wondered if that little blond mouse could read. She looked smart, but he didn't know how long she'd lived here at the village. Or where she'd come from. He didn't know much about her at all. She wasn't exactly the sharing type. Tended to clam up at anything that even hinted at a personal question. But that was okay. Jesse had time. He knew he could eventually crack her, find out what she was all about. All he had to do was wait, then use that charm the girls back home couldn't resist.

CHAPTER 14

Target Practice

When Jesse returned from the river, he was met by Dustu. The scowling warrior was leaning heavily on a thick branch that had been stripped of bark. He used it because Jesse's wicked twist had done a painful number on Dustu's ankle. It was going to be a long time before the warrior was able to stand on two feet again.

"U yo," the smaller man said, his upper lip lifted in a sneer. "Too bad river does not clean ugly skin off. You are still white."

Any pleasant thoughts of Adelaide and the river instantly vanished. Jesse kept walking. He had his own limp, but he did his best to mask it as he passed Dustu. "Yeah? And you're still a turd."

He was surprised to hear a steady *shuffle thump shuffle thump* behind him, then realized Dustu was following him.

"What is turd?" Dustu wanted to know.

"What comes out the back end."

A moment, then Dustu laughed. "Turd. I will use this."

"Go ahead. It's all yours."

"I say you will burn, turd."

Jesse stopped and took a slow breath. He turned and met Dustu's spiteful glare. "What?"

"You will cook like *awi i nage ehi*."

Jesse stared through his lashes, then shook his head very slowly. "Eh?"

"Awi i nage ehi," Dustu said slowly, like he was talking to a two-year-old. Then he raised his free hand and spread his fingers over his head like antlers.

Jesse started walking away again, but Dustu wasn't finished. Relentless little bugger kept on limping behind him, tossing barbs.

"I will sing song for you while you burn, *Awi i nage ehi*. Special song. I will dance."

Jesse snorted. "One-legged dance. Sounds great."

They kept moving, and Dustu surprised Jesse with how fast he could go. He'd hoped to simply outpace the man. Just like a cockroach to keep on going no matter how many times you step on him.

"I will take your golden hair. It will fly like bird's wing over my house."

Jesse spun to face him, gritting his teeth. "What is your problem, bat face?"

Dustu's smile was broad. Satisfied. And missing a couple of important teeth. "You are problem. I do not want you here."

Arms crossed, Jesse leaned closer. "That makes two of us."

"Leave."

"You'd like that, wouldn't you? Of course, since I already busted your leg, you wouldn't be able to be in the war party that guts me, but you could watch."

"You are not Cherokee. You do not belong here."

Wasn't that the truth? "Thanks for the information. I'll be sure to think on that."

Dustu either didn't understand the sarcasm or chose to ignore it. His snicker didn't sound the least bit contrite. "You will die, white man."

"We all gotta go sometime," Jesse muttered, then squinted

hard at the warrior. "Some of us fall faster than others." He stepped toward Dustu, set his hands on the man's chest, then shoved hard. Dustu, already off balance, flew backward and landed in a gasping heap a few feet away.

"I kill you," Dustu growled.

Jesse pointedly observed him, letting his eyes travel over Dustu's fallen form. Then he nodded and turned away. "Or I'll kill you first, little man."

Dustu didn't follow, but his shadow did, casting darkness on Jesse's entire outlook. The man had been right. He *didn't* belong here. They probably *would* kill him eventually. But he had no say in anything. He was stuck here, left to wait and wonder and bang his head against a wall if he wanted. The only thing he wasn't allowed to do was leave the village. That was driving him crazy.

He stormed past a house and purposefully whacked his hand against a fish-drying rack, knocking the thing over and dropping a dozen fish into the dust. A little boy with shoulder-length black hair stood nearby, looking up at Jesse with round, nervous eyes, and Jesse drew back his hand as if he was going to hit him. He'd never have done it. Wouldn't hit a woman or child if his life depended on it. But he wanted to scare the kid. God help him, he wanted to terrify him. It worked. The little boy took off without a word, the weathered soles of his feet pounding the earth as he ran.

Furious energy buzzed through Jesse, taking his mind off all the aches and pains in his body and pushing him to walk faster. He needed to get some of this anger out. He needed to take it out on something or else he might just explode. When he passed the next house he slammed his fist against the wall and growled like a trapped animal but kept walking. A woman popped out of the house, squawking, demanding to know what he was doing, he supposed, but he just flapped a hand at her.

Half a dozen horses milled around in the corral, and Jesse had to fight the need to vault onto one of those broad backs and race far from this place. But that would mean certain death, and he was too angry to allow that just yet.

He'd had to deal with anger before, obviously. But then he'd had the wide-open outdoors, where he could run all by himself. He could gallop across the spaces, navigate through the forest paths, or simply hide out awhile in a cave or by the water. If he could just keep moving, maybe this need to throttle something would fade.

A pile of still-hot ash from an earlier fire sat directly in his path, so he kicked it, scattering dust and gray coals, then stepped over the mess. When one of the friendly village dogs came pounding over to him, leaping and curling its tail in anticipation, he leaned down and roared at it, teeth bared, until it slunk away.

He reached the other side of the village and stood on the outer edge of the forest, looking in. He couldn't run, obviously, because they'd kill him. And because of the restless fury pulsing within him, he certainly couldn't just sit and ponder the situation. He wasn't that kind of man, anyway. He needed to keep his hands busy. Needed to take out some of his anger on something. On impulse, he stooped and grabbed a rock at his feet, then threw it into the trees. The thud it made when it hit an unseen tree trunk or ricocheted off a boulder hidden within the shadows was mildly satisfying. He scouted the ground, looking for more, then stopped short at the sight of a weathered pair of moccasins beside his own. He looked up into the slightly amused gaze of Soquili.

The Indian didn't say anything, just narrowed his eyes and studied Jesse for a second. It was unexpected, Jesse thought, seeing so much calm in those black eyes. Something you didn't expect from what he'd always known as savages. Then Soquili set his hand on Jesse's arm to move him out of the way, and Jesse was instantly back on guard, fists raised. But Soquili only laughed and shook his head. He turned away and stepped a few paces back, then waved at Jesse to get out of the way.

Jesse frowned, not understanding. Eventually, when Soquili jerked his head to one side, he gave in and moved. As soon as he was far enough out of the way, Soquili drew his tomahawk from its place around his waist, swung it back over his head, then flung the weapon toward a large dead stump a few feet away from where Jesse now stood. The blade did a perfect spin, then planted itself in the middle of the wood with a rewarding thunk. Soquili walked up, grabbed the handle, and tugged it out, then walked back and did it all over again, this time from a little farther back. He repeated the same action five times, then stopped in front of Jesse and folded his arms over his broad chest.

"You."

Jesse looked up at him from under his lashes, then huffed. As he walked back to where Soquili had thrown from, he muttered, "It'll be you I'm aiming at, brother."

He'd thrown knives before, when he was younger. Aimed them at a certain spot on the barn wall. One he'd set in his mind as his father's face. He wasn't bad at it, but he'd admit to not being the best. Never thrown a tomahawk before, though. He pulled the one from his belt and stared down the five long paces from the trunk. He wondered if he'd even be able to hit the thing. Might just lose it in the woods. He started to swing his arm back, then stopped and glanced at Soquili, whose wry grin didn't help Jesse's confidence one bit.

"What?"

Soquili moved his hand, thumb edge up, in a straight line, indicating how Jesse should throw.

"Yeah, yeah." Shaking off the tip, Jesse drew back the tomahawk and hurled it with all his might at the trunk.

It hit the trunk, which was a great start. Then it hit it sideways, then fell uselessly to the ground. Unable to stop himself, Jesse looked over at Soquili, but the big brave had his eyes glued to the ground at his feet. At least he didn't have to answer to any teasing. Jesse picked up the tomahawk, moved his arm in a practice swing, then hurled it again.

Same result. This was not helping Jesse's mood one bit. Twice more he tried, and twice more the tomahawk ended up lying like a stick on the ground.

"Forget it," he finally said, jamming the weapon back into his belt.

"Do not kill it."

"What?" Jesse snapped. The last thing he wanted right about now was a lesson.

Soquili didn't seem to notice. He walked to Jesse's side, holding his own tomahawk as an example. He showed Jesse how loosely he held the weapon, then slung it back and casually nailed the trunk.

Jesse eased his grip a little, weighing the thing in his hand. Soquili stepped away and nodded, looking confident, then folded his arms again while he watched. Nothing like a little pressure, Jesse thought, setting his feet one ahead of the other. He'd tried to look like he didn't care when Soquili was showing him what to do, but in truth he'd studied every move. The hard part, he figured, was not making it hard. Easy does it, as they say. So he pulled his arm back and swung through in one fluid motion, and the tomahawk floated end over end, planting itself in the dead wood. Just like Soquili's.

Jesse stared at it, shocked it had been that simple. Soquili was smiling easily now, and he nodded in the direction of the weapon, but he didn't have to. Jesse was already walking over to pull it out and do it again. After a few perfect throws, Soquili carried over another log, one that was a little smaller in diameter. He took a turn, hitting the centre with annoying accuracy. Jesse missed a couple of times, then sunk the blade nice and deep. He experimented, moving back farther from the target, twisting his wrist to see what happened, then let Soquili coach him on how to make his shot even better. Then Soquili left and Jesse stayed.

For an hour, he threw that thing, throwing harder and farther until his shoulder screamed at him to stop. But the satisfaction of seeing and hearing that delicious success was exactly what he'd needed. He took out his aggression, his frustration, his indecision on the little trunk, and when he finally came away, it was with a feeling that he could, after all, survive all this. He hadn't answered a single question about any of it, but he'd at least gotten ahold of his anger and used it in a good way, rather than getting himself in trouble by starting a fight or something. It wasn't the last time he went out to that spot for target practice.

CHAPTER 15

Tloo-da-tsi

He'd gone hunting with Soquili and a few others, showing them he knew how to use a bow and arrow. They watched him constantly, suspicion thick in their black eyes, but they all assumed he'd fall in line eventually. Join their Cherokee family. As if he had any choice. Over time, he forced himself to become more polite with Salali and Ahtlee but could never call them Mother or Father—though, God knew, Ahtlee was without question a better father than the one he'd originally been given. But to look these black-haired people in those slightly slanted eyes, set above flattened noses and broad cheekbones, and call them his family? How could any white man do that?

Adelaide didn't seem to be part of any one particular family, but she was close to Soquili's. He would have to ask her about that someday.

He'd noticed that among the Cherokee, there were elders, people who looked after the decision making in council, and who decided the fates of others with a blink of their milky eyes. The women seemed to be the ones in charge, even over the elder men. Above them all floated an ancient crone named Wah-Li.

"Come," Soquili said one day in his halting English. "Wah-Li see you."

"What if I don't want to see her?"

"Not a question."

So he'd gone, after some last-minute primping by Salali, and ducked under the opening of the big council house in the middle of the village. The heat of the place sucked his breath away, yet the only warmth radiated from a small hearth fire where the old woman sat, tiny and shriveled by time, wrapped in blankets Jesse would have found smothering.

"Sit," she croaked.

Jesse didn't sit immediately. Nor did he speak. He paced the entryway of the house, studying every corner, making himself aware of exactly what he was getting himself into. But the room was almost completely black, save the red embers and the wrinkled woman. He squinted, trying to adjust his eyes to the darkness, but could see nothing. He didn't like the darkness behind her. It felt . . . occupied.

At length he sat, but he kept his gaze on the hidden place behind her. He didn't think she'd notice anyway, since her eyes were masked by a murky layer of white.

"Tloo-da-tsì," she muttered with a smile, then poked a twig into the fire. "I thought so."

Jesse frowned but said nothing. He wasn't sure what she'd said, but he thought it'd been English. He'd been told the old witch spoke the language, that she'd learned along the way, with help from Adelaide's sister. He hoped so. Otherwise this was going to be a waste of time. Not that he had a great many things to do with that time, but still.

"You are uncertain of this place, Tloo-da-tsì." When he didn't speak, she smiled and he saw only more darkness within the toothless jaws. But it wasn't threatening, that smile. Curious, like a child's. His muscles loosened just enough as he began to relax. She cast a quick glance over her shoulders, toward the back of the house, looking for whatever it was that held his attention. Maybe she wasn't so blind after all.

"You hide in the shadows, but you do not like when the shadows hide from you."

She definitely spoke English. That woke him up. "I don't like surprises," he admitted.

She smiled. Her face seemed to have collapsed in on itself, lacking either bone or teeth to keep it in the right shape. Age had had its way with the woman and left her with a hideous face, yet the air around her felt soft and comforting.

"This life brings many surprises," she assured him. "Your life with the Tsalagi is a surprise, I think."

That roused a crooked smile. "Oh, I'd say it most certainly is."

"And are you unhappy?"

Unhappy? Hardly seemed to scratch the surface, did it? Jesse dropped his chin to his chest and bit his lip, willing himself to keep calm. Wouldn't do to reach across the fire and throttle an old woman just for asking a stupid question. One he wasn't about to justify with an answer.

Unhappy. Huh. How about furious? How about, What the hell is going on? Would that qualify as "unhappy"?

Jesse got to his feet, debating his next move. His first instinct was to turn and leave, stomp out of the stifling house and maybe head to the river. Get away from the crazy woman and the looming shadows.

But he didn't go. The old woman intrigued him. What was it about her that had the whole village so entranced?

"Where will you go, when you run from here?"

He glanced at her, startled. He didn't like learning he was so transparent. It was a decent question, though. He couldn't go home, though his father probably assumed he was already dead. That was maybe a good thing. He could let Thomas keep on believing that.

"I have to get home to my family," he bluffed.

The woman tilted her head like a sparrow. "I hear you have only a father. The Catawba took the others."

It was as if an Arctic wind suddenly whistled through the house. Jesse remembered suddenly the shapes of the men who had killed his family, even though they'd been in the distance. He remembered how their wild eyes had been painted with rings of black and white. He stared at the old woman through cold, cold eyes, but she didn't even blink.

"You hear right."

She continued as if nothing had changed between them. "You have a family here now. You must trust the new family."

"I don't trust easy."

"No. I see that." She hesitated. "Permit me to touch your face, Tloo-da-tsì?"

He frowned, startled by her request. "Why?"

The curious smile lit up again. "What have you heard of me, the old woman of the village? What have your new people said?"

"That you're in charge."

She chuckled. "I do not know those words, but I think I understand. The People come to me for answers because I can see what they cannot. May I touch your face?"

He jerked away and stared at her, not understanding. It seemed like an invasion, letting someone touch him like that. Not like when Adelaide had helped him out, though. That was different. That was to fix his injuries. But the old woman just smiled up at him, so obviously harmless he could find no reason not to stoop and let her do what she wanted.

"Here," she said and patted the ground beside her.

Jesse puffed out a breath through his nose, but he sat where she said.

"Now. Just sit," she said calmly.

Her fingers were shriveled and soft as deerskin, her joints twisted at strange angles from their losing battle against rheumatism. In spite of the pain he assumed would come from doing so, she pressed them firmly against his cheeks, her forefingers on his temples. She smiled at him, then closed her eyes. Without thinking about it, his did the same.

He floated. He had no other words with which to describe what happened in that moment. The air around him churned, like someone had poured the boiled kettle into a cold bath, then swirled the water around. Part of him wanted to jerk away, demand to know what was going on, but most of him didn't really care. Didn't want to move at all. He felt relaxed, more soothed than he could remember ever feeling. He saw things he hadn't remembered until that moment, pictures and sounds from his past flowing before him like the globe in Doc's house when he spun it slowly. He recognized the old privy and the mangy brown dog sitting outside of it. He kind of remembered that ugly dog from when he was little. The mutt had ended up with a muzzle full of porcupine quills and had to be shot. There was his mother, her face so long forgotten, beckoning. He ran to her, his little boy body melting into the promise of security in her arms. Then she was gone, and he ran with his brother, laughing in the summer grass.

But his life contained much more, and that dwelt in the dark. He waited for the old woman to unlock the door, unsure. Part of him feared what she would see, wanted to keep it hidden and thereby stay safe from it himself. Part of him cowered in shame at the truths his memories would give her. But he also knew that when she saw it, he would somehow . . . feel all right. He might even understand a little better. He had been so young, after all.

But he found no comfort in the picture of his father, loosing his belt to teach him one lesson or another, tightening fists to use on his sole surviving son. He saw no peace in the images of torture and killing his father and his gang had inflicted on others. He had nowhere to hide from the shame that threatened to shadow all his dreams. He tried to hide, tried to shield the old woman from it, but she was there, her thoughts with his. She was *in him* somehow.

Then he saw the girl, Adelaide. Her expression was tired and sad, as it so often was. She gave the impression that she was very much alone, and though she obviously ached with loneliness, she seemed petrified of connecting with anyone. Her pain, from whatever source, penetrated almost as deeply as the old woman's thoughts. He wanted to touch her, comfort her in exchange for all she'd done for him, but her image vanished in the next breath, and he felt a lingering sense of loss when she was gone.

The pressure of Wah-Li's fingertips eased on his temples, and he coaxed his eyes open, not wanting to rush back to reality. But the ancient crone was waiting. Sadness floated in her eyes.

"You do not trust for many reasons," she said, her voice more gentle than it had been before. "The Tsalagi will help you."

Jesse didn't know what to say. Even if he had, he wasn't sure he'd be able to form the words. He was suddenly exhausted beyond belief, his body close to collapse. She saw it and smiled. "You had much in your mind. Sharing has been difficult. You will sleep well tonight."

He had no doubt of that.

CHAPTER 16

The Importance of a Name

The cat moved in. Just to annoy Soquili, Jesse called the little feline Gitli, which he knew very well meant "dog." After Adelaide assured Soquili it was a joke, Soquili had joined in, calling Jesse "A-ta," or woman. That wasn't the only nickname Jesse got. The old woman called him Tloo-da-tsì. Adelaide pronounced it "Loo-Dot-See," and told him it meant "cougar."

"Why cougar?" he asked. "My scar?"

She shrugged. It was a small gesture, her slight shoulders lifting and falling like a sigh under the faded deerskin tunic. Everything about Adelaide looked sad: her gestures, her expressions, her eyes, even the way her white-blond hair hung weakly over her shoulders when it wasn't braided. Such a deep sadness. As if all hope had been sucked from her soul. Sometimes the sadness got so all-consuming that he didn't want to be around her, because it wanted company. Being sad just wasn't Jesse's way.

Mostly, though, he did want to be around her. A lot.

He'd gone to her house that morning, needing to hear a little English, wanting to see a little of her. She'd been startled when she saw him there, but her immediate pan-icked glance—which he'd noticed was the expression she always used first—faded swiftly into amusement. And later softened into an actual smile. Yep, he had a way with the ladies, he thought proudly. Usually he used these natural gifts with the purpose of reaching his ultimate goal: kissing and cuddling never did anyone any harm. And though he would dearly love to experience that with Adelaide, he had a different reason to use his charm this time. He needed her to like him so she could help him. This village was an entirely different world, and it didn't appear he'd be getting out anytime soon.

"The Cherokee believe your animal chooses you, so the scar could be part of it. But it's not just that, I don't think." She squinted at him, her head cocked a bit to the side. "No. It's more than that. It's in your eyes."

"There's cougar in my eyes? Come on, Adelaide. What's that supposed to mean?"

She smiled at him, though even then she couldn't quite manage to slip the sadness out of her expression.

"Let's go for a walk," she suggested. "I'll tell you a bit about Cherokee legends. It might help you understand things better."

He shrugged, trying to keep the motion casual. "I got nothing else to do. Lead on, my lady."

They strolled along the edge of the village, and on impulse Jesse stooped to pluck a daisy, then handed it to her. When she raised her eyebrows, he blushed, surprising himself. He felt vaguely exposed, letting this stranger see a weakness, and he looked away, pretending to study the line of the trees. From the corner of his eye, he saw her touch the petals of the daisy, one by one, then gesture toward the forest.

She stepped into the trees ahead of him, deftly finding a deer track and following it straight up the mountain, winding through rocks and shrubs, ducking under branches of loom-ing oak and maple. He was quiet behind her, admiring how the smooth deerskin dress clung to the lines of her body as she moved, waiting for her to start up the conversation. Jesse was hungry for all the information she could give him, but he sensed she needed to be handled with kid gloves. That was all right. He could give her room.

She stepped into an open space at the top of one of the peaks, and the view just about took his breath away. The ancient gray of the granite cliff, smoothed by time, extended like a hand over the Keowee Valley, so he and Adelaide seemed to stand on God's palm while they looked out. The view almost didn't seem possible; the forests were so lush below them, it was as if the trees were grass. As if he could just step off this cliff, and they'd be soft under his feet. Through the green snaked the Keowee River, tumbling through bubbling white rapids, then calming and continuing its journey as if nothing had happened.

"Careful you don't step out too far," Adelaide said, her voice soft behind him. He'd almost forgotten she was there, he'd been so distracted by the view. Almost. Not entirely. Now he was more than aware of her, standing close enough that he could turn and set his hands on her waist if he dared. "When the wind comes up, it feels like it could snatch you right off," she explained.

"I can handle it."

As if she'd called it, a sudden gust nudged him, checking to see if he was attached or not. It stroked up his side and ruffled his hair, then moved on, searching for easier prey. It was a cool breeze, but he kept warm within his deerskin shirt, relieved the Cherokee had let him keep his trousers after Adelaide patched the holes. He never had gotten used to those breechclout things. Seemed awfully close to naked in his opinion. And though he was as happy as the next man to wear nothing but the hair on his body, he didn't think it was proper for the ladies to see that. Not even the Cherokee ladies.

Adelaide had settled against a pile of boulders and looked comfortable lounging within its edges. She watched him with blue eyes that shone like stars within her tanned face, pale in comparison with the cloudless sky. The breeze had roused a red glow in her gentle cheeks, which were being tickled by blond wisps of hair that had blown from their ties while she'd climbed. Jesse stared at her, momentarily tongue-tied. She looked like a fairy, her sweet pink mouth relaxed in a calm smile, her colouring almost ethereal. He wondered if she had any idea how beautiful she was.

"Soquili brought Maggie and me here a long time ago," she said, not appearing to notice his hesitation. "He told us a Cherokee legend about how the world began."

"Sure is a pretty place," he replied, finding his words again. He walked toward her, looking for a place to sit, and eventually claimed a large boulder with another behind so he could lean back. He closed his eyes, letting the sun bake his lids.

"You wanted to know about your Cherokee name, Tloo-da-tsì. Cougar," she said, and he opened his eyes again. She was looking at him in that way, like she was thinking carefully about every word she was about to say. "I think it's more than your hair or your eyes. I'm not sure the Grandmother even thinks about colour. It's what is *in* you. She can see it, you know."

"That's one strange old lady," he muttered.

She chuckled. "Don't say that in front of the others. I thought she was pretty frightening in the beginning, but she's an amazing woman once you get to know her. Just nothing like what you and I knew before we came here."

Jesse didn't say anything. She'd inadvertently revealed a tiny gem about herself, and he didn't want to scare her back into hiding. He wanted to ask her all about her life before she'd come here, find out what invisible bonds tied her here. Because it seemed like being in the village was her choice, and he just couldn't understand that. She never seemed able to open up about herself, but Jesse was determined to wait patiently. He was good at that. He focused on her, trying to appear both attentive and harmless. It seemed to work, because she started speaking again in that almost whisper.

"The Grandmother is teaching me a few things about myself, too," she said shyly. "My sister . . ." She stopped, looking shocked at her own words. "I'm sorry. I can't tell you about her."

He frowned. "Why not?"

"Because you might think she's something she's not. She just . . . can do things other people can't."

"Like what?"

She sighed, her expression tortured.

"I don't judge folks," he assured her.

"It's not that. It's, well, we never used to tell anyone, but since we came here, it seems so . . . normal. It's just that I haven't spoken with a white man in so long . . ."

As he watched, her gaze seemed to cloud, her expression to tighten so that her cheeks sucked slightly in. She didn't blink.

"Adelaide?"

Her eyes snapped back into focus. "I'm sorry. What were we . . . ?"

"Your sister? Me not judging?"

She gnawed on her lip, then blurted, "Maggie sees things in her dreams. Things that are coming. She's always had those dreams, but Wah-Li showed her how to become stronger and use them better. Wah-Li thinks I can do some of that, too, but I'm not very good at it."

Jesse's eyes narrowed despite himself. "You have visions? Don't that make you a witch?"

She shot him a glance, and fear spread across her face. "I'm no witch."

"Hey," he said, raising open hands in surrender. "Just asking. I'm not about to string you up for some kind of witch talk."

"I'm not a witch," she insisted, then frowned and looked away. "Maybe you don't want to hear what I have to say."

"Now you're just being stubborn."

She looked back at him and gave a little half smile, one side of her mouth quirking up and lighting her eyes. Jesse liked the look of that, and he was determined to see more of it. Her smile both calmed and excited him at the same time.

"Maybe so," she admitted. "You being a cougar, you'd recognize that."

He rolled his eyes. "What are you going on about now?"

"Okay," she said, letting her smile broaden. "The Cherokee think we all have animal partners. Like our spirits are similar to the ones in specific animals."

"And I'm like a goddamn cougar. How's that?"

Her eyes looked at his, the blue surprisingly intense as she assessed him. "I'm guessing you like to be alone, and that you can be patient."

"Sometimes," he said, starting to grin. He liked games like this.

"You're obviously not afraid of challenges and are quick to fight. Pretty strong, too."

"You got that right," he assured her.

"And when people need a peacemaker, they come to you."

He looked away. "Yeah, sometimes. So? What's that have to do with anything? Cougars solve problems for folks? Never heard of that before." Yeah, that happened, and he never enjoyed those requests. It usually got him in trouble with both sides. But he did usually seem to be the only one with the guts to stand up and say what needed to be said. He'd give her that one, too, though he'd rather skip over it.

"Hmm," she tilted her head to the side. "That's just another one of the qualities the Cherokee say are part of the cougar. It's interesting, her thinking you're a cougar. Because there's a lot more to it—and for you to be here with the Cherokee, well, it makes a lot of sense. Or rather . . . it *could* make a lot of sense."

His smile faded. "I lost you."

"Okay. Here it is. The Cherokee believe that when you are a cougar, you are climbing to a higher place in your life. You are changing, becoming stronger in your heart."

He didn't speak for a moment, letting her words stew a bit before he tasted them. They felt eerily real.

For so many years, Jesse had cried in his sleep, cowered in panic, hid from his father's wrath. He'd been so young, for God's sake. He hadn't understood. He'd witnessed his father's crimes, and he'd known Thomas was a very bad man. But no one else appeared to see Thomas in that light. They all looked up to him, vied for his attention, did his bidding without question.

Despite Thomas's apparent intentions, Jesse had grown into a man. And while he didn't try to kid himself into thinking he was a particularly good man, he felt pretty confident that he was a better one than Thomas. He took his beatings when he had no other choice, but he also challenged his father on occasion. He even led a separate life by going to visit Doc. He learned about the world, and he learned about himself. He'd grown from being a helpless victim of his father's madness to being an independent man who knew right from wrong.

Changing? Growing stronger in his heart? Yeah. That was safe to say. Kind of an interesting coincidence, that cougar connection.

She had stopped talking and now watched her fingers as they drew circles on her skirt. She looked anxious, as if she was unsure if she should have said anything. She was a nervous little filly, half-broke, needing a gentle hand.

"And what kind of animal are you?" he asked.

She blushed, still looking down. "I don't know."

"I kind of see you as a mouse."

She glanced at him, her expression torn between amusement and disappointment. "A mouse? Why, no one likes mice."

"Oh, that's not what I meant. Do folks like cougars? No. I was only saying you're small and timid. Kind of nervous."

That seemed to reassure her. She nodded a little. "I guess so. I'd rather not be a mouse, though."

"You'd like to be a cougar?"

"No, not quite." She sighed. "I know I deserve to be called a mouse, but if I could change, it would be something a little braver. Maybe that'll come with time."

"What's got you so scared, little mouse?" he asked, then bit his tongue. He should have kept his big mouth shut, waited a little longer, because those pale blue eyes stopped twinkling, stopped smiling. It was as if a door slammed shut in her mind.

I'd like to kill the son of a bitch that hurt her.

She looked away. "It's nothing. I've always been that way. My sister's the brave one." Her gaze dropped back to her hands, clasped on her lap, and she looked very young indeed. "But I need to get stronger. I will. I can't hide behind other people my whole life."

He couldn't stop his hand from reaching over and settling on top of hers. It just seemed so natural. "You don't have to be scared. I'm here."

She froze at his touch, but he was encouraged when she didn't pull away. Very gently, he squeezed her hand, then pulled his own away again. He suddenly wanted very badly to know her better, to be there for her. He'd meant what he said. He'd watch out for her as long as he was there. He'd take care of her. She didn't move, but some of the colour had started to flow back into her cheeks, the brightness into her eyes. It was like watching spring come into bloom, and something about that made his breath hitch in his chest. He wanted to lean over, touch that angelic face, kiss her. But he fought the urge. What was he thinking? This wasn't the time to fall for a girl. Besides, how would the Cherokee react to his taking an interest in one of their own—even if she was white?

Then again, like she'd said, the cougar in him was always up for a challenge. When she finally looked fully at him and shyly smiled, he stopped worrying. He reckoned he was more than ready to stand up for Adelaide.

CHAPTER 17

The Hunt

Time changed Jesse. Life changed him. Forced to spend the past few months with his sworn enemy, learning their ways, following their rules. That had been interesting, to say the least. He had fought it with everything he had in the beginning, refused to give their ideas even a ghost of a chance in his mind. He still hated that he had no choice. That he was stuck in this in-between life of prisoner and adopted brother. But he'd found less resistance in his soul as he went along, saw glimmers of insight that made him reconsider not them, but himself.

Adelaide had started that, pointing out that his arguments were ridiculous, based on nothing but old stories told to him by an ignorant man. Thomas would have been livid, hearing himself described that way. *What right did this insignificant woman have to judge him?* Jesse'd felt that way in the beginning, then realized with a start that she had every right. She'd lived both sides. She'd probably fought the same changes he was fighting, though maybe with a little less fire.

Over time, Jesse began to listen, to learn, to appreciate the way the Cherokee lived. All his life, he'd been taught that he and the Indians were completely separate creatures. He was on the good side; they were unquestionably and infinitely bad. At first he'd stared at them from the edge of the circle, dumbstruck at their craziness. Their wailing, shrieking songs made his head ache, and when they stomped around fires, waving their sticks and stones, beating drums until it made a man want to run, well, he just didn't understand it.

But after a while, after he'd accepted that he was going to have to put up with it, he'd taken a deep breath and stepped inside that circle. He'd learned the tales their dances told, studied the passion that consumed their painted faces as they spun and thumped worn moccasins on the dirt. He managed to loosen the knots that tied his tongue when he tried to speak their language. And on the night that he rose with Soquili and joined the dance, letting colours and emotions swirl through his mind and body, his life changed.

At first, he was self-conscious, painfully aware of how fluidly they moved and how his jerky, amateur attempts to move made him look like a wooden soldier. Then he looked around and realized no one was watching him. He closed his eyes like Adelaide had advised, stood still in the middle of them all, and let their wildness sweep through him. He began to sway, to shuffle his feet, and when the hair rose on the back of his neck, he didn't fight the sensation. As he sweated alongside the shining, copper-skinned men, following their lead, letting the noise wash through him, something—some energy, some strength, some spirit, call it what you want—rose from within the flames. It plunged deep within him, grasped the pain he'd carried for so long, and yanked it loose. The flames of the huge fire around which they all danced reflected the rage as it took ahold of him, and he let his body express the hatred, the grief, the loss he'd never truly acknowledged before. He lost track of where he was, what he was doing. It was Soquili who led him from the circle and left him in a quiet place where he could weep with bewildered relief.

All the wrongs he'd seen and done seemed suddenly

forgiven. These people had brought him into their family despite his stubborn refusals. They'd shown him he was accepted. More than that, though, they'd shown him he was *wanted*. These people he'd hated with everything he had became his family, and he decided to stay.

Soquili came for him the next morning, ready for the hunt. They gathered with the half dozen others who were all talking loudly, gesturing, clearly excited to be on their way. Jesse's first impulse was always to shout back, to answer their unintelligible yammering with a sharp retort of his own language, but after the first time, he realized doing that wasn't going to get him much more than another fat lip. His Cherokee was nowhere near good, but Adelaide was teaching him. Trying to, anyway. They made understanding it easier through their constant hand movements, gestures that spoke almost as clearly as words. It was easier speaking than listening, but he was working on that. He had to. He couldn't stand not knowing what people were saying around him. The fact that they might be—and probably were—discussing him and his shortcomings frustrated him to the point where he'd decided he should at least try to learn the savage tongue. When the Cherokee spoke slowly, he could take the words apart in his head, see them one at a time. When he got lucky, he could stick them back together so they made sense. That meant that every time they said anything, there was a pause before he answered, but at least he got it right some of the time. And he seemed to have made enough friends that by now they only teased him for making mistakes, didn't beat him over the head with something for doing it.

It was humid and hot as hell in the forest. The leaves practically dripped with sweat. Jesse felt it trickle down his back and wondered how close they were to the river. He sure would appreciate a sloshing of cold water on his face and a drink to soothe the aching in his throat. They'd followed a game trail deep into the forest, then stopped close enough to the water that the animals would have to come this way sooner or later.

When they reached their first hunting spot in the woods,

he squatted beside Soquili, daydreaming about the river while the others muttered in quick Cherokee. He didn't bother trying to interpret when they did that; they knew they could say just about anything around him if they said it quickly. He didn't care. As long as they weren't plotting to kill him, he was all right with missing some of their jokes— even if those jokes were about him, which he was sure most of them were. Now they were laughing in that way they had, low and strange, like they didn't want the creatures of the forest to know what the sound was.

These boys were all right, but he wouldn't have chosen them as friends, let alone brothers. Unpredictable sons of bitches. Your best buddies one minute, knife in your gut the next. Jesse was not looking forward to the day when they asked him to come on a raid with them.

It didn't take the snap of a branch underfoot to alert them to their prey. Something in the air must have told them, because the Cherokee stiffened around Jesse before he even heard a sound, then they kind of melted. Like snow on spring grass, only faster. That's how he saw it, anyway. Like their bones and muscles and skin took on the shape and feel of the forest around them. He had to admire that in them. That and the fact that they had an uncanny ability to always be downwind. They belonged here in the trees. Jesse was trying to learn those skills, but he still felt . . . white. He knew his blond hair was a giveaway, but when Adelaide had braided one dark feather into it the other day, he tried to convince himself he blended a little better.

Adelaide. That was the closest they'd gotten so far, her doing that with his hair. He found himself always trying to make her smile these days, wanting to explore the warm currents flowing beneath her icy façade. Sometimes those blue eyes flickered and he saw the life within, and he thought—or maybe only hoped—that was happening more often lately. But when she was lost in sadness, when her memories took her away from him, those eyes were almost translucent, a blue colder than any winter sky.

Soquili shifted beside him, a subtle, sliding turn of his

broad chest toward the hidden path. Jesse peered into the dark, knowing what he was looking for, waiting for the shadow of something that hadn't been there a moment before. Something that belonged, but didn't. Kind of like these Indians. He frowned, staring harder. Then Soquili's breath came out in a long, nearly silent whistle, and Jesse saw the deer. A large buck, judging from the flicker of an ear by the ground. Jesse narrowed his eyes and watched the animal mouth at the grass with soft black lips, then jerk his head up at a suggestion of danger.

The Cherokee didn't move. Jesse didn't even breathe. The buck stepped onto the path, long legs at once tentative but strong. Yes, he was big. Older, too, with faded scars cutting across one side of his face. Probably about ten years old. His fur didn't look too shiny, but that could have just been shadows camouflaging his tawny coat. A second leg followed, then he moved with more confidence, encouraged by the familiar sight of the trail to the river he'd undoubtedly followed for every one of those years.

Jesse's eyes slid toward the river, and he noticed the Cherokee had all adapted, their forms moulded to the curved veins of leaves, to the indifferent bark of the trees. And their arrows had been silently nocked.

The buck was downed with one shot. The turkey-feathered arrow protruded from just behind the foreleg in what was, as usual, a clean heart shot. Jesse knew the importance of that shot. If it wasn't a mortal shot, the animal could run, bleeding out slowly, leading his trackers for miles. Because of their skill, the Cherokee rarely had to go far.

Jesse had tried to contest the fact that these men were superior hunters to him but had eventually, grudgingly, given up. They'd taught him how to work a blowgun for hunting small game like rabbits and quail, and though the crowd had enjoyed a few guffaws at his expense, Jesse had declared the lessons worthwhile. He'd seen the craftsmen in the village making the weapons: drying river cane for the darts, then holding it over an open fire so it would bend and straighten over their knees. They smoothed the joints inside the cane with a piece of rough metal attached to a stick, then cut the tube into eight-foot lengths. They seemed ridiculously long and awkward, and Jesse had doubted, at first, he'd be able to master the strange weapon. The men laughed and shook their heads when he toppled over from dizziness after trying to blow the foot-long dart through the tube. But when he struck his first rabbit, he didn't bother to contain a hoot of victory.

Hunting with the Cherokee was quite an ordeal. The first time he'd witnessed the preparations, Jesse had stared, open-mouthed, as the warriors went through the routine. It was even more extreme when they were hunting for a major festival, which Jesse assumed this was. The whole process began about seven days before they even headed into the forest, and included a whole bunch of fasting, sitting in the sweating tent, and throwing up, before they finally bathed in the river and headed out with the garbling priest's blessing. One thing about the whole ordeal really bothered Jesse. It was what they did to the first deer they shot. After gathering around the carcass and singing some thank-yous to the gods, they skinned the animal, cut it up, then laid the meat over a fire . . . and burned it. Just burned it. No eating, just burning and watching. They stared at the meat, watching when the fat popped. If it popped to the east, that meant the hunting would go well. If it popped to the west, there was a unanimous sigh of disappointment.

Just plain old strange was what that was. Jesse'd tried to point out that if the hunt didn't go well, at least they'd still have the one deer if they didn't just go burning it, but the hunters paid no attention to the raving white man. After all the preceding fasting, Jesse's stomach could be heard over the fire, and he fairly drooled, smelling that meat crackling over the fire. But he could do nothing about it.

Fortunately, this wasn't the only kill of the day, and the first poor buck had popped to the east. So everyone was feeling confident. Jesse thanked his lucky stars. At least they'd eat that night.

Hunts went on for days, with a lot of wandering through

the woods, then trooping through long stretches of grassy areas. It was easy going on the way there, but a long, thirsty route when they returned, carrying the village's meals on their shoulders.

When they finally returned to the village, they were met by a greeting like nothing Jesse'd ever experienced before. The women and children flocked to the hunters, jumping around them, laughing and embracing them. Naked children bounced around them like nymphs in Doc's mythology books, relieving the hunters of quail, rabbits, squirrels, whatever their little hands could hold. The men puffed their chests and held in their smiles, trying not to let the women see how pleased they were to receive such a welcome.

Jesse watched one woman reach her husband, convince him to set his prize aside and instead gather her into his exhausted arms. She brought her round, beaming face to his and said something through quick-moving lips—something Jesse had a feeling he could never interpret, and figured he'd be embarrassed if he tried. It felt intrusive to even look. The hunter didn't see anything but her. When they kissed, Jesse looked away.

He was surprised to meet the quiet eyes of another female when he turned his head. Adelaide's blue gaze was such a contrast to the black-brown eyes with which he'd spent the last week that it took him back a moment. She stood quietly a few feet away, watching him, so he seized the moment and walked right to her. Why put things off when they could be done right then?

His mind still on the reunion he'd just witnessed, Jesse threw caution to the wind. He dropped the deer from his shoulders and seized the solid curve of Adelaide's waist in his hands, loving the way her eyes flew open at the contact. She was apparently too surprised to react, so he bent to her level and kissed her lips. So soft. Jesse had dreamed about those lips, knew they'd be soft, but had no idea just how soft.

But those lips stiffened, and she twisted her beautiful body out of his grasp, just as slippery as that damn cat of his. Then she slapped his cheek. Hard. That was one reaction he hadn't foreseen, though he probably should have. This was the first time Jesse had ever been slapped by a girl. Being the handsome golden boy he knew himself to be, he had always known the right moment to approach a woman and get exactly what he wanted. Up until now, anyway. Maybe he was out of practice. Maybe if he just tried again . . .

He reached for her, but stopped, seeing tears crest. Her fingers came to her lips like a shield, and she shook. She actually shook.

"Hey," he tried, stretching out a hand to help. She shook her head, her chin trembling, and took a couple of steps backward. Then she turned and ran, leaving him alone with the dead deer.

Another slap, this time much heavier, landed on his shoulder as Soquili came up beside him. The man wore a strange expression of amusement and sympathy.

"Not all women are happy to see husbands come home," he said and walked in another direction.

"Huh?" Jesse asked, but he was alone again.

CHAPTER 18

Lesson Learned

Despite that memorable encounter, Adelaide didn't stay away. She always seemed to be waiting for him, though it didn't exactly feel that way. It was like whenever he looked for her, she just appeared, her soft, forlorn figure like a breath of air on a sweltering August day. He wondered at the courage it took for her to wait like that, since she obviously had such a fear of men. Then again, maybe it was out of desperation. They were the only two white folks in the village. Maybe she just needed a little something to bring back memories.

Except memories, with her, were apparently so fragile she didn't share many of them. Sometimes she said little bits and pieces about her sister Maggie, and maybe remembered this and that from their old life, but not much more. And most of the time, she berated herself afterward for having said anything. He wanted to know about her, but he was never sure whether he should bring up the subject or not. Sometimes being around Adelaide made him so edgy, so nervous, he hardly knew what to expect, and that wasn't like him. Jesse was used to being in charge of everything and everyone around him. Everyone but his father, that is.

He gnawed on a twig, cleaning his teeth, enjoying the satisfying crunch when he bit down. He sniffed and watched a couple of dogs chasing each other around, tried to distract himself from ugly recollections of his former life. Guess he wasn't so great with memories, either.

He'd have to come up with some new ones. Should he give up on his plan to escape? Would it make any sense for him to stay in the village with the noisy whooping warriors? He'd surprised himself by toying with the idea lately. Life was relatively good here. He ate better, laughed more, even had what he might call friends.

But no. No matter what the People said, no matter what crazy notion they had about him, Jesse wasn't a Cherokee. He was a white man, and that meant he belonged in a white-man's world.

Except he wasn't sure what that meant anymore. The only white-man's world he'd ever known had been the one in which he and his father had lived. But if he left here, there was no way he was going back to Thomas. He wasn't sure where he'd go; it didn't matter as long as it was far from the old man.

He could stay. They'd made him welcome. After all, Adelaide was here. He enjoyed her company more than he'd expected, and the idea of carrying that further stirred a craving in his belly. But now things were different. Especially after she'd shown him his kisses weren't going to get him anywhere. So he wasn't about to stay here on her account.

No. He didn't belong here. He'd get out at the first opportunity, run the other direction.

Problem was, he couldn't seem to make himself forget about Adelaide. Couldn't drop the feel of her, the way her eyes softened when they looked at him—most of the time, anyway. They didn't do that for anyone else, as far as he'd seen. Maybe she'd come with him when he left. Maybe they could escape together.

He'd seen her head off in the direction of the river earlier, a basket hung over one arm. Jesse stooped under a low-hanging branch and stepped over a log, then straightened and followed the trail toward the sound of rushing water. He'd dropped the stick from his mouth aways back, and now he spat a bug off his tongue.

She sat on the edge of the river, in the shade of a willow. Its weeping branches seemed even more limp than usual, suffering in the heat. The songbirds were quiet, saving their strength. They'd come out later, like they did first thing in the morning, singing loud enough to wake the dead. Ah, there she was. Her profile was clear but dark, and he couldn't spot the distinctive blond of her hair in the shadows. When he got closer, he noticed she had left it untied that morning, and it hung loose, reaching the small of her back. She sat facing the water but frowning at the leather she was sewing, paying no attention to his approach. He didn't want to startle her but didn't have much choice, since she seemed oblivious and he wasn't about to turn around and go back.

"Adelaide?" he said quietly.

"Oh!" she exclaimed softly, clutching the soft leather in a ball against her chest. Moccasins then. Too small to be a tunic.

Her eyes adjusted, the startled flash warming to recognition. "Hi, Jesse. Do you need something?"

"Just a little company," he said, then gestured at a spot in the shade beside her. "May I?"

She smiled and nodded. They sat in awkward silence for a few moments, neither of them moving, until Adelaide eventually lowered her hands and searched for her most recent stitch. She frowned at the leather again, then her brow cleared when she spotted it. She pierced the leather and pulled the thong through.

"Moccasins?" he asked.

"For Kokila," she said quickly.

"Good of you."

"Hers are worn out."

He nodded, then sat quietly for as long as he could stand it. "Oh, hey. I almost forgot," he said, deciding to go for a nonchalant approach. He reached into the small leather pouch at his waist and pulled out the handful of beads: two dozen, all blue. "I brought these for you. I figured you could use them."

She peered into his palm, then her eyes opened wide and she blinked up at him. "For me?"

"Uh-huh. I figure you'll have more use for them than I would."

In fact, he was rather proud of the trade he'd arranged, bringing one of the other women a couple of fish so she'd give him a few beads. He knew Adelaide liked sewing those things, putting them on tunics, moccasins, whatever needed prettying up. He held the beads while she prodded at them, studying them carefully. Ignoring her resistance, he took her other hand and turned it palm side up, then poured the little beads into her hand. She examined them a moment longer, then slipped them into her sewing bag.

"That's very nice of you, Jesse."

"Yeah, well." His smile went a little crooked. "I can be nice."

She smiled. "Maybe I'll use those in a pair of moccasins for you, if you'd like."

He looked at his own, black from plodding through the dirt, fraying around the edges. "I'd appreciate that. I've just about worn these out."

She sewed a few more stitches, and Jesse gazed out at the rushing stream. How the hell did this girl make him so nervous? Did he have the same effect on her?

"Hot today," he tried. She smiled serenely and kept sewing. No, she didn't appear to be as nervous as he felt.

"Aw, hell," he muttered, and she glanced over, startled. "Sorry. It's just I always think of things I wanna say, until I'm actually with you. Then I can't seem to remember a single thing."

"Maybe you're thinking too much in Cherokee," she teased. "Can't remember the English words."

There was another reason he'd wanted to talk with her, and this was as good an opening as any other. "Ha! No chance of that. I just hope it's good enough for the powwow."

The Cherokee had decided they trusted him enough to ask him to attend a powwow with Ahtlee. He was to be their translator. A lot of the Cherokee spoke a fair bit of English, but it was important that the details of this meeting be understood. They didn't want any fast talk coming from the settlers' side. None that they didn't catch, anyway. He recognized the invitation was an honour, or at least a symbol of trust, being asked to do that. And he had to admit he was flattered. They could have brought Adelaide to translate instead of him, since her Cherokee was so fluent. Then again, she wouldn't have left the village without a fight, and Jesse would have stood up for her, so he would have ended up going anyway. The idea of translating in front of all those people was intimidating, but he didn't have much choice.

"You leave for that tomorrow, right?"

He nodded.

Her needle paused, then pierced the leather again. "You're still planning to run?"

"Not at the powwow."

"That's not what I meant," she said quietly.

He shrugged. "How can I stay here? What is there here for me?"

She lowered her hands to her lap and blinked at him. "Well, there's lots of things. Lots of reasons to stay. I bet you eat better here, for one."

He'd give her that. He plucked a long strand of grass, slid it between his teeth and worried it a bit while he considered what she had said. "Yeah, I guess that's right. But other than that—"

"There's me," she blurted and turned an immediate crimson.

Jesse nearly choked, taken entirely off guard. "What—"

Her back was straight as an arrow, her hands flat on the grass on either side of her. As if she were anchoring herself there. The moccasin rolled over and away from her hand, a forgotten prop. She glanced away, but the breeze lifted the hair at the back of her neck, confirming his suspicions. Miss Adelaide blushed for him? Well, now.

"Huh. And there I was, thinking you couldn't stand the sight of me."

"Did you? Do I give that impression?" She shook her head, looking concerned. "Sure, you can aggravate a person, but I don't hate you."

He grinned. "Well, that's better than a kick in the head at least."

"I mean," she said, blinking furiously, the red in her cheeks even deeper, if that were possible. "I think we're friends, aren't we? I mean, sometimes we talk, and . . ." She stopped, eyes wide, words apparently gone.

Jesse's smile peeked out then, slow and intrigued. It was the same smile that had worked on girls for just about as long as he'd had teeth. "Well, now," he said slowly, his voice dropping to a smooth, deep rumble. "I'd have to say yeah. You and I are friends."

The red was starting to drain from her cheeks, leaving her awfully pale. Then he noticed the hand holding the sewing needle had started to vibrate. Jesse shook his head, shocked at how quickly this girl could change direction. A man could get dizzy around her. He sat up straight.

"Hell, Adelaide. Calm yourself. I'm not gonna do anything to hurt you. You know that, don't you? You don't need to get so worked up."

Her stare lowered to the grass between them, where her fingertips grasped at the blades. "I'm so embarrassed. I don't know why I do that. It's the strangest thing. One minute I'm all right, the next I'm a mess. It's just that I . . . I . . ."

He had no idea if it would help or hurt, but Jesse did the only thing he could think of, gently laying his hand on hers. He was shocked at the coldness of her skin. It should have been warm like his in this heat. Her muscles tensed under his hand, but she didn't pull away. Taking this as encouragement, he curled his fingers around hers, and with a barely audible sigh, she let him. He turned toward her, willing her to meet his eyes, to read the reassurance he offered. Eventually she blinked shyly up at him, and he took a deep breath, keeping his mind clear for her.

CHAPTER 19

A Question of Trust

Through Jesse's experience with women, he'd learned a few things. The most important one, in his opinion, and the one that definitely applied here, was that women could be a lot like horses.

There are two methods a man can use to break a horse, but only one for Jesse. Restraining them, blindfolding them, and whipping them into submission usually worked, but that resulted in an angry, fearful, unwilling ride, sometimes a wasted animal altogether. Some even died during the process, and Jesse thought that though the poor creatures' bodies were beyond help at that point, it was actually their hearts that had broken in the end. That was his father's approach, the way a lot of men he'd grown up with believed it should be done, the way Jesse'd been taught.

But Jesse had seen a man once, fragile and old as dust, bring in an animal the others would surely have ruined. He'd heard stories about the crazy old horseman. The others joked about him, but even then Jesse heard a hidden respect inside their gibes. Jesse had wanted to witness the man working his magic, so he'd hidden in the barn, watching a three-year-old filly prance, her hind legs kicking out unpredictably between steps. Her eyes rolled with nerves, and the sweat that completely covered her black coat shone in the sun, despite the dust she stirred up under her hooves. Foam fell in soft balls from her lips every time she snorted.

The old man had simply waited, leaning on the fence, a rope dangling harmlessly between his fingers. He'd hummed a bit, spoken softly to the horse as if she were a lady friend. It took at least an hour for the filly to come to terms with her captivity, then to eye this strange man with more curiosity than fear. Eventually he pulled an apple from inside his shirt and took a noisy bite, then tossed the rest of it so that it rolled to a stop a few paces away from his feet. Puzzled, she'd taken a couple of reluctant steps toward him, then stopped and glared. As human an expression as Jesse'd ever seen. Eventually, she took a couple more. A second bitten apple landed in the dirt, a short distance from the first one. When she got to within a couple of feet of the old man, she lowered her head, snorted at the first apple, then sucked it between her lips and chomped loudly on the sweet fruit. A half step more, and she'd swallowed the second.

Jesse watched, rapt, sure the man's rope would fly any second, but it did not. In fact, nothing happened. So the horse came closer. The man kept talking, telling her what a pretty girl she was. He pulled out another apple and took a bite, still talking. Then he held out the rest of it on his palm in invitation. When her muzzle touched the wrinkled old hands, he didn't move, only waited for the apple to be accepted. Slowly, slowly, the man's other hand reached her cheek and caressed the coarse hairs there. By the end of the day, the horse followed the old man everywhere, seeming more content with him than she was on her own. Jesse wanted that kind of horse when he could afford one.

The old man had known he was hiding there, of course. Pretty difficult for a man to stand motionless for that long and not sense everything around him.

"You can come on out now, boy," he said eventually. His voice was a little tougher now. No cajoling needed for Jesse.

Jesse, disappointed to find out he hadn't been invisible, stepped sheepishly out of the barn. "Sir?"

"You see what I did there, boy?"

"I did, sir."

"Think you can do that?"

"Sure would like to," Jesse admitted. "She's a pretty thing."

The old man's face relaxed a bit, the deep crevasses of old age smoothing as he turned toward the mare. He stroked the smooth neck. "She is that." He looked back at Jesse, and the wrinkles returned. "Don't you never treat a horse with nothing but kindness. You do that, and she's sure to take care of you till the end of her days. Just like a woman, boy. You remember that."

Jesse'd had a horse like that once, when he was seventeen. He bought her wild at the market, using every penny he had. She was a pretty bay filly that constantly tossed her head with frustration, snorting angrily at everyone and everything around her. When he'd gotten her home, Jesse'd taken her out to the far paddock, where the other men wouldn't come. At first it was hard to resist following the lessons he'd been taught early on. He wanted nothing more than to leap on the horse, force her to set still under him, accept him as her master. But he'd seen too many horses ruined that way, and he liked the look in this one's eye. Smart girl. Jesse had the ability to wait it out, the patience his father said came from Jesse's mother. It obviously hadn't come from dear old dad, whose temper flared like the stomp of a hoof: unpredictable, sharp, and crushing.

Jesse spent two days doing what he'd seen the old horseman do. He could still remember the feel of his own mare's soft muzzle when it finally pressed against his hand, the hot puff of breath as she sniffed for threat, the wet lips claiming the apple as her prize. He'd called her Breeze after that, because in the dry, baking heat, he could think of nothing more beautiful than that. Jesse had never been anything but good to her, and she had come to him at the slightest invitation. Man, that filly could run. And he was right. Breeze was smart.

But she hadn't been able to outrun Thomas Black, whose own horse went lame at an inconvenient time. Thomas and the boys had needed to go out for some reason, and Thomas had taken Breeze instead. Jesse was working in the fields, oblivious to her absence when Thomas rode her straight into a gopher hole. Furious, and unable to admit it was his own fault, Thomas stomped home and demanded Jesse go back out and put her out of her misery. Claimed it was Jesse's horse, Jesse's responsibility.

Jesse had always feared and disliked his father. But on that day, his feelings grew to include hate. The way Thomas hated Indians was how Jesse hated Thomas. He knew he couldn't leave Breeze out there alone, dying slowly, attracting predators. So Jesse borrowed another pony and headed out to where his beautiful mare lay alone in the grass, her dark, sweat-soaked side rising and falling with exertion. She had given up the fight and no longer screamed as he'd known she would have, but her massive body trembled with shock. Jesse couldn't say anything to her, not when she was like that, though he knew that's what she needed most at that moment. Some kind word from her friend. But he felt too weak with grief. He saw the pain and pleading in Breeze's dark eyes, and something hardened in his chest. It was as if she knew what had to be done, and she was giving him permission.

"Yeah, Breezie. I'm your boy." He cleared his throat and shoved a bullet in the rifle, then took a deep breath, eyes closed. When he looked again, she seemed calmer, knowing he was there to help. It was hard for Jesse to aim with the gloss of tears flooding his vision. It was even harder to walk away when it was all done.

There had been other horses since then, all of which he'd loved, but Breeze always watched him. He felt her gaze. He knew she'd forgiven him, which was a stupid thing for a man to think about a horse, but there it was.

Adelaide reminded him of when he'd first bought Breeze. Skittish but needing him. Her eyes, sky blue whereas Breeze's had been mud brown, wanted to trust him, but terror had formed a protective armour over them. It was less now, that armour. She was coming closer, like when Breeze had first touched his hand. There was no way he'd hurt this filly beside him. And no way anyone else would, either. Not while Jesse Black was around.

"You've got nothing to worry about, Adelaide. I'd never hurt you."

She stared at him with such an intensity, any other man might have looked away. But Jesse had been drawn into the blue, admitted entry into her private thoughts, and he didn't plan on running away from that. She leaned toward him, bending at the hip, her movement barely perceptible, but he caught it. He covered the distance between them, touched his lips gently against hers, sensed no resistance. Her trembling breath tickled his cheek, the air warm and encouraging. He kissed her a little longer, fighting the devil to keep his urgency in check.

He opened his eyes, but hers were closed, faded lashes touching shadowed cheeks. So defenceless, this girl. A surge of protective instinct flowed through him at the sight, and he closed his eyes again, savouring the exhilarating fact that it was to him she had turned. To him she had finally come. To him she had opened her scarred heart.

Their lips parted, but he pressed his forehead against hers, knowing her eyes were still closed. "I'll keep you safe, Adelaide."

He felt her response before he heard it. Her fingers touched his cheek, light as a child's caress. She was watching him this time, and he kept his eyes closed just a moment longer, let her experience the same feeling of belonging. When he couldn't bear to be in the dark any longer, he opened his eyes and looked at her, intoxicated by the potency of the space between them, and saw the ice in her eyes had melted.

"I know you will," she whispered. "I feel safe with you, Jesse."

Her trust roared over him like a wave, and he could do nothing but ride it. He cradled her face in his hands and brought her against him again, kissing her and feeling the tentative movement of her lips against his. The tips of her fingers pressed on his upper arms, and her pulse galloped against his skin. He moved closer, curling one arm behind her neck, inhaling something herbal in her skin and hair, the remnants of smoke from a hearth fire, and the sharp, unavoidable tang of something he called fear. She made a little sound, almost urgent, and he slid the other hand down to her waist, swathed in soft, strong buckskin. Her arms had gone around him now, her fingers pressed urgently into his shoulder blades, and the taste of her tears touched his tongue.

She relaxed against his arm as he laid her gently back into the cool grass, kissing her the entire time. Then he drew away, leaning on one elbow and gazing down at her, admiring the pink flush that had consumed the white of her skin. Her hair was a pale pillow against the green, white loops and bows he wanted to feel between his fingers. She looked up at him, eyes shining with ready tears, a nervous smile trembling on lips that looked more full than they had a moment before.

"God, you're beautiful," he said. She threw one hand over her eyes and giggled. That was an unexpected sound. "What?"

She shrugged, unable to stop laughing, but at least she moved her hand away. He could have laughed himself, seeing the happy twinkle in her eyes. He leaned down and kissed her again and the giggle died away.

"Guess what, Adelaide?" he finally said. She opened her eyes wide, waiting. "You kissed me, and you're still alive to tell about it."

A shadow flitted across her eyes, but it passed. As if a bird had flown overhead, cutting them off from the sun for only an instant.

"I am," she agreed. "Jesse?"

He ran one finger down her tear-dampened cheek, amazed by its smoothness. She was like a china doll, like the one his father had kept in the blanket box after his mother had been murdered. "What is it?"

"That was nice," she said.

He smiled. "I've got more where that comes from," he assured her.

Her chuckle was slightly lower this time, but her eyes flickered with concern. "Oh, I imagine you do," she said. "But that's enough for now."

He rolled onto his back so they lay side by side, staring up at the underside of the willow. They listened to the water and birds, then he sighed and closed his eyes.

"You okay, Adelaide?"

She hesitated before she spoke, but her voice was confident. "Yes." He heard the swish of the grass as she turned her head towards him, so he knew she was watching his reaction. He kept his eyes closed.

He smiled. "You'll be fine."

Her fingers brushed his, and he took her hand.

"I think maybe you're right," she said softly, and he drifted off to sleep, warm with the knowledge that for the first time in his life, he had a reason to stay.

CHAPTER 20

Family Reunion

Jesse and Ahtlee headed out with three other warriors the next morning, riding to the powwow. It was the most unlikely of meetings in so many ways. Cherokee and white politicians, all assembled in the August heat under the pretext of bettering their relations, faced each other across a small piece of grass outside the gates of New Windsor. The day was too hot to do any business inside. Everyone had shown up in their finery, the chiefs in their newest clothes: bright, beaded moccasins, a half dozen or so battle feathers hanging in their hair; the politicians wore coats, hats, and matching moustaches. Jesse wore simple trousers and a buckskin shirt, and he had graciously allowed Adelaide to weave a feather into his hair. Normally the feathers were reserved for warriors who had fought in battle, but Soquili had insisted that applied to Jesse, since he had fought bravely that first day, when Soquili had brought him home.

Something told Jesse that any kind of deal making at this powwow might involve his father showing up, and that little voice had been right. Thomas stood back a ways, leaning casually against an oak, arms crossed. Although his father intended to appear disinterested, Jesse could see Thomas's hungry eyes taking in every man in the area and measuring him. Didn't matter that Thomas had nothing to do with the men in charge. He had a way of wheedling his way into things, taking what he needed, and using it however he saw the most benefit to himself. Thomas didn't spot his son right away, so Jesse got to his feet, dusted off his trousers, and made himself visible. He wasn't surprised that his stomach rolled a bit, queasy with nerves. Now that it was time to talk, he wasn't sure what he'd say.

Thomas's eyes popped open at the sight of him, and Jesse watched a variety of expressions cross the old man's face: confusion, bemusement, then something more calculating. Not once, Jesse noticed, did the gray eyes register anything resembling relief at the knowledge that his son had survived. Jesse nodded shortly, hiding his grin. Felt good to give the old man a shock. Maybe he'd drop dead of it. Thomas's stunned expression snapped back in place, leaving a smile that hinted at amusement.

Ahtlee said something quick under his breath and Jesse grunted back. "My father's over there," Jesse explained. "I should at least tell him I'm alive."

Ahtlee shook his head slowly, distrust swimming deep in his eyes. "He sees."

"Well, he'll come over here if I don't go over there."

"He will not."

Sure enough, Thomas came loping across the square of flat, dry earth they'd designated for the powwow.

"Jesse, boy!" Thomas called cheerfully, waving as if they were the closest of friends.

"I told you," Jesse told Ahtlee. This time Ahtlee said nothing, only narrowed his eyes speculatively at Jesse.

Jesse grinned. "I'm coming home with you," he assured the Cherokee. "I just gotta talk to the guy is all."

Ahtlee nodded, then glanced toward Thomas as he approached. "He call you "boy"? Not "man"? He not know son too good." Then he turned toward the other Cherokee, leaving Jesse alone. Jesse couldn't hide the grin that popped out at the unexpected words of praise from his foster father.

"So," Thomas bellowed as he drew close. "The boy's alive after all. And would you look at you now? All Injun, you are." He flicked his fingers at Jesse's hair. "Even a little feather. Suits you."

"Yeah, I'm alive, no thanks to you," Jesse replied, giving nothing away. "And you look the same as ever. Old, dirty, and mean."

Thomas's expression resumed his typical sneer. He hooked his thumbs in the waistband of his trousers. "What's going on, Jesse? Why ain't you dead?"

Jesse shrugged, looking unconcerned. "Guess I was too pretty to kill. They'd have no trouble with ending you, though."

His father grunted, then examined Jesse with his piercing gray eyes, hunting for something Jesse had no wish to give. He owed this man nothing, and Jesse held his stare. "And the other fellas they brought in when they caught you?"

"Not pretty enough."

A couple of seconds passed with nothing said but what passed through their eyes. How many times had Thomas glared at him this way, forced him to look away? Jesse wasn't budging this time. He wasn't afraid anymore.

"So what happens next? You gotta stay with 'em?"

Jesse nodded, said nothing. He watched a calculating thought pass through his father's face, linger in his eyes, then stop on the tight line of his mouth. "You and me stand to do good on this deal, boy, if we play it right."

Jesse recognized the expression. Thomas had just tossed the dice, and now waited to see which way they rolled. He had no idea what his son was thinking. Jesse loved that. Wanted to keep it that way.

"Yeah? How's that?"

"I figure you know things we can use, you know? Make the deal even sweeter."

"Is it a bad deal, then?"

Thomas winked and Jesse's stomach fell. He knew that wink. The Cherokee were in trouble.

"I tell you what, boy," Thomas said, coming closer. "I never thought I'd be happy to see you, but I guess I am. Y'all head back and have your little pipe-smoking party, then bring me everything these dogs say. That way I can get it to the men here. Easy pickins. That's what it'll be."

Jesse nodded slowly, remembering so much about his life with Thomas. The beatings he'd been given when he spilled anything, when he left a broom in the wrong place, when he asked a question his father couldn't answer. The wicked things he'd seen Thomas do that had always haunted his soul, and the way Thomas had told him, over and over, that what he'd seen was how it was supposed to be. All those times when Thomas had bellowed it should have been *him* that died, not his brother. What a waste of time and food Jesse was.

"Is that right? Easy pickin's?"

"Sure 'nough. Why, you and me can have just about anything we want after that."

Jesse sniffed and crossed his arms, staring directly at his father. "Ain't no 'you and me,' *Thomas*. Never has been." He got a visceral thrill from calling his father by his first name. It was the first time Jesse had felt strong enough to stand up to him that way, and he figured he had the Cherokee to thank for that. How ironic that the people he'd set out to hate, the people who had captured him and forbidden his escape, had freed him.

Thomas's eyes hardened to pewter, clashing against the fire in Jesse's golden eyes. "Is that so? Why the hell did I bother feedin' you all these years, then?"

"Got me," Jesse said with a shrug. "Your mistake. You made a lot of mistakes."

He didn't give his father a chance to answer.

"I'll see you in three days, old man. If you want this thing so bad, you'll have to do it on your own. I ain't helpin' you." He winked, feeling deliciously dangerous. "I gotta go back now, see to my new family. You have yourself a good day, now."

He turned and headed back to the scrum of Cherokee

that no white man would dare enter without an invitation. He ignored the curses his father threw at his back and nodded at Ahtlee when the older man glanced over his shoulder, checking. Jesse couldn't stop smiling. Never turned to give Thomas any hint of that, though. Didn't want to give Thomas anything. He owed him nothing.

The speeches began shortly after that, and Jesse sat cross-legged on the mat, glaring across the grass, watching Thomas's reaction. The old man was listening hard to what everyone was saying, looking for opportunity, and wearing that arrogant grin Jesse knew so well. As if he had the most delicious secret and was just daring someone to ask. Whatever happened to the poker face he always preached about?

Just where Thomas fit into all this, Jesse didn't know, but wherever it was, it wasn't good. It made Jesse smile, though, thinking about what Thomas would say if he knew the wickedly narrowed black eyes behind him belonged to a man claiming to be Jesse's new father. If this meeting wasn't so damn important, Jesse would have thrown back his head and laughed. After the years of lessons he'd been taught, learning the countless reasons why all Indians were evil savages who deserved nothing better than to die slow deaths, now he regarded his birth father with more suspicion than he did his new family. But Thomas Black didn't have much of a sense of humour. And Jesse still had to be careful.

Deep inside Jesse there lurked another, deeper concern. Truth was, Jesse was Thomas's blood son. What was that old saying about the apple falling by the tree? How much truth was in that? Enough that it kept Jesse from entirely trusting himself at times.

Chief Standing Trees, the host, sat tall as his name, towering over the rest of the men despite his advanced years. The day had started out with ceremony, the old chief receiving arrows from the other chiefs, then holding them aloft to signify strength in numbers. Five villages stood before the white men, and pretty soon they'd all be listening to Jesse's pathetic attempts to interpret. For this meeting, he was mostly supposed to translate English into some sort of Cherokee, which was the biggest challenge. At the next meeting, in a few days time, he would have to pull together the village's thoughts, put them into English, and declare them to the entire crowd.

Chief Standing Trees's face, sagging in weary pouches, said nothing. In fact, Jesse wondered if the old man had fallen asleep during one of the drawn-out speeches. He studied the ancient Indian's eyes, watched them cross momentarily, and figured he was right. Either that or he'd had a long puff on that peace pipe of his.

Beside Standing Trees sat the other four chiefs, all of lesser status and looking exactly that. The smallest, Runs Quickly, didn't look as if he were going to run anywhere for a long time. His face had been badly scarred by the rampage of smallpox that had decimated the tribes ten years before, and his back seemed to be developing a hunch. His eyes, interestingly enough, reflected the same blurriness as did Trees's. The other three seemed alert. They also bore ugly smallpox scars, and one had a thick white knife scar running down one cheek. Other than Runs Quickly, the men sat straight, their eyes moving with suspicion over the white men, occasionally glancing off the paper they were expected to sign. Of course, there would be no actual signing, since none of them knew how to write his name. All they were expected to do was make a mark of some kind with the ink they'd be handed. Their names could be nothing but a blotch of ink or an 'X.' The white man's contract didn't care which, as long as there was a witnessed mark.

Ahtlee stood boulder-like behind Jesse, living up to his name of Does Not Bend, and glaring through ebony eyes at those he trusted least. Jesse figured that of all the powerful men here, Ahtlee was probably the most intelligent. The most . . . vital. He included Ahtlee's own chief, Standing Trees, in that. Ahtlee had said little about this powwow ahead of time, keeping his thoughts to himself, but Jesse was aware that his adoptive father was there not only to be Trees's right-hand man and learn about what the white men offered. He was also there to monitor Jesse's reaction. Soquili had never doubted who he believed Jesse to be; Ahtlee knew better.

Jesse's role in all this was to sit among the People and tell them what was being said. It was a difficult assignment, since the white men all postured with magnanimous gestures and generous overtures that weren't exactly translatable into Cherokee. Jesse assumed most of them were lies, and he had yet to hear a Cherokee tell a lie. The gist of it was that the whites were offering a better trade proposal in exchange for a fair parcel of land they could call their own. The Indians would promise to stay off the land and leave the settlers alone, and the whites would do the same for the Indians. There would also be a neutral portion of land along the Keowee that was open to both for hunting and fishing.

It all sounded reasonable, but Jesse was concerned about this neutral land they kept talking about. The moustaches were going on about how everyone would live together in a harmonious, beneficial partnership, sounding to Jesse like they were just talking garbage. That kind of partnership would never happen. Jesse knew it, Ahtlee knew it, probably they all knew it.

Standing Trees had long been an advocate of better trade with the white men. He wanted his people to have everything the white men had, and if it took giving up a little land, which he didn't believe anyone but the gods owned anyway, that was fine with him. So the big old man stood firm in his backing of this new initiative. He spoke in his tired, croaky voice, raised his gnarled claws to the sky, and intoned to the gods and the ancestors, chanting about the goodness of this plan and how the Cherokee would only be strengthened by signing. Runs Quickly nodded sagely, then joined in with his own little yips and howls.

When the old men were done agreeing and the ones with the hats had thrown out their last highly questionable promise, there would be three days of deliberation in each Cherokee village. Then everyone was expected to return with answers. With a last glance at Thomas, Jesse rose and followed the others out of the meeting area and toward the corral.

CHAPTER 21

Smoke

The moment Jesse and Ahtlee returned to their village, they were ushered toward the council house with some ceremony. There they would be expected to go over the story again and again, slowly and painstakingly inspecting every statement, which Jesse prayed he'd translated right. Before they even stepped through the entryway, the council house had been what Adelaide called "smudged." The People had burned sage and sweetgrass, letting the smoke clear evil and anger from the room, as well as from the men's hearts. Jesse was stopped at the door and had to wait while one of the elders held the bowl of smoking herbs before him, then used a feather to fan the stuff over his face, head, and body. He was starting to get used to this kind of thing, though he still found it strange. Adelaide had tried to explain how all of this worked, how the earth and the sky and the spirit world were all connected or something. Jesse had no idea what she was talking about, but he'd given up fighting it.

After the smudging was complete, all the men sat in complete silence, and the head priest came in. He said prayers, turning to the four walls of the council house as he

did so: east was first, then south, west, and north, praying
to the four symbols of air, water, fire, and earth. When the
prayers were done, the sacred pipe was offered around.

Jesse'd heard about this pipe from Adelaide. She'd never
smoked it—claimed she never wanted to—but had tried to
explain to him what it was all about. A mixture of trumpet
flower, sumac, and tobacco was packed into the pipe, along
with dried leaves of another plant. After a man inhaled the
traditional mix of herbs, he was expected to speak, to share
his innermost thoughts. Those thoughts were supposed to
come out with brilliant clarity, embracing facts and possibilities with intelligence and intuition. Adelaide had called
the stuff Indian Truth Serum, saying a man couldn't lie at
that point. Jesse was very curious.

The building was comfortably quiet, though almost suffocating with the heat and stink of so many bodies sitting
close together on this sweltering day. Jesse could only hope
the whole thing wouldn't take too long. Soquili, sitting on
his left, jabbed him with his elbow to get his attention. When
Jesse lifted an eyebrow in question, Soquili explained how,
when the pipe was offered, it would be his turn to speak.
Jesse should let the smoke come into him gently, let it mingle
with the air in his lungs, then let it drift out. It all sounded
pretty easy.

"Little smoke, Jesse. *Little* smoke. No big smoke," he said,
watching Jesse closely to make sure he paid attention.

"Yeah, yeah," he said, waving Soquili off.

Jesse studied the men as they smoked. They looked
relaxed, puffing at the long clay pipe, letting smoke drift out
of their mouths and noses. When a man exhaled that sweet
smoke, no one looked away, and no one else spoke. Jesse
wondered if it was his imagination, but it seemed to him the
words seemed to come slower upon the man's exhalation,
his thoughts calm as the ponderous tendrils of rising smoke.
When the pipe was handed to him, he reached for it, turned
his hand over, as he'd seen the others do, and inhaled, trying
to assume the expression of a man who knew what he was
doing.

The smoke was harsh in his throat, but he controlled the reflexive coughing. He closed his eyes, filled his lungs, then waited. He'd seen the other men take their time before blowing the curls of gray through their lips, so he forced his lungs to freeze, take in whatever they were supposed to take in, before he slowly exhaled.

Clarity of thoughts. Intelligent insight into possibilities. That's what the pipe was supposed to bring.

Well, he'd obviously done something wrong. When he opened his mouth, Jesse couldn't even speak. Just the idea of using his voice seemed impossible. Words? Any words he'd planned before had snuck out and left him completely empty. His gaze floated lazily over the sea of eyes and he noticed there seemed to be more of them all of a sudden. Every dark brown iris was completely focused on him.

Jesse blinked, then marvelled at the simple action, at how his eyes had simply known to do that without any prompting from him. Fascinating. He blinked again, on purpose, noticing for the first time in his life the slick sensation of his lids passing over his eyes. The feeling struck him as funny, and he adopted a wide, blank grin. Soquili was quiet beside him, but when Jesse turned his head, ever so slowly, toward this "brother" of his, Soquili smiled back.

"You're not so bad," Jesse managed to say, tripping through the words. His tongue had gained weight. It felt thick and foreign. He frowned, considering. The only other time he'd had so much trouble speaking was when he'd gotten into Thomas's whisky that time, and how funny—actually, he couldn't remember what had been funny, but he was sure it had been. He chuckled, and Soquili joined in.

Soquili said something quick to the others and a unanimous snicker simmered through them. It was the kind of sound that might have set Jesse off at other times, but at this particular moment he found the very concept of laughter hilarious. Mirth rolled out of him, turning his muscles to jelly, sending his empty thoughts to float among the smoke. Eventually, he realized he was the only one laughing, and dedicated a lot of effort to keeping his face neutral. He wiped his hands over his eyes, looking around the room and trying to fit himself back into the goings-on. The pipe had moved on. It was three men down now, which meant he'd missed three speeches. Huh. No one had waited to find out what the amazing Jesse Black had to say. He frowned. They couldn't just keep going, could they? Weren't there rules?

"Hey," he said, reaching for the pipe.

Soquili put his hand on Jesse's arm and gently pressed it down to his side. He shook his head. "You don't need talk," he said.

Jesse wanted to object, wanted to contribute something. He pictured the scene at the powwow, the smug look on Thomas's face. He knew that expression, knew it meant nothing good could be in it for the Cherokee. He searched his mind for the right way to say these things, but thanks to the pipe, the words got garbled and lost in the thick space between his ears. Truth serum. Ha! Jesse rested his elbows on his knees, let his head slump into his hands, and fell asleep.

He had no idea how long the meeting went on before he was shaken awake and shoved into the cool night. The air felt brisk against his hot skin, and his head suddenly seemed as clear as the starry night. Soquili walked beside him as usual, but he wasn't speaking. He didn't look angry, only thoughtful.

"What'd I miss?" Jesse asked.

Soquili looked at him, at a loss.

"Big talk?" Jesse tried, jabbing his thumb back at the council house.

Soquili shrugged and tried to speak English. "We talk more in morning."

"Did Ahtlee tell them—"

"My father talk, other men think."

Not much he could do then. Not that there ever had been. "Damn, I'm hungry," he muttered.

Soquili lifted an eyebrow, inquiring.

"Hungry," Jesse said, a little louder. Soquili grinned and nodded, then took him home and gave him the most delicious snack of dried venison he'd ever had.

It all started again in the morning: the smudging, the sitting, the prayers . . . and the pipe. Soquili and he headed inside the council house, then went through the routine. As they sat, Soquili glanced at him, his expression giving nothing away.

"What?" Jesse asked, already on the defensive, regardless of Soquili's frame of mind.

"Smoke not so much today," Soquili suggested, the corner of his mouth twitching.

Jesse scowled. "Okay."

The pipe did the rounds, and Jesse watched closely when Ahtlee stretched out his hand for it. Everyone was quiet, waiting. Ahtlee spoke slowly, outlining what had happened at the powwow. His deep voice rumbled, every word heavy with meaning.

One by one, the men took their turns voicing questions and opinions. It was obvious from the start that the elders, for the most part, were going to side with Standing Trees and Runs Quickly, if only for duty's sake. The younger men, the warriors, argued emphatically, pointing out the weak points that Jesse had shown Ahtlee. Their youthful gestures became more urgent, more frustrated, and the elders grew louder as well, demanding more attention on the basis of their status.

Ahtlee gazed around through narrowed eyes, studying each man and his reaction. He was leaving it up to them, Jesse saw. Why would he do that? Ahtlee was usually so smart. Why wouldn't Ahtlee step in and show them the answer?

Resisting temptation, Jesse behaved. When it was his turn to accept the pipe, he took a short puff and blew the smoke out almost immediately. By doing that, he was left in relative control of his thoughts, though he rode a pleasant, dizzy wave as it passed through his mind at first. Despite the attention aimed his direction as a result of the pipe, Jesse wasn't nervous. It frustrated him that Ahtlee wasn't saying anything constructive. He wanted to be heard. He knew his Cherokee would sound wrong no matter what he said, but he couldn't stand to keep quiet any longer, to let all this go without at least saying something. Two dozen pairs of eyes stared through the firelit room, waiting for him to say something more intelligent than he'd attempted the night before.

"I say," he said in stilted Cherokee, "this is bad. I say Tsalagi no go there. These bad words hurt Tsalagi . . ."

He stopped, immensely frustrated when he couldn't find the right words. How could he explain Thomas's nefarious character in a room full of honest men?

Soquili took the pipe and did what he could for Jesse, trying to elaborate. Voices rose and fell again, the old men railed against Jesse's lack of evidence, and Jesse dropped his forehead back into his hands. In the end, he realized, he could do nothing about any of this. He was a translator. A pawn. The whole thing was damn frustrating. He told himself he didn't care one way or the other.

Now if only he could believe that.

CHAPTER 22

In the Village

He didn't see her the next morning, but he wasn't overly surprised at that. She was probably a bit spooked after their little interlude by the river, though he hoped she'd gotten past that. For a moment, he questioned whether he should have kissed her or not that day, then dismissed the question. She hadn't objected, as far as he could recall. And it had been something he'd needed to do. But now, since she'd disappeared, he figured he'd have to tread carefully again, let her take the next step.

Soquili took him to a different site along the riverbank in the morning, passing between houses, pausing to speak to women hard at work skinning the recent catch, then stopping where three men worked on a forty-foot canoe. The massive yellow poplar had been felled months before, and small curls of smoke still rose from the fires lit along its top. In places the carefully tended fire had finished its job, leaving cooling grey ashes in its wake. The men used axes to remove the ash, hollowing out the boat as they went.

Taking his cue, Jesse pulled an axe from his belt and chipped away at the burnt wood, trying to ignore the heat from the contained burn as it baked his skin from below. Overhead, the sun seethed from a cloudless sky. Sweat soaked the waistband of his trousers, and he wiped streams of it from his face with the back of his arm. The men worked in silence, none of the Cherokee showing any surprise or concern that this white man was included in the process. Of course not. They weren't stupid. It was damn hard work. Any help was good help.

Jesse was all right with hard work. He was used to it, and he actually preferred working, because it gave him a chance to stop thinking. He and the others worked a few feet at a time, moving slowly, so everything would be completed perfectly. It had taken months to get to this stage, and when they finished this part, they'd spend just as long sealing off the wood with animal fat and pinesap, making the canoe entirely waterproof. After a half hour, Jesse stood back, one hand on his waist, one scratching his head, and looked at the thing, estimating twelve warriors would eventually row from within its sturdy shape.

After a couple of hours, Soquili'd had his fill of labour, so he and Jesse left and headed to the promise of the river. Hard work might be good for the soul, but cold water had never felt so good as it did in the moment when Jesse dove into the deep pool. He swam without surfacing, keeping his eyes open, running his fingers through meadows of reeds and underwater grass. When he finally burst through, blinking at the suddenness of the sun, he spied Soquili loping along the bank, headed toward a thick oak.

Jesse paddled his feet in place, staying deep enough so he could dip under whenever he wanted, but keeping his head up so he could watch Soquili. The Cherokee scaled a gnarled old tree using the outstretched limbs as a ladder, until he stood twenty feet in the air. Then he called down to Jesse and flung himself into the air, landing with a huge splash in the river. His head popped to the surface, black as an eel except for the flashing white smile that clearly invited Jesse to join in.

Grinning, Jesse followed Soquili, climbing up to the thick

branch and hanging on while Soquili sidled out to the edge. Soquili waved, beckoning him, but Jesse shook his head. He looked up, spotting another branch six feet higher. Waving Soquili off, he scrambled up, then stepped carefully toward the thinner branches at the end, his toes clinging to the rough bark to keep from slipping off before he was ready. Soquili, standing almost directly beneath him now, laughed.

"Ah, my brother. You always must be better. Some things do not change."

Jesse grinned maniacally at him, then sprang off the branch, screaming his version of a Cherokee war cry. He could run, climb, crawl, and swim with the best of them, but Jesse had never flown before—other than leaping off a roof, and that hadn't been anywhere near as high as this. The sensation twisted his belly, sent a bolt of crazy, wonderful fear through him. He whooped with the thrill of it, then plunged into the silence underwater, sinking into the weeds until his toes touched on the silt beneath. Like one of the river frogs, he bunched his legs under him and shot back up, rising weightlessly again.

Waterlogged and glistening under the sunshine, the men climbed and jumped for an hour, as if they were young boys, swimming until neither had the energy to go another step. They dragged themselves to the shore and fell asleep on their backs under a big oak, sharing the first real peaceful moment as brothers they'd ever had. They woke at almost the same instant, both struggling up onto their elbows and saying nothing as they came back to the sunshine and shadows.

"More council today," Soquili muttered.

Jesse sighed. At least this would be the last one before they headed back to meet with the politicians. He'd had more than enough of these things. Nobody paid any attention to him anyway. What was the point?

"You don't need me there. I'll see you after."

Soquili frowned. "You come. No question."

"I don't have a choice?"

Soquili shook his head. "You come."

"Why? No one wants to hear what I say."

"You come."

Stubborn son of a bitch. Jesse plucked a blade of grass from beside him and peeled the outer layer off, slowly enough that the blade stayed whole by the end. Then he tossed it and grabbed another. This one he stuck in his mouth and chewed for a while. Maybe today he could say something that mattered.

Ahtlee silently acknowledged them when they arrived at the crowded council house, then took up his observation post again, braced against the council house wall with his arms crossed, keen eyes reading every expression. Once again, nothing was decided, and the meeting seemed to go on for much longer than three hours. Both Jesse and Soquili came close to nodding off. Jesse felt as if he'd been in there for years, surrounded by pipe smoke and snarling Cherokee. He didn't know if he contributed to the arguments with his occasional obligatory comment or not—he tried to sound impartial but knew it didn't come out that way. It's just that he knew his father, and his father had been smiling. Therefore, the Indians were getting cheated.

Jesse was surprised to see Adelaide waiting when he finally came outside. It was after dusk, but the warm summer air was still heavy as it played with her hair. She had tied it behind her, he saw, in one long tail that flicked up with the breeze as a horse might twitch its tail at a bothersome fly. She leaned against the wall at one corner of the building, arms crossed, and gave him a small smile. Such a pretty smile, he couldn't help thinking.

"Good evening, Miss Adelaide," he said.

That prompted a wider smile. "Miss Adelaide? Sounds like I'm an old woman or something. I don't think I've been called that since I was a little girl. And only when I'd done something I shouldn't have done. Miss Adelaide, Miss Margaret, Miss Ruth . . ." Her smile faltered, but she forced it back and stepped away from the house. He walked alongside her, unexpectedly elated by her presence. After all the dark feelings he'd dealt with during the powwow, after the hours of male cussing and posturing within the sweltering confines of the council house, she was like a cool drink of water.

"How was the meeting?" she asked.

He shrugged. "Do you really want to talk about that?"

She glanced up and met his gaze, then chuckled. "No, I'd rather not. I think I can imagine enough without your stories."

"Good. I'm tired of thinking about it."

The wind puffed, lifting her blond tail and draping it over one shoulder. She reached for it and silently stroked its length a few times before tossing it back. So this was how Adelaide did her thinking, he realized. She walked. And maybe, since she'd been waiting to bring him along for the walk, well, maybe she wanted his thoughts as well.

"The Cherokee tend to talk a lot," she said. "That is, when they want to. Other times, they won't say a word, but their faces say it all. They're interesting people."

"If you say so," he said. He decided he'd do best to stay neutral, let her say what she wanted. He found that when he tried to start up a talk with a woman, they usually ended up being angry at him. So most times, he let them do it without his help.

"I'm glad you're back," she admitted, watching her feet.

That was a pleasant surprise that raised a little heat in his chest. "You are? I thought you'd be thanking whatever gods these people worship the minute my horse left the place. Especially since I didn't see you around when I got back." He peeked at her face, saw her hiding a smile, then turned back. "Where we heading?" he asked.

She shrugged. "Nowhere in particular. I just wanted to walk around. If it was daytime, we could go up to the rock, but it's too dark now."

Quiet little Adelaide just wanted to walk around with him. Huh. She'd missed him. Jesse had to hold his own grin in check.

They meandered across the field, the day's heat soothed by the cool swish of grass against their moccasins and the songs of crickets. It was closing in on a full moon, and the big white circle glowed with confidence, surrounded by an endless audience of stars that blinked, one by one, as they came out. Jesse wondered, as he always did, what was going on out there. He remembered Doc's books, tried to remember some fact from them, thinking maybe if he impressed her, she'd like him a bit more. Then he figured if he got it wrong, she'd only laugh. Best to keep quiet.

A small, untended fire outside one of the council houses had faded into embers. Jesse headed toward the remnants and picked up a couple of sticks along the way.

"Let's sit awhile," he suggested.

She nodded, then smiled as he sat beside her on a thick log. Still nervous, he could see, but maybe less so. He dropped one stick gently onto the small fire and jabbed it with the other, shooting sparks into the darkening sky.

"You warm enough?" he asked. She nodded quickly, a nervous movement, but she didn't speak.

The dying fire sparked, then caught on the stick and started to chew, picking up strength. Jesse poked it some more, encouraging the flames. Adelaide sat quietly beside him, the orange light flickering on her face, brightening it, then dropping it into shadow. He tried not to stare at her, tried to make it look as if he was concentrating on something beyond her. But he couldn't help being drawn to her simple profile, the occasional blink of those long, pale lashes.

Through the entire dreary, frustrating, unsettling day, Jesse'd wanted nothing more than silence. Now he ached for conversation. Words struggled to get out, then jammed in his throat. Most of them were trite and unimportant anyway, just an excuse to say something, get her talking. He wanted to hear her speak, hear her thoughts, but she was quiet as the moon.

So he stared into the fire as she was doing, letting his mind play tricks with the flames. A breeze flitted through, flaring red to orange, and he imagined he saw black silhouettes dancing, twirling, disappearing. He remembered sitting like this as a boy, as a young man, as a grown man, always the same, stretching his face as close to the heat as he could, daring the fire and himself. And when his eyes burned he'd close them, still relishing the sensitivity of his lips against the heat. When he drew away, the cool air washed over him, tickling the heat of his skin as if it were a feather, and he started wondering how long he should stay this way before seeking the cool—

"What are you thinking about?" she asked.

He sat up abruptly, trying not to appear startled. "Nothing much," he admitted. "You?"

"A quiet fire makes me remember being happy with my sisters, my mother . . . even my father sometimes," she said.

He nodded, encouraged. This was what he wanted, for her to reach out, share something other than the strange world in which they both now found themselves. He had questions, but the careful whisper of her voice was like a hand holding him back. She sighed, but it wasn't a sound of peace. It was more like she shoved the air from her lungs.

"It seems like another life," she said.

"I thought you were happy here."

"I am, I suppose. It's just not what I thought my life would be like."

He chuckled and watched a shower of sparks as the fire popped. "No, I guess not. Me either."

"And I miss my sisters."

Her loss had been recent, he remembered Soquili saying, though no one would elaborate on what had happened. His had been oh, fifteen years or so. He'd been just a kid. Barely thought of his family anymore, other than his father, who he'd sooner forget. Did she want to talk about it now? Should he ask? Should he wait? Damn. He never got this right. He decided to take the easy route and keep silent.

"What do you remember?" she asked. She leaned down and picked up a small stick, worrying the bark off it in thin strips.

He glanced at her. She was studying the stick, eyes averted from his gaze. "About what, my family?"

She nodded, her flickering orange expression impossible

to read. He stared back at the fire, wondering. What did he remember? He remembered his aunt's scalp. He remembered Thomas and his fists. And he remembered feeling scared he'd end up just like his father.

"Not much. It was a long time ago."

"Do you remember being happy?"

That got him. He had to think hard on that. "Nope," he finally admitted. "Sorry to say, I don't."

She turned to him, frowning. "You don't remember ever being happy?" He shook his head, shrugging. "So were you *always* angry?"

Huh. That felt like an accusation. He stopped himself before he could say anything that might upset the applecart. If he jumped down her throat for saying something like that, well, then she'd be right, wouldn't she?

"No, I'm not always angry. Do I seem that way?"

"Mostly. To me, you do."

"Well, are you always sad?"

That stopped her, and he silently congratulated himself. Then he felt bad, because she didn't speak for a couple of breaths.

"I wish I could say I'm not. Sometimes I'm not. Sometimes I even laugh. I used to laugh more . . . before. But I was never a really happy, outgoing girl. Not like my sisters." Her brow creased as she considered his question. "Careful. That's what I'd call me. Not so much sad, but careful." She looked up at him. "I was always afraid of what might happen."

"That's no way to live."

"No. But that's how I am. Can't change that."

The crickets were out in full force now, their chorus festive. Almost too much noise for the type of conversation they were having. Jesse squinted into the darkness, wondering if he and Adelaide were on their own or if anyone watched. He didn't sense anyone, just wondered. Every time he was with Adelaide, the Indians left them alone. He figured it was maybe a let-the-white-people-be-together thing, and he appreciated it.

"I wish I was more like you," she said quietly.

"What, angry?" he asked, flipping a sarcastic eyebrow she never noticed. She was too busy with the stick, which was now about half its original length. She dropped it with a huff.

"Yeah. Angry. I wish I was angry. I wish I could do what you do. When you get angry, you just jump right back in there and fight for yourself. Not me. I just want to hide."

Jesse was quiet, watching. The air around her seemed taut, as if her worries held onto it for reassurance. She looked very small. He had no right to do this, to reach out and offer security. He knew the potential of his own rage, knew his bloodline only too well. He knew how Thomas would have handled a delicate flower like this. What if Jesse's own nature snuck up and forced his hand? But she was looking at him now with such trust, her need for answers shining in those blue, blue eyes.

"You just need to believe in yourself a bit more," he said gently. She gave a tiny nod and looked back at the fire as if she were thinking about that, but he wondered if it was just something she'd never figure out. "Hey. Don't worry about it. You ever need someone to fight back for you, Adelaide, I'll do it."

A tear appeared like magic at the corner of one eye, a shiny orange reflection of the fire. "Are you ever afraid, Jesse?" She looked up again, and his breath caught when he saw more tears threaten.

"I am. I'm afraid a lot," he admitted quietly. "But you can't let folks see that. They'll take advantage if they see you're scared. But nobody's gonna get the best of me. Never. You let 'em get to you, you'll never win." He reached up and brushed a tear from her cheek as if it were the most natural thing in the world. "You don't need to be afraid, you know. I'm here."

CHAPTER 23

A Son's Lesson to a Father

When Jesse and Ahtlee travelled back to the meeting place for the final decision, Jesse claimed a spot farther from the centre of everything, so he could lean against a tree. Otherwise, his back got sore, sitting so long, not moving. Now here he sat on the hard earth near the Cherokee, staring across at his son-of-a-bitch father. Thomas Black sat off to the side, out of hearing distance, the old man's hard eyes boring into Jesse like a pair of hot pokers.

The Cherokee in the crowd were from other villages, other representatives chosen to speak for their clans. Jesse had expected to be treated with a certain amount of abuse, but after Ahtlee made all the official introductions, none of the others had looked twice at him—though he did hear a few chuckles when he said the wrong words at the wrong time . . . which he did fairly often, which made it even funnier that he was their translator. Ah well. He was the best they were going to get around here. Ahtlee had told him what to say to the chiefs. He wanted Jesse to relay the information to the white men that his village had decided—despite Jesse's best attempts to persuade them otherwise—to agree to the terms. In exchange for a nice, neat neutral piece of land they would all share, the white men agreed to increase trade with them. Sort of sharing all the way around. In Jesse's opinion it sounded good, felt bad.

When Jesse was called to the front to give the vote from his village, he took his time about it. Ahtlee had told him exactly what to say, but the truth was, Jesse had never been good at doing what he was told. He'd figured out what he wanted to say the whole journey there, hoping he was getting it right. Now that it was time, Ahtlee approached the chiefs with him, then stood just behind Jesse's right shoulder. Jesse couldn't help but notice the startled looks on the politicians' faces. Sure, they'd seen him in the crowd, but they clearly hadn't expected to come face-to-face with a white man, and the expressions surrounding their moustaches made it clear they weren't altogether pleased to see him there. They looked as if this was supposed to be an easy process, getting the Indians to sign. Jesse represented trouble. Just for the hell of it, Jesse gave the white men a wide grin and a bow. As an afterthought, he turned to Thomas and did the same thing. The politicians smiled stiffly back. Thomas did not.

After formal introductions had been completed, Standing Trees began to chant in his tired, rocky voice, his Cherokee syllables strained by years of fighting, singing, laughing, and general chiefing. Jesse listened closely and barely made out, "Greetings Jesse, son of Ahtlee. We . . . Tsalagi . . . truth . . . future . . . sun . . . Mother Earth . . . gods . . ." then something that sounded like "mountain and fish . . ."

Jesse didn't want to turn around and ask Ahtlee for a better translation. He figured it was all just fancy starting-up talk anyway, and it was important that he appear as if he knew what he was doing. When it was time, Jesse faced the politicians and proceeded with his own kind of greeting.

"Greetings to our distinguished white friends from the great chiefs Standing Trees, Runs Quickly, One-Foot Bird, Lives in the Woods, and Quill Cheeks," he said in English, then let out a puff of relief. He had been worried he wouldn't remember all those names once he got up there, and he figured if he got those wrong, no one would listen to a word he had to say after that, no matter what it was. He returned to his choppy Tsalagi and faced the other audience, saying what Ahtlee had advised. "I am happy to speak for the village of Standing Trees," he said slowly, careful with every syllable. "We listen to the talk here and make talk in village for three days. White men promise great gift of trade and Tsalagi understand."

He looked at all the faces, most of them bored, but maybe a little entertained at hearing a white man attempt to speak their language. It was a pretty novel thing, from what Jesse'd seen. He glanced quickly at Ahtlee, then swallowed his nerves and dove in headfirst. "But I, Jesse," he said, thumping one fist meaningfully against his chest, "know the hearts of these white men. There are good white men, and there are bad white men. There are good ideas and bad ideas. I do not believe this idea is a wise thing for the Tsalagi."

Ahtlee grunted behind him and punched Jesse's back. "Say what I told you."

Jesse closed his eyes and sighed. "I want to say what I know."

"No. Not your place."

Jesse shook his head, then opened his eyes and looked around at the questioning Tsalagi. He'd known his opinions would never get heard but had figured it was worth a try. He had nothing upon which he could base his argument, but every nerve in his body screamed that this deal was bad. He knew Ahtlee understood as well, though he couldn't say anything without proof. He had given Jesse enough room that he'd gotten away with saying that much, but Jesse was at a loss about where to go from there. He glanced at the politicians for inspiration, and his eye was caught by the flutter of paper, weighted under inkwells and stones. The answer clicked into place like a ball in a musket. He had one more opportunity to prove he was right, but he'd have to take a chance. After this, he'd either look the hero or the fool.

After an apologetic glance over his shoulder at Ahtlee, Jesse continued. "The Tsalagi need know all words. I read paper so all is good." Then he addressed the white men, who were busy chewing lower lips and flexing fingers nervously. "I would like to read the paper to the Cherokee," he told them, smiling politely.

That was an unexpected request, apparently. He saw a jolt of concern pass through the politicians.

"It has been read many times, sir," said one.

"Not to the Cherokee," Jesse argued.

The politicians faced one another, their moustaches moving like fat, hairy caterpillars as they discussed Jesse's request. Jesse nodded, hiding a smile. He had a good feeling about this.

"Good," Ahtlee muttered behind him.

This was going to be a pleasure. A chore, definitely, since translating that many words was akin to choosing one particular salmon out of a school of four hundred. But hopefully it was worth it. If he didn't read, if he simply told the group he believed the deal required more negotiations, he would be silenced. But if he read what was actually written, and the deal included what he thought it might, no one could argue.

The white men had no other option but to acquiesce. Jesse was given the contract with great ceremony, and he accepted it the same way, hiding the nervous tremor in his hands. As he unrolled the paper, he noticed Thomas's face, twisted in a sardonic grin. The old man thought this was a ploy, because he knew perfectly well his son couldn't read.

Jesse ran his finger across and down the paper, combing through the artfully written words. What he read was what they already knew: the white men's plan to have free access to the Keowee Valley, including not only hunting and fishing but eventually establishing homes and towns as well. In exchange, the price on rifles, blankets, and other goods went down, and the trade value of pelts went up. They all knew that. Far from fair, but Jesse knew there was more. Had to be.

He kept looking, reading to the very bottom, which was where he saw it. The words jumped out at him as if they'd been painted in red war paint instead of black ink from a fine quill. Jesse wanted to punch the air, hoot with victory, but that would be inappropriate. Instead, he lifted his gaze from the paper and met Ahtlee's searching eyes. Jesse nodded slightly, then gave him a quick wink. And Ahtlee smiled.

Jesse looked farther, making sure he had everyone's attention, enjoying the theatrics he knew the Cherokee admired. Then he spoke in Cherokee as clear as he could manage. "My Cherokee family, I bring you the words of the white man. He talks of the Keowee Valley. They want to share fishing and furs. They want to build houses. We know this, yes? And we understand they need a home." He glanced around, making sure his words were getting through. The men watched him with sober expressions, nodding.

Jesse held up the paper, holding the corners so they could see the entire sheet, though it was illegible to anyone who couldn't speak English. He turned slowly, letting everyone see. As he moved past Thomas, he caught the old man's hostile glare, but also made out the tight, smug smile beneath. He averted his eyes to keep from laughing. *Oh, Thomas, my dear man, you ain't gonna be smiling in a minute.*

"For three days we talk. We know Mother Earth is generous but we must stop and see." He pointed at the paper. "The white man wants to settle on Keowee's eastern shore, yes? What they did not say, but what they wrote on this paper, is they also will have the *western* shore. The Cherokee, who have crossed the Keowee River for thousands of years, will not be permitted to cross here anymore. They can only cross twenty miles away. Twenty miles away from the water and the game trail you always hunted."

The faces before him, some of which had been frowning with impatience, were suddenly uneasy. Men leaned in to speak with other men. It was probably the most satisfying moment Jesse had ever experienced. Not only did he get to see how the Cherokee adjusted their thinking, how they suddenly respected him enough to believe his hard-won words, but he got to enjoy the sight of Thomas suffering the surprise of his life. Thank you, Doc Allen, for all those hours spent teaching him the value of letters and words. Yes, it was a good day.

"Paper say Tsalagi put sign here, say yes to deal," Jesse finished, then held up the contract again. He brought the paper to Standing Trees and presented it to the old man, who frowned with disbelief and frustration. He had been made to look a fool in front of all these people. Jesse saw his anger and tried to ease it. He spoke quietly so as not to upset anyone else.

"The brave heart of the great Standing Trees does not lie. It does not expect others to lie. These men have lied."

Standing Trees studied him, the tough old man holding him securely with nothing but a heavily jowled look. His chin trembled slightly with old age, but the gaze didn't wander. Finally he nodded.

"Tloo-da-tsì speaks clear as mountain water. This lie chills Tsalagi hearts." He stood abruptly and dropped the paper to the ground. "Standing Trees will not sign." The other chiefs followed suit after glancing quickly at the paper. And just like that, it was done.

As the Cherokee walked away, Jesse turned back to the panel. "I believe that concludes today's business, gentlemen." He nodded smugly at Thomas, whose own expression looked nothing short of murderous, then followed the Cherokee toward their horses.

It was a long ride back to the village, but Jesse felt good for most of the journey. He rode beside an expressionless Ahtlee, who had never been much of a talker to begin with. He spoke even less now, it seemed. Around them rode the others, some still digesting the truth of the day, others celebrating the loss they hadn't suffered, due to Jesse's revelation.

About an hour before they reached the village, Ahtlee spoke to him in slow, digestible Cherokee. "This day, Tloo-da-tsì, you grew to a man. You said words against your own people. You said words against my orders. You did something I told you not to do, but you made the better choice. I was proud."

He was proud? Because Jesse'd disobeyed? Would Jesse ever understand these people? "It was the right thing to do," he said.

Ahtlee agreed with a short grunt. "And you had courage, going against what I said."

"I apologize for that," Jesse muttered, not sure if that was the correct response. He looked straight ahead, between his horse's ears, waiting for Ahtlee to get to the point. When Ahtlee started a conversation, he had a reason for it.

Ahtlee smiled gently. "Yes, it is brave to follow your heart when you know you are right and the path you are on is the wrong one. But for you that is easy." He chuckled. It was a low, pleasant sound, like a dog's playful growl. "This test was not difficult for a man like you, a man who should have my name: Does Not Bend. I thank you, Tloo-da-tsì, for what you did today, and for honouring my village with your loyalty."

Jesse didn't know what to say. An apology from Ahtlee *and* a compliment? He followed Ahtlee's example and made a noncommittal grunt in reply.

"You have been in my village as my son for four changings of the moon. You have made my heart proud, and you have soothed the grieving which tore my soul. I thank you for that as well."

Jesse didn't even bother grunting this time. Just waited. Something was coming.

"You have earned my trust, Tloo-da-tsì. The village approves of you as well. When we return, you may decide if you wish to remain with us or return to the white man's world."

Jesse blinked. "I can leave?"

Ahtlee looked straight ahead, rocking gently with the horse's uneven steps as she picked her way down a slope. "If that is your decision, you may go. You will always be a part of our family, no matter where you are."

"I thought—"

"We hope you will stay."

"But I thought . . ."

From the expression on Ahtlee's face, he had no more to say on the subject. Then Jesse was glad his travel partner wasn't talkative, because all of a sudden he had a lot of thinking to do.

PART 3

Adelaide

CHAPTER 24

Terror From Trust

Of course I knew they would give Jesse the choice of whether to stay or go. I suppose I could have told him that would eventually come, but for some reason I hadn't. It was strange, because initially I couldn't wait for him to leave, and then, well, then I hoped they would change their minds and not permit him to go. Then he wouldn't have a choice. He couldn't leave. He'd have to stay . . . with me.

I had always had a choice. I had chosen to stay with the Cherokee when Maggie married Andrew, when she moved into her beautiful home with him, near her new friends who had come all the way from Scotland. They were good people, and I had never felt even the slightest fear of those men, for some reason. Every one of them was large, gruff on the outside, intelligent within, and yet I'd never thought twice about being around them. They treated me like glass. As if I were their little sister. I could have been happy with them had I chosen to stay there. And I would have been kept safe.

But I hadn't. I had chosen to stay here in the village, with people who lived with their ancestors forever perched on their shoulders like angels, people with a passion and dedication to their world, with an unselfish need to love one another with ferocious loyalty. With people who accepted me despite all my fears and oddities, people who taught, included, and understood me. These were the same people who wore practically nothing and shrieked like demons around a fire, singing primal, ancient songs that froze my blood every time I heard them. People who thought nothing of slitting an enemy's gut open then rejoicing at his suffering.

As a result of my decision, I lived an uneasy life, not knowing where I belonged, not liking either option. Something had always been missing.

Then Jesse had come along, clearly not belonging either.

"You see?" he asked.

I shook my head, trying to clear my thoughts. "I'm sorry. I wasn't listening. Say it again?"

He closed his eyes, then opened them again. He frowned at me, frustrated. "How much didn't you hear? I've been talking awhile now."

"Since you told me about Ahtlee's decision, and how you weren't sure what to do."

"Huh."

We sat side by side on cold granite boulders, wrapped in an extra layer of deerskin. The breath of warm summer air had chilled to a brisk warning of what was coming, stirring greens into golds, shaking the first layer of loose, dead leaves from rustling branches. I'd led Jesse back to my favourite place atop the mountain, the place where I had first explained Jesse's Cherokee name to him. Where Soquili had once told me about the beginning of the world. On our way up, the pathway had been slick with fallen leaves, rain-soaked, and rotting. Jesse caught my hand when I slipped, and I'd wanted both to cling to him and to run from him. What was I doing?

"So that's all you heard."

"Sorry. I . . . My mind was elsewhere."

He rolled his eyes. "I see that. But . . . Could you help me out a bit? I need to understand. I mean, you're so comfortable here with these people. Like this is how it's meant to be for you. Obviously that's not right. You're white, in case you'd forgotten." He gave me a wry grin and tugged a bit of my hair in illustration. "As white as they come." He paused, and something in his eyes softened. He wasn't angry at me anymore. But I felt bad. He had opened his heart to me, and I'd missed it.

"Tell me what you're thinking. Why is it so hard? I thought you hated it here. Hated these people."

He gave that a quick, dismissive shrug I'd come to know so well, looked doubtful. "I did. Sure I did. But you know everything's changed. It's been a real interesting time here. I feel . . ." He hesitated, frowning and scratching the pale blond hair where it curled above one ear. He had washed his hair that morning, I could tell, then let it dry with nothing more than a cursory run-through with his fingers. He never smeared in the bear fat that so many of the other men used, so he never carried that harsh tang with him. His hair was much longer than when he'd arrived, the gold waves licked his shoulders now, and he often tucked them behind his ears.

"I feel different from how I felt before."

"I can tell," I told him. "You're not so angry anymore."

He chuckled. "No? Maybe not. But I still have a temper, you should know. Boy, I was angry at that powwow. Seeing my old man there, it just brought back all that. I was rarin' for a fight, is what I was."

"Ahtlee said you were very controlled," I replied. That wasn't exactly what he had said, but close enough. Actually, Ahtlee had uncharacteristically taken me aside and told me he'd been proud of Jesse, of the way he'd held back when he clearly wanted to unleash his opinions and his frustration.

"Yeah, well. Anyway, I don't know. I don't think I could stay here forever, but I don't know how I could ever go back to what was."

I had no answers for him. How could I? I had none for myself.

It was still early afternoon, the sun still burned high overhead, but the autumn air was cool. A storm was coming, spotting across the sky in clouds that grew heavy with rain.

The chill cut through my tunic, but Jesse was watching me. He saw my inadvertent shiver and stood to give me his shirt. In the moment when he looked down at me, blocking the light, my sad little mind transformed him into nothing but a black silhouette. A strong shadow cutting out the sun. The shape of a man looming over me, his body solid, real, and able to inflict so much damage. He pulled his shirt over his head and held it out. But for me, he had ceased to be Jesse. Blackness and strength and cold . . . fear and helplessness and pain . . . sweat streamed from my forehead and my breath was hard to catch. Jesse stepped out of the sun and squatted instantly beside me. I gasped and pulled away reflexively.

"Hey, what is it? One minute you're fine, and the next you're looking at me like I'm some kind of monster."

I turned my head to the side, hating myself, as I always did when this kind of thing happened. No, it was more than that. I hated myself almost all the time. Hated my weakness, my ridiculous inability to control this panic. I would not cry. I would *not*. I was so tired of crying, and Jesse had to be getting tired of seeing it. His fingers were gentle on my cheek, and warm. I turned back toward him and tried to meet those golden eyes.

His voice was gentle. "Somebody hurt you bad, didn't they?"

I sniffed but couldn't look away. "I don't remember." That was partially true. I remembered wicked flashes of things I'd seen: my mother's dead stare, Ruth's blond curls rolling down her back as she was carried away . . . but the details were gone, hidden deep within me. I would never let them see the light of day again. I couldn't.

"We gotta fix you, Adelaide. We gotta. You can't just take off like a doe for no reason."

"No," I corrected him, my voice straining through the thickness in my throat. "You don't have to worry about it. I'll take care of myself. It's got nothing to do with you. It's my own problem."

He frowned, looking puzzled. "But Adelaide, it does have something to do with me."

"That's sweet of you, Jesse, but it doesn't. It's my problem, and I'll understand if you don't want to be around me because of it. I'm . . . just having a little trouble. I guess I heal slow."

He wouldn't give up. "It ain't sweet of me, Adelaide," he said, shaking his head. "Seeing you like this makes me feel bad." He frowned, chewing on his lower lip while he thought about what he wanted to say. "See, I've gotten to know you pretty well, I think. And I like being with you, even though I'm never sure if you want me anywhere near you. I have a feeling . . ." His expression hardened briefly, like he was thinking deeply, but he cleared it with a breath. "Whether it's a good or a bad thing, I think you're something I'm always gonna want to take care of. I don't know, I . . ." he said quietly, then cleared his throat. "No."

"What?"

"Sounds stupid."

"I won't know until you tell me."

"Well, fact is, I can't stop thinking about you. It's gotten so I look for you all the time, and when I can't see you, I'm too distracted to do much else. I want to make sure you're safe all the time. But it's more than that." He looked at his feet, swallowed hard, and shook his head. Then he met my eyes again, his own intense with a kind of desperation. "Who am I trying to kid?" he almost whispered. "The thing is, Adelaide, I've fallen in love with you."

His smile wavered, unsure, and the rain-tinged wind tossed the hair that fluttered at the sides of his face. But his eyes . . . the gold was almost hidden now, swallowed up by deep black circles of hope. He looked so young all of a sudden, his confidence and bravado replaced by the unreasonable trust of a child.

He loved me?

He heard my hesitation. I imagine its silence was ferociously loud to his ears. He held up his hands as if to show me they were empty. "And I understand that you're scared," he said. "I get that somewhere along the line someone didn't exactly leave a great impression on you. But . . . I'd be different."

He shifted from a squat until he was on both knees, his face on the same level as mine. But despite his closeness, to me he sounded far away, as if he spoke through cupped hands. All I could do was stare at his lips, watch them shape around his words. "I would be. You know I would. And we have a choice, the two of us. If you loved me, well, we could do what we wanted, right? We wouldn't have to stay here— or we could, if that's what you wanted, I guess. We could be on our own, though. We could—" He stopped, at a loss, his hands spread wide.

I stared at him, feeling the flush that had stolen my breath slowly die away.

"Adelaide?"

I blinked and forced my jaw to close.

"Have you got anything to say? Anything at all?" He chuckled nervously, running his fingers through his hair so the ends of one side stuck out like a wing. "Because if you don't, well, I guess I'd understand that, too. I kind of just up and sprung this onto you without any lead." He shook his head, marveling at his own error. "And that's like taking a green mare and throwing a saddle right there on her back without any warning."

Such an unexpected comment. I had to smile. "A green mare?"

Now it was his turn to blush, and a charming colour flooded his cheeks. "Well, no, that's not exactly what I . . ."

As he blustered through his words, I tried to pay attention, but I was distracted, aware of a stirring within me. As if something rose to the surface. It was just an emotional reaction, but it was so real I imagine I could have seen it if I'd had no skin. A bubble grew from deep in my belly, warm and soft and pushing against the walls of my body. It pumped up, spreading through my arms and hands and heart and veins, tingling like blood.

Hope. That's what it was. Hope.

"Jesse?"

"Yeah?"

A half smile played at the corner of my mouth, the start of a grin I didn't want to let out—not just yet. "I have something to tell you. It's kind of a funny thing."

He frowned and nodded, dropping his hands to his sides. "I'm listening." He didn't have to tell me that. His focus was intense, centred on me and me alone. No one else on earth existed but him and me, and suddenly that didn't bother me at all.

"The Cherokee have plans for us."

Concern creased his brow further. "What?"

Oh, he was going to be surprised. What would he do? All I could hope was that he didn't get angry and storm off like I'd seen him do. I swallowed. "I never mentioned this, because I didn't know what you'd say, and I had kind of hoped I wouldn't have to for a while, but now I think that if I don't, well, things might just get even more complicated. It seems like the right time to let you in on this, except I don't know if—"

"Adelaide?"

"I was supposed to marry Wahyaw," I blurted, watching his expression, which didn't change. "So when you came to the village in his place, they told me I would marry you."

He tilted his head, as if he hadn't quite heard me right. "You would . . ." Without changing expression at all, he scratched his jaw. "Huh. And so . . . You . . . Sorry. Tell me again? Why didn't you say anything before?"

"How could I? You and I are both so lost most of the time—"

He stiffened. "I ain't lost. I'm just still deciding."

"Oh. All right. Well, *I'm* lost. And I lose myself even further when I dream, and I didn't want to start something that might hurt all over again."

"Huh." He looked away from me, gazing into the forest. When he looked back, his smile was lit with humour, and he was so, so beautiful.

"So I didn't even need to ask you. It's already been decided."

I shook my head. "I told them I wasn't going to follow that tradition, and so far, they've left me alone—other than the pestering, that is."

His grin grew, and it was contagious. He laughed out loud, startling a resting crow overhead, who fluffed shiny black wings, then glared down at him. I'd never seen him like this before, and the sheer energy of his happiness made me dizzy. He leaned forward, cupping my cheeks in his warm palms. My skin buzzed, and my heart thundered so that my pulse tripped through my lips and fingers. I was afraid, I was excited, I was confused. And I think I was ready. He dropped his hands to my waist and brought his face to mine, then closed those golden eyes just before I closed mine.

His lips were warm and soft and not afraid. I wanted that so much, to be able to carry confidence like that, to own it, to share it like he did. I tried, putting my hands on his bristled face and pulling his lips harder against my own. That fed whatever he was craving, and I felt a jolt of celebration, knowing I'd done something right, even if it was something that terrified me to my core. Or maybe it was because of that. I sensed his energy building, racing through him, and I longed to be a part of that.

Except I knew what was coming. I knew what he would want, and I vibrated with fear.

"It's okay, Adelaide," he whispered against my lips. "You're safe."

His voice was like fingertips brushing the hair from my eyes, like a breeze when the sun was so sweltering it threatened to take my breath, like water in my throat after that horrible, horrible day . . .

He lowered me gently to the ground, his breath warm, the feel of his hands reassuring on my arms, my waist, my face. His warmth took away the cold the storm was bringing. And slowly, without ever feeling an actual change, I realized my trembling now rose from something I'd never felt before. Not fear, not the familiar vibrations of terror that had shaken within me for my entire life. This was something deeper. Desire. Desire and need and . . . love? Could he be right? Could this be love?

My arms went around his shoulders, pulling him down, and the weight of him settling against me was a good weight, a healthy pressure, a welcome pleasure I'd denied myself for so long. His hands explored the curves of my body, but I felt no fear. The need I felt in him and for him urged the bubble of hope inside me to rise higher still, its shimmering border growing larger, holding me, binding him to me, until I wanted everything . . . and that was a good want.

I had no idea anything could feel as wonderful as this man's body pressed against mine. I touched the warm skin of his chest, ran my fingers over the definition of muscles in his upper arms, explored the ridge of hard muscle across his shoulders and up his neck. When he nuzzled his face in to kiss my neck, my mind began to journey, like sinking into a dream, swirling among the warm shades of passion that wound through my heart. It was as if my thoughts reached out and searched for his. I felt it there, my dream, moving like a river, pouring into him, exploring, like a hand in the dark, searching . . .

Then everything crashed.

CHAPTER 25

Warning in a Kiss

The dream descended like a landslide, submerging me under layers of sharp, heavy images. Within my mind, the gurgling of rushing water was silent, the songbirds' fluttering and chirping gone. The trees had ceased whispering, as if the forest paused to witness the violence I knew was coming. I had come there on my own volition. Something in me had needed to come, though I couldn't yet place the reason.

In the dream, he was as clear as he'd always been on waking days. Except in the dream, Jesse lay facedown on the ground, unmoving. Fresh blood shone on the side of his face, dark with the fading light of day.

He couldn't help me when I stood to face the demon. The creature's face was shadowed by the vanishing lines of the sun, but I saw it well enough: a man with sunshine hair and a halfway smile just like Jesse's. But these eyes were feral—no longer golden but gray as an approaching winter storm. Demanding hands gripped me, tore at me, and my struggles did nothing. I sensed Jesse everywhere in the violence—even *smelled* him—yet I knew it couldn't be him. Jesse loved me. He could never hurt me. And there was so much hate in the grasping fingers, so much madness. I couldn't escape, could do nothing but scream and wish myself somewhere else.

The wall I had so carefully constructed in my mind began to splinter under the onslaught. Chunks of the barrier crumbled into the abyss of my mind, opening me up to something I couldn't bear to witness. But I had no choice. The hands were no longer part of the Jesse dream. They came from beyond, from the nightmare I thought I'd sealed safely away. So many strong hands, rough, dirty, hungry. I felt pinned in place like the skins we stretched to dry, inhaled pine and sweat and whisky. I couldn't come up for air, and I couldn't break free like I usually did. Both dreams wrapped around me like a braided rope, sending flames through my wrists as they burned . . . the burn I could never completely forget—

"Hey!"

No no no no no don't touch me don't hurt me please please

"Adelaide! Wake up! God, girl, wake up!"

No no no no no Jesse! Please, no no no!

Then a whisper, a soft tickle in my ear that brought the world spinning back with horrible clarity. "It's me. Jesse. I'm here, you're safe. Remember?"

My eyes opened, and he was there, kneeling beside me, eyes dark with concern. But it was all different. I scanned the trees around me, feeling my heart pound with a need to flee. No one else was there. But they had been. They'd broken through, come to find me again. I had to get away. How could he . . . The sounds were still fresh in my mind, the pressure of fingers bruising my skin, the stench of Jesse's blood on the dirt. Oh, Jesse, *Jesse* . . .

I pulled away, slid my body from his reach.

"What is it?" he asked. He started to reach for me, saw me flinch, and pulled back.

My pulse hammered frantically in my temples, loud in my ears. I struggled to my feet and backed farther away from Jesse, and he wisely did nothing but watch. Words weren't forming right in my mouth, but they escaped nevertheless, tripping awkwardly over my tongue. I stared at him but saw instead the man with the gray eyes who looked so like Jesse. When I heard my voice, it was no more than a whisper, like the hissing of a snake.

"You have to stop him. It's you. He'll kill you."

"Wha—"

"His hands . . . his eyes. God, Jesse. He'll kill you, then he'll take me . . ."

"Adelaide, please. What are you—"

I looked up at him, pleading. "He looks like you. But his eyes . . . So wild, so hungry. Not like yours. And yet he . . ." My eyes flew open with realization. "Your father! Your father, he—"

Jesse frowned. "Don't you worry about Thomas Black. He has no place with you and me."

"He wants to kill you. He wants to kill me, too."

That stopped him. One eyebrow flicked up, and he hooked one hand on his hip. His voice changed, sounding skeptical. "Aw, come on, Adelaide. You can't just say things like that. It makes no sense."

I couldn't explain, and my head spun with questions. I had to get out, get away. If I left Jesse, would the gray-eyed man leave my nightmare? Would he let me live? And the others, those men who had come crashing back through my mind—were they coming for me? Could I outrun them? I couldn't see any answers, couldn't know them because Jesse had woken me before I'd seen the end of the dream. The pieces of it were still there, shards of threat and fury ripping through my mind. My head felt as if it might split before I could get it all out.

But he couldn't possibly understand. It was too much for me, so it was far beyond him. "I need to think about some things," I told him. "I need some time to myself, all right?"

His hands opened at his sides. "Okay. I'll just wait."

"No. You have to go," I said. I was gasping, having trouble catching my breath. "Go back to the village. I'll come later."

"But—"

"Please, Jesse. Just go."

He frowned. "Hang on a minute. I don't understand. One minute you're fine, the next you're making no sense. Don't I deserve some kind of explanation?"

Of course he did. But how could I explain something to him when I couldn't figure it out for myself?

I puffed out a breath and wrapped my arms around my stomach, trying to contain the panic. "You remember that day I told you about my dreams, and you asked if that meant I was a witch?" He nodded warily, remembering how I'd reacted at the accusation. "Well, remember I told you that sometimes I dream things that are going to happen?"

"Yeah, but you said you were just learning how to do that."

"I am. But something just happened, Jesse." I clamped my fingers around my head, digging my fingers into my hair, trying to hold everything in so I wouldn't completely lose my mind. "When you kissed me, the pictures in my head came so clear. And they were so scary. I just . . ." I took a deep breath and let it out slowly while he waited, still looking baffled. "I need to sort through what I saw, Jesse."

"I'm listening."

I shook my head. "No, I can't do it with you. Not yet, anyway. I need to do this on my own."

"I don't understand."

"I don't, either."

His eyes were soft with hurt. He stepped carefully toward me, as if I might spook and run away, which I was tempted to do. But I made myself stand and waited until he'd come right up to me. "I want to help you, Adelaide. I want to be the one you come to."

"I know," I said, dropping my hands from my head and touching his cheek lightly. "But I can't. Not now. Not yet. Please, Jesse. Leave me for now. I'll follow soon. I just really need to think."

His expression made me want to cry. How could I both fear and need him so much?

"I'm sorry, Adelaide. I'm sorry I scared you. I love you. You gotta believe that. I thought you were okay with me—"

"I am. I'm okay, Jesse. I'm . . . I just—I'll come down soon. Please?"

He frowned, then nodded slowly. "All right." He glanced down at my waist. "You got your knife, right?"

I gestured toward my hip, to the protection I always carried there. He backed away, then turned toward the path. He stood without moving for a moment, his back to me, and I could tell from the angle of his head that he was staring at the ground, trying to figure all this out. He glanced over his shoulder at me, chewing on his lower lip and looking torn.

"I don't want to leave you here alone like this."

I wrapped my arms around myself again and said nothing. He blinked a couple of times, then was gone.

I leaned back against a huge pine, staring at the ceiling of branches over my head. My breath was coming fast enough that I felt dizzy. What was happening? What had I seen, and why was the past returning after so long? And why, why was Jesse in the middle of everything?

I dropped to my knees and vomited, my body trying to get rid of the poisonous thoughts coursing through me. When I felt steadier, I stood and turned the opposite way from where Jesse had gone, then headed toward a small stream. I cupped cold water in my hands and splashed my face, trying desperately to think. Jesse loved me. He wanted to help me, but I'd sent him away. And yet I'd lied to him. I couldn't do this on my own. I was lost.

No, I wasn't. Maggie. I needed Maggie. I got back on the pathway and started on the familiar path to her home. I hadn't been there in a few months. Not since Jesse had come. But I needed her now. I needed Maggie like I needed water and air. I started to run.

CHAPTER 26

Maggie

The rain caught up to me after about an hour, falling slowly at first, like a warning. Then it came faster and harder, until I was drenched through and shaking with every step. I ran much of the way, clutching Jesse's shirt around me, following deer trails that snaked around heaps of granite and through groves of great oak and poplar. I ran to keep the blood pumping, trying to keep warm, ducking under soaked leaves that slapped my face, watching my steps so I didn't stumble over slick rocks and roots.

It took a couple of hours before I saw their little cluster of houses by the river. Seeing them made me smile, because I knew Maggie was there. Her life had become so normal and good. I'd come running to a place where I could ask for help and receive something solid in reply. They had chickens now, I saw, and their four horses had welcomed a fifth. Strong draft horses—they'd have to be, since they had to carry the big Scotsmen. I started wearily down the last of the path toward her house, and though my body buzzed with happiness, I was too tired to run. I was here at last, and I felt I could barely go another step.

The lone cow heard me. She glanced up from behind the barn, big brown eyes blank as the wall beside her.

Andrew appeared first, emerging from the barn and standing under a protective overhang while he wiped his hands on a rag. Catching my movement as I exited the trees, he looked up the hill toward me and smiled, a line of white in his ruddy face, then I saw him lift a hand in greeting. He always made me happy, Andrew did. His soul was so open, though his thoughts were always hidden beneath. Like the Cherokee, he didn't seem to be a man who knew how to lie. And his love for Maggie came before everything else. How could I not love a man like that?

But my steps faltered. It was strange to see him there, welcoming me. Maggie *always* greeted me first. She always knew when I was coming; dreamed it, I supposed. But she wasn't there.

"Adelaide," he called, his soft Scottish brogue changing the sound to "Ah-dlaide," a distinction I loved. "What are ye doin' in the rain, lass? Come warm yerself by the fire."

"I can think of nothing I'd like more," I assured him. "Is Maggie in there?"

Just the mention of her name changed his expression. He was at once soft and proud and charged with an energy I could actually see. "Oh, aye. An' she'll be right pleased to see ye. She's a bit of somethin' to tell ye. Go on in. We've broth o'er the fire to warm ye."

And fresh bread. I could smell the heavenly aroma wafting outside the house as I came closer, pressing through the cool rain to warm my heart. My stomach growled, and I realized I hadn't eaten since early that morning. The journey through the woods, combined with the afternoon's frightening experience had left me famished.

I didn't bother knocking, just walked in. Strange again. If she hadn't met me outside, Maggie should at least have been there to open the door. And yet Andrew seemed unconcerned. Happier than ever, if that was possible.

She was just taking the bread out. Steam rose in perfect curls from the three loaves she set on the table, though the room was warm, almost overly so. She always cooked more than was necessary, as did Janet in the other house. The men with whom they lived were big and always seemed hungry. I'd watched them devour a table full of meat, bread, cheese, and broth, as well as ale or scotch, without appearing to pause for breath. I was positive that no one in South Carolina cooked as much oatmeal as Maggie did every morning.

She glanced up when the door opened, and her face lit up. "Addy!" she cried, rushing toward me.

Suddenly she stopped, held up one finger for me to wait, then grabbed a blanket from near the fire. She slung it over my shoulders and grabbed me, bundling me inside the warm wool. I hugged her hard, breathing in the familiar scent of her, sweetened around the edges by the baking, and tears burned in my eyes. Maggie, my big sister, the one who always knew what to do, and not only because she dreamed of the future.

I pulled back so I could study her face. Most of her long, dark hair was tied behind her neck in a healthy tail, but wisps dangled on both cheeks. She looked like she'd lost weight, and her eyes were tired. I frowned. "Are you okay?"

Her eyes widened and she laughed, sounding strangely unconvincing. "Okay? Why would you ask that?"

"Because you didn't know I was coming."

She bit her lower lip, but her eyes were smiling. "I'm fine. Let's celebrate your visit with some hot bread and butter with tea. Bo makes delicious butter."

"Bo?"

She chuckled and set a plate of sliced dried apples on the table, then went back to pour tea. "I promised I'd try to learn some of Andrew's language. Gaelic, it's called. *Bò* is cow. I thought I might remember it better if I called her that."

I could smell the sassafras tea, sweet and tart, as she set it aside to steep. My hands felt half-frozen from the trek through the rainy forest, and I dragged my chair closer to the hearth fire to soak in some of its warmth. I watched her flit from table to pot to larder, moving like a hummingbird, then hesitate, seeming to prop herself up against the long stone counter. In a moment, she was up and moving again, slicing two thick pieces of bread and drizzling honey on top, just as she knew I liked it. When at last she was done, she pulled her chair up near mine, but slightly farther from the fire. Then she handed me the bread and let out a deep sigh.

"I'm so happy to see you, Addy. I've missed you. Have you been busy?"

I nodded vaguely. "I guess you could say that."

I wanted to unload everything, tell her about Jesse and my vision, but more than anything I wanted to soak in her presence. Sometimes when I got caught up in day-to-day events, I forgot how much I loved her. How just seeing her made me stronger. Except this time was different, I realized with a start. Because I already *was* stronger. Jesse had made me so.

He had taken it all away just as easily, and he hadn't even known how.

"I came to tell you lots of things, Maggie, and to ask for your help. But I want to talk about you first. Tell me what's happening. I'm sorry I've been away so long."

She twisted her beautiful face into a frown, half-mocking, half-curious. The firelight flickered, turning her pale skin gold, but only making the dark shadows beneath her eyes look even deeper. She bit into the soft, doughy bread, chewed for only an instant, then swallowed. "But I want to know about you."

"Oh, you will. But tell me your news first. Andrew said you had something to tell me."

Her smile was immediate. "I do."

"And why didn't you know I was coming, like you always do?"

"I . . . I've been ill," she said, looking away. "I haven't been seeing much lately."

"Ill? Why didn't you send for me?"

"Because I thought I could handle it by myself." She sat a little taller. "And I did. Andrew and I did."

"So you're all better now?"

I was relieved to see the sparkle dance in her eyes and know it wasn't just a trick of the fire.

"I'm pregnant," she blurted, her face shining with joy. "Almost four months, we think."

My stunned glance went reflexively to her belly, then back to her eyes. She wore a long homespun gown under a stained white apron, and I could see no telltale bulge. Not yet, anyway. But her hands dropped, fingers spread like a protective fence around the tiny inhabitant. Pregnant? I supposed I shouldn't have been so surprised, considering how much she and Andrew loved each other. It was just that it seemed so . . . unexpected, I guess. Like she'd moved to a new level without me. Again.

Despite the shock, I was thrilled for her. "Oh, Maggie!" She was close enough to hug, so I leaned in and squeezed her tight. I felt nothing different about her physically, save the fact that her breasts pushed a little harder against me, so I assumed they were growing at least. The rest of her seemed smaller, not larger, and I realized she really had been ill.

"I'm going to be an aunt," I said, smiling against her. "That's the most wonderful thing I've heard . . . in at least two hours."

That was cruel and unfeeling. I hadn't meant to say that. And yet her eyes opened, the smile replaced by a look of curiosity. "Oh? What could be more wonderful than that?"

"I'm in love," I said quietly.

That surprised her. Her jaw opened, only slightly wider than her eyes. "What?"

I gave her a half smile and shrugged. "I guess I am. He loves me. He told me a few hours ago."

"Who is it? Not Soquili, surely. Adahy? Tsiyi?" She took another big bite of the bread, and I was glad to see she seemed to have recovered her appetite.

"Actually," I said, grinning wryly. "He's the one I'm *supposed* to be in love with, so it all works out."

She narrowed her eyes. "What are you talking about?"

It was so strange to me that she even had to ask. Her whole life she'd known all the answers, never needed to ask anything. In the beginning, it had been dreams, visions, things she saw when she let herself drift into what I called the "half-place." Not awake, not sleeping. Maggie had always known how to find that place. And after she'd met Wah-Li, it became so easy for her that she could simply close her eyes and just . . . know. She could speak with animals. She could cry out silently and speak to people's minds. I tilted my head, studying her right back. It must have been odd for her, too, not being able to see what I was thinking. The gift she'd hated for most of her life, then valued, but never had to do without.

"Maggie, hold my hand." She did. "Now," I said, "tell me what I'm talking about."

She didn't even try, though I thought I saw regret when she shook her head. "I'm too tired, Addy. I'm trying to do the opposite. Trying to close my eyes to everything around me but Andrew and the baby."

"You're doing it on purpose?"

"In the beginning, it was just because I couldn't. Oh, I was so sick, I couldn't stand. I couldn't pull my weight around here, and of course everyone is needed." She lifted one eyebrow and smiled sheepishly. "I was angry and terrible to be around, too. Andrew told me not to worry and tended me like I was a lame puppy." She frowned. "I hated that. Hated feeling helpless. I . . . hated it so much I almost didn't want the baby for a while."

I blinked, shocked. Why hadn't she sent Andrew or Iain to get me? I would have taken care of her, would have helped with whatever needed doing. But Maggie had always been independent. And stubborn.

"Does Wah-Li know?" I asked. She shook her head. "I'll tell her," I assured her, and she smiled. "Are you happy now? About having the baby?"

She nodded. "It's easier now. I'm not as sick these days, though I feel like I've been dragged behind a running horse for three months. Now, well, now I can get around and do things. Small things, of course, because Andrew won't let me lift a finger, but at least I'm not just lying around."

"Wow," I said quietly as the reality settled in. "You're going to have a baby."

She squeezed my hand. "And you're in love."

We let the flush of happiness die down and were quiet for a while, lost in our own thoughts. Maggie gazed at the fire, her hands absently caressing the flat plane of her stomach. I stared into the flames, appreciating the warmth while I scrubbed my fingers through my hair, helping it dry. I was so tired. The heat was lulling, the sweet, warm bread filling the hole in my belly and encouraging me to seek sleep. I wanted to tell her all about the village, give her the news, share all the stories with her, but for now it seemed right just to be sisters.

A thought struck me. "Maggie . . ." I mused. She glanced at me and lifted her eyebrows. "Have you thought about what this baby will be like? The child of you and Andrew? Two people with gifts no one else can imagine?"

"Of course," she said with a slow smile.

The door opened and Andrew stepped inside, bringing with him the *shushing* of rain as it battered grass and leaves. The noise made me even happier to be warm and dry by the fire, and I snuggled deeper into the blanket. Andrew shook water off his coat and hair as if he were a big black dog, then latched the door behind him, leaving the room suddenly quiet again, with no sound but the occasional crack of the fire.

It took him no more than three steps to reach her, to lean down and claim her lips. She was lost to me in that moment, so complete was their connection. I loved seeing that their affection for each other hadn't weakened even the slightest. Every time I saw either of their expressions when the other entered a room, it was as if they hadn't seen each other in ten years. It was so beautiful, that love. The unquestionable connection I knew was so rare.

The connection I wanted more than anything in the world.

"We'll go to Iain's for supper this eve," Andrew said. I glanced up, and he smiled at me, the lines of his dark, handsome face soft with ease. "Aye, I told him ye were here as well, and he was right pleased to hear of it. Seems he and Seamus have had enough of waiting for last month's deer to age. Your visit only encouraged them to make a meal of it."

It was understood I would stay at least one night. And though I ached to open up to Maggie, to somehow ask her for help, I also looked forward to an evening with these friends with nothing to worry about save how much I would eat. I lived day to day suspended between worlds, loving and hating both. When I spent too much time with one, I craved the other. This place was an escape for me. One where I didn't have to live in constant division, trying to figure out where I fit. And yet I had chosen not to live there.

The evening was close and raucous, the small pine room crowded with laughter and loud Scottish voices. The voices hushed with sorrow when I gave them the news they hadn't heard from the village, telling them of Wahyaw's death. I lightened the mood somewhat by recounting the story of the furious white man they'd adopted in his place, and Maggie shot me an inquiring look. I smiled briefly, as did she, knowing we'd speak more of it when we were just two sisters alone, behind a closed door. But by the time Maggie said it was time to go home, I could barely keep my eyes open.

When he'd built the house, Andrew had constructed two bedrooms as well as the large front room. The second bedroom served as an extra, for anyone visiting. Sleeping in my own room gave me a luxury I had never known: privacy. As a child, I had shared a bedroom with my sisters, now I shared a council house with my Cherokee family. Being so alone was an odd feeling. I curled into the bed, pulling my knees against my chest, listening to the sounds outside my door. It seemed too quiet.

A gentle knock on the door, then Maggie came in. I sat up, and she eased down on to the side of the bed, looking quietly at me.

"You came here for a reason, Addy," she said softly. "Don't you think we've put it off long enough?"

CHAPTER 27

A Sister's Connection

So I told her everything, despite the fact that both of us had been drooping from exhaustion five minutes earlier. I told her of Jesse. Of my initial fears and the dreams that had come to me before he ever had. That brought a thoughtful expression to her eyes. I admitted my instinct to flee, then the grudging friendship that had bloomed so rapidly between us. Her eyes glistened as I described him, though my confession shyly listed his faults along with his better points. I laughed, telling her the stories I had found infuriating in the past, like the way he was always so ready to fight the entire Cherokee nation to prove he was right. I told her Wah-Li's name for him, and comprehension dawned in Maggie's eyes. It was easy for her to visualize the wild side of him, the curious, up-front, enthusiastic man, the daring cougar with a mind that never stopped and eyes that suspected the world.

She heard more than what I told her: she heard the need she'd once known herself. She felt my pain, then the embrace of relief when I'd realized someone loved me—and I could actually love him back.

"But you're here now," she said quietly, settling herself onto the middle of my bed. "Not with him. Why?"

"Because I had a dream. I had the most real vision I've ever had, and it scared me to death."

She sighed, looking sad. "You know you don't need to be afraid of dreams, Addy. They—"

I stopped her by putting up one hand. I didn't want to hear that. I didn't need her to look down on me, treat me as if I were a little girl again. I knew what I'd seen; I'd come a long way from when I couldn't bear to think of the dreams. I couldn't stop the harsh tone when it burst from my throat.

"Like the dreams *you* had? Are you telling me you weren't afraid that day? I saw you so many times when the dreams took over your mind, scaring the life out of you. I held you when you could barely breathe. When I had this dream today, it took over. It attacked the secrets I'd hidden away, the ones I'd never wanted to see again. But in this dream, I saw Jesse, and *I saw that day*, Maggie." I broke down, sobbing. "I felt the men on me, Maggie! I heard them. I remember *everything*."

Maggie's expression hadn't changed, but she blinked and her eyes welled. This was new. Maggie didn't usually cry. I instinctively wanted to apologize, to change the conversation, to step back into safe territory. But this was why I had come all the way out here. This was why I'd run from the only man I'd ever loved. Because I knew what I'd seen. I wasn't going to let her tell me not to pay attention.

I sniffed loudly and wiped my eyes with my arm. "But it's not just that. There was something about the way that nightmare happened in the midst of another violent dream. There was another enemy, and Jesse was . . . Well, that's why I've come. I need help, and I need the help that only you can give me."

Her expression was tired, her eyes liquid with regret.

"But you can't, can you?" I asked.

I saw the battle going on behind those deep eyes of hers and felt horrible. I had no right to ask her for this. "It's okay,

Maggie," I said. "I'm okay. I just wanted to talk with you and see—"

"Okay," she said quietly. "I don't know if I can help, though. I'm still so . . ." She lifted her shoulders in a shrug, then let them fall. I could see her exhaustion, feel the weight of it just as she tried to cast it off.

"Are you sure?"

We stared at each other for what felt like a long time. Then she made up her mind and scrambled forward so she sat beside me on the bed, and we leaned back against the cool pine wall. She sighed.

"What do you think, Addy? How do you want to do this?"

I closed my eyes, fighting the panic that was starting to eat its way into my mind. "I want to try and bring that dream back. I want to show you Jesse, and I want to understand what I saw today. Like what we do with Wah-Li, you know? If you see the same thing, maybe you can tell me what it means. What I should do."

Trying to see each other's dreams was something entirely new for both of us, but she nodded, ready to try. She closed her eyes in a deliberate manner, her mouth straight and inexpressive, the muscles in her face relaxed. Her hands lay at her sides, palms up, and I seized the one between us. Our fingers intertwined, and I closed my eyes, feeling the pull of her powers—though they were shadows of their former strength—and gratefully sank into whatever she could offer.

I had done this—purposefully recalling my dreams—twice before: once with Wah-Li, once on my own. But I knew Maggie—or at least the Maggie who hadn't been pregnant—had powers that could outshine even the wise woman of the Cherokee. I took a deep breath, prayed for strength, then dove into memories of my dream, bolstered by her support and by the knowledge that I was safe with her. Our connection, strong as an ancient oak, was solid and held us together. We stood side by side, more one person than two, inside the dream I conjured.

The vision returned, the forest shadowed, sucked of air

by the witnessing trees. Jesse lay bleeding and motionless. Then the face so much like his, aged and tinged with gray, his hands on me . . .

Maggie tugged on me—not my hand or arm or body, but my heart. She sensed the threat and wanted to be away, to escape what I had warned her about. But I held her, forced her to stay. I needed to know—was what I saw real? If I could hold on to her, use her as an anchor, could I stay in the dream until its completion? Had Jesse and the Cherokee given me enough courage?

On the other hand, if her perception of the dream changed from mine, maybe it had all been a mistake. I had never been able to control my dreams before. Maybe this had just been one of those times when I'd misinterpreted. God, I hoped it was.

But the man's hands on my throat were thick, calloused, and tightening. His teeth, yellowed over time but straight and bared. Words hissed through them, words I couldn't hear but understood regardless. His eyes burned cold, gray metallic flames fueled by hate and lust. But that mouth was so familiar, the lips I had kissed . . .

Stars flew in my head, and the earth beneath my feet dropped, melting into a black, bottomless pit. I couldn't grab on to anything and couldn't find Maggie. Thomas Black wasn't alone anymore. The others were back, those men I'd thought gone forever. I was choking, my defences draining. When I could see no more, I could still feel hands on my tunic, the fingers demanding, rabid. I tried to wriggle free, but the hands only fought me harder. I screamed—

The door slammed open, and Andrew was there, deep brown eyes wide with concern. "What is it?" he demanded. "Are ye all right?"

Maggie had screamed, too. Our voices lingered like ghosts within the fragrant pine walls. Andrew waited for an answer, but I couldn't speak. I was not all right, but I was alive and unharmed. And once again, I'd escaped the dream before it ended. Maggie held me while I shook. I felt her own small gasps, felt her tears and sweat, warm on my cheek.

"There is a man coming," she said to Andrew over my shoulder, then swallowed. Her tone, though interrupted by tiny sobs, was smooth and ethereal, as it was so often when she saw visions. She sounded as if she were still halfway in the dream world. I couldn't see Andrew's expression, but I knew he would believe every word she said. "He is coming for Addy. He must be stopped. He *must* be. You will know him, Andrew. He will seek her with a passion you cannot douse. He will hunt her through the eyes of a killer."

With her cheek pressed against mine, I felt her summon Thomas's image in her mind, felt her reach out to Andrew. His thoughts reached toward her, taking the offering, reassuring and promising all in one breath. It was a strange and beautiful experience, being included in their intimate exchange.

"Where is the devil?" he asked, his voice husky.

She shook her head. She didn't know. "The forest. Soon. A day? Two?"

My eyes squeezed shut against the pain. Now I knew. She'd seen it just as I had, and it had frightened her. She'd seen the connection between the dreams. It was real.

PART 4

Jesse

CHAPTER 28

Another Protector

Shouldn't have left her. Godammit. Jesse pounded his fist against the council house wall with frustration. He would never, *ever* understand women. There he was, thinking he'd finally pulled it all together, had even told the girl he loved her.

And he *did* love her. He did. Scared him how much he loved her. It was a foreign, terrifying feeling, knowing she was what he needed to complete who he was. He even felt slightly lost now that she was out of his reach. Bit by bit, little Adelaide the Mouse had become the most important thing in his world. Having her in his arms had felt like the first bite of fresh bread, the river on that scorching day with Soquili, the sight of a purple sunrise when the last of the clouds faded away. She had been soft and warm in his hands and had tasted like berries, her lips welcoming and giggling under his.

Then it had stopped. She had sat up, stared at him as if he were a ghost, and run off. To make matters worse, she hadn't come back like she'd said she would. She should have been back for supper, should have been there in the evening for him to share a fire with. She should have come back and let him kiss her again, let her soothe whatever crazy fears had taken over this time. She was a funny little thing, his mouse. And she needed him.

But she hadn't come back. Not that night, not the next morning. Jesse had stomped around the village, questioning everyone. No one had seen her. And no one really worried, because, well, these were Cherokee, and they damn well did what they damn well pleased, didn't they? How was a man supposed to get any answers? Kokila was normally the one he'd go to, or Soquili, or even Soquili's mother, Salali. But they all just shrugged.

Ironically, it wasn't until he bumped into the little weasel, Dustu, that he finally got an answer. He'd been walking past, trying to ignore the bastard's slimy grin, when the man laughed, pointing at him.

"Shadow Girl leave you, white boy," he said, grinning through a chipped tooth. Jesse always claimed to have broken that tooth, but he wasn't actually sure if that was the truth. He didn't recall much about the man's appearance before that first fight had broken out.

Jesse glared at him, fists clenched. "You know nothing, weasel face."

"I do know. Girl gone, white boy *soooo* sad." His smile drooped into a cynical frown. "Poor, poor white boy."

"You should stop talking before I *make* you stop talking."

Dustu's grin was immediate. He cracked his knuckles and flexed his fingers in preparation. "You ready?"

Jesse wasn't in the mood for a fight. Actually, he was, but he didn't have time for one. And he didn't have time to recover from one, either. He wanted to find Adelaide, and his sense of urgency was building. Where could the girl have disappeared to? Dustu waited a few feet away, hopping on the balls of his feet like a dog on a tether, raring to go. Jesse leaned in and peered closely at the warrior's face, startling Dustu, who backed up a step. Jesse stayed close. He poked Dustu's cheek, looking impressed, then teased him in Tsalagi.

"No bruises? What's happening, Dustu? You keep pretty for a girl?"

Dustu's joy disintegrated. "I'm not pretty."

"Truth," Jesse agreed. "Adelaide say Gauri thinks you pretty. I say she wrong."

Dustu frowned, looking unsure. "Gauri . . . Gauri say this?"

"Yes," Jesse replied with a scowl. "Woman has bad taste."

The fight evaporated from Dustu's face. He frowned, stroking the sharp line of his jaw while he considered the possible implications of this. "She say—"

"That's all I know," Jesse assured him, turning to go. "I must find Adelaide."

He got about ten paces away before Dustu spoke up. "She is at sister's. She always goes to Maggie when she needs to know something."

Jesse wheeled around. "You sure?"

"Nah. But I think maybe." In a rare moment of charity, Dustu gave him instructions on how to get to Maggie and Andrew's place, and the men went their separate ways.

Her sister, Maggie. Now this was interesting. More insight into Adelaide. What did he remember her saying about Maggie? Trying to remember gave Jesse more to think about on the journey. Dustu had drawn him a map in the dirt, and Jesse'd used that to come up with a shorter route, though he knew there'd probably be some bushwhacking to be done. He knew the first half. They did a lot of hunting up this way. He remembered the major fork in the trail. The right fork led toward the path Dustu had drawn for him. The other led to New Windsor and the home of Thomas Black.

In the beginning, Jesse had been tempted to take that fork, disappear into the trees when he was out hunting with the men. Occasionally the Cherokee had forgotten about him, caught up as they were in the hunt. Then Jesse'd reconsidered. If they could catch deer so easily, how simple would it be for them to track a full-grown human who wasn't nearly as quiet? But still, it was comforting knowing the path was there, an option if he got desperate.

He didn't care what the Cherokee thought of him. Not at all. Except maybe Ahtlee. That old guy had a way of making Jesse feel good, with a regal nod of his head. And maybe his wife, Salali, whose twinkling eyes were filled to their black brims with patience. Soquili had ended up being a pretty good friend after all. Nechama was sweet and patient. Of course, Kokila was a good friend to Adelaide, so he approved of her as well . . .

As usual, he went left, then eventually swerved off a bit, aiming for the landmarks Dustu had given him. He cut through the woods a little carelessly, slipping on rocks but catching himself in time, the dirt map clear in his mind. He ran when he could, wanting to make up for lost time, which is what he called the time between when he'd last seen her and that particular moment. All of a sudden, nothing on earth seemed as important as finding Adelaide.

He was going to get her to explain everything. Then he was going to make her marry him. How could she not? He knew she loved him. Nobody could kiss like that if they weren't in love, could they? He grabbed the edge of a waist-high shelf of granite, hopped up and over. All right. His little mouse had gotten spooked. That much was clear. She had to get over some memories—whatever they were—and he was determined to help her with that. The latest declaration about Thomas Black had come out of nowhere, but he'd figure that out once he had her back in his arms.

Jesse's mind held pictures as tight as a snare holds a rabbit. He saw the map Dustu had drawn, and despite the fact that he strayed to try and save time, he kept to the general directions and arrived safely at the little piece of land that had been claimed by Maggie and the others over a year before. He knew it by the number of houses, the first cluster he'd seen since leaving the village, though he'd seen quite a few singular homes along the way, all in different states of upkeep.

He stepped out of the trees and gazed down at the peaceful scene before him. A flock of chickens bobbed at the side of the house, and Jesse licked his lips in anticipation. What he would give for a couple of eggs right about now. And a bed, maybe. He was damn tired. It had been a long journey, and if he was being honest with himself, he didn't actually think his shortcuts had helped much. He'd stumbled off a few sharp edges, twisted an ankle on a stubborn root when he wasn't paying attention. He was cold, too. At least the rain had spent itself the night before.

Adelaide had said these folks were Scottish, and Jesse knew from years back that Scottish people pretty much always opened their homes to visitors. Jesse could practically taste the supper, feel the warm hearth fire that crackled under the stone chimney, see Adelaide's welcoming smile.

At least he *hoped* she'd smile when she saw him. Forgive him for whatever he'd done to set her off.

It was close to dusk, after a long day, the last offering of warmth pulling away as the sun retreated. A rooster mistook night for day and crowed, but he was entirely ignored by the few horses feeding beyond the barn, and the cow as well. A fine domestic scene. Where would Adelaide be? In the house? Or maybe in the stable? He knew she wasn't overly fond of horses, but he also knew she wasn't afraid to work with them. Maybe she was cooking with her sister. He'd like to meet that sister. She sounded interesting. What would she look like? Adelaide had said she was dark-haired, not blond like they were. Jesse shivered and headed down the little slope, hoping for a warm welcome and a bit of supper. Sure would sit well just about now.

"Hold, stranger," he heard.

Jesse froze. He held his hands out at his sides, palms open, clearly offering no threat. "Hey, I'm not here for trouble," he said.

"No? What for, then? What business would ye have here?" Jesse recognized a Scottish brogue, like the ancient trader McCulloch who'd run the trading post near his old home. Short, squat, and dark, with glowering eyes that didn't take nonsense from anyone. And ugly. That man had been memorably ugly. He wondered if this voice belonged to someone similar. He glanced to his side, toward the source.

No, this was nothing like McCulloch. The speaker was about the same height and age as Jesse, but his body was more solid. His hair fell in dark waves, almost as black as Cherokee hair, sweeping the tops of his shoulders. Dark eyes—again, almost black—forbade even the suggestion of light conversation. Even the rest of his face was dark, shadowed by a short beard Jesse judged to be maybe three days old.

"I'm looking for a friend. I heard she might be visiting here."

"Is that right, then?" The Scot crossed his arms over his chest. "Who is it ye seek?"

"Adelaide's her name. You know her?"

A moment's hesitation, then the dark man's eyes narrowed perceptibly. A touch more aggression edged into the stone-cold voice. "No one here by that name. Ye might as well head back to where'er it is ye came from."

Jesse frowned. That didn't seem right. He was sure this was the place. He mirrored the man, folding his own arms. The Scotsman had seemed just a bit too quick to answer. As if he'd been prepared. Was Adelaide here? Had she told this man they'd had a disagreement or something? Because if she had, well, that wasn't right. He hadn't done anything wrong. Hell, he deserved the opportunity to speak with her, get all this out into the air. She'd kissed him back, dammit.

Then something in his chest tightened. Was she hurt? In danger? What if this bastard had done something?

"I think she *is* here," Jesse said, meeting the stranger's eyes.

"An' I said she's no'."

Jesse nodded. So that's the way it would be. "Listen. I don't want any trouble. But I have to see Adelaide. I need to talk with her, and I need to bring her back to the village with me. I don't know what she told you, but—"

The fist came out of nowhere, slamming into Jesse's jaw and knocking him flat on his back. Solid rock, that fist. Jesse stayed down for a moment, blinking back the wetness that sprang to his eyes, spitting a shot of blood to the side. He frowned up at the man, sizing him up in a completely different way now. So the man could fight and was obviously well equipped.

Well, that was just fine. Nobody was gonna tell Jesse if he could or could not see Adelaide. He slid his jaw from one side to the other and back again. It seemed to still be working fine.

"You shouldn't have done that," he told the man.

The dark eyes glared down a straight nose, nostrils flared as if he scented the air. Jesse felt the slightest twinge of apprehension. The eyes of a wolf glared at him, the gaze of a man he maybe shouldn't cross. But it was too late for that. He had come for Adelaide, and this man was blocking his way.

"Ye shouldna have come."

Jesse got his feet under him and stood slowly, lifting his own fists in readiness, but the Scotsman was ready. A quick shot to Jesse's gut that bent him in half, then one to the other side of his face. Stars danced in his vision like sunlit dust motes, and he staggered back, hating his inability to get the upper hand on this fellow. He backed away, still hunched over and breathing hard, watching the man's feet as he got out of the way of those quick hands. The leather shoes of the Scotsman never moved. So the man was waiting, not pursuing. Defending his property.

"I ain't here to cause trouble, like I said."

"Turn around an' go back," he was advised.

"Can't do that," Jesse grunted, straightening and wiping sweat from his eyes. "Can't leave without Adelaide."

The man's feet moved then, but Jesse stood straight and braced himself, determined to win this round. The punch came, but he'd expected it. He blocked it, pushing it to the side and opening the other man's body for his own attack. It felt good, pounding his fist into the wall of his opponent's stomach, proving he was more than a punching bag. But this was no inexperienced, wild young warrior from the village. This was a man hardened out of necessity. Jesse'd seen that in the unflinching set of his eyes. The Scotsman grunted from the impact but barely winced, ready for the next and the next.

Why was this happening? What had set this stranger against him in such a determined manner? Why did it seem he'd rather kill Jesse than let him past? She couldn't have told him something terrible about Jesse, could she? No. Not Adelaide. He knew her too well. She had opened up to him, let him into her secret, tortured world, and sought solace in his arms. She wasn't afraid of him. She needed him, and she knew it. So why the armed guard?

The slugging went back and forth, neither man willing to back down, though Jesse felt weak with hunger, and he needed both food and sleep in a bad way. Both men's blades slid out of their sheaths, and the closing darkness stole any telltale reflections off the metal. The men moved smoothly, like beasts: a wolf and a cougar, circling, waiting for an opening.

"I'll tell ye once more, man. Go back. Ye dinna want to test me wi' a knife."

Jesse sucked in his breath, keeping the pain from his voice. "Don't tell me what to do, Scotsman. I don't know if anyone ever told you, but you don't listen too good. Understand this," he said deliberately, trying to hide his exhaustion. "I will have Adelaide. Nobody's gonna stop me." Jesse lowered his voice to a growl. "Nobody."

With a roar, he dove toward the big man, knife at the ready, but his target spun out of reach. Jesse used his momentum, spinning as well until he faced the stranger. He sliced his blade downward and met a thick, resisting barrier of flesh. The knife went in, and the man grunted, quick and deep, but he still didn't go down.

Jesse did. The broad Scottish dirk had gone deeper than his own knife had, cutting into Jesse's side and opening a hole he knew Adelaide could have healed easily if only she'd come out of that damn house. He dropped to his knees, pressing both hands as hard as he could against the wound. Doc had told him he should always do that. Push on a wound to stop the bleeding. But there was a hell of a lot of bleeding, and he wasn't sure he could push quite that hard. His knees gave way, and he collapsed with some relief onto his back.

His opponent still stood, but he clutched his side as well. Less blood, less damage overall, lucky bastard, though blood did seep from beneath his hand. The man walked toward Jesse and glared down, lips tight with pain, eyes narrowed in a forbidding expression.

"No one hunts my women," the man growled.

His *women? Who the hell was this guy?*

"Ye were warned. Get yerself gone now, if ye can, but know this: I am no' the only man here, an' I'm no' the strongest of us. Ye willna get past us to Ah-dlaide. She's safe from ye here."

He turned and headed toward the houses, which were sinking quickly into the murk of night. Jesse watched his attacker get smaller with every step, finally stopping outside one of the doors. The dark man looked back up the hill, toward Jesse, hesitating just a moment, then stepped inside and shut the door.

Jesse lay back and squeezed his eyes shut, still pressing hard against his side. The cut burned, cold and hot at the same time, feeling much wider than the thin slice he could see. He grabbed a handful of wet leaves and stuck them under his other hand, hoping the cool touch would soothe the pain. It did. It helped. A bit.

"I'll find you, Adelaide. I'll save you," he whispered to the stars, and they winked back.

CHAPTER 29

Not Dead Yet

Jesse was shaken awake by tremors. They rolled through his body so that he shuddered from toes to teeth. His body ached from the hard bed of wet dirt on which he'd tried to sleep. Fortunately, his side, where the blade had gone, had stopped bleeding but still burned, and when he rolled carefully to his side, it began to ooze again. The hand he'd pressed against it was stiff, caked with dried blood. He grabbed another handful of leaves, now soaked by dew, and pulled up the side of his shirt. He swept the leaves gently across the wound, gritting his teeth when the shocking cold hit his hot skin.

"Not dead, you son of a bitch. I ain't dead. Not yet."

But he wasn't ready to challenge the big man again, either. No, the kilted man, whoever he was, had effectively taken care of Jesse's immediate future, meaning he didn't foresee any more fights for a while. Damn the man. Why was he so bent on keeping Jesse from Adelaide? Seemed a little off. He should have at least let Jesse speak. Then again, he'd heard Scots were stubborn.

The cut, once it was relatively clean, didn't look all that

wide, but it did stretch about three inches long. Clean but not deep. The man kept his blades sharp. Killing Jesse at that point would have been easy. Scary how easy, actually. That suggested he'd used this altercation as a warning. The rest of Jesse's stomach was a mottled and swollen red and purple, reminders of the Scotsman's wicked fists. Jesse dabbed the leaves at a bright dot of blood that had surfaced, then moaned and lay flat again.

He wasn't going to die of this. He could tell. His body always healed well and quickly, though it was covered in scars that had tried to prove him wrong. But it would need some time. So what to do next? Damned if he was going to head back to the village and have Wah-Li or one of the others sing chants over his body, praying their gods would fix him up. He was tired of Cherokee medicine and Cherokee minds right about now. He'd had enough of their ridiculous fights and arguments and talk about honour. He needed Doc. But he thought he could maybe last a little longer before heading that way.

Adelaide was his priority right now. Jesse groaned and braced his hands against the dirt, then forced himself to his feet. No point in lying around feeling sorry for himself. He had to do something. He glanced into the trees, imagining what might be going on in the village, then looked across the yard toward another, more travelled road. A road he thought probably led to town. He sniffed and chewed on his lip, deciding, but his gaze kept returning to the little cluster of houses at the base of the hill. Adelaide was there. Of the three paths, the narrow one to the houses was the one he most wanted to follow, but that wasn't going to be possible just yet.

He could wait. It wasn't as if she'd stay forever. He wished he could see her just once, get a glimpse of that shining white hair, that dazzling smile. It wouldn't be such a shy smile if he saw her with her sister, and he'd like to see that. Yeah. He'd wait. He'd stay here for a couple of nights, lick his wounds, then talk her into letting him walk her home. Scots weren't the only stubborn ones.

PART 5

Adelaide

CHAPTER 30

Reconciliation

"What should I do?" I asked.

"You sleep. We'll talk about this in the morning."

Maggie tucked me in, then accepted Andrew's hand and let him lead her to their bed. I had thanked her and closed my eyes, then fought sleep with all my heart. I couldn't allow the images back into my head. Couldn't. I didn't understand, and I didn't want to believe.

Sleep claimed me anyway, and the fates saw fit to give me at least one calm, sweet night of sleep. I woke to the songs of birds and lay without moving for a few minutes, relishing the fleeting peace. I listened to the calm, rhythmic *whip-poor-will! whip-poor-will!* and prayed the rest of my day might be similar to this moment.

But the hoarse shout of a raven disturbed my thoughts, and my chest tightened, remembering that Maggie had seen what I had seen. If only I could have dreamed a few moments more, stayed submerged long enough to see the ending, I'd know what to do.

All I could think was that I had to tell Jesse, explain to him about the dream. He wasn't connected to the nightmare

from before. That I knew. So the only thing I could think
was if I told him about that day in the woods, it might affect
the dream I'd had about Thomas Black. I could see no other
reason the two visions had intertwined in my head. But my
heart sank at the thought of that conversation. I would have
to open my heart and tell him of the men, tell him what
they'd done to me, to my sisters. And by doing that, I would
reveal myself, showing him I was no more than a dirty,
loathsome whore, a defiled woman no man could ever truly
love.

"Well, you said you wanted to help me," I said softly,
staring at the ceiling. "You said you loved me."

Maybe he wouldn't hate me. Maybe he'd just walk away,
not wanting to see the disgusting truth every time he looked
at me. I wasn't sure which would hurt more.

I heard movement in the front room and quickly
pulled my clothes on. The autumn morning was chilly, so I
wrapped a blanket around me as well, like a cloak. When
I stepped into the front room, Andrew's friend, Janet, was
leaning over the big black pot, stirring something that
smelled wonderful. That woman could cook anything.

"Good morning, Janet. Sleep well?"

"Oh!" she exclaimed, startled by my sudden appearance.
"Good morn to ye as well, Ah-dlaide. Can I get ye some
parritch?"

Janet was an absolutely beautiful woman, with ebony hair
like the Cherokee and eyes the colour of summer grass. She'd
come from Scotland with Andrew and the others, the only
woman among them, and she seemed to me as brave as they
were. Besides being attractive, she was efficient, smart, and
funny. And she could cook. All the best aspects in a woman.
Yet she remained unmarried. Maggie had told me it was by
choice, that Janet had been approached by a great many
neighbouring farmers, and some eligible bachelors in the
town as well. But Janet was headstrong and wasn't about to
accept anything not exactly right. I didn't worry for her. Maggie had assured me Janet would be very happy, and that she'd
seen it would happen soon.

"Porridge would be lovely, thank you. Is everyone awake?"

"Aye, Andrew and Seamus are huntin', but yer sister is still a-bed," she said, leaning over the pot and dipping in a deep ladle. The porridge steamed as it was spooned into a bowl for me. Janet turned and pulled a jar from the pantry behind her, then held it up in question.

"Honey?"

I smiled and nodded.

Janet bustled around the kitchen, then set my bowl and spoon before me. Beside that sat a plate of biscuits and some cold slices of ham. A pungent, light brown dollop of honey spread over my cereal as the heat melted it.

"There are mornings when she's up wi' the sun," Janet said, carrying her own bowl so she could sit across from me at the table, "and other times when the wee one tells her to sleep a while. This is one o' those mornings."

We talked about this and that, about nothing at all, really. Janet was a wonderful girl, but we knew little of each other's lives or pasts. And I wasn't one to start that kind of conversation, since I didn't want to share my history. If Janet needed to know anything, Maggie would tell her. But I did like sitting with her, listening to her talk about what was going on around their little cluster of homes, and hearing how sweet and attentive Andrew had been since Maggie had told him he'd be a father.

"I ken some folk say it's evil luck to talk o' the child afore it's born, but, well, ye ken Maggie well enough. She'd see if something bad were comin'. An' she sees no clouds in her sky. She canna tell yet if 'tis a boy or a girl, but they've told us what they might call the bairn when it arrives."

"Really? What if it's a boy?"

"They'll name a wee laddie after Andrew's older brother, Dougal," she said, her voice distant. A sad smile flickered across her lips, and she looked down into the porridge. "He was lost, ye ken. At Culloden."

I did know. They had told us about the massacre in Scotland, the one that had convinced the group of them to leave their devastated country. I gave her a moment of grief, then asked what they would name a little girl.

"Ruth," she said, her smile bright again. "Little Ruth. For yer wee sister."

It was my turn to turn away, lose myself. Little Ruth. Golden curls and laughter like tiny bells. Little Ruth, forever ten years old. I closed my mind, solidly refusing to remember anything more.

"Sad," she said softly. "And yet 'tis a good thing. To give the names of the dead to the livin'. We remember the dead, but with less sadness when it is connected with the joy of a bairn."

I swallowed the familiar lump in my throat. "Ruth would be happy to know Maggie decided to do that in her honour."

We both looked at our bowls a moment longer, then Janet started eating her porridge. I had lost my appetite but hated the idea of wasting food. I emptied the bowl, then discovered I had been hungry after all and helped myself to a slice of ham. By the time I was finished, Maggie was coming out of her room.

"Oh, good. I was afraid you'd left already," she said. "I'm sorry I slept late. I should have been out here with you."

"No, you needed the sleep," I assured her. "Janet's been taking good care of me, don't worry."

Janet rose and took our dishes away, leaving Maggie and me to talk alone. She reached across the table and took my hands in hers. She frowned at me, waiting for my full attention. Then she spoke.

"Addy, Andrew met the man you dreamed about."

The hair on the back of my neck stood straight up. Thomas had been there? I hadn't imagined it would be so soon. "What?"

"Last night. They fought. Andrew said the man insisted he wasn't leaving without you, so Andrew scared him off with his knife. Got him pretty bad, he says. Didn't kill him, but by now he should be far away."

My sister and I looked into each other's eyes, saying nothing, then Maggie closed hers. I closed mine as well, preparing myself for the strange yet comforting feel of her in my head. But the gentle prodding of her questions never came. No pictures flashed through my mind as they usually did. She let go of my hands and let out her breath. I opened my eyes, and she was already looking at me, her expression apologetic.

"I can't see anything. I'm sorry."

"It's all right. I've decided, Maggie. Knowing that you saw the same thing makes all the difference."

She nodded. "And how do you feel about that?"

I gave her a half smile. "Like I was right all along. I never should have learned about my dreams. It's terrifying, Maggie. I don't know how you live this way."

"I never had a choice," she said quietly. "It's only now I'm learning how to turn away from them, but it's not easy."

"At least I know I'm out of danger for now, since Andrew got rid of him." *Except for those forgotten monsters who ripped our lives apart, Maggie. I'll never get away from them, will I?*

She sighed, and I knew she understood even without reading my mind. "What are you going to do?" I shrugged. "I have to go to the village and speak with Jesse, try to convince him of what I dreamed. He has to understand that because my dream was real, there was a reason I ran off on him. Maybe with Wah-Li there to help, he'll believe. Poor man. He must be so confused. We were just getting close, and I sent him away without an explanation. I have to convince him."

"And what about . . . the other part of the dream?"

"I'm going to tell him."

We stared at each other in silence, both of us knowing that by doing that, I was changing everything about my life. Maggie eventually nodded. "Good."

"I have to go this morning."

She sagged. "So soon? You just got here."

I felt bad, but it had to be that way. "I have to find him. I can't let him stew on it. I'm sorry."

"Oh Addy. Of course you have to do what you feel needs doing. I only wish you could stay longer."

"I'll come back and visit soon. I want to see you get big and fat."

She grinned. "I'm working on that." She picked up a biscuit and took a small bite, swallowed and waited, as if wanting to ensure her stomach accepted the offering before she continued. When it did, she settled in with a hungry grin, helping herself to another after that, and two slices of ham. "The baby's hungry. Sometimes it won't let me eat much at all," she explained. She finished the first slice of ham, then pointed her knife at me while she talked. "Iain will come with you. Andrew and Seamus have gone, but Iain will go."

"Oh no. There's no need—"

"Yes, there is. I saw what you saw, Addy, and we're keeping you safe. Andrew scared the man off, but he's not dead. You still need protection. If anyone can do that, it's big Iain. Once you're back at the village you can stay safe with Jesse and Soquili."

I turned to go, but she spun me back around to face her. She wrapped her arms around me and held me against her. Her breath was quick and warm on my neck. "Those men are all dead, Addy. You're safe from them. It happened, but it's over now. Don't let them win."

Tears burned in my eyes, but I didn't let them go. I nodded silently and swallowed, choking down the grief in my throat, then I moved out of her embrace.

"Thank you, Maggie," I whispered, then stepped outside.

Iain *was* big. Like a bushy, red-maned animal, part bear, part lion. And though his size and the gruff tone of his voice were forbidding to strangers, to me it was a comfort. During our breakfast, he had been in the stables, repairing something for the horses, and now he returned, slapping his hands together to rid them of dust.

"We'll take my beast," he offered, and I happily accepted. Riding back to the village would take less than half the time it had taken me to get there, and I suddenly felt in a great hurry to get to Jesse. Iain helped me onto the big chestnut mare and mounted behind me. When we ran out of things to talk about, we drifted into a comfortable silence.

The horse's rocking gait checked when he tripped on something, then he began to step awkwardly, listing a bit to the side.

"Stone," Iain grumbled.

We stopped at a pond so he could inspect the hoof. While the animal drank, Iain dunked his head into the water, then flung his massive red mane back so that it sprayed everywhere. He blinked at me with a dazed expression, and I giggled.

"Dizzy?"

"Aye."

"Hey, Adelaide."

Jesse was suddenly there. He stood, leaning slightly to one side, at the edge of the pond across from us, a bouquet of wildflowers clutched in one hand. Iain was on his feet in an instant, sword drawn.

I'd had no idea it was possible to miss anyone so much, but when I heard his voice, I wanted to run across the surface of the water to him. Iain held me back, extending one massive arm to block my path.

"D'ye ken this man?" Iain asked, suspicion thick in his narrowed gaze. "Or is this the wicked creature MacDonnell told me of?"

"Yes, I know him. This is Jesse." I grinned. "He wants to marry me."

Iain looked unsure, but Jesse took a few experimental, limping steps toward us, wisely careful around Iain's blade. He kept his own sheathed, posing no threat to the giant. I was shocked at Jesse's appearance. He was filthy, and swollen with bruises. He raised one eyebrow while he looked Iain over.

"Did ye meet wi' a bear?" Iain asked, wary.

I stepped closer, my hand out when I saw the large patch of dried blood staining his shirt. "What happened?"

He glanced down toward the place where I was staring, looked at me, then back at Iain. His bruised expression seemed impressed. "That other fellow wasn't kidding about him not being the biggest of you. You Scots must eat well."

Iain flicked his own bushy red eyebrow, unimpressed. "What say ye, lass? Am I to trust this man?"

I stepped closer and pulled back the torn cloth at the side of Jesse's shirt. The wound wasn't terribly deep, but it was long. Blood had crusted along its edges, and the surrounding skin was black with bruises. I glanced at his face, but his eyes were trained on Iain. "What—"

"Sure you are," Jesse said. "Isn't he, Adelaide?"

"Isn't he . . . ?"

"Able to trust me. Come on, Adelaide. Pay attention. The big man wants to know if you're safe with me."

Our eyes met, and I saw the pain in his, the questions I'd put there. He'd promised never to hurt me, but I'd hurt him, leaving him confused and alone. And yet here he was, half-way to Maggie's. He'd come for me, and something bad had happened to him along the way. Guilt rushed in, leaving a bitter taste in my mouth.

"Yes, Iain. You can trust him." I put my hand on Iain's forearm, encouraging him to lower his weapon. "And even better news for you is that you can leave me with him. He'll take me back to the village."

Iain's sword slowly and noisily slid back into his scabbard, as if he were making sure Jesse knew it was still there and ready to be used at any time. Looking relieved, Jesse limped up to him, hand outstretched.

"Jesse Black," he said. "Good to meet you, sir. And thank you for taking care of Adelaide."

Iain's grunt was one I recognized as grudgingly giving way. "Fine then. Iain MacKenzie," he said, accepting Jesse's hand. He squinted at me. "Ye're sure, lass? He looks a wee bit black and blue. Bit shabby for my taste."

"You can thank your countryman for that," Jesse muttered.

"He looks that way a lot," I told Iain. "I don't mind. I'm getting used to it."

"And here I thought you liked me for my peace-loving spirit." The wink he gave me looked painful. "Are you on your way back?" I nodded, and he held out the flowers, then his arm. "Might I have the honour of accompanying you?"

I felt strangely shy around him. The last time I had seen Jesse, he had been a gentleman, to be sure, but one entirely physical, and one I couldn't help wanting to grab onto. Now he played the formal role of a man courting, as if he were afraid of my reaction, and I hated that I'd made him feel that way.

"It would be my honour, Mister Black," I said, smiling and accepting the stems. I glanced up at Iain. "Thank you for bringing me this far, Iain. Please tell Maggie I'll be just fine. I'm with Jesse."

Iain frowned down at Jesse, then nodded. "Right. I will. Keep yerself safe, the two of ye. There's undesirables afoot." He turned back to his horse, who was contentedly munching on clumps of grass at the pond's edge. She lifted her head when he swung onto her back, then the pair disappeared into the trees.

CHAPTER 31

Revealing Dreams

We hadn't touched yet, other than the warm hook of his arm through mine. We hadn't spoken, either, and I had a feeling he was waiting for me to start up the conversation. He was unsure, which was sweet, but it also reinforced my guilt. I'd taken some of his confidence when I'd run from him. I'd have to figure out how to give it back. After walking maybe thirty feet, the quiet got to me.

"What happened to you?" I asked.

He shrugged, one eyebrow lifted over a crooked smile. "Some angry Scotsman wouldn't let me past. He was pretty . . . serious about that."

"What Scotsman? Where?"

"Back at your sister's. I came to get you, and he wasn't inclined to help me out with that."

I stopped dead in my tracks. "You came looking for me, and a Scottish man fought you?"

"Yep. Dark-haired bastard with a mean left. I got him, though. He'll have a limp for a bit."

But if Andrew had hit Jesse . . . "Was his name Andrew?"

"I have no idea. I only got to know his fists. And they

weren't too welcoming. He said something about protecting his women. Hell, that's what *I'd* come for. To protect you. Bastard never let me explain. Just kept telling me to leave, which I couldn't do, of course."

"Oh." I bit my lip and frowned at the bruises colouring his face. "Did he—"

"Man's got a sharp blade." He lifted up one side of his shirt, giving me a better view of the slice on the side of his stomach, just barely healing. I couldn't help sucking in a gasp at the sight. It cut across one of the claw marks of his cougar scar, like a *Y*. "Protective son of a bitch, that one. Stubborn, too."

"Will you let me help you with it?"

"Not right now. I want to keep walking for a bit."

"Okay," I said sarcastically, walking beside him again. "As long as he's the only one who's being stubborn."

His smile quirked, forming a funny sort of lump where it was swollen. "Yeah, yeah. I just can't figure out what put that bee in his bonnet."

"I think that was my fault," I admitted, looking down the path ahead of us.

"How's that?"

"I went to see Maggie, to ask for her help." He didn't change expression. "But I guess you knew that."

"Uh-huh. Learned it from an unlikely source. Dustu told me."

"Dustu?" I couldn't hide my surprise. I didn't think the two of them ever spoke.

He frowned. "Yeah. I had to get the news wherever I could get it, since you never came home."

"Sorry."

We walked a few more quiet steps before he nodded, forgiving me—at least for now. "So what happened when you got here?"

"Maggie saw my dream with me, and she told Andrew a man was coming to kill me."

"She saw your . . ." He puffed a breath through his lips and shook his head slightly. "I'm not even going to ask how that works. But then they assumed—"

"Sorry." I bit my lip again and stepped ahead of him on the narrow path. I heard the slightly uneven pattern of his limp as he followed me. "I never thought he'd come after you like that. He was . . . expecting someone else. But I'm very glad to see you, Jesse, even though you look like you've had better days."

"Are you?"

I glanced back at him, surprised at the vulnerability of the question. I was more than glad. Being with Jesse made me happy. Just talking to him eased my fears. I felt safe again. Nothing bad could happen to me if Jesse was there. "Yes. Of course. Why?"

"Well, you kind of ran off the other day. Remember that? Remember telling me to get lost and you'd be back in a bit?"

"That's not what I said."

"That's what I heard."

"Oh. Sorry."

A few more steps of silence, but this time the tension between us was edged with his anger and my embarrassment.

"I told you I'd come back. You didn't have to come for me."

"I figured you meant in a couple of hours, not days. I got worried is all."

Prickles of pleasant heat rose up my neck and filled my cheeks. "I'm sorry, Jesse. I am glad you're here. Thank you."

As the trees parted, he stepped up beside me and shrugged good-naturedly. "Hey, I hadn't had a fight in a couple of days. It's good to keep in practice."

Just like that, the tension was gone. He unhooked his arm and reached for my hand, and I gave it to him, clutching his gift of flowers in the other one.

"Can you tell me now?" he asked. "What's going on? About your dreams and all that?"

"I can try, but you can't interrupt. Want to sit down?"

He shook his head. "Seems to me, you think better when you're walking."

I was surprised to hear that, mostly because it was true.

I'd always felt easier dealing with questions when I was on the move. I suppose it could have frightened me, finding out he'd been studying me that way, but it had the opposite effect. I liked knowing he'd cared enough to watch. And that made it easier to speak about things I'd never said out loud to anyone else.

"I'm not great at dreaming. Not like my sister. She sees what will happen, and she can even make things happen. She can read people's minds and communicate with animals. I can't do that. But I do see things. I get caught up in a dream without meaning to. I might be sleeping, or just sitting, but it'll come and show me things I don't want to see. My problem is, I don't have the courage to stick with a dream long enough to see the ending. I never see what's going to happen, because I'm too scared."

"Most folks are like that, aren't we?"

I shrugged. "I guess. But most folks don't get told important things in their dreams. Things I should pay attention to, you know?"

He nodded, looking as if he were taking it all in, and I was relieved to see it. Maybe explaining this wouldn't be so difficult after all.

"All right. I think I'm with you so far," he said. "So what happened the last time? You know, when you ran off on me?"

I blushed, remembering. "I am sorry about that. Really I am. But when you and I . . . when we . . ."

"It's okay, Adelaide," he said, smiling. "You don't have to say it out loud. I remember what we were doing."

"Okay. Well, something happened—"

"Sure did!"

"Are you going to let me explain?"

He slapped his palm over his mouth and nodded for me to go on.

He was a beautiful man. I could see that through his bruises and cuts, when I ignored the deep circles under his eyes that told me he hadn't slept for a while. And when he smiled like that, when his eyes danced for me, I felt completely undone. He loved me. His torn shirt was filthy, his golden hair ratty with dirt and leaves. This beautiful, wild creature was mine if I chose to accept him. My heart skipped, and I tried to hide the pleasure that thought brought me.

"All right," I said, forcing my mind back to the present. "Something happened between you and me that brought back my dreams. And whatever it was, it made them even stronger."

"What'd you see?"

"Two different things, but they're tied together somehow." I ducked under a branch, focusing on the ragged deer path. I didn't want to watch his reaction. "The first part is that you weren't moving. You were lying on your stomach on the ground, and your face was bleeding. Your eyes were closed, and I couldn't tell if you were breathing." I looked sideways at him. "Oh, Jesse, it broke my heart, seeing you like that."

"Go on," he said, suddenly serious. "What was the second part?"

I swallowed. This was where it would get a little harder for him to believe. "I saw a man, Jesse, and he looked a lot like you but older. He was very strong, and he grabbed my throat, backing me into a tree, and he ripped at me, and—"

His hand squeezed mine before I could give in to the panic. "That's why you were going on about my father."

"Yeah," I managed. "There was something so familiar about him, I almost thought it was you at first. And the idea that you might do that, that you could—"

He interrupted without giving those dark thoughts the time of day. "Listen. Maybe it was him. If your dreams really can do that, see folks, it *could* have been my father. Thomas Black hates me. He always has, but even more now since I foiled whatever plans he had at the powwow. And yeah, he'd be glad to see me dead. But you don't need to worry. He ain't as quick as I am, and I know all his tricks. As long as I'm around, you have nothing to worry about. You're safe." Any hint of hardness left his eyes when he told me, "I'll tell you that forever, Adelaide. I'll always keep you safe."

"But in the dream you couldn't. I was by myself. And you—"

"Was there anything else to the dream? Anything more?"

I sighed, defeated. The courage I'd felt before abandoned me. I couldn't tell him about the other part of the dream. I couldn't. So I lied. "I don't know. That's when I escaped from it. But you have to understand, Jesse, that there is nothing I fear more than a man—I mean a man who is intent on—"

"It's okay, Adelaide. You don't have to explain," he said, squeezing my hand again. I was mildly surprised to discover it had started shaking again. He stopped walking and tugged my arm so I came around to face him. Then he took my other hand, and the look he gave me was nothing like what I'd expected. I had thought to see maybe indifference, disbelief surely, but not this sober expression. His eyes caught mine and held on.

"I will not let anyone harm you ever again. You have to believe that. And Adelaide?"

"Yes?"

"I love you. You know that's true. But I won't rush you. I won't demand more than you're ready to give. I can't deny I want to touch you and hold you and love you 'til you can't stand the sight of me, but I can wait. I'll never do anything to scare you off, I promise. You've got me . . ." He hesitated, his eyes searching mine, then he let his breath out, and his shoulders dropped. "You're too important to me."

Something in my heart released. My blood sang through my veins as if it had just been freed. No one had ever looked at me that way before, talked to me with so much truth in their eyes. Even my sisters had been careful with my feelings, guarding their words when they wanted to tell me anything. And here stood Jesse, rough, straightforward, holding his heart out there for me to accept . . . or crush.

I was filled with a longing like I'd never felt before. A need, really, to let Jesse fold me into his arms, guard me with his body, protect me with his life. As if I could step off the highest mountain and just float through the air without a care, because I'd be safe knowing he was waiting to catch me.

Then a cold fist grabbed my heart, stifling everything. The truth of it was that I couldn't allow myself to love him.

And I couldn't let him love me, either. Because I wasn't what he thought. I wasn't the perfect, quiet little mouse he thought me to be, all white and clean and innocent. All that was gone. They'd taken it. They'd ruined me, and I would never be good enough for Jesse's love. So I chose to crush us both.

I shook my head. "You don't know me, Jesse. Not really."

He stared at me, his head tilted a little to one side. He hesitated, then asked, "Are you ever gonna tell me what happened to you?"

I shook my head and his mouth opened a bit, as if I'd stopped him mid-word. Then he shut it and frowned, his expression not angry, but probing. He wanted to know, and I'd told both Maggie and myself that I would tell him. But I couldn't. The wall held me up, kept me alive. The wall I'd built in my head was the only thing that kept me from losing my mind.

I stepped away. "You really don't know me."

He was quiet, blinking slowly as thoughts raced behind his beautiful eyes. "I think I do," he said quietly. "But I'd like to know more."

I shook my head, but he only nodded. "We can keep walking if you want. I know it helps you think. But Adelaide, I get the feeling you need to get whatever this is out of you. I think if you talk about it, you might not be so scared anymore."

"I *want* to be brave, Jesse," I whispered, staring into his eyes. "I have always wanted to be brave. But I never had to be that way. I was always in Maggie's shadow, and it was safe there." I looked into the trees. "At least it was until that day. And now she's here with Andrew. Gone."

"I'm not, though," he said and used his thumb to brush a stray tear off my cheek. "You're safe with me."

"I can't."

"You can." He held my hands between us. "Adelaide, I want to be the one you trust."

He wasn't going to give up. Maybe that was a good thing. Maybe if I told him, if I showed him the truth, I could help him get away from me. Instead of walking, I sank down until I sat on the path, all the wind sucked from my sails. If I could let it out, tell him the entire story, at least then he'd understand why he could never love me. I was dirty and damaged with a history no one could possibly look past. I knew well that I wasn't good enough for any man to marry, let alone him.

"I haven't thought about this in a very long time," I told him. He sat quietly beside me, backing up so he leaned against a tree. He didn't seem to be in pain, but he looked more comfortable now that he was sitting. "It's like I *can't* think about it. If I do, it takes over. Maggie says I need to move on, try to forget, but it's like an itch that won't go away. If I scratch it, let myself see what happened, it only gets worse."

"But if you ignore it, it might kill you."

I smiled vaguely. "Yeah, maybe."

"Nah. It won't kill you," he assured me. "It's stuck in your brain, though. Let me help you."

"You'll hate me when you hear it."

He shrugged lightly, his gaze confident. "Not possible."

I took a deep breath, closed my eyes, and let myself fall back into the nightmare.

CHAPTER 32

From Behind the Wall

We had gone weeks without rain. Our mouths and eyes burned constantly, dry as the fragile blades of grass that scratched the door frame of our sagging little house. The sun attacked our bedroom as if it were a beast, sinking hungry rays into the worm-eaten wood of the walls, licking our skin until it shone. Maggie, Ruth, and I shared a bed, making the heat even more difficult to bear. I slept each night with my head pressed to Ruth's, breathing the essence of her sweat. She was ten, five years younger than I, and while her body was still young enough to be called that of a child, it had begun to seep the musk of a woman.

Maggie always woke with a different expression on her face. Sometimes she appeared distracted, as if trying to remember what she had just seen. Sometimes she awoke with what I can only describe as the most wonderful halo around her. I could actually see the colours, the ethereal shimmering, breathing along with her. Those were the best mornings. The air around her seemed to glow like the sun when they came, like it was thick with something delicious. And when she'd reach over and touch me, or when she'd hug me, still warm from sleep, I could almost share whatever she'd dreamed. Not the visions, of course. Just the feel of them. It was beautiful.

But on that morning Maggie woke with terror carved into her face, and her sweat-soaked hair stuck to her cheeks. No colour brightened her face, nor the air around her. In fact, the air in our room was still as death. Wet with the kind of viscous slime an earthworm oozes as it burrows through the earth. Cold, even, though it was the hottest summer anyone could remember. As if our room had become a tomb. She clung to our faded yellow walls with fingers like claws, beads of sweat rolling down her cheeks. She stared at me and tried to speak, but nothing passed through her lips save a trembling breath.

"What is it?" I whispered, but still no words came.

I turned to Ruth, who blinked like a blue-eyed owl. "Get Mama," I said.

Ruth rolled to the edge of the bed and set her little pink feet on the floor. She ran from the room, mussed blond curls bouncing down her back. Ruth always ran on her toes. Like a fairy. Ruth was just like a little fairy.

Mama appeared in the doorway, and Maggie wrapped her arms around her, clinging to the old white nightgown as if she was a child, not a grown woman of seventeen. She didn't cry, only stared without blinking. It was the most frightening thing I'd ever seen.

Breath by breath she came back to life, though she seemed reluctant to drop her hands and step away. It was only when our mother put her hands on Maggie's shoulders and pressed her a step back from her that my sister was able to stand on her own. Her chest rose and fell as it had in younger days, when she'd chased me up and down the hill outside our home until we both giggled and rolled in the stiff, golden grass. There were no giggles this time, only a silence at last broken by the croak of a raven in the woods beyond our land.

Mama, her fair hair pasted onto her neck in sweaty curls, looked just as terrified. I wasn't brave, but I was the calm sister, the one to speak reason when the others spun in circles. Perhaps that's why I was so afraid most of the time. It seemed reasonable to me. Anything unknown should remain unknown, because it posed a possible threat.

"Let me help her, Mama," I said.

Mama smiled at me through bewildered eyes, and in them I saw my own fear. I had inherited my timid personality from her. How a woman as slight as she survived the bleak South Carolina grasslands, I will never know. Then again, I am still alive, so maybe I do know. We do what we must. We survive, though we would often rather not. It is the way of man and beast to refuse our own deaths, though we're never really given a choice. I often wonder about that. I wonder if, after the cruelest day of all, might I have chosen otherwise if I'd only been brave enough?

I helped Maggie dress, guiding her arms through the short sleeves, handing her a comb to slide through the tangles the pillow had tied in her hair when she'd rolled, attempting to escape the dreams. She sat on the side of the bed and stared at the comb for a moment, frowning, like she couldn't remember what it was for.

"Comb your hair, Maggie. You'll feel better."

When she looked at me, her eyes were so sad. As if she carried the worst possible news in them. Maybe if she'd cried, it might have eased their burden. But Maggie rarely cried. In fact, I couldn't remember ever having seen her cry.

She combed through her dark hair in long, smooth strokes and watched me clean my face and teeth, using the tepid water from the old tin bowl on the table. She braided her hair, then helped me with mine, but her fingers shook while she tied the bow.

In appearance, Maggie was what people called plain, though it never would have been a term I used. She was dark and strong, like our father, God rest his soul. Ruth and I were blond and slight like our mother, though I was never as beautiful as Ruth. No one could have been. People stared at her when we went to town, and she smiled at everyone. She made them smile. Like she cast a spell over anyone she ever saw. I often wonder what she might have become had she been given the chance.

Maggie was seventeen at the time, and I was two years younger. Both she and I had developed the bodies we would carry as women. Hers was always in motion. Like her mind. It was always moving, digging into problems, unwilling to stop until the answer was revealed. She was also our defender, standing up to our father more than once when he came home reeking of whisky. Unafraid, my Maggie.

But on that day, I marveled at the change in my older sister. She startled as if she were a fawn, wild-eyed at any unexpected noise. She eventually settled into whatever she could find to keep her hands and mind busy. Despite the crippling heat, the broom was busy in every corner of the decrepit house, her sewing needle winked in and out of anything needing to be mended, and she wove me a bracelet out of long, dry grass. It was rough work because without rain to soften the ground, the grass splintered when she tried to bend it. When it was done, she sewed a little dress for the shabby, yellow-haired rag doll Ruth carried everywhere.

Ah, Ruth. I have to stop thinking of her, because my heart breaks anew every time her face flits through my memory.

And yet the story must be told, and Ruth played a part in it, no matter how brief.

A dozen men came in the afternoon, their sweating horses stirring up dry dirt as they slowed in front of our house. We weren't often visited by anyone, living as remotely as we did, and Mama reflexively pulled our father's rifle from the wall. I remember the clouds of dust lingering around the men, how hot air pressed urgently against my skin as we stepped through the door to see what they wanted. The heat had pushed any hint of a breeze away; the horses barely lifted their tails when flies lit.

Maggie went still beside me, then she started to shake. Mama stepped in front of us, holding the rifle as if she knew exactly how to use it, though I don't think she'd ever shot anything in her life.

"Good afternoon, gentlemen," she said. "My husband will be here shortly. Is there something I can help you with?"

One of the men seemed to be in charge. He wore a tattered blue shirt while the clothes on the others faded, almost camouflaged into the dirt. He grinned and shifted in his saddle, looking at his men while he spoke. "Well, now, missus, we all know that ain't true, don't we?"

Another man called out from somewhere in the group. I only knew where he was because the others turned to laugh with him. "Ain't no husband, 'less you's married to a ghost," he said.

He was right, of course. My father had died in a wagon accident one night, and Mama had never remarried. There weren't a lot of men to choose from out there, if a woman were looking to get married, and until that day we had done well enough without one.

Five of the men got off their horses and started walking toward our house, carrying frayed coils of rope. It was a moment before I realized those ropes were for us. My skin prickled, and my lips felt oddly numb. Mama's skirt trembled, but her voice was strong.

"Hold it right there. Get right back on those horses, please," she said. I was proud of her in that moment, but the feeling passed rapidly. She shook like Maggie did, trembling like a cornered squirrel. She lifted the rifle and pressed it against her cheek, aiming it at the men. I hoped it was loaded. "I have no wish to shoot any of you."

The next instant brought something I've tried hard to forget, but I doubt I will ever be able to do that. Why is it so easy to forget the happy times, but the ones that cut out your heart are forever etched in your mind?

The man in the blue shirt said something to one of the men behind him. His name, I think.

"Yes, sir," the young man said. Quick as lightning, he pulled a pistol from his belt, aimed it at my mother, and shot her through the head. Mama flew backward and hit the door with a thud. Her bones seemed to melt, and she slid down the wall, dirty-blond hair bunching in loops behind her.

Ruth screamed. The tortured sound went on and on, like the howls of a dog in a trap. Her voice probably carried for miles across that flat nothingness of land, but I barely heard her. I don't know if I screamed.

Maggie grabbed Ruth and shoved her into the house. I reached for Maggie, but a man's arm, big enough that it felt like a tree branch, wrapped around my stomach, jerking the wind from my lungs. I inhaled a sour gust of grime and sweat as he pulled me hard against his chest. I screamed and kicked backward, jerking my head around, doing anything I could to loosen his grip, but failed. I was nothing against him. A flea on a dog. He spun me around and slammed me into the wall right beside the place where my mother's life had ended. If I'd wanted to—if he'd let me—I could have reached out and touched the place where the bullet had pierced the wall after passing through her brain. He held my throat, but from the edge of my vision, I could see her eyes were open. Dead eyes, pale as the sky just before it clouds over. I looked away. I couldn't bear to remember her eyes that way. And yet I do.

I screamed through the pressure of his hand, choking on tears. I grabbed at the wrist pinning me in place, its leathery skin thick with black hairs. I yanked and twisted, but his hand didn't budge. Through swollen, disbelieving eyes, I watched another man tie my hands in front of me. I saw the calloused fingers grip my wrists, saw him wind the rope around once, twice, then knot it with a jerk.

"Shut your mouth," the first man growled. He reached behind his neck with one hand, the other still anchored against my throat. He loosed the knot on the kerchief he'd had tied around his neck and yanked it off. It was filthy and smeared with old sweat. He balled it up in his hand and thrust it toward my mouth.

"Open up," he said.

I clamped my mouth shut and squeezed my lips as tightly together as I could, but in the end, he jammed one disgusting finger into the side of my mouth and wedged it open. I bit down hard, and he grunted but kept at it. The stiff cloth touched my tongue, and he shoved the rest in. I didn't want to breathe, couldn't stand the sweet stench wafting from the cloth as it soaked in my mouth. I gagged, but he held me still, like a bug on a pin. Bile rose in my throat, but I had to swallow it back. He had no intention of letting go.

"Lewis," he bellowed, turning toward a couple of the men who still held the horses. "Bring me your kerchief, boy."

One of the others nodded and came toward us, pulling off his own neck cloth as he came. I stared at him, pleading with my eyes, sniffling, hoping he might stop this madness. Instead, he smiled. It was a half smile with something cruel lurking in it I'd never seen before. He winked, then tied the kerchief at the back of my head, pulling tight so the wad of cloth completely filled my mouth and I had no hope of shoving it out. My jaw ached from being forced open, and now the kerchief bit into my lips. I kept yelling, praying they'd stop, have mercy, but my cries were muffled and more pathetic than ever. It was getting difficult to breathe through my nose because of all the crying, and I realized I could actually suffocate. I collapsed helplessly against the man when he leaned over and scooped me up, carrying me in his arms as if I were a weightless baby. He lifted me onto his horse's saddle, then swung up behind me, pressing his body to my back. His hands were hard as granite, holding me in place.

I had to stop crying or I wouldn't be able to breathe for much longer. I chewed through the constricting cloth until I could at least get my teeth around it. That way I could breathe easier through my mouth. I gasped in my sobs, trying to slow them, trying to calm myself so I could think. I had to find some way to escape.

My sisters were dragged out of the house, and I tried to call to them, but nothing could get past the gag, wet and heavy on my tongue. Ruth was slung over a man's shoulder, looking small for a ten-year-old. The man hardly seemed to know she was there, despite the fact her entire body struggled against his grip. A screaming Maggie fought every step, pulling against a rope until I saw blood smear her wrists. The man finally gave up the battle of towing her behind him. Avoiding the wild swinging of her arms and desperate kicks, he picked her up and carried her to a different horse. He handed her to the rider, who held her between his legs, then jammed a gag into her mouth as well.

Fear had ruled my life for as long as I could remember, and yet I'd never really had cause. Now that I had reason, fear seemed to shrink into something far away. It was as if I lost who I was the moment the man behind me kicked his horse into a gallop. I forgot to care. Hooves pounded beneath me, forest branches slapped my face, the man's hands gripped my thighs, holding me in place. And yet none of it seemed real.

Part of me was terrified beyond belief. Part of me wasn't even there. From the safety of my perch, I saw myself tied to a tree. I saw the rope had cut into my skin, rubbing it raw. I noticed I sat slumped over, unable to do anything but wait. My sisters were gone. I couldn't see or hear them. Nor could I sense them, which I normally could do simply by closing my eyes. It was as if my world had died, leaving me alone in this nightmare.

The first time a man put his hands on me and tore my dress, I screamed and kicked, flailing against the ropes. My arms bled, and my legs, ripping on the bed of rocks and branches, bruising against the man's iron grip. When he reached beneath my skirt and tore the rest of my life to pieces, I went numb.

The second man knelt beside me, saying nothing at first, but I was so lost, so overwhelmed, I barely saw him there. When he said something, I heard just a rumble of syllables. When I didn't look up, he grabbed a fistful of my hair and yanked it back so I had to meet his eyes.

Somewhere in the back of my consciousness, I noticed the twists of silver in his beard, the dark spots of age mottling his weathered cheeks, the mangy, matted beard. He seemed about the same age as my father, and he stunk of old tobacco, and worse. In contrast, the skin of his naked thighs was as white as a fish's belly.

228 GENEVIEVE GRAHAM

"Just be quiet. Be quiet," the man kept saying. "Be a good girl."

Be a good girl. My father had said those same words. He'd told me to be quiet, be a good girl, when my sisters and I played too loudly or sang when he wanted to sleep. This man threw one leg over me, and I twisted like a worm on a hook, but he took my throat in his hand and jammed it against the dirt. When he was done what he'd come to do, he sat back and grinned.

I said nothing, only stared, unable to rouse a sound from my battered body. It was no longer me on the pine needle–strewn forest floor. It was a shell containing nothing. Everything was gone from me: the fight, the hope, my voice.

But that wasn't enough. His grin hooked on one side, then drooped into a frown. Through a fog of disbelief, I watched him flex his fists, then pull one back so it poised by his ear. His fist crashed into my cheek, my vision went white, and a sharp sting told me the skin had split beside one eye. My head snapped back, slamming into the hard ground. I squeezed my eyes closed as tightly as I could, trying to push out the pain, praying he wouldn't do it again. I didn't want to ever open my eyes. I feared what I might see if I looked.

My heart thundered, and my empty stomach, for the hundredth time that day, rolled over. I wondered vaguely if I might vomit into the gag. What then? Would anyone untie it? Because if they didn't, I was sure I would die.

And yet I didn't panic. Somehow, living no longer seemed all that important.

While I lay motionless on the ground, I heard a sound I hadn't heard before. A small mewling sound that didn't belong in this place. Could that be a cat? Here? I opened my eyes but gasped at the tiny movement. I tried to see past the pain, concentrating on lifting my eyelids. Greens and browns blurred together, the heady aroma of dirt and leaves smeared forever into my memory. The pathetic mewling grew louder, and I realized the sound was my own weeping.

After that, all the men and everything they did, all the violence and pain and disgust and loathing, were lost to me.

I saw it all from far away. Far enough that I felt nothing. I thought, and I hoped, that I would never feel anything ever again.

The next day, I learned they'd killed Ruth. Broke her apart, then left her in the woods to rot.

They set Maggie and me back on horseback and headed back on the path, and when we stopped again, I knew I would rather die than face another moment with these men.

The Cherokee saved us. They burst from the trees, sending arrows and tomahawks into the bodies of our abusers, of our mother's and Ruth's murderers. When the white men lay dead, bloody lumps around their dying fire, the Cherokee turned to us. They tended our wounds as well as they could, and we drank the foul tea they coaxed through our swollen lips. I remember little beside that tea, how it wet my tongue when I'd almost turned to dust. It made me sleepy. They bundled us in furs and secured us onto travois their men had fashioned and eventually dragged along the trail. Our little beds rocked and bumped behind them, but we were cushioned by a pillow of furs. For the first time since the nightmare had begun, I slept.

When I woke, we were in a different world.

CHAPTER 33

What Happens Next

It was out now: the nightmare that had consumed me for almost a year. The hardest part had been the first few words, braving that first step back into the dark. I was exhausted now. The strain of tears shed and grief relived weighted my eyelids down, yet I felt oddly light within. The memories had taken me far, far from Jesse's side, dragging me through what I'd never wanted to see again, and in the end, I held the truth of my captors' deaths as a solid, undeniable truth. They were gone. I was free of them. Because I had been courageous enough to face the horrors again, the hole that had gaped in my heart since that day began to ease closed, like pulling the tethers of the deerskin bags I made at the village.

Ruth was gone, of course. That would never change, but my pain over losing her would. I'd miss her until my last breath, but now I could accept that I'd be doing that without her by my side. And having stepped into that dark world and emerging unscathed, I felt stronger again. I would survive. I might even find joy again someday.

"Sometimes it feels as if the nightmare happened yesterday," I told Jesse. I drooped, feeling like a cloth wrung out and hung to dry. "At others, it is more like it took place in another world, another time. To another person."

Jesse blinked occasionally through the story, but other than that, he didn't move. He was so quiet I forgot he was there for a time. But I was finished now, and the silence kept on filling the forest, the weight of my confession heavy and disgusting on my shoulders. He would leave now, knowing what I was, and I would never see him again. But he'd been right. I'd needed to say it out loud, no matter the consequence.

"So that's why you live there," he finally said, his voice calm as a breeze.

I seemed to have used up all my words. My face was wet with tears, but they'd stopped rolling down my cheeks for now. I felt empty of everything. I had nothing left. Soon he, too, would be gone.

"I had wondered what kept you there, you know. I see now." The gold in his eyes had melted into a soft amber, like the liquid brown of tree sap in the spring. "Those men," he said softly. "They're all dead now? Cherokee took care of 'em?"

I nodded, so he did, too.

"Good. One less thing for me to do."

He left the support of the tree and slid closer to me, still sitting. "Can I touch you, Adelaide?" I didn't move, so he took that as permission. He put one hand out and gently wiped the tears on my cheek with a dirty, calloused finger, gentle as the pat of a kitten's paw. "So do I know you now?"

"What?"

"Sounds to me like that was the one thing between us, and now you've told me all about it. So do I know you now?"

It took a shaky breath before I could nod.

His fingers moved down until they cradled my chin. "Then it wasn't you that I didn't know, was it?"

"I'm confused."

He dropped his hand and linked my fingers with his. I looked down, seeing the damage he'd done to his knuckles, to his arms, all done while he'd been trying to find me. The knowledge twisted in my gut.

"It was what *happened* to you that I didn't know," he said. "But I was right. I knew *you* all along."

He leaned in and kissed me, his lips light as a butterfly's wing against mine. A farewell kiss. Because now he knew. He surely couldn't feel anything for me now, save repulsion.

"And knowing this," he continued, as if I'd spoken out loud, "changes nothing about how I feel for you. I love you, Adelaide. I think I knew that from the first time you looked at me. I knew you were scared, knew it was something awful, but it was up to you to tell me."

It couldn't be possible. "You still . . . love me?" I whispered.

His smile was so sad, trying to be brave enough for both of us under eyes that mourned with me. "I love you," he repeated. "And whether you'll have me or not, I'll always love you."

I stared at him, swallowing hard, terrified this was some kind of illusion that would end if I blinked. I'd seen him in my dreams for so long, but I'd never imagined the reality of him would become so important to me. I'd tried to ignore him, to pretend he didn't exist, to hide from any threat of another heartbreak. And he'd just kept coming, stubborn as ever. My Jesse. He kissed me again.

"Marry me, Adelaide," he whispered against my lips. I caught my breath and felt his crooked half smile, the soft curve of his lips barely touching mine. "What? I did ask you before, you know."

I shook my head, suddenly angry. "Weren't you listening, Jesse? You *can't* marry me. I'm . . . ruined. There were five of them, Jesse. Five men."

His smile was stronger than my confusion. "I don't care about any of them. All I care about is you. Marry me."

"You still—"

"You're a lousy listener, Adelaide." His smile was so tender, so full of promise. It reached in and roused my own smile, shook it awake.

"You didn't really ask me before. Not exactly," I said

quietly. Nerves buzzed through my fingers, raced through my gut.

"Sure I did."

"No. You went on about how we could be together, but you never actually—"

He scrambled, suddenly and painfully, onto one knee, gripping both my hands in his. "Marry me, Adelaide. Please."

"Get up, you fool," I said, blushing. "You'll open that wound in your side again."

"Not until you give me an answer."

"You already know my answer."

"Then say it."

I sighed, wrestled my hands from his and traced the smooth, swollen lines of his bruised face with my fingertips, followed the crooked, oft-broken nose. So beautiful, my Jesse. I imagined his features in a few years, then a few years after that. I banished the memory of his father's face, similar, but sliced with deep lines of strife and anger. Jesse wouldn't have that kind of life, I promised myself. I would give Jesse a good life. One filled with love.

"I love you, Jesse Black, and yes. I will marry you."

I had thought he was handsome, kneeling at my feet. When his expression lifted in a self-satisfied grin at my answer, well, he went beyond handsome. He rose and took my face in his hands. "You won't regret this," he said.

"I know."

He narrowed his eyes, serious again. "Really? How do you know? Did you dream something?"

I laughed, and he joined me. *Marry me*.

Yes. I would be all right, I told myself. I would. As long as I had Jesse, I would be all right.

CHAPTER 34

Ambush

The afternoon wore on, oblivious to the story I'd had to share, then to a wonderful, passionate moment where Jesse and I celebrated what we'd found in each other.

I didn't tell him that when he locked his arms around me and we kissed, I saw his father again. I saw the meanness in the older man's eyes and the intent burning there, but this time I was braver, believing in myself just enough to keep the shadows at bay. I shoved the image from my mind, directing everything I had at the man who held me. The man who loved me.

Our kisses grew stronger, but it wasn't only he who brought heat to our passion. I had discovered a part of me I had never experienced before, except with him. His chin scraped gently against mine, like a slow burn, but I didn't care. I tasted his breath, warm and delicious in my mouth, inhaled the strong, powerful reality of him, and loved what I breathed.

He suddenly stopped kissing me and sat up fast. As if he'd forgotten something. "We should go now," he blurted.

I blinked up at him, bewildered. "Did I do something wrong?"

His crooked smile flashed, and he shook his head. "Oh no, darlin'. Problem is, you were doing too many things right. I don't exactly trust myself at this moment."

I didn't think I could blush any deeper than I already had, but I did. I sat up beside him, and he took my hand.

"We should go," he repeated.

A cool reminder of approaching evening agreed with him, blowing through the trees so that they swayed above us, graceful dancers preparing for the night. Jesse and I stood and walked on, this time holding hands and sharing a beautiful secret. Wouldn't Wah-Li and Soquili be surprised when I told them that I would indeed be marrying Jesse! Then again, Wah-Li never seemed surprised by anything. I wondered if that was a good thing for her or whether it took all the joy of discovery out of life. I found myself considering spontaneity and wondering if it was really as dangerous as I'd always feared.

Jesse held out his arm, keeping a branch from my face, and I saw him wince and press his hand to his side. "You have to let me tend that," I said.

"Later. I want to get to the village."

"I am sorry about—" I shrugged helplessly. "About everything he did to you."

"Yeah. Well. I still don't understand that whole thing."

"I know. I've lived with this my whole life, and I still don't understand it all that well. But the thing is, Maggie saw my dream with me, and she sent Andrew out."

"But why me?"

I was surprised. "Because the dream—it *looked* like you, but it couldn't have *been* you. Maggie's never seen you, so she couldn't know that."

"I suppose. It's just . . . You told the Scotsman some guy was coming to get you? That's it? Nothing a little more specific? Like there was also a man coming to take care of you, but in a good way? Nothing like, 'The guy you want to avoid is older and real mean'?"

"I'm sorry. He just wanted to protect me. Please don't hate Andrew."

He sighed and shook his head, but the quirk on the side of his mouth told me he wasn't angry. "No matter. I'll recover. And don't you worry about your Andrew. I guess I gotta thank him someday for lookin' out for you."

He stopped and turned to me again. "I don't hate many folks, Adelaide. Truth is, I don't like many, either. But you're different. You are the only person on earth that really matters to me."

How could I argue with that? I put my arms around his neck and kissed him as if I'd done it a thousand times.

One would think that if one had a dream, then found oneself living that specific moment in time, they would avoid the darker aspects of that dream. If they knew they were going to fall off a cliff and the mountain plunged suddenly beside them, they'd choose another route. But it doesn't work that way for my dreams. It hadn't worked that way for Maggie's, either. We saw what would happen, regardless of what we did.

So when I saw the familiar group of trees around me, felt the air tighten with quiet, I knew it was almost time.

Jesse and I had gotten into a silly challenge that had me giggling until my ribs hurt. I didn't remember ever laughing so hard without reservations. The game had started innocently enough. I'd plucked something pink from the greenery along the path and asked him what it was. He made up a ridiculous name for it, then told me he knew of another one in the same family that was useful for curing hiccups. We took turns finding a new plant that the other had never seen before and giving it a story. I scouted deeper into the trees and came back with a fern of some kind, which I claimed had fallen from the moon. In turn, he brought me an extremely rare, brown flower that ate bugs. In fact, it was a nondescript green something he'd rolled in mud. It was just a silly game. Now he was looking for something yellow. He was about fifteen feet ahead of me, peering into the forest, when he froze.

"What is it?"

He held out a hand in my direction, telling me to stay put, but his eyes darted through the trees. Clearly, he'd heard

something I hadn't. My heart thundered in my chest, and I
suddenly knew.

A man leapt out of nowhere, bursting from the trees and
roaring like a grizzly. Jesse turned just in time to meet a
solid fist as it slammed across his face. Echoing the roar, he
pounced on top of the man, and they rolled down the path,
screaming obscenities.

"Think you can get back at me, do you? Miserable cur!"
The man was on his feet first, and he kicked Jesse hard in the
stomach, one kick for every word he yelled. "Damn . . .
waste . . . of . . . my . . . life!"

I ached for Jesse, remembering the mottled black and
blue already staining most of his body. He was rolled into a
ball, trying to cover himself, hands over his head.

The man kept on. "Goddamn Injun lover!" He paused for
a moment, catching his breath, and Jesse took the moment
to roll away and get to his feet, though he was curled in on
himself with pain. Blood flowed from his nose, dripping off
his chin, but his eyes were on fire. They flicked to me for the
briefest of blinks. A warning. *Stay away.*

But his enemy saw the signal. He spun around and stared
at me, his expression wild. Just as I'd seen in the dream,
Thomas Black had so many of Jesse's beautiful features,
though crevasses of hate had dug into his face. He took a step
toward me, and Jesse tackled him from behind. This time,
it was Jesse's fists that flew and Thomas who covered his
face, but both men were bloodied.

I heard my own voice, screaming, sobbing. I knew the
outcome, didn't I? Jesse would never get up, and I would be
in this man's hands.

Thomas rolled so quickly to one side that I didn't see it
happen, and Jesse fell off him. Thomas grabbed his son by
the throat and slammed his head to the ground. Except it
wasn't the ground that he hit. It was a rock.

The light died from Jesse's eyes. I saw it flicker, then
disappear.

"Goddamn right," Thomas growled, getting to his feet.
"Think you can get the best of me, do you? Goddamn

mistake from the get-go." He gave Jesse's body another kick, then reached back and pulled out a pistol. Its black barrel rested on one arm, and he pointed it directly at Jesse's head. "Should've been you them Injuns got, not your brother."

No no no no no!

My fear forgotten, I stooped, grabbed a thick branch lying at my feet, and ran toward Thomas. "Get away from him, you bastard!" I screamed, striking at the gun so it fell uselessly to the ground.

Thomas stared at me, incredulous, and turned from his son to me. I wanted to run, but he was right there in my face, as I had seen him before. He was quicker than I'd imagined he would be, ripping the branch from my hands and coming up close. Just as he had done with Jesse, he gripped my neck, shoving me hard against the solid trunk of an oak. His breath was hot and reeked of alcohol.

I knew that stench. Whisky, sweat, hate, lust . . . the day, that night, that nightmare suddenly resurrecting itself . . . *Oh God, what am I doing? Why am I here? Please no, no, no, no, no* . . . Every bruise, every tear and slap came back to me. It was all happening again. If only I could escape again, like I did every time the dream reached this point. But I couldn't move at all. His bristles scratched against my face, and his face came clear, that face I loved . . . and yet it wasn't. His lips were the same, but they'd twisted into a feral grin that made me shake almost convulsively. His eyes terrified me the most. This wasn't Jesse at all. The eyes narrowed at me, bloodshot and shining with conquest, were gray, not gold.

His other hand tore the neck of my tunic straight down, and the quick blast of air on my stomach told me he'd bared everything I'd tried to hide before. I fought harder, pushing at him with my hands, screaming, and trying to scratch at his face, but his fingers tightened around my throat until stars wobbled in my vision. My knees weakened, but I used one in a desperate motion, thrusting it hard between his legs. He stepped back to avoid my pathetic kick, then slapped me hard across the face. I stumbled to the side as my vision flashed white and my cheek burned. I landed on my back and he'd straddled me before I could move. At least my attempt to hurt him had accomplished one thing: his hand had left my neck for that moment, and I gulped down air.

His eyes were wild, and his hungry grin had widened. I had given myself a moment of lucidity, but he meant to take much more. His hand clamped onto my face, and one thick thumb slid over my lips. My nose was bleeding; I could see the evidence on his thumb just before he licked it off.

"You're a tasty chicken," he said, his voice raspy. Spittle shot from his mouth, hitting my face as he spoke. I squeezed my eyes shut, shaking helplessly. "And guess what? I'm one hungry son of a bitch."

"That's one thing you got right," came another voice, one that sent a shock through my system. My eyes flew open, and I would have wept with relief if I could have. Jesse sounded weak but aware. And cold with rage. "You *are* a son of a bitch. And this here's my woman. Let her go."

Thomas grinned down at me, blood from their earlier fight leaking onto his teeth. "Don't be telling your Pa what to do, whelp."

Jesse leaned in so I could see him. He stood behind his father, eyes glued to mine, his lips drawn tight. "I said let her go, old man."

Thomas Black's smile was a wide crack in a face that might have once held charm. Might have, long before, said pretty words to someone. Now it offered only violence, promised only pain. He held my chin in one large hand, squeezing my cheeks so my lips puckered between his fingers. He leaned in, and I whimpered, squeezing my eyes shut again, unable to move.

The hammer of a pistol clicked, and I looked up again. Jesse had come around and now squatted behind me, the pistol Thomas had once pointed at his son shoved hard against Thomas's own forehead.

"Uh-uh," he said. "You don't wanna be doing that. Nobody kisses my girl but me."

Thomas straightened slowly, his eyes hard with wariness

but still focused on mine. The grip on my chin eased, and I bit my lower lip hard, tasting the blood that leaked from my nose.

"Put that thing down, boy."

"Let her go." Jesse's voice was deep and deliberate, and final as death. The skin on Thomas's forehead indented around the barrel as Jesse pressed, a white circle cutting into sun-darkened flesh. The finger on the trigger was tight, not the least bit tentative. When he spoke again, it was done slowly, hatred sharpening the edges of his words. "I will kill you. You know I will. I've been waiting for an excuse to do this for near on twenty years."

The steely gray eyes finally blinked and left mine, drifting calmly toward his son's face. The rough hand slipped once more to my throat and stayed there, as if waiting for instructions.

"You'll kill me, will you, Jesse? You'll shoot your Pa over some whore of a girl? After all I've taught you, you still don't get it. You're stupid, boy. Always have been. And now you're half Injun, you've gotten dumb as that old mule McKenna shot last week." He nodded, then grinned. Something in his face shifted, hardened further and one of his shoulders rolled back. "Well, if you're gonna kill me, then this girl of yours—"

His fist exploded into my stomach at the same time Jesse's pistol went off. The instant, blinding pain was incredible, like stubbing a toe hard, but having it start deep inside and resonate throughout my stomach. Both Thomas and I rolled to the side, but he wasn't moving or making any sound. I curled into a ball, gasping, desperate for air I couldn't find, fighting a haze as it settled over my vision. Jesse knelt beside me but seemed to float just out of my reach. I saw his mouth move, but I heard nothing beyond the ringing in my ears. Something pressed on my head, and I squirmed, feeling trapped, until I realized it felt good. Soothing. Jesse's hand on my hair, calming, his lips brushing my ear.

"Breathe, Adelaide. Slowly now. He knocked your wind out, but it'll come back. You're all right, my girl. Just breathe. That's right."

Aided by his touch, I began to unfold my body, letting the muscles loosen as the tension in my stomach released bit by tiny bit. Jesse settled some kind of blanket over me, and I felt even weaker with gratitude. The first whispers of air snuck into my lungs, and I gasped for more.

"That's it. Breathe now. You're okay. Just breathe. Now don't you cry. You need to worry about breathing, not crying. You can cry later."

CHAPTER 35

A Soft Place to Fall

Slowly, after much coaxing, my breathing returned to normal, though my ears still felt as if something had been stuffed into them. I lay flat on the uneven ground, staring at him, delirious with relief. I was alive. The worst had not happened. Had I allowed the dream to finish way back when it had started, I would have seen Jesse save me. I would have known things would turn out all right. And now he looked down at me with such tenderness I was hard-pressed to behave when he told me not to cry.

When he saw my colour return to normal, he slid one hand behind my neck and helped me sit. The blanket started to slide off, and I grabbed it and pressed it hard against me. I used one edge to wipe the blood from under my nose and caught a whiff of the material as it passed. Jesse. It smelled like Jesse. I smelled horse and dust and trees and his own sweet sweat. It wasn't a blanket after all. It was his shirt. He'd torn it off so he could cover me.

Jesse's father lay unmoving beside him. I couldn't see more than his back, but a dark puddle seeped from behind. I turned away.

"I'm sorry," I said.

His frown was incredulous. "You're *what?* Why?"

"Your father. If I hadn't come here, you wouldn't have had to—"

Jesse drew back, looking as if he couldn't decide whether to laugh or cry. "Don't you ever apologize for that. Thomas Black was a snake who got what he deserved." He glanced behind at the body, then grimaced and turned back toward me. "He shouldn't have touched you. It's me who should be sorry."

We watched each other in silence, then I shivered. Night was closing in, and the forest was getting dark. A chill cut through the shirt he'd layered over me.

"Wait a moment," he said, then got up and rustled around in the forest.

I curled around my stomach, wrapping my arms around my knees. My body still throbbed on the left, where Thomas had struck me, just under my ribs, but it didn't feel as if he'd broken any of them.

Jesse returned with his arms full of sticks. He heaped them on top of dried grass, leaves, and a pale fungus I recognized as coming from the bottom of a birch. His flint struck, sending cheerful sparks into the dusk. A spot of orange appeared and was almost entirely swallowed up by a puff of gray smoke from the wet leaves. Jesse crouched low, breathing life into the young fire and adding sticks when it was capable of catching. I shivered again and drew nearer to the little flames.

Jesse stood and plodded toward the lump of his father's body. I watched him squat and look down at something—a memory, I imagined, and hoped he had at least one happy time he could bring back. I looked away. When he returned to the fire I noticed he wore his father's shirt and Thomas's haversack was slung over his shoulder.

"I'll move him out of here as soon as I get you a little warmer."

The light of the fire helped, but warm? I doubted I could ever stop shivering, and it was only getting worse. It wasn't just the chill of the night. My body shook in reaction to what had happened and what *could* have happened. My teeth chattered hard enough that it would have been difficult to speak, had I any words that needed saying. I didn't. I couldn't think of a thing. As the fire caught, Jesse looked across it at me, the orange glow against his face showing his worry, then taking it away as the fire jumped and fell. He came back to me, then we sat, side by side, staring at the growing flames.

"Your poor head," I said, touching the side of his skull Thomas had struck against the rock. Blood had painted half of Jesse's face a ghoulish red, flickering black in the firelight. When I touched its sticky source, he flinched.

"I've had worse," he mumbled. "I got a thick skull."

"We should go to the water, clean you up—"

"Let's just sit, all right?"

I wiped my arm across my face, then smiled as he did the same. "Look at us. We're a mess," I said.

His eyes searched mine, asking without saying a word.

"I'm all right," I whispered.

He looked into the flames, which had grown into a respectable fire despite the wetness of the wood. When he looked at me, his eyes were so sad my heart threatened to break.

"Adelaide, I feel awful for what happened. I don't know what to say," he said. "Or what to do next. God, Adelaide, I should have been paying attention. He almost . . . When I think of him hurtin' you, I just . . ." His fingers curled into claws, and he combed them through his hair for the hundredth time. "And now, well, the thing is, I don't know how to comfort you. I'm afraid to touch you," he admitted softly.

I pressed the side of my arm against his, trying to tell him I not only wanted but needed his touch. If only his strength could somehow work its way into my mind. I rested my cheek against his shoulder, which seemed to surprise him. He drew away at first, then wrapped one arm around my shoulders so that I was closer to him. We stayed like that awhile, both of us aware of my shivering as it subsided and eventually dwindled to tremors. They travelled down my body and pulsed against the pain in my stomach. I felt heavy all over and let my weight sag against Jesse. My eyes closed. I craved sleep.

"You tried to tell me this would happen, didn't you?" he asked quietly. His voice rumbled through his chest, a pleasant vibration against my cheek. I nodded. "How? How did you know?"

I hadn't used my voice in a while, so I had to clear my throat before I could answer. The words came out softly. "I told you. I dream."

"Then . . . if you knew it was coming . . ."

I shrugged, the movement a monumental effort. "I couldn't have stopped it. I knew you and I would be there, that it would happen. I know it's hard to understand, but there was no way we could *not* be there."

His chest rose and fell as he breathed. I rode the soft swell and felt completely at ease. I could stay here forever.

"So . . . did you know you would end up here, with me?"

"No. I never saw the ending."

"Huh." He shifted against me, and I felt the soft press of his lips on the crown of my head. "I like that. It's like I'm the happy ending."

The fire shot a spark into the dark, and I sighed, content.

"I'm so tired, Jesse," I said, yawning despite my need to talk with him.

"Of course you are. Quite a day." He'd carried a pack with him, as had I, so we were each able to pull out a blanket. He laid one out and rolled the pack at one end for a pillow. He was looking at me, watching my reaction. How I wanted to lie down, to rest, to forget for a while. But the memory of strong male hands on me—

"I'll sleep on the other side of the fire," he said gently. "You can have my blanket. You'll be safe and warm."

I followed the magnetic pull of the earth. I lay on my side, drew my knees toward my chest, and closed my eyes. Jesse covered me with a blanket, then leaned down to kiss my cheek.

"Good night, Adelaide."

Tears threatened immediately. "I don't want to be alone," I whispered.

Without a word, he lay behind me, his body curled against mine. He covered us both with the blanket, then wrapped one arm possessively around my waist. He tugged me tightly against him, where it was warm and soothing and filled with love.

"Good night, my Adelaide," he whispered, and I fell asleep.

CHAPTER 36

Welcoming the Demon

He was still beside me in the morning, but the arm that had held me so tenderly was now flung out to the side. Jesse lay flat on his back, mouth slightly open, breathing deeply. The blankets had fallen into a lump between us and over me so that he was uncovered. I propped myself on one elbow and gently pulled the blankets over him again, examining the lines of his face, the long lashes, the slight upward curl at one edge of his lips while he slept.

He was rugged, to be sure. A man who had seen—and caused—violence. His face, still relatively young under bristled cheeks, bore scars of experience, but the overall shape of his face was kind. Soft, almost. Life had been hard, but he wasn't. Not unless it was called for, anyway. I recalled the metallic set of his eyes the night before, when he'd pressed death against his father's forehead. I hadn't seen those eyes when the gun went off, since I'd been doubled over in pain, but I imagined they had changed again, becoming harder still.

A pillow of soft curls was trapped behind his head, their colour a shade or two lighter than I knew his eyes to be. One loose curl had taken up residence in the middle of his forehead. Another flicked like a wayward wing just behind his ear, and I touched it without thinking, wanting to feel the spring of it under my fingers. Jesse's eyes popped open, then relaxed at the sight of me.

"Hi," he said. He smiled slow and lazy, reminding me of his ridiculous cat, Gitli, when she did a low stretch over her front paws. As if he read my mind, Jesse reached his arms over his head and made a satisfied groaning noise, not unlike a purr.

"Good morning," I said. "Sleep well? How's your head?"

"Still attached to my neck. How about you? Are you all right this morning?"

"I am, thanks to you."

"Shall I find us something to eat?"

I frowned, then shook my head. My stomach still hurt from the night before. "Not for me. I'm not actually hungry."

He snorted. "I am. But I can wait." He reached toward me and brought my face to his for a kiss. "God, you're beautiful," he said. I blushed, which made him smile. It was a smile that flashed with a child's laughter, though it rumbled with what I recognized as the need of a man. He tucked my hair behind my ear and kissed me again. "Tell me, Adelaide. When you ran away from me, did it have anything to do with what I'm doing now?"

"I got scared," I admitted, unsure how to explain. Thinking of the last time we'd been together made me regret so many things. I should have stayed. As usual, I should have tried harder. I shrugged, wanting him to think I was unconcerned. "Like I said. When we were . . . together, it was like all the dreams got stronger. It all happened at once, and I felt trapped—"

"Not by me, though, right? It wasn't that you felt trapped because I wanted to kiss you, was it?"

He was a little boy, begging to be set free from guilt. I had to smile. "No, Jesse. I wanted to kiss you right back, if you recall. But the dream . . . I saw your father and felt his hands. It was so clear—"

He shook his head briefly, dismissing my words. "He's gone now. No new dreams?" I shook my head. "Then we should be fine." The twinkle started up again, lighting his eyes, though they looked tired. "So if you weren't scared of me kissing you, maybe we should try again, see how that goes."

I kissed my fingertips, then pressed them against his lips. "Yes, I think we should try again."

They were so warm, so soft. Gentle yet taking possession of mine in the most exquisite way. When he kissed me, my entire body buzzed, thrumming like the thick vibrations of a cicada's wings in the depths of summer. His thumbs, one on either side of my face, stroked my temples over and over as his kisses deepened, and my hands went to his shoulders, to the hard muscles that flexed when he raised his body up and over mine. He kissed the side of my neck, and every hair on my body stood straight up in appreciation. I lifted my jaw toward the sky, welcoming more, and he gave. His breath was warm on my ear, tickling across my cheek.

"Adelaide," he whispered, lifting his face so he could look down at me. "I need to touch you."

How was it possible that the idea of one man's hands repulsed me to the point of near suicide, and the idea of Jesse's left me dizzy with desire? Just the sound of his voice, hoarse and wanting me, untied any of the ropes still imagined on my limbs. His desire overwhelmed my fear, took away the panic that had always come with physical closeness.

I removed the shirt he had covered me with. I still wore my tunic, but it fell in shreds, exposing everything above my waist. His eyes flicked to my chest, then returned to my face. I could see the cougar in him as clearly as he could see my breasts—and my own need.

"You're sure?" he asked quietly.

I stared into his eyes, mesmerized. "I dreamed of you for years before Soquili brought you to the village. I'm yours, Jesse. I've always been yours."

He pulled off his shirt—his father's shirt—and my hands went to his warm skin, tight against the muscles of his stomach and chest, soft when I pressed my fingers against him. I had never explored a man's body before, not this closely, though I had been drawn to his ever since the first time I'd healed his wounds. The new wound, the one Andrew had given him in an attempt to keep me safe, was dark and ugly, craving attention. I saw the neat scar of the gash I had cleaned on his arm after his battle with Dustu, and the deep, short scar above his right breast. My fingers explored the soft pink pucker of it, traced the four lines left by the cougar so long before, then went looking for more.

Jesse stayed where he was, on hands and knees, letting me get used to him. He flinched when I touched a spot that tickled, but other than that, he didn't seem the least bit bothered that my eyes and fingers travelled over him, curious.

"You're the most beautiful thing I've ever seen, you know," he said softly, pulling me from my trance. "I think I fell in love with you the first time you gave me that adorable frown."

"I thought you just wanted me to translate."

He grinned. "That, too," he said, then kissed me again.

He held himself up on one elbow while his other hand cupped my shoulder, fitting perfectly, then slid down my arm and back up again. When he touched my breast, his hand was firm, not shy, yet it remained in place briefly enough that I knew I could escape if I needed. But escape was the furthest thing from my mind. Before I'd understood what he was doing, he set his lips on my breast and I caught my breath, taken by surprise at the sensations that flooded through me with that little action. When he moved his face to my other side, I was momentarily afraid he might stop.

Surprising both of us, my hands slipped down his sides, taking ahold of the waistband of his trousers and inching my fingers toward the buttons in the middle. Wide eyes watched my smiling expression as I undid one button, then the other.

"What?" I asked, trying to slide his trousers down. He chuckled and stood up, dropping them carelessly to the earth. "Here. Let me help."

I stared long enough that he covered himself with his hands and flushed slightly red. "Um . . . you okay? Is there something wrong?" he asked. "If I recall correctly, this was your idea."

"I'm sorry. It's just that I've never seen . . ." My eyes lowered again, but he blocked my view. What I could see of the rest of his body was a rainbow of cuts and bruises. "Sorry."

He frowned, confused. "But I thought—"

"I never looked at them," I said quietly. "I closed my eyes and wished I was dead. I never saw anything."

His expression melted with understanding, and he came back to me, letting his hands fall to his sides. I could tell he was still self-conscious, but he lay beside me instead of on top, and gave me a brave smile.

"Go ahead and learn whatever you want. I am happy to tell you what I know."

I giggled. "It's okay, Jesse. I don't need a lesson. I just didn't know they looked like that. Kind of funny."

He bristled slightly. "Hey."

"Sorry." But the giggles came through anyway, and Jesse stopped them with kisses. He straddled me again, then lay flat, squeezing me under his weight, muffling my laughter. Within moments, I was under both his body and his spell again. I gasped with pleasure as one of his hands moved to the outside of my thigh, gently massaging just above my knee, sliding upward in long caresses, rolling waves through my belly and below. My tunic skimmed up my leg, following the lead of his palm. His other elbow rested beside my head, supporting his body. He was taller than me by about a foot, so his bare thighs brushed against my knees.

I felt vulnerable when the material was entirely out of the way, when air touched me where I had been protected before. And I felt the shift in his urgency. He eased onto his knees so he was closer to me, until the shape of him pressed against the inside of my thigh.

I caught my breath, and his eyes opened wide, questioning. It wasn't that I wanted him to stop, just that I remembered that: the readiness of a man, the moment when he was so roused there was little or no hope that he could stop. A shudder ripped down my spine.

"I . . . I can stop," he managed. "If you want."

I watched every blink of his eye as if it might give away a secret, then shook my head. "Don't stop," I whispered. "Show me what it's like to make love."

He kissed one of my cheeks, then the other. "It won't be 'like' making love, my Adelaide. It will be the real thing, because I love you with everything I am."

"*Gugeh yuhi,* Jesse." I love you, too.

He watched me closely, ready to stop if I asked. I felt the hesitancy in his movements, the tentative touch. I smiled to encourage him. "Make love to me, *please*," I said softly.

He watched my reaction when he entered me, and I saw his eyes dull a bit, hiding behind heavy lids. I would have watched him, would have studied every beautiful angle of his face, but I was distracted by the sensations within me.

It didn't hurt. That was my first observation. I felt no pain at all. A feeling of something . . . wrong in me. No, not wrong. Something foreign, obviously, but not wrong. In fact, it felt entirely right.

Oh Jesse. I kissed his neck and closed my eyes, making love for the first time in my life.

CHAPTER 37

Daylight

We awoke later, curled around each other, and he reached
for me again. I was there, welcoming him as I always would.
I loved the smell of him, the sweat, the strain, the lust that
no longer frightened me. Far from it. Knowing he wanted me
roused feelings I never could have imagined before, making
my blood race. I wanted more every time.

When we lay exhausted, my head on his chest, a thought
struck me. "Where's your father?"

"In the woods." His words vibrated through his chest,
through my ear, my cheek. "Moved him while you were
asleep last night, in case of animals."

"I could have helped you."

He looked down at me and smiled, vaguely amused. "As
if I would ask you to help get rid of the man who tried to
violate you." He touched the blanket, then tugged it to my
chin as if to keep me covered. "I would never ask that
of you."

"Jesse, he was your father. How did you feel—"

He rolled to his side and held up one finger. "You should
know something about Thomas Black, Adelaide. He was a

bad, bad man. He was not a man I would like to offer as a father-in-law." His smile was grim. "He was so bad, I'm a little concerned about offering his son as a husband."

"What do you mean?"

"I mean I work every day of my life trying not to be like him. But sometimes I wonder, when I get really angry, if it's just something I can't avoid. If it's in my blood or something."

I frowned. "That's ridiculous."

"Is it?" He smiled gently, but his gaze looked distant. As if the thought resonated in his mind. When the echoes died down, his eyes came back into focus and he changed the subject. "God, you're beautiful, Adelaide. I'm the luckiest man in the world."

"I hardly think so," I said. "Not when people find out you killed your father and made love to an unmarried woman."

He laughed, tapping one finger on my chest. "Ah, but I intend to marry her as soon as I can. That's gotta count for something, don't it?" He leaned toward me and kissed me a long, long time. "Hey," he said, watching me regain my breath, "I never thanked you for saving my life."

"How'd I do that?"

"Loads of ways, but right now I'm talking about Thomas and his gun."

"But you couldn't see. You were—"

"No, I didn't see it. But there's no other explanation for why he'd leave his pistol lying by my head."

I touched his cheek. "He was going to shoot you."

"I don't doubt that," he said, kissing my forehead lightly. "And he would have. Thank you. Pretty brave of you. I don't think I can call you 'mouse' anymore after that."

That made me smile. The idea of having even one brave image in my head. "Not bravery. It was selfish. I didn't want him to kill you, because I wanted you."

"Whatever it was, it was brave. Don't doubt yourself so much."

"I never had a brave thought before I met you. Then I

started dreaming of you, and I knew something was going to change. Something big."

"When did you first dream of me?" he asked, his tone teasing.

"Long before you came to the village. I saw your eyes, I saw you were white, and I saw that you were very, very angry. Full of hate." I touched his face again, let him rest his cheek in my palm. "You don't seem so angry anymore."

"Not right now," he admitted with a lopsided smile. He pulled a strand of my hair off my brow and hooked it behind my ear. "I've found life ain't always pretty, and sometimes it's even less than that. But there are times when it's so goddamn beautiful, it's hard to breathe. That's where I'm at right now."

I blushed and enjoyed the prickles of heat as they spread over my cheeks. He rolled onto his back again, and I laid my head on his chest, in the spot I had claimed as mine forever. It was a hard place, set between his ribs and his collarbone, and the muscle that pillowed my cheek was taut and warm. But the heart beneath, the heart I had believed so well protected, was soft and vulnerable. And it belonged to me. I would protect it with my own. The night breeze didn't bother me. The rustling and secret noises in the trees barely touched me. I was safe and warm with Jesse. I closed my eyes, and Jesse stroked my hair, my cheek, down my neck as I fell asleep again.

I dreamed we walked along the path again, but no threat lurked in the trees. Nothing waited to leap upon us, shoot us, rape us, or beat us to death. It was just Jesse and me. His hand was warm around mine, and he was laughing, telling me something I couldn't hear in my dream.

But I was distracted. My left shoulder was stiff, which I assumed was from sleeping on the hard ground, and my stomach pain had grown worse. It was higher now, as if I'd damaged something within my chest. I stopped walking, and we both stared at my torso. It slowly turned blue while we watched, as if with a massive, spreading bruise. I collapsed onto my knees and looked up at him, but he was still staring at my stomach. I shook my head, and he frowned at me, not understanding. Then all at once the skin over my ribs began to tear, opening into a yawning wound that seeped, then poured blood. I fell backward, seeing him there, reaching, but never quite getting ahold of me.

Jesse! I screamed, but my voice was lost, drowned in the rush of blood that rose higher around me, rising until I feared it would cover me—

"Adelaide?"

A hand on my shoulder, trying to pull me out, but I'm too heavy. Drowning. Can't—

"Wake up, Adelaide. You're at it again," came Jesse's voice, soft and sweet in my ear.

Jesse!

"Yeah. It's me. Wake up, sweet thing. Sounds like you got something you need to tell me."

CHAPTER 38

From Within

The pain came in waves, an aching pressure becoming a fist, twisting deeper. In my mind, I could see it, something within me that would explode, that would devour me. Thomas Black had broken me. Thomas Black would have his vengeance, take me from Jesse, kill me even after he was dead. Thomas Black, just like Jesse had said, was a bad, bad man.

Jesse tried to question me when I'd awoken, but I could offer little. I told him about my dream, then said, "I've seen it, Jesse. I'm broken inside. I'm not going to survive."

"That's hogwash," he said, hoisting me into his arms as if I were a child. The pain shifted and subsided, then came back full force, so that I grasped him tightly around his neck.

"Careful," he teased. "I can't run far if you strangle me."

He ran forever, or so it felt, heading down a separate path from the one we'd been on before. I dimly recognized it as the one from which his father had come. I moaned when the pain caught me, feeling so weak my arms slumped from his neck. He stopped running and laid me on the ground while he caught his breath. I curled around my stomach, aching inside.

"Don't you do this, Adelaide," he puffed, frowning down at me. "Don't you go and do this."

"Take me to Wah-Li," I begged. "Or Nechama. They'll know what to do."

"No time for witch doctors. No time to get there anyway," he said. "Doc'll know."

"Doc?"

"Yeah. Doc. You'll like him."

I lost the rest of the journey, receding to a place where the pain had trouble finding me, hiding behind the sweat of Jesse's body as he ran. He spoke to me, telling me stories to distract us both, occasionally stopping to catch his breath, but not resting for long. He set me by the riverside and bathed my face, helped me drink the water, but I was weak. Dizzy. Disconnected from my limbs.

"Hang in there, girl. Almost there," he said at least a dozen times.

I woke to silence. A complete silence. No trees blowing, no water trickling along a pebble-lined edge. No birds or insects. No soothing voice of the man I had come to think of as home.

But pain, oh, that was there, roaring through me like a hurricane. I moaned, pressing my hands against my chest, and the sound brought me help, or what I assumed was help. A tiny, white-haired man stepped close, his hard-soled shoes causing the floorboards to squawk in protest. A strange, deeply creased face appeared, squinting down at me through spectacles badly in need of a cleaning. I watched him from as far away as I could get, clutching the sides of the bed on which I lay, then reverted back to the words I'd said so often in my past: "Don't touch me, don't touch me, don't touch me . . ."

"Hello, my dear," said the man. "I am going to help you."

"No, no, no, no, no," I cried.

"Ah, now. There's nothing to fear."

"Jesse?"

"Yes, Jesse. Jesse brought you to me. So you see? You have nothing to be afraid of. I will help you."

His words seemed muffled, far away, and my tongue with them. "Jesse?"

"My name is Doctor Allen. I am an old friend of Jesse's. He brought you here."

I was captivated by how his small, pointed beard moved like a trapdoor when he spoke. "Where is he?"

"Out. But don't worry, my dear. He will be back momentarily. I have sent him to pick up something I thought you might like."

The stomping of boots in the next room jerked me alert, but Doctor Allen merely patted my wrist. "See now? Here he comes. Ah, Jesse," he said, turning away from me. "Were you successful in your quest?"

"Yes, sir."

Jesse. I relaxed, breathing easier again, though the pain seemed to have spread through my ribs as well. Were they broken?

"How's the patient?"

"Just waking up in time to go to sleep," the doctor said.

"So you really—"

"Come along, then, Jesse. Let's not worry the lovely girl. She has enough on her mind. Speaking of which, she's been asking for you. Seems she's rather fond of you, my boy. Can't imagine why."

Jesse laughed, a sound that was rapidly becoming one of my favourite sounds in the world. It was lower than his regular speaking voice, and rolled gently. Like a purr.

"There she is," he said, coming to my side. "How are you?"

I smiled, trying to still my quivering chin. I didn't want to start crying again. God, he must be so tired of seeing it. But I was relieved he was there. As friendly as Doctor Allen seemed, it wasn't enough.

"What's going to happen?" I whispered.

"Doc's gonna fix you like I said he would. Remember that? I told you about him. He's fixed me up so many times I've lost count." He gazed down at me, golden eyes soft with concern. The roughness of his calloused fingers slid down my cheeks and curled my hair behind my ears. "I ain't going nowhere, Adelaide. I'll be right here with you the whole time."

The monster in my chest twisted. I gasped and squeezed my eyes shut.

"Yes, yes. Time to move along, children," said the doctor. "Jesse, bring me that bottle there, would you? The brown glass. Yes, there. And bring me the honey as well. Thank you, my boy. So excellent to have your assistance. Now, my dear, I suggest you not smell this before swallowing. Just drink quickly. There. There you go. That's right."

He touched the bottle to my lips and I choked on the foul stuff, sputtering brown liquid, but he was persistent. "There, there," he said, his voice calm. "You must drink this down or I will not be able to help you with the pain in your stomach. Jesse? The honey, if you please."

Jesse pressed a spoon to my lips, sticky with honey. "Try a lick of this, Adelaide. Takes the edge off the other. But you gotta drink it. You'll get past the taste soon enough."

I managed to get it down, swallowing whatever they gave me, alternating between the sweet and the repugnant. After a while, my limbs felt heavier, my stomach pained me less. Or if it didn't, at least I wasn't aware of as much. My mind drifted, Jesse's face faded in and out, and I clung to it, as if he could anchor me with his eyes.

"You sure, Doc? That's enough?"

"She's too small for more, dear boy. We shan't encourage her to expire on my table."

"But—"

"She feels very little now, but I imagine she will drift further soon."

And I did. I floated above the bed, around the room, through the meadow that stretched beyond my family's forlorn little house, listing slightly to one side, like a ship taking on water. Ruth and Maggie and me, skipping through the faded yellow grass. The faraway mountains that held the Cherokee, Wah-Li's toothless smile and ancient hands, the baskets in her council house with their tightly woven reeds.

Then a burning. A pressure, a pain so sharp I screamed.

I was back on the table, in the white room, with the little spectacled man. Jesse's face loomed just behind, his brow creased with worry. He had grasped my hand to hold it down, and I needed to raise it, to protect myself. But his hand was too strong, my own strength almost gone. I gave up, aware I would either survive by some miracle or I would never see Jesse again.

"There, there," the doctor said, clearly distracted. "So you see, Jesse, the spleen is located . . ."

CHAPTER 39

What is Right

He pressed, and it came again, the cutting, the burning, and I fled. I dropped into darkness where nothing moved, nothing spoke, nothing existed. Then shadows began to shape from that nothing, rising, taking on the silhouettes of men on the move, an army of hunters. Colour seeped into their features, and I saw they were Indians.

I was there now, close enough to the attackers that I could smell their excitement as it sizzled in their sweat, shone in their copper pores. They yipped in words unfamiliar to me, and I stared, trying to figure out what I was seeing. Who were they? The painted circles around their eyes—one black, one white—gave them an eerie skeletal appearance. Like an army in which each warrior consisted of two halves of a skull, one in the day, one at night. No hair grew on their faces or bodies, but four or five feathers stood in a spray over each head. Not Cherokee. A people I didn't know. A furious people.

One of the skull faces appeared suddenly, unavoidably, an inch from my own, and though in my head I wanted to scream, to disappear, to fly like a shrieking bird from this place, my hands had other plans. They moved without hesitation to the sides of the painted skin, and my fingers pressed against the hairless temples. The black eyes seared mine, raging at my intrusion, but he was as captive as I.

My mind crept into his as Wah-Li's had into mine. My questions stretched like tendrils within, dragging through his thoughts, curling around images that threatened to tear me apart. The strange Indians waited on one side, a town of unwitting whites went about their daily lives on the other.

The townfolk would be obliterated. That was what was in this man's mind, his sole purpose: slaughtering the unsuspecting families in the town below.

I had to get out. I couldn't stand to learn how this might end. I tried to do as I always had, to shove myself through whatever invisible bonds held me in the dream, pressed me into the boiling reality of the nightmare, but I couldn't move. No matter how hard I struggled, the medicine I'd been given forced me to remain a prisoner to the devastating images in the man's brain.

Then the demonic face was gone from before me, and I turned freely to survey my surroundings. About a mile in the distance I recognized the outskirts of New Windsor, the town I had visited in my childhood. We had travelled this way to trade, and the people of the town had treated us as if we were nothing but an irritation. My sisters and I had enjoyed seeing the sights of the town, but the people left us feeling small and unimportant. When our errands had been completed, our dilapidated wagon limped home, carrying our little family and our meagre possessions across the grasslands, then sat in the yard and rotted in the sun until the next trip. We were nothing like the townspeople, and they made sure we knew it.

New Windsor was also the place where I had first seen the men who had stolen my sisters and me from our home. That was the final time we'd gone to town. The men had been leaning against the wall of the blacksmith's shop, observing our mother and the three of us girls from across the road. A few days after that visit, I saw the same dusty, feral smirks, only then they were inches from my face, contorted with the thrill of destroying my life.

I had no love for New Windsor and its inhabitants.

But in this dream, the people of the town were about to be slaughtered like sheep. Why? Why had I been shown this vision? What was I supposed to do? Maybe it would happen in spite of me, but I knew I couldn't let it go without doing something. When I turned back to the unknown Indians, Jesse was there. His horse stood beside Soquili's, and more Cherokee warriors lined up beside them. Their own faces were painted for war, their expressions fierce. The heinous skulls crept closer, and for a moment it seemed Jesse was the only barrier between the savages and the town. But he stayed, staring them down with angry eyes. In the next moment, the enemy was gone. Jesse and Soquili sat quietly, and the town stood undisturbed.

"Jesse!" I screamed, and the dream was over.

Jesse was beside me immediately, taking my hand in his. "What? What is it? Are you all right?"

"They'll die," I whispered, then grunted and flung my hand over my body, seeking the source of the pain. From the sensation, I feared my ribs were on fire.

Jesse caught my hand in midair. "Nope, sweetheart. Keep those pretty hands at your sides for now, all right?"

"Hurts!" I managed.

He nodded, but it was a small movement. "I imagine it does. Here's some water. See how that feels."

It felt wonderful. I didn't realize how thirsty I was, but when he poured a few drops in my mouth, the water reached inside and soothed the fire. I sighed, then closed my eyes and opened my mouth, wanting more. He poured a few more drops onto my tongue, but it wasn't enough.

"Slowly, girl. You gotta go slow."

"What happened?"

"You've been sleepin' for a couple of days. Doc's been givin' you medicine, letting you heal a bit before you woke. He . . . he had to cut you, Adelaide. You had something going on inside that had to come out."

Cut me? "But—"

"*Shh.*" He turned away, then tugged a stool over so he could sit beside the bed. I grimaced at the sharp sound as the legs scraped across the floor, but he didn't notice.

I noticed everything. Mostly the pain. But it was a different kind of pain from before. Sharp, intense, as if my stomach had been removed and shoved back inside. But I didn't feel as if I might die. The pain wasn't taking over my entire body like it had been. As if the worst was over. I prayed it was.

"Doc was amazing, Adelaide. Truly," Jesse said, giving me that lopsided grin. "I've never heard of this kind of thing, but Doc seemed to know exactly what he was doing. He gets all the latest journals from the big cities, knows all the newest stuff. He showed me a diagram of what's under your bones, and told me about the thing that was hurtin' you."

He looked at his feet, his frown softened by shame. "Thomas broke somethin' in you when he hit you. It started bleedin' inside you, so that's why you were so weak and hurt so bad. But that thing, well, Doc took it right out."

I closed my eyes, unable to battle the weight any longer. "So tired."

"G'nite, sweet girl. I'll be here when you wake up."

But the darkness only brought back the creeping Indians, the light of madness in the warrior's eyes. I burst back into the light, gasping.

"We have to get them out!"

It took Jesse a couple of seconds to get to me this time. I wondered how long I'd been asleep. But time was running out. I sensed it.

His hand was warm, soothing on my brow. "You're back. It's good to see those blue eyes of yours, Adelaide."

"We have to get the people out."

He stared at me, his expression blank. "Oh really?"

"They'll all die." Frowning, he pulled the stool back and sat beside me. "Now, that's what you said the last time you woke. What's this all about?"

"The town. The Indians are going to attack. The town

isn't ready. Oh, it's awful, Jesse." I gripped the sides of the bed, needing to sit upright. I had to do something. No one knew but me. "We have to go."

"No, no, no," he said gently, uncurling my fingers one by one from the mattress. "Settle back down. You ain't going nowhere. Doc just did some major surgery on you, and your body won't be ready for anything for a long while now."

"Jesse, they'll all die."

He crossed his arms. "You had another dream, huh?"

I nodded, then winced as pain broke through my shock. My concern for the town had taken priority at first, but now my body demanded attention.

"They'll kill the town," I whispered.

He looked doubtful. "You should think again on this one. Ahtlee and the rest have no fight with these folks."

"Not the Cherokee." I squeezed my eyes closed, needing to see them again, but the images were gone. When I looked again, the sun shone directly onto Jesse's face, turning it a deep orange. Morning sun. Jesse squinted through the light, watching me closely. "Their heads," I said. "No hair, but four or five feathers straight up. They'd painted circles around their eyes."

"One black, one white," he murmured, and I nodded. He saw the images even if I couldn't. The muscles around Jesse's mouth tightened, and the soft gold of his eyes sharpened. "Catawba," he said.

"They're coming. Soon."

He shook his head and ran his open palm over the rasps of a new beard, looking at the floor while he thought over what I was saying. He returned his attention to me. "You know this for sure?"

I nodded, then slowly moved my right arm so I could feel what Doc had done. Jesse observed my every movement, making sure I was careful.

The bandage covering the site was thick but clean. I could smell old blood in the air, but it wasn't on the cloth.

"Jesse?"

He nodded, waiting.

"It has to be you. You and Soquili. You have to bring the Cherokee to stand against them."

His expression was skeptical. "The Cherokee stand up against the Catawba for a bunch of white folks? I don't see that happening, Adelaide."

Slowly, very slowly, a smile crept over my face. "But I did. I saw exactly what will happen."

"What do you mean? You told me yourself you never see the endings to these dreams of yours. It could end up totally different from what you're saying."

"I didn't want to see it," I admitted. "I tried to get away. But I couldn't wake up, couldn't escape—"

"Laudanum," he said, his crooked smile hitching up as he figured it out. "It kept you under."

"It was awful, Jesse. But I had to stay, so I saw what you have to do. If you go, it will work. You can do it."

He ran his fingers through his hair and gazed out the window. "Me and the Cherokee against the Catawba, saving a town full of white folks neither you or I care about?"

"Yes."

The smile left his eyes, but he nodded. "I'll go to Soquili for help."

"You will?"

His smile popped back up at my expression of surprise, and his eyes creased with humour. "Never thought you'd hear that from me, did you? 'Ask the Cherokee for help' doesn't really sound like me, does it?"

I shook my head. "But you believe me?"

His smile wavered and was lost. "If you say so, Adelaide. If you truly believe this will happen, it will have to be done. I guess I gotta go."

Of course he did. If anyone knew the urgency of his mission, it was me. But selfishly, the idea of his leaving was terrifying. My stomach clenched, and pain washed over me. He saw that, too.

"Don't you worry. Doc'll be here, and he'll keep you safe. Not much I can do for you right now other than sit here and go on about nothin' anyway. You've given me a job to do, so I'd best go do it." He put his hand on mine. "You can trust Doc. I've trusted him my whole life. Actually, until you came along, I guess he was the only person I've ever trusted."

I nodded and tried to relax. The door squealed closed behind him, and I heard the muted sound of his boots as he stepped from the wood floor to the grass beyond. I wanted to sleep. Wanted to stay awake. I needed both. I ached for Jesse, hating the task I had put before him. He hated Catawba as well as the people from the town; I hated white men. Now he had to ask the Cherokee to defend people we both hated.

But it had never been a question for me. I saw the deaths being planned in the Catawba warrior's mind and knew it was up to us. Up to Jesse. But would the Cherokee see it as something they must do? Would they set themselves against other Indians for our sake? Would the people I knew stand up for their enemies? I wished I could have gone with Jesse. I wanted to be there when he told them, to be witness to Wah-Li's expression when she saw what we had become, Jesse and I. Because he would have to go to Wah-Li. She would reach the truth he held out, then bring it to the People. It was up to her. She would send them. Unless . . .

I had never before been able to see my dreams to fulfillment, but if I sat before her, presented myself to her, she probably could. What if I'd seen this one wrong? What if she saw what Jesse told her, then saw a different ending? If she saw needless death, useless sacrifice, would she still send the men?

PART 6

Jesse

CHAPTER 40

Lesser of Two Evils

Catawba. The name stuck in his mouth like a piece of gristle. Jesse spat to the side, tasting bile. Goddamn Catawba. They'd slaughtered his family, and now, if he was going to believe Adelaide's crazy dream, they were coming for the town. Something big must have gotten into them. They usually went for small settlements of houses, unprotected, helpless victims. Then again, a bunch of shopkeepers and ladies wasn't exactly a well-prepared army. Goddamn Catawba.

He did believe in the dream, though. Wild as it was, he was determined to put his pride aside, and his life in danger, on the basis of one girl's imagination. He believed, and he would do what he had to do.

Doc kept two horses. Before he'd been taken by the Cherokee, Jesse had given them to Doc as a thank-you, and he had trained them as well. When Jesse stepped out of Doc's little white house, he spotted Doc leaning on a fence post, watching the mares. The early morning sunlight caught their matching chestnut coats and turned them a burnished copper. Soft black muzzles mouthed at grass wet with dew. At first, Jesse had wondered if bringing the horses to Doc was maybe a bad idea, that Doc wouldn't know what to do with them. But he'd been pleasantly surprised by the way it had turned out. The horses tended to Doc the way Doc tended to folks. They healed whatever Doc needed, just by being there. Jesse guessed it was the mindless ease of their company that did it. The old man could be the picture of concentration, of courageous medical skills like he had been with Adelaide, then he could flip entirely. Like a page in one of his books. The animals calmed him. Jesse'd once seen him take an hour just grooming one of them, talking to them, carrying on a one-sided conversation the horse seemed to enjoy.

"I have to leave for a bit, Doc. Can I take Blue?" The mare didn't register her name, but both horses looked up at Jesse's familiar voice, delicate ears perked with interest.

"Certainly, certainly you may, my boy. She'd be happy to take you. And your lady friend? You will leave her in my care, of course."

"Is that okay?"

"Of course. I would have it no other way. But tell me. I'm curious. What is it that has the power to pull you away from her, when I haven't been able to do it for three days?"

Jesse chuckled. "I gotta go save the world, Doc."

"Ah. Of course." He hooked his long fingers behind his back and stared up at the cloudless sky. "Well, it's a good day for it anyhow."

Blue was the quicker of the two, though River was a fine mare as well. Blue was a bay, so her mane and tail were mid-night black against her copper coat. Both were friendly, but Blue listened a little better. Just that slightest bit brighter, Jesse figured. He was comfortable riding without a saddle, but chose to use one this morning because he thought he might need it later for carrying things. And it looked like it might be a long day ahead, and the leather would provide a bit more comfort than Blue's knobbly back.

He didn't ride her hard, but kept up a steady pace. It was a couple of hours to the village from here. He had plenty of time to go over things in his head.

This raid on the town seemed extreme, even for the Catawba. But they were unpredictable sons of bitches. Even the Cherokee hated them. He could picture the warriors, their painted faces and lack of hair making it difficult to tell one from another. He'd heard horrible stories about killings done by Catawba, about things they'd done to the dead, too. They had sick senses of honour, those men.

And they were vengeful. He wondered what had set them off that might make them go to this length. The Catawba weren't actually thinking too far ahead, he realized. If they attacked an entire town, the army would take revenge. Problem was, he doubted the army would bother differentiating between the Catawba and the Cherokee, or any other kind of Indian for that matter. He sure hadn't. Until recently, one Indian had always been the same as another to him.

That had changed. At first, everything they said or did evoked his father's voice, stirring up hatred Thomas had planted and tended in his son from early on. The Cherokee asked him to turn right, he'd go left. Set out clean new clothes for him to wear, and he'd tug on his old stained breeches instead. He'd do just about anything but be agreeable.

Adelaide had turned him around. She had no problem with them and had told Jesse a lot that made him more curious than disapproving. He learned some of their hunting techniques, carved out an arrowhead or two, eventually gave in about the clothing. Except the breechclout. That was not for him. No thank you. But the tunics and the trousers one of the women had made for him, well, he'd been surprised at how good the deerskin felt against his skin. And he'd seen some of the successes these people had had with their healing. Of course, some of them were disasters, but he doubted even Doc could have done any better in most cases.

They'd eventually treated him as an equal, like when they gave him their trust at the powwow. They'd included him in things no white man would normally experience. Like that game of *Anejodi*—or whatever it was called— when the men used sticks with nets to toss a deerskin ball at a carving of a fish on a pole. He grinned, remembering the comradery he had experienced for the first time in his life. Out there in the field with Soquili and the others, chasing that goddamn ball and tackling each other just to get to it, well, that was fun. He'd never fit in with Thomas Black and his crew, never had friends his own age as he'd grown up. Doc had been the closest thing he'd had to a friend, and Doc was old and unusual.

Thinking of Doc made him think about Adelaide again. He didn't worry about her health, because he knew Doc could handle whatever came his way. It still made him ill, though, thinking about Thomas's fist in her stomach, breaking her apart inside. Took away any feeling of guilt he might have felt over ending Thomas Black's life. He smiled and checked Blue's canter, slowing to a walk. Both he and the horse needed a water break, and he knew the stream was close.

Yeah, his Adelaide was a flighty little thing, but damn, she was the prettiest woman he'd ever seen. Seemed to him the braver she got, the more beautiful she became. He loved seeing the fire spring up in her eyes when he teased. Even more though, he loved the way the icy blue of them grew dark, her pupils dilating into perfect black circles when he kissed her, when he touched her like she'd never been touched before.

He shouldn't have made love to her. He knew that. He should have waited until they were properly wed. But the opportunity had been there, and she'd seemed to welcome it, to want him as much as he wanted her. No, it was more than wanting. They'd *needed* each other in that moment, and they both gave what they had to give. He'd never regret doing it, not for the rest of his life, but he did wonder how she felt about it now. It had certainly brought them closer—in a number of ways. Ever since then, she had been more open with the things she said, less shy in the way she said them. So maybe it was all right that they hadn't waited. He wasn't sure.

Jesse guided Blue toward a stream, but he needn't have bothered. The mare was already going that direction. She'd heard the silvery sound of the mountain water rattling over pebbles and stepped up her pace. When they got to the edge, he hopped down and dropped her reins, tossing them casually over her neck. She strolled to the edge of the water, lowered her head, and cooled her throat. Jesse squatted beside her and filled a flask, then cupped his hands and drank. He stayed there a moment, squinting against sparks of late morning sun on the water, and spotted a trout wriggling across the riverbed. Too bad he hadn't brought a hook. He didn't feel patient enough to do it Cherokee style, stabbing at the thing with a spear. No time for that anyway.

He did have time for a short wash, though. He peeled off his trousers and kicked them into a pile over his boots, then started to wrestle his filthy shirt over his head. He changed his mind halfway and tugged the shirt back down, thinking the thing could do with a wash anyway. The itchy wool fibres clinging to his body had once belonged to his father, and he wanted to wash any trace of Thomas from the shirt.

He waded in until he was knee-deep, relishing the slippery cold of pebbles sliding between his toes, then bent over to scrape dirt from his skin. When he'd almost gotten used to the frigid temperature of the mountain water, he sat in the stream and splashed the rest of himself—including the shirt— then shuddered in reflex. Finally, he dunked completely under and gasped at the welcome shock of cold against his still-healing face. He shook his head like a dog, spraying water into a fountain around him, then shoved his hair back from his eyes.

When he got out and headed to Blue, he noticed he'd accidentally tied Thomas's haversack alongside his own on the saddle. He reached up to grab something to eat from his, but curiosity made him unwind the strap from his father's as well. With the bag hanging over one arm, he carried a chunk of cheese and a piece of Doc's fresh bread back to the edge of the stream and took a seat.

"What you got in here, old man?" he wondered aloud, unravelling the ties and emptying the contents onto the grass. Not much. Kind of sad how little was left to represent a man's life. A small knife, a rusted fishing hook stuck into a chunk of deerskin, some kind of biscuit that had hardened into near rock. Jesse sighed and dropped the items back into the bag. He could use them. Might as well keep the bag, too. He was just getting up when something grabbed his eye, and he crouched back down.

The item was a shell about the diameter of an apple, but it was like no other shell he'd ever seen. He wrapped his fingers around the little treasure, amazed by its colours. He supposed the base colour was white, but the shell seemed to catch fire whichever direction he turned it, iridescent blues and greens dotted or rippled throughout.

"What are *you* doin' in Thomas's bag?" he mused.

He turned it over and noticed there was more to the beautiful shell than its colours. His thumb skimmed over a series of scratches on the concave surface, and when he squinted he could see the lines were white and purposefully etched. Peering closely, he was able to make out a vague shape, a carved, intricate pattern of triangles. The pattern looked much like something a Cherokee might have used.

Now where would Thomas have gotten something like this, and why keep it with him?

Blue nudged his shoulder from behind, and Jesse reached back to stroke her warm, wet nose. "You're ready, are you, girl? Keep going and we might get there before this sun gets too hot. You're right, as usual."

The little shell slipped with a clatter into the sack he'd tied to Blue's saddle. He'd give it to Adelaide. She'd like something pretty like that, maybe.

He slid on to the saddle and nudged Blue back in the right direction. Before long they were on the path where Thomas had attacked them, and Jesse couldn't help but glance nervously around him. The old man was dead. He knew that better than anyone. Nobody was liable to come back after a bullet did that to his head. Just the same, the air held whispers Jesse'd rather forget. Even Blue seemed to step more gingerly through the path, as if she sensed the violence that had occurred there.

CHAPTER 41

Gift of Persuasion

As he rode into the village, Jesse was spotted by eight-year-old Ahsdahyaw Deela, or Loud Skunk, and the rest of his little gang. They shrieked something that Jesse was sure was supposed to sound fierce, then raced ahead, announcing Jesse's arrival to the entire village.

Kokila ran toward him, her brow creased with worry. "Tloo-da-tsì!" she cried in English. "I cannot find Adelaide! She is gone many days!"

Jesse slipped off Blue and smiled with reassurance. "Don't worry. She's with me. In town."

She stared at him, wide-eyed, clearly taken aback at the idea of Adelaide mixing with white people. "In town? Why?"

He tried to speak in Cherokee, then decided to stick to English. His emotions ran too high at the moment to try and translate. So he compromised by slowing down.

"She's fine now, Kokila. She was hurt and sick. My friend healed her. She is getting better now."

Her eyes flickered over his face, searching for anything he wasn't saying, but Jesse didn't have time for this. She wasn't who he wanted to talk with about his mission. He

needed to talk to Ahtlee. Kokila shrugged when he asked
where the man was.

"Soquili is at canoe. I do not know about Ahtlee."

It was a different boat from the one Jesse had originally
helped with. Smaller but no less impressive. Soquili was busy
carving into the sides, sweat streaming down his chest despite
the autumn chill. He looked up when Jesse approached.

"Brother," he said, frowning. "Where you go? You tell
no one."

"Not true. Dustu knew."

Soquili twisted his mouth with disgust, and Jesse was
hard-pressed not to laugh. "Dustu." Soquili spat, then left
his carving tools and went to Jesse. "Where you go?"

"To find Adelaide."

"Ah," he said, his expression lifting. He peered behind
Jesse. "Where is she?"

"Not here."

Soquili's frown was back, dark with suspicion. "Where—"

"Listen, Soquili. I need to talk with Ahtlee."

"He not here. He hunt many days."

It was Jesse's turn to frown. He sighed and hooked his
hands on his hips. "Many?"

Soquili nodded, wiping sweat off the tip of his nose.
"Why you need him?"

Jesse stared at him a moment, considering. It would have
been easier to ask Ahtlee for help, but he didn't have much
choice. He sighed again. "Okay. You'll do. Come and sit
with me. I have a story for you."

They sat by the river where they had once leapt from the
creaking old oak. The leaves along the edges of the water
were gold as sunshine, quivering with the slightest of breezes.
One by one they gave in to exhaustion, twirling toward the
soggy carpet of those that had fallen before.

"I have a problem," Jesse admitted, grabbing a broken
twig from the ground beside him.

"Ha! You have many problems," Soquili assured him
with a grin. "But you do not often come to me for help. What
problem makes you look this way?"

"What way?"

"Old. You look old."

"Fine," Jesse snapped. "Respect your elders and keep quiet a minute."

Soquili beamed and nodded amiably.

"You know of Adelaide's dreams, right?"

Soquili looked doubtful. "You speak of her sister, Maggie."

"No. I know Maggie has dreams, but so does Adelaide. They're just not quite as . . . developed. She's worked with Wah-Li on them."

Soquili's left eyebrow lifted with surprise, then he nodded, accepting the idea. "I did not know this. But I believe you. Maggie is very powerful. Her sister should be, too. Adelaide dreamed something?"

He didn't want to tell Soquili about Adelaide's surgery or the initial cause of her injury. He wanted to keep the message clear and direct. But Soquili was too astute for that. He pried with questions, asking over and over where Adelaide was, not accepting Jesse's evasions. So he told him everything.

Well, not everything. He told him he was going to marry Adelaide, which made Soquili hoot with laughter, but didn't tell him anything more about the two of them. Those memories were for him and Adelaide alone.

He told him of Thomas Black and his subsequent demise. Told him Adelaide was being cared for by his friend, who was an excellent doctor. Soquili looked confused when he explained about the surgery.

"I do not know of this healing. We must speak with Nechama."

"No, that's not the point here. The point is, we need to get the men to town. Keep the Catawba away."

Soquili tilted his head. "You want Cherokee to fight Catawba for white men?"

Jesse nodded, but Soquili disagreed.

"I do not think this is wise. Cherokee may die fighting for white men. Why? They would not die for us."

Jesse had to agree. And in truth, the men in New Windsor

meant nothing to him, either. They'd ignored him when he'd staggered into the town as a young boy, bloodied from yet another encounter with his father. Teased him about crazy Doc Allen. And now he knew all about the men from New Windsor and what they'd done to Adelaide and her sisters. For that alone, he didn't think any of them should live.

But Adelaide had told him those men were dead. Now Thomas was dead. So, technically, it set them back to even. And it was wrong, wasn't it? Knowing someone innocent was going to die and doing nothing to stop it?

But Soquili had a point, too. Why put his people in unnecessary danger?

Jesse had so many questions about Adelaide's dreams, though he doubted he'd ever learn all the answers. But it seemed to him there had to be a reason they were dreamt in the first place. Why else would a deep-rooted evil take hold of her mind and refuse to let go, unless she was supposed to do something about it? She rarely saw the endings. So could the dreams be made to end the way she wanted? Did she change history when she dreamed these things? Did it matter?

"If the town is killed, the army will come." Jesse held Soquili's gaze. "And white men often do not see any difference. You are all Indians," he said, then waved at Soquili's head, "with different hair and paint. You and all other Indians are their enemy whenever that's convenient. You're their friends when they need something. Well, I'm saying they need you now. And if your people don't do anything about it, the army will wipe *all* of you out."

"They cannot! They do not have that power."

"You have no idea how many white people are in this world," Jesse said, his voice rising as he remembered some of Doc's lessons. "And they are all coming here, to your beautiful land. If the Cherokee are friends with the white men, things will be all right. If the Cherokee allow a slaughter like this to happen, there will be no hope for the Cherokee."

Soquili's eyes burned. "You are wrong, Jess-see. The

Tsalagi have lived here forever, and will always live here. The white men are like geese, landing, then flying, coming back when the weather is good. It is not their land."

Jesse closed his eyes, praying for patience. "I'm not here to argue with you about white men and Cherokee. I'm really not. I'm telling you it's wrong to let someone kill someone else if you know it's going to happen." Time to spice it up a bit. "And with enough mighty Cherokee warriors there, the Catawba may run in fear."

That worked a little. He saw the defiance ease in Soquili's eyes, but not the suspicion. "Come," Soquili said, standing.

Jesse followed him to Wah-Li's house. He wasn't comfortable with the old woman, didn't like the way she could read his thoughts, but with all the dreaming going on, this might end up being the best idea after all. The men called in through her door, waited for a signal, then stooped through the low door.

Wah-Li sat with Nechama and another woman, watching them enter.

"Ah," she croaked, stretching out hands that shook from age. "Handsome young visitors. Come. Come. Sit. What news of my Shadow Girl?"

Soquili started speaking, his tongue lightning quick over the syllables that always tripped Jesse. Jesse listened hard, wanting to make sure his side of the story was heard, but other than the occasional reference to Adelaide and himself, he couldn't grasp much. Wah-Li's shrunken face stayed neutral through the summary, the only movement coming from her lips as they rubbed contemplatively against each other.

When Soquili had finished, she turned her attention to Jesse and gave him a brief smile. "Come, come," she said again, reaching for his face.

Jesse had been afraid of this. The way he felt when she did that crazy mind-reading thing was disturbing. Some of it was wonderful, as if he flew through the rare joyful moments in his life, seeing them all again. But the bad always goes with the good. He shifted closer so she could press her dry old fingers against his temples.

As if she held a warm rock to his face. That's what it felt like initially. Then the heat from her fingers spread throughout his brain, sharing his thoughts and everything else about himself. Jesse wasn't fond of sharing. Never had been. Usually when he shared, things were taken. But he had learned that Wah-Li never took. Or if she did, she left him with his own share, and never used any of it against him. Now he rode with her, racing through his childhood again, touching on the past and moving swiftly into recent days.

The inevitable scene came to his mind, the memory he would very much like to forget: the struggle with his father. How he'd turned to see Thomas holding Adelaide, how all the blood had left her face, and her eyes were squeezed shut. He saw Thomas's fist ram into her side, felt the pistol's sharp recoil as he blew his father's miserable brains out.

Wah-Li saw them together, wrapped around each other on the forest floor. He sensed her surprise as their passion flitted through his mind, then her approval as Adelaide's happiness shone in her eyes. Jesse felt no shame, only a strong need to be with Adelaide again.

She smiled, sensing his love for her Shadow Girl. "Yes, yes," she purred, eyes still closed.

Wah-Li felt him sweat as he carried her all the way to Doc's house, saw what he saw as he gazed at her pale, semi-conscious face. She followed him inside Doc's place and watched him explain to the old man. Then she saw Doc plunge a knife into Adelaide.

"*Ayah!*" she exclaimed, releasing his head. She turned horrified eyes to Nechama and told her what she'd seen. The healer looked shocked, glancing from Jesse to Wah-Li, then back again.

"She lives?" Nechama asked him. Wah-Li's clouded gaze shot to him.

He nodded. "She does. Doc is keeping her safe."

"He kill her!" Wah-Li cried, wrinkled features sloped with horror.

"No, he didn't, E-Lee-See," he said, addressing her as "Grandmother" for the first time. "He took a part of her out that was broken. It was . . . amazing. She was in a great deal of pain when I left, but Doc says she will live."

Nechama leaned forward, eyes bright with interest. "I want learn from this Doc!"

Jesse couldn't help grinning at her. "I'm sure he'd love to teach you, Nechama. I think he would like to learn from you as well."

She clapped her hands together. "Oh yes!"

"No, no, no," Wah-Li muttered, flicking a hand at Nechama. "Come, Tloo-da-tsì. No time for this. Story not over."

He nodded and leaned forward, submitting to her seeking fingers again. Then she was given proof, hearing Adelaide speak to him, hearing the pleading in her weak voice.

"Soquili," said Wah-Li. "Call meeting. You will lead. You and Tloo-da-tsì stop Catawba."

Soquili couldn't argue with her. When Wah-Li said something, it would be so. Before they left, Jesse turned back and took the old woman's hand again.

"E-Lee-See?"

She peered curiously at him. Her skin was warm and smooth, waxy with age. Jesse felt an unfamiliar pang of regret, realizing the old woman couldn't live forever.

"Thank you for blessing Adelaide and me. She has agreed to marry me."

"I know," she said, then covered her toothless mouth and giggled like a young girl. "It was you. It has always been you."

CHAPTER 42

Warrior

Wah-Li kept her smile hidden the next time she reached up to touch Jesse's face. It was quite a stretch for her, but when he stooped a bit to make it easier, she shook her head. She had become small and hunched in her old age, but her pride hadn't shrivelled with her body.

She slid her finger down his nose, tickling his skin with the cool stickiness of paint. "Red is for war," she murmured, her voice weak in sound but strong in meaning. She stroked five lines across each cheek. "Red is also for your clan, the *Aniwahya*. You are pure in spirit and proud in your heart, Tloo-da-tsì. The Tsalagi are proud of you."

It was a new feeling, this whole pride concept. In his past, Jesse had experienced apprehension and a spattering of excitement on the eve of battles or raids, or whatever his father wanted to call them, but never before had he felt as if there was a purpose for what he was about to do. As if it mattered what he did. When Wah-Li had finished, Jesse stood a little taller. He wore the same single feather as everyone else. It was an identification method for use during the thick of battle, should things get out of hand. Anyone with a white, red-tipped feather was friend. Anyone else was fair game. The feathers also served to help identify the dead when it was all over.

Soquili stood beside him, and Jesse chuckled, studying the red pattern that had also been painted on his own pale skin.

"Looks better on me," Soquili said. "You stick out like gull in middle of crows."

Jesse snorted. "Looks better on you? That's not what the ladies say."

"Stand beside me when the Catawba come, brother," Soquili said, sober. He clapped a hand on Jesse's shoulder. "I will not lose you again."

"Ha! Can't lose me. I stick out like a gull, remember?"

"Oh, you will be lost," came a snide comment. "You do not belong on battlefield unless you are prisoner, like before."

Jesse flushed at the reminder. "Didn't nobody ever tell you that if you ain't got nothin' nice to say, don't say nothin' at all? You're a pain in the ass, Dustu."

"Maybe, but I *belong* here," Dustu retorted.

"That's enough," Soquili snapped in Cherokee. "Having the same skin colour does not mean you belong, Dustu. You would fit in better with weasels, I say."

"*I* say," Dustu continued, speaking so quickly Jesse almost didn't understand. He poked Soquili on one side of his chest. "That if you want to keep this *brother* of yours alive, today is not a good day. He does not know how to fight, and the Catawba will eat his liver."

Soquili shoved the shorter man out of his way, and Jesse followed him through the circle of warriors. He'd had enough of the flexing and posing anyway. Sure, sure. All right. They were all tough and ready to go. *Let's get on with it,* he kept thinking. He didn't know exactly when the Catawba were coming, but Adelaide had said it would be soon.

But Dustu wouldn't leave it alone. Jesse grunted when a sharp punch landed in the centre of his back. He spun around, glaring at Dustu. As usual, the man was spoiling for a fight, always wanting to tempt Jesse's fists. Hadn't he had enough?

"I teach you," Dustu said, grinning. "I teach you do not put your back in a man's face. Unless you running. Or maybe you like to run."

"Keep walking," Soquili muttered. Jesse turned back and moved alongside Soquili.

"Like now," Dustu continued. "Show him your back, same as give him your throat."

"Don't you have somewhere to be?" Jesse growled, glaring back at him.

Dustu shrugged and moved up beside them, offering the guileless smile of a child. "I do not think so. It is important I teach you. You die make Soquili sad. So I ask do you have knife? Weapon is important in war."

Jesse's hand dropped to the hilt of his knife, which was always at his hip. He turned so his face was an inch away from Dustu's, but the impertinent grin never wavered from Dustu's face.

"My knife hasn't had a taste of you yet, weasel," Jesse growled, "but it sure is hungry. What do you say? Wanna give it a sample?"

Soquili stepped between the two, shoving them apart. "Enough," he said. "Save it for Catawba." He was right. Jesse stepped back, but Dustu didn't move.

The smaller man sneered. "Stay away from me, white man. You will get us all killed."

When the horses finally headed out, forty or so of them, Dustu's words were what stuck in Jesse's mind. And that made him angry. Dammit. He knew what he was doing. Always had. He'd known how to fight his whole life. If he hadn't been born with the skills, he had learned them from necessity. So he shouldn't have worried. But he did. He knew the Catawba from a distance, and from reputation. While his blood growled with lust at the opportunity to finally get some sort of revenge for the killing of his family, a part of him trembled with something close to fear. Dustu was right. They were coming for white-men's blood, and though the

Cherokee would be standing against them, Jesse was an obvious target. Even so, before they'd left the village, something in him had rebelled, and he'd decided not to bother smearing anything into his hair to darken the colour.

They stopped a mile or so from the town, and Soquili held up his hands, beckoning the group closer. They left the protective forests behind and passed scattered homes— either huddled together in clusters or standing separate and fragile—which had popped up like bubbles across the grasslands. The war party was still far from the bustling streets of New Windsor, but Jesse could see the narrow roof belonging to Doc, imagined he could see River, grazing calmly in the field.

And if he imagined even harder, he thought he might just be able to visualize the pale pink oval of Adelaide's face where it pressed against the lone window in Doc's healing room. The velvet fall of her long blond hair. The haunted combination of fear and hope in her eyes. He sat a little taller, rolled back his shoulders as if to settle everything. The plain fact was he couldn't get killed today, because he couldn't bear to let her get hurt again.

Leadership was new to Soquili, but Jesse was impressed by the settled look in his eyes. He seemed born to this. The role draped over his shoulders with pride, like a mantle handed from father to son. From his place beside Soquili, Jesse smelled the sweaty thickness of the air around their leader, heavy with nervous energy, excitement mingled with anxiety. Every man bore a variation on the same scent of natural intoxication, the fervour and thrill of impending bloodshed. The horses felt it as well and pressed closer together, eyes wide and aware. When all the men had gathered around, they ceased talking and waited respectfully for whatever Soquili had to say. As if he held the pipe.

"Today is an important day for the Tsalagi," he announced in their language, sitting comfortably, though his mount pranced with nervousness. He kept the words simple so Jesse wouldn't miss anything. "What we do today will change everything. We stand against the Catawba to defend another enemy. A weaker enemy. An enemy with white skin." Then he sneered, nostrils flared as he looked over the men. "The Catawba are too low to lick the fleas from our dogs. They have no reason for killing these people today. But we have reason to kill the Catawba."

Soquili's horse shifted under him, another mare snorted loudly from somewhere in the group, and Blue pawed at the dust, tossing her head with impatience. Jesse patted her neck, and she settled, but Jesse did feel a little bad for her. She'd no experience in fighting. Other than when they went hunting, the stench of blood was relatively new to her.

"If the Catawba kill the white people, the white army will come to kill Mother Earth's children: Cherokee, Creek, Choctaw, Chickasaw, Shawnee, and Catawba as well. We are all the same in the eyes of the ignorant white man. So today we must defend that white man." He gestured with an open palm toward Jesse. "We stand with my white brother, Tloo-da-tsì."

The moment was surreal: sitting on Blue's creaking saddle in the midst of these savages, being called one of them, knowing they were all here and would fight because of him. A part of him wanted to laugh at the irony of the situation. The other part wanted to wriggle even deeper into the throng of men, mingling and sharing their ancient strength. Something had happened to Jesse since he'd lived among these people. Well, of course it had. But not in the way he'd expected. He was not a starved, beaten slave, subjected to torture and constant ridicule—except at the hands of Dustu, of course, who he could handle easily. Instead, he had been accepted, respected, and included. His opinion mattered for the first time in his life. He felt new. His back was straighter these days, his heart a little stronger. These people believed in him, so he did, too.

He wondered what Adelaide might think, seeing him at the head of the Cherokee like this: lone feather pointed skyward, face painted with red lines like the claw marks of a cougar. Then again, she said she had seen him there already.

The breeze kissed the powerful men's cheeks, ruffling feathers and coarse tufts of black hair, lifting manes and tails. Like a whisper, a response from the heavens. It roused the horses and a few tossed their heads and snorted, ready to go.

They didn't have long to wait. The Catawba was a tribe used to ambush, adept at sneaking up on their enemies. They were soundless until the last moment, when a man could practically die of fright as a result of their sudden, wild shrieks. They would have sent scouts ahead, and the unexpected parade of forty Cherokee warriors painted for battle would have compelled them to regroup, change tactics.

Somewhere in the back of Jesse's memory he saw them again, heard the screaming, smelled the burning, then remembered the torn bodies of his family from when he'd helped his father lay the poor souls to rest. The memory awoke an ancient rage in him, and he ran his thumb down the smooth edge of the *galuyasdi usdi* at his hip, tied there alongside his knife. Soquili had taught him how to throw the wicked tomahawk, how to split a log from thirty feet away, and he'd learned well.

On his other hip, he carried his father's pistol. The one that had left Thomas rotting in the woods, exactly where he belonged.

CHAPTER 43

Battle

The Cherokee war party stood in a line facing the distant woods, Jesse near the centre. No one spoke. Even the horses stilled, as if they knew what was coming, but their heads jerked up at the unexpected sound of hooves approaching from behind. A dozen armed white men, scouts from the town it appeared, rode to within thirty feet of them and stopped. Their expressions seemed determined, and though they tried, it was impossible to hide the fear in their eyes. Not a man alive could approach a war party of this size without it. No one spoke for a moment, and Jesse realized it was up to him.

"Good afternoon, gentlemen," he said, nudging Blue toward the line of townsmen.

One of the men, wearing a tricorne and a droopy moustache, seemed to be in charge. He encouraged his horse forward, appearing relieved to hear English spoken.

"Good afternoon yourself. Do I know you?"

"I can't be sure. Jesse Black."

The man's eyes narrowed. "Thomas's boy."

"No. My own boy," Jesse snapped, hating the idea. "I'm here with the Cherokee."

The townsman, jaw clenched, looked away from Jesse, and his eyes scanned the proud row of Indians. "Might I ask why we are honoured with this unexpected visit by the Cherokee? Something we should know about?"

Jesse nodded. "Well they have a bone to pick with you folks. Someone do something they shouldn't have?" The man frowned, looking puzzled, then shook his head. "Seems the Catawba have a plan to teach your town a lesson. They're on their way now. The Cherokee have decided that's hardly fair."

"Is that right?" The man sounded unconvinced. He gnawed on his lip, making the greasy strands of moustache disappear inside his mouth, then slide back out again. "Doesn't sound right somehow, Cherokee helping us out."

"That's fine, but that's what it is. Maybe you'll keep that in mind the next time they could use a hand. Since you're here, we could use a few good men with rifles helping out today. How's that sound? Join the Cherokee and save your town? The alternative doesn't sound near as nice."

Soquili called from the crowd. Movement had been sighted at the top of the next hill.

"I have to go, gentlemen, but I invite you all to stay and help out."

Giving the men a brief nod, Jesse wheeled Blue around and galloped back to the Cherokee, leaving the white men to huddle in a confused group. Having done what he could, Jesse forgot about them and moved up beside Soquili, letting him point out the slightly uneven sway of grass that shouldn't have been happening, the shadows that seemed to move on their own. Blue muttered to herself, bumping flanks with Soquili's horse, her ears alternating between seeking sound in front and flattening with concern. Jesse's heart beat quickly, pounding against his ribs, his blood surging with excitement. One horse by the end of the line gave in, unable to stand the anticipation any longer. She screeched and reared straight up, pawing at the air as if fighting an invisible attacker. Her rider muscled her back down, but by then the ground had erupted, spewing Catawba from the grass, reminding Jesse of the summer the locusts had come.

The air was suddenly quick with the whispers of arrows, cheered on by whoops and answered by grunts and cries of those caught unaware. With a wild yipping that made Jesse's hair stand on end, the Cherokee swarmed forward, and the two tribes crashed together like opposing waves.

For a moment, Jesse was paralyzed by the sight before him. The tribes seemed evenly matched, meaning almost a hundred ferocious warriors wrestled before him, fury and bloodlust shining in their eyes, sweat and blood flowing down the lean lines of their naked thighs. Cracks of musket fire clouded the air, and men fell back with jagged, smoking holes torn through them. Such a close battle meant muskets lost their use quickly, and the smoke gave way to blades. Within the first minutes, bodies lay still or writhing in the long, broken grass, many partnered by crouching enemies whose bloodied hands hacked or sliced life out of the fallen. For the briefest of moments, Jesse's mind begged him to run, to flee this field of certain death, but he couldn't consider the thought.

Blue shied under Jesse, prancing backward, tugging at the reins, but he leaned forward. "Come on, girl. Show 'em what you can do."

She seemed to take courage from his voice. When he nudged her forward, she ran into the midst of a group of attackers, but a hand gripped Jesse's thigh and held on tight, yanking him from her back. He landed hard on the ground, on his back, just in time to block the killing blow coming at his face. The young Catawba warrior, eyes wide in their painted circles, was unprepared for Jesse's quick reaction and lost his balance for a breath, giving Jesse all the opening he needed. His knife arced up, slicing the man's neck, and Jesse rolled out of the way as a hot spray of blood coated the grass. The body twisted, the voice made gurgling noises Jesse knew would be burned into his brain forever, then the body lay still. Jesse stared at it with fascination. He'd killed an Indian. He'd killed a goddamn Catawba. *For you, Mother.*

He jumped to his feet and spun toward another Catawba staring straight at him, this time from the side of a bow about fifteen feet away. The nocked arrow was aimed directly at Jesse's eye. He sensed it there, knew without any doubt that the warrior would not miss. He was about to throw his knife when a musket cracked, cutting the archer down from the side. The bow released, the arrow flew straight up, and Jesse nodded thanks to the shooter: one of the few remaining white men from the town.

By now, most of the Cherokee were off their horses, and the animals had fled to safety as the men plunged into the thick of battle. He had no time to check, but Jesse was sure Blue would have found her way back to the herd. It seemed important, knowing she was okay. He shouldn't have brought her—but what choice did he have?

Ten feet from him, Jesse saw a tomahawk fly, spinning blade over handle, handle over blade, with perfect accuracy, chunking into the centre of a Catawba's chest. The man fell flat on his back, and the thrower raced in, digging the blade out and hammering it back in, over and over, the meaty thudding of the weapon lost to the noise, as if it had been nothing but receding footsteps.

"Tloo-da-tsì!"

At the sound of Soquili's shout, Jesse leapt to his feet, bloodied knife in one hand, tomahawk in the other, surprised to discover two leering Catawba standing before him. Their eyes—one circled with black paint, the other with white—sizzled with ferocious anticipation. As he'd predicted, he was an easy target, his hair practically glowing in the midst of all the black heads. Soquili, still on horseback, sent two arrows in, both of which lodged in the throat of one of Jesse's attackers.

Jesse ran at the other one, bowling him over. The warrior reached up and thrust his blade at Jesse's throat, but Jesse grabbed the man's sinewy wrist and shoved it out of the way, then punched the Catawba across the side of his face, wincing as the man's teeth cut through his knuckles. He pulled back his hand to slug the man's bloody face again, but his opponent managed to lift his other arm and shove Jesse's fist sideways, throwing him off. Now the Catawba rolled on top, his knife hand an inch from Jesse's throat. Jesse gritted his teeth against the man's strength. He had to drop his knife so he could grip his opponent's wrist with both hands, and both men's arms shook with exertion. Then the Catawba leaned down, pushing his weight harder, bringing his bloody face so it was mere inches from Jesse's. Blood dripped off the dark lips and landed on Jesse's cheek, and the warrior sneered through teeth painted almost black with more.

"Now you die," the man hissed in slow, distinct English.

But Jesse heard a different voice, and the power of it sapped the strength from the warrior's blood. Instead of the gore, Jesse saw a sweet pink smile, eyes as blue as the sky overhead. He felt a rush of strength pour through him, felt he could suddenly take on so many more than just this one warrior. He'd felt this surge of energy only once before: as he'd staggered through the gauntlet in the village, suffering the beating meant to either prove him or kill him. It had been too much, and he'd almost fallen, almost given up, then he'd heard that voice in his head, the one he thought he'd imagined. This time, he recognized it.

Be strong, Jesse. Come home to me.

He lashed out with the power Adelaide sent him, seeing again the moment when his father had struck Adelaide. With a roar, he shoved both hands up, forcing his attacker to his feet. Jesse rolled to his own, then used all his strength to deliver the same devastating blow Thomas had used on Adelaide, destroying the man before him. The Catawba warrior's quick, surprised squawk went silent as he crumpled to the earth, then rolled into a ball. Having no desire to ever meet the man again, Jesse grabbed his knife from where he'd had to drop it before, then jerked it across the warrior's throat.

There was no time to study his second kill. Soquili had

dropped from his horse and was still screaming wildly, sweeping his knife through one enemy, his tomahawk through another. Jesse saw his mouth open wide, heard him roar when a knife caught him on his thigh, but it didn't stop the big Cherokee.

Another Catawba stood before Jesse, ten feet away. The two stared at each other, eyes burning with determination. Then the Catawba started to run at him, knife held over his shoulder on an obvious path to Jesse's neck. Jesse ran forward to meet him, too angry to be afraid. At the moment when the warrior's knife arced down, Jesse dropped to his knees and slid under the outstretched arm, then swept his own arm backward, slicing his tomahawk through the Catawba's side. The man dropped; Jesse stood and ran deeper into the fray. All around him copper skin shone with sweat and blood, black eyes of the ancients burned with fresh kill. Jesse joined them, losing all English words to his new Cherokee tongue, losing his past to the present, becoming the brother Soquili had always claimed he was. And he felt no fear. He imagined these unfamiliar painted men bearing down on the town, crawling like spiders toward Doc's little white house, and practically lost his mind with fury.

Most of the men were locked together or stalking prey. When Jesse caught up to Soquili, he was coated in blood and kneeling over a fallen foe. He grinned maniacally at Jesse, looking disturbingly like a fiend with his wide eyes and gore-painted face, and Jesse knew he looked equally gruesome. Jesse glanced away, searching for his next target, and spied a victorious Dustu crouched just beyond Soquili. The weasel dropped his lifeless adversary, then howled ecstatically into the air, so caught up in his own euphoria that he didn't notice the Catawba warrior approaching from behind.

For an instant Jesse stared, paralyzed. He hated Dustu. The man would like nothing better than to take Jesse's golden scalp. But no one stood near enough to jolt Dustu from his daze, to warn him. And the Cherokee were Jesse's family now.

"Damn weasel. What'd you say about turning your back to your enemy?" Jesse muttered. He stood and slid his hand to the base of his tomahawk handle, then stepped forward and launched the weapon, using all his skill and strength. The blade planted itself between the attacker's shoulders, shoving him forward so that he landed with his arms outstretched, just behind Dustu. Dustu, startled, jumped back up, looking wildly around to find out what had happened. He met Jesse's eyes and narrowed his own in question, looking skeptical. He pointed at the man Jesse had just killed, and Jesse lifted his chin. A reluctant smile snuck across Dustu's face, and he nodded. A well-earned nod of thanks. Of acknowledgement. Of respect.

Then Soquili shouted, his voice overpowering all the wails around him. He called to his men, his warriors, his brothers, and the Cherokee went to him, grouping together as an invincible—though battered—army, standing as one against the scattered Catawba. Faced with the concept of having to fight this many-limbed monster, the Catawba turned and fled.

Jesse watched them go, the thrill of the fight still singing in his veins. The grass, stained black with blood, shimmered with the breeze as if nothing had happened, though patches of it were buried beneath bodies from both tribes. A lone vulture circled high overhead, and the Cherokee wandered the field, collecting their wounded. Nechama and a few of the other women had come with them, staying well out of danger, and now rushed in to do what they could.

Soquili stood beside Jesse, breathing hard, watching the aftermath of the battle. "Tloo-da-tsì is good name for you, brother. You have eyes, claws, and teeth of cougar. Yes. That is good name." He chuckled and tilted his head toward two dead men on the grass nearby. Two of the men Jesse had killed. "Catawba should have asked your name first."

Jesse laughed at that, the idea that he could frighten his lifelong demons. He gave Soquili a sideways smile, showing he was impressed. "And you are a powerful war chief, Soquili. You did well out there."

Soquili tried and failed to hide how happy Jesse's words

made him. He nodded once, then changed the topic. "Now we go to village. Feast our victory."

The horses had gathered in a familiar herd behind the battlefield. They began spreading out, calmer now that the noise had stopped. Blue perked up her ears when she saw Jesse looking at her. He shook his head.

"No feast for me tonight. I gotta go to Adelaide."

Soquili frowned, his gaze dark and assessing. "You will not come back to Tsalagi."

"Says who?"

"Says me," Soquili said, lifting his smile halfway. "You and Shadow Girl will leave us."

Jesse shrugged. "I don't know what we'll do. But I have to make sure she's all right before I make any kind of plans."

Soquili nodded, his smile gone. "You fight like Tsalagi today, Jess-see. You make us proud." He cleared his throat and nodded again, briefly. "You make my brother pleased. I hope you come back."

Jesse nodded thoughtfully, strangely moved by the sentiments. He slapped Soquili's back. "You have not seen the last of me, my Tsalagi brother."

Jesse had never called him that before, and he was surprised the words came so easily to his tongue. They'd just felt right. Over the months he'd lived with the Cherokee, he'd come to accept that these people knew what they were talking about some of the time. That maybe something actually did exist between him and Soquili, something a little deeper than friendship. That perhaps some kind of connection did forge a link between their spirits.

He kind of hoped so. He liked the idea. And with the Cherokee's belief that they always carried their ancestors on their shoulders, Jesse figured he'd never have to feel alone again.

"I think," Soquili mused, "I will feast later. I want see Ad-layd. Make sure this Doc is good man."

Jesse grinned. "I bet she'd be happy to see you."

Nechama, finished with the wounded, waded through the grass until she stood before Jesse. She was a small, solid woman with silver-streaked braids that reached halfway down her body. Years had cut lines in the leathery skin of her face, but most of them swept away from the corner of her eyes. She smiled more than she frowned.

"I meet Doc now," she said, beaming like a young girl.

CHAPTER 44

Confirmation

A respectable-looking group of town officials was waiting at Doc's house when Jesse's bloodied party rode in, confirming Jesse's earlier suspicion: it had been Doc who had sent the armed white men to the battle before it had started. He had to smile. Little Adelaide had convinced him as well. Blue trotted in first, and the gruesome sight of the battle-worn riders held the white men still as stones. They clung to their rifles and held their ground, watching warily as the Cherokee drew closer. When Jesse and the others pulled their horses to a stop, the exhausted war party stared down at the white men, just as unsure.

Then Jesse slid off Blue and headed toward Doc, his broad grin the only bit of him not covered in filth.

"Jesse!" cried the doctor, rushing forward to embrace him. "You are well! You see, gentlemen? Your messenger brought you the truth of the matter. I said all would be fine and Jesse would be back soon, bearing only the best of news. Is it so, my dear boy? Have you come with glad tidings?"

"I have indeed, Doc. I have indeed. It wasn't pretty, but the Cherokee came through," Jesse said, holding the fragile

old man against his grimy chest. When he glanced at the
officials over Doc's shoulder, a wave of nerves passed over
him. He leaned down and muttered in Doc's ear. "What are
these gentlemen here for? They ain't here to arrest me
because of Thomas, are they?"

Doc Allen grinned and shook his head, stepping out of
the embrace. "No, no, my boy. They're here to see you all
receive the gratitude which is due."

"How is Adelaide, Doc? Is she gonna be all right?"

The smile remained. "She will be better when she sees
you. But might I suggest you clean—" His words fell away
as Jesse bounded inside.

She was propped partially up in bed, still pale, but alert.
She had heard the indistinguishable rumble of voices outside
and waited quietly for Doc, agitation flickering in her eyes.
Then fear that filled them, panic at the sight of Jesse's bloody
face coming toward her. It wasn't until he was close enough
to see her worry that he grinned.

"Hey, little mouse. It's me."

"Jesse!"

He was beside her in a heartbeat and had to restrain
himself from pulling the beautiful invalid hard against him.
But he did wrap his arms carefully around her, pressing his
nose to her hair and breathing in her scent. *She doesn't smell
sick,* he thought, relief flooding through him. Tired, needed
a bath, sure. But Doc had done it. She would be all right. He
closed his eyes, feeling like he'd come home, and he clung
to the feeling.

"Oh Jesse. I was so—"

"Stop that, Adelaide." He moved so they were eye to eye.
"You knew I'd be all right. You sent me to do a job, and I did
it. I always said I'd take care of you, didn't I? You ain't got
no call to be scared no more."

He kissed her, a gentle press against her lips. He didn't
want to hurt her. But she pulled away.

"You smell awful," she said.

He didn't let go, only pulled her back against him and
chuckled into her ear. "So do you."

A short knock on the wall grabbed his attention, and Jesse drew reluctantly away from her. Doc stood in the doorway, grinning nervously.

"Em, Jesse, my boy, I do dislike the idea of separating the two of you, but would you mind terribly coming with me for a moment? It seems we have a slight language barrier with your friends, and some of the town's gentlemen are a tad bit concerned."

"Language barrier? The Cherokee are here?" she asked.

"Just a few of them," Jesse replied. "I'm comin' Doc. Oh, and Doc?"

"Yes, my boy?"

"That ol' woman out there, she wants to talk with you. Her name's Nechama. She's their healer and wants to know what you did for Adelaide. I told her you'd be happy to tell her all about it. Shall I send her in?"

Doc brightened. He loved to teach. Jesse was always a disappointment in that department, and he was well aware of that. Just as quickly as he'd smiled, Doc's brow furrowed, and he clasped his hands in front of himself, looking unusually nervous. He wasn't used to visitors.

"Certainly. Certainly," he said. "Should I prepare tea? I confess, I have not had a Cherokee in my house before. I'm not sure of the proper etiquette."

Jesse snorted. "Don't worry over that. Just set her beside Adelaide for now. So she can see for herself that you ain't killed her."

"Of course!" Doc exclaimed, mortified. "My manners are appalling."

"I'll be right back," Jesse said, turning back toward Adelaide. She had relaxed, and he thought her cheeks looked slightly pinker than they had even a moment before. He leaned in and kissed one of those cheeks, savouring her soft skin against his lips. "You're lookin' better, you know."

Her gaze was warm on his. "I'm getting better. Especially since you're here."

Jesse heard a voice raised, coming from outside, and he identified it as Soquili's. "I gotta go," he said.

"Jesse?" She reached carefully toward the table by her bed and retrieved a wet cloth. "Use this, would you? I think the men will be more likely to listen if you don't look like a corpse."

He used it to wipe the grime from his face, managing to clear away most of the war paint beneath, started to hand it back to her, then realized how disgusting that idea was and decided to keep it with him. He followed Doc outside and handed the filthy cloth to Soquili, who frowned and tried to pass it back. But Jesse stepped back, giving him a nod of encouragement. Soquili grudgingly used it to wipe his own face, then passed it to his friends.

"Gentlemen," said Doc, addressing the townsmen. "This is Jesse Black, of whom I had spoken earlier. He will be able to tell you all that happened."

Jesse nodded, but before telling them the story, he turned to Nechama and smiled. "Adelaide waits for you in house," he said in Cherokee. "She is good." He switched to English and spoke slowly. "Nechama, this is my good friend, Doc Allen. He is happy to teach you."

Doc stepped forward, holding out his hands. She gave him one of her own.

"I come to thank you, Doc. And to learn," she said, tentative with her English.

Doc closed his hands over her strong fingers. "It is my pleasure, madam. Please, allow me to present the young lady for whom we were all so concerned."

Jesse turned back to the men of the town and explained everything that had happened, choosing to skip over the actual reason he'd known about the planned raid. When they asked, he said he'd simply heard through someone and left it at that.

"Does it matter?" he asked. "Your town's still standin'."

He introduced Soquili and the small group of warriors with him, and after an awkward hesitation, the townsmen held out their hands in greeting. The Cherokee stood stiffly, unfamiliar with the gesture. Jesse put himself between the two groups and shook the men's hands, leading by example.

He nodded to Soquili, who followed suit, along with the others.

Doc's house was too small for him to invite them in. Jesse didn't think his friends would be comfortable in the small space anyway. But it was inconceivable, after all they'd been through, for him to let them leave without at least offering something. Holding up one finger, asking them to wait, he ran inside and returned with some of Doc's baked bread and muffins, which he'd known would be waiting for him. Doc always prepared Jesse's favourite things, and since Adelaide was there as well, the old man had prepared extra. The Cherokee sat on the ground and ate as if they hadn't seen food in a week. Jesse excused himself, saying something noncommittal, but Soquili knew. He smiled at his brother.

"I say *osiyo* to Ad-layd, yes?"

Jesse nodded.

When they entered the house, Nechama and Doc were sitting on two stools on one side of Adelaide's bed. Doc chattered quickly, moving his hands in illustration while Nechama sat silently by him, her eyes slightly glazed, her jaw slack. Then Adelaide spoke up, stepping weakly into her role of translator. Nechama listened intently, nodding and asking questions. Doc glanced between Adelaide and the healer, obviously fascinated by the language.

Grinning, Jesse stepped to the other side of the bed and took Adelaide's hand while Soquili waited in the doorway, soaking everything in. Doc launched into more explanations, so Adelaide paused in her translation just long enough to glance up at Jesse with a tired but warm smile.

When the next round of translations had been completed, Nechama nodded and spoke directly to Doc. "I thank you for your teaching," she said. "I would like teach you. You come to village?"

Doc's mouth opened and closed a few times. He rarely left his house, let alone travelled as far as the village. Jesse waited, one eyebrow raised.

Finally Doc smiled, and Jesse could see how hard he was trying. "It would be my great honour."

Grinning, Adelaide interpreted again.

"Nechama," she continued, reaching for the older woman's hand. "Wah-Li saved the town today by believing Jesse's thoughts and my dreams. How can we ever thank her for this?"

Nechama's eyes almost disappeared, swallowed by the grin she gave them both. "The Grandmother has only one wish. She told it to me two moons ago."

Adelaide and Jesse exchanged a glance, then nodded. "Anything," Jesse said.

Grinning, Nechama clapped her hands together, obviously pleased to share Wah-Li's words. "She wishes you to name your first daughter after the Cherokee."

Jesse swallowed, surprised, then glanced at Adelaide, who had turned a healthy shade of pink. Their first daughter. Jesse's heart got so big in that moment that he was afraid Doc might have to fix it later. He leaned down and kissed his girl, then walked around and kissed Nechama as well.

He grinned. "Nechama," he said in careful Tsalagi, "please take this message to the Grandmother. We will name our first daughter after the Cherokee, and she will name her first daughter after the Cherokee. We will continue this for . . ." He glanced at Adelaide for help.

"For many generations," she said for him. "To thank the Cherokee."

The old woman smiled. "And the Grandmother wishes you to know, Tloo-da-tsì, that she hopes you understand now. We are your family. You are our son and brother. You have shared your spirit with us, and we give ours to you as well. She wants to tell you it is time for you to trust. That you have done right and well, and you will get the happiness you deserve. She has seen it."

"Thank you," he said. "And yes. I understand now."

"Be well, Jes-see and Ad-layd," the older woman said, getting to her feet. "I must go now. There will be a big celebration tonight. Especially when I tell them you are both well."

While Doc showed Nechama to the door, Jesse and Soquili took their places on either side of Adelaide. She was pale, but her lips seemed less gray now. Jesse took that as a good sign.

"Soquili," she said quietly. "You are well?"

He grinned. "It was a good day. And I have decided you, Ad-layd, must change your name."

"Oh?"

"You cannot be Shadow Girl. You stepped from the shadows today. Once the Cherokee carried you from the white people. Now you bring the Cherokee and the white people together. The Cherokee nation is proud of you."

There was another flash of pink in her cheeks, and Jesse squeezed her hand, thinking he'd missed that sweet reaction of hers while he'd been away.

"I'm proud of you, too," he said. That's when he remembered the little shell he'd found in Thomas's bag. "Hey, I brought you something you might like."

He fished in his sack, which lay on the floor by his feet, then handed her the shell.

At first, she didn't move, just held the little thing on her palm, staring at it with a wide-eyed expression. She brought it closer, then turned it over and rubbed her thumb over the carving.

"You like it?" he asked, grinning at her stunned reaction.

Her breath hitched. The girl was crying. What the hell? Jesse looked to Soquili for help, but Soquili was also staring at the shell, his own expression incredulous. "Where you get this?"

"It was in—"

"Look, Soquili," Adelaide said. She sniffed and handed the shell to him. "Where did you find that, Jesse?"

"It was in Thomas's haversack. I was looking through his stuff and found it. I thought you might like it. But hey, if it's gonna make you cry—"

"Your father carry this?" Soquili demanded, eyes sharp.

Jesse shrugged. "Yeah. I don't know—"

"This belonged to Soquili's brother," Adelaide explained quietly. "I made it for him. He never took it off. When they brought his body back to the village, it wasn't with him."

"Oh, Jesus. I didn't know—"

"Of course you didn't. Jesse, this must mean your father killed Soquili's brother and took this as a trophy."

Jesse frowned, suddenly nervous. "Yeah. I guess it might mean that. But on the other hand, Soquili took me. Kind of works out in the end, don't it?" He watched Soquili closely, wondering what was going through the warrior's mind. Did this mean it was time for "an eye for an eye"? Was he going to die because of Wahyaw's pendant? Had Thomas managed to kill Jesse in the end, like he'd said he would?

"Listen, I'm sorry that—"

But Soquili's expression had softened, losing its tight mask of hatred and easing into what Jesse recognized as a smile. His voice was calm, warmed by an emotion Jesse couldn't place.

"You killed my brother's killer, Jess-see. My brother, he gave you this." A broad grin brightened Soquili's entire face. "I was right from the beginning," he said. "You carry my brother's spirit. You *are* my brother."

Just a few months before, Jesse never would have considered the idea. Now it felt natural and wholly possible.

"I thank you, Tloo-da-tsì," Soquili said quietly, folding both hands over the shell.

Jesse watched Soquili get up and leave, his step lighter than it had been. When he was gone, Jesse glanced back at Adelaide, who appeared slightly bemused.

"That was interesting," Jesse said.

She shook her head. "It was something."

Adelaide wasn't well enough to stand and bid the Cherokee farewell, but Jesse was able to gently carry her closer to the window so she could watch them ride away. The day was done, the excitement over; the feast at the village beckoned the Cherokee. Jesse stood behind Adelaide, loving the gentle pressure of her body in his arms as she leaned against him for support. But at the same time he felt a tug on his heart, watching the riders disappear.

You are wrong, brother, he thought, smiling to himself. *You will see me again. You can't get rid of me that easily.*

CHAPTER 45

By the Hearth Fire

It had to be a dream. And yet . . .

I stood in the middle of a wide-open field, my parents'
home a stark, wasted skeleton in the distance. I knew the
trees bordering the field, saw the contrast of vivid green
against the faded yellow grass swaying at my feet. I knew
the endless blue overhead, though the clouds were forever
new. I didn't want to see the house. Didn't want to be back
in this place. Too much of me had been broken there, on
that day, in that other lifetime. Despite that, something in
my heart yearned to step closer so I could run my fingers
over the splintered boards I knew so well, to reach out for
the memories that clung to the yellowed walls.

Time and place do not matter in dreams. They do not
exist. And so it was that I found myself at the front door of
the house, averting my eyes from the spot on the wall. But
while time and location have no place in dreams, neither do
self-imposed rules or desires. My eyes were drawn inexorably
back to the place where my mother had died. The bullet had
flown so swiftly into her brain that she hadn't had time to
cry out, though I knew my sisters and I had screamed. But

now, when I looked, the blood was gone. Any sign of her was gone . . . except for a small hole. A bullet hole. Would the murderous piece of metal still be inside? A narrow passage, but wide enough that my smallest finger fit inside. The passage was splintered, unconcerned with the intrusion, but not very long. At the end of it, I touched cold steel.

"Good-bye, Mother," I whispered.

I wandered inside, my eyes taking in familiar knotholes in the walls, my ears listening for the distinctive creak I had come to expect from each board underfoot. My hands braced against the walls as I mounted the stairs because I knew the steps weren't trustworthy. But I reached the top without stumbling, and I followed the corridor to the room where my sisters and I had all slept, curled together under pungent wool blankets. The world was a dangerous place, but as long as I was with my sisters I had always believed I was safe. That belief was long gone.

Once upon a time, we had played in that room, giggled about silly little girl things, cried in each other's arms, whispered deep into the night when we could hear my father's snores in the next room. One time, little Ruth carried a jar of raspberry jam in there, then sat in the corner and dipped her tiny fingers into the sticky red fruit. She wasn't allowed to have it in there, and she knew it, but who could take it away from her, as sweet as she looked with the telltale jam smeared over pudgy lips and cheeks? When she dropped the jar, Maggie and I did our best to wipe up the spill, clear away any evidence, but the juice soaked quickly through the wood floor, staining it forever. We slid our dresser over top, and no one ever knew but the three of us.

The dresser still stood guard over the damage, and in my dream I twisted the rickety piece of furniture out of the way. The stain had faded into a dull gray, disappearing along with the echoes of our childish giggles, but it was still there. I stooped and touched the spot, my heart finally calm, finally strong enough to accept the truth.

"Good-bye, Ruth."

Then I was outside again, but far from the house. I stood

at the entrance to the forest, at the place between the trees where the monsters had ridden through, carrying the three of us as if we were mere sacks of flour. Once we'd crossed into that dark, cool world, we'd lost all hope. I'd lost any sort of courage I'd ever had. I'd lost myself.

Now I stared at the forest, aware of small hushed sounds moving within. A bird fluttered by, and leaves rustled under tiny, scraping claws, but I heard no sound of horses, no gruff male voices. I knew the feel of that cold earth under my back, the unyielding rocks and roots that lined the forest floor, cutting and bruising bodies and souls. I knew the canopy of branches overhead that stretched out limbs to cut off the sun.

"Good-bye fear," I whispered, then stepped into the trees.

Jesse stood just within, waiting.

"You're safe," he said. I wrapped my arms around his waist and nodded into his chest, breathing in his scent, feeling calm and complete.

"Adelaide?"

I sighed and held him tighter, but he asked again. His voice sounded far away, as if it drifted overhead like a wisp of cloud.

"Are you with me, Adelaide?"

The dream. I had followed it here, and yet . . .

I'd never once needed to flee what might happen. And I knew that when I opened my eyes, I would meet Jesse's intense, golden gaze. A long time ago, I'd wanted to run from him as well, I remembered. A very long time ago. But he'd never given up on me.

His fingertips grazed my brow, lifting the fringe of hair and letting it tickle back into place. I sighed with pleasure at the exquisite sensation of goose bumps rising through me. I was aware that I was smiling, but I wasn't yet ready to let the hazy dream go. But when his lips touched mine, warm and gentle, I floated to the surface like a bubble underwater, reaching for the air he breathed.

"There she is," he said quietly when I opened my eyes. "There's my girl."

He lay at my side, propped on one elbow, watching me.

I reached over and touched the soft gold curls at the back of his neck, then pulled him back to me, needing more.

"Dreaming?" he murmured against my lips.

I nodded. "Saying good-bye."

He didn't blink, just stared into my eyes, his own alive with questions. Then he looked away and relaxed onto his back. "It doesn't have to be that way," he said softly.

"Yes it does. We've talked about it, Jesse. It wouldn't work," I told him, squeezing the words through a tightening knot in my throat. I turned my head toward him and tried to laugh. "Besides, you wouldn't want to live with the Cherokee forever."

A gentle, cool gust pushed through the trees, waving the thinning branches like flags over our heads. The season was about to change, but I didn't fear the cold, dark days ahead. Instead, my mind conjured the warmth of a hearth fire, its crackling cheer spread over a gathering of flickering orange faces. The faces of my family, including a little girl new to the family . . . a tiny, dark-haired child named Ruth.

Jesse chuckled. "You're gonna have to make the introductions this time, you know. I wasn't exactly welcomed the last time I dropped by."

So much had happened since then. Since the day he'd first said he loved me. Since the day I'd run away, fleeing to Maggie. I was a different person now.

"Everything has changed, Jesse. You'll be welcomed like a brother."

The look in his eyes held doubt, but his lopsided grin made me smile. "But what about the village?" he asked. "Won't you miss them?"

"Sure. But I need my family, and they need me. And I need you." A thought occurred, and I sat up quickly, shocked that I hadn't asked before. "Why? Did you want to stay in the village?"

He shook his head, but it wasn't the definite motion it would have been before. "You're right, though. Everything has changed. I never would have pictured wanting to stay there, but now . . ."

"You're not angry anymore."

"And you're no mouse." He shrugged, looking content. "Why should I be angry? Everything bad in my life is done, I figure. From here on in, it's you and me and only good stuff. We'll set up our own place—"

"Beside my—"

"Beside your sister," he assured me, "and make some kind of life." He narrowed his eyes. "What about your dreams? Seen what we're gonna do yet?"

"I'm not going to look."

He frowned, but I shook my head. I knew the question in those eyes.

"No, it's not because I'm afraid," I told him, lying back down. "It's because I want to see it with you for the first time."

That wasn't exactly a lie. I hadn't looked ahead with the intent of envisioning our future life, and in truth, I had no idea about how it would be. But without meaning to, I had seen something. On a blanket by the hearth fire, in a room I'd never seen before, little Ruth played with a doll, making the little thing dance and sing just like her namesake had done years before. Also on the blanket, staring up at Ruth with guileless adoration, sat a smaller girl. One with long blond hair, golden eyes, and a smile of tiny teeth that filled my heart with light.

I stared up at the sky, seeing that sweet little face, and felt my entire body tingle when Jesse reached for my hand. We would name her Cherokee.

IF YOU ENJOYED *SOMEWHERE TO DREAM*,
DON'T MISS THE COMPANION NOVEL
BY GENEVIEVE GRAHAM

Under the Same Sky

AVAILABLE NOW FROM BERKLEY SENSATION

PART 1: MAGGIE

From This World to the Next

CHAPTER 1

A Dubious Gift

He has always been there. That fact is as important to me as my own heartbeat.

I first saw him when we were children: a young boy with eyes as dark as rain-soaked mud, staring at me from under a mane of chestnut hair. I kept him secret, invisible to everyone but me. He should have been invisible to me as well, because he was never really there, on the same windblown land, under the same sky. We never stood together, never touched as other people did. Our eyes met, and our thoughts, but our bodies were like opposite banks of a river.

When I was little, I thought of him as just another child. One with a slow smile and gentle thoughts that soothed me, as if he held my hand. When he didn't fade with my childhood years, I began to wonder if he were a spirit, communicating through my dreams. In my heart, I knew he was more. His world was the same as mine. He was as human as I.

I was born in the year of Our Lord 1730 on a patch of grassland in South Carolina. Our pine-walled house, dried to an ashy gray, stood alone, like an island in a sea of grass. Its only neighbours were a couple of rocky hills that spilled mud down their sides when it rained. They stood about a five-minute run from our house, just close enough to remind us they were there. The house barely stayed upright during the mildest of storms, and we had no neighbours to whom we might run if it ever collapsed. When winter struck, the wind sought out gaps in the walls, shrieking around bits of cloth we stuffed into the holes. The cold pierced our skin as it had the walls, and we wrapped our bodies in dried pelts that reeked of tanned leather. Our barn offered even weaker shelter to one aged horse and a few poorly feathered chickens who, fortunately, were good layers. My father owned a rifle, and he occasionally chanced upon a prize from the nearby forest. He also ran a tangled line of traps that provided most of our meals. Beyond that, we had little. What we did have we mended many, many times.

I was never a regular child, spending my days with nothing but play and chores on my mind. How could I be? My dreams showed me what would happen an hour, a day, a year before it did. I had always dreamed. Not symbolic imaginings of flying or falling, but dreams that showed me where my life would eventually go.

I could also see what wasn't visible, and hear what made no sound. When I was a toddler, my mother encouraged my odd abilities through games. She would pry a toy from my grip and hide it somewhere, then return and say:

"Go, Maggie. Go find your toy."

I ran to the target and came back every time, prize in hand.

Mother said I had "the Sight." I never told her there was more. I never told her about the boy I could see, who spoke to me without words. I wanted to keep him safe within secrecy, as if sharing him might make him disappear.

My dreams introduced me to people I had never seen, and took me to places I could never have known existed. Most nights they appeared and vanished, leaving vague memories in the back of my mind. Other nights I awoke bathed in sweat, drowning in images I didn't understand: hands flexing into fists, bristled fibres of rope chafing my skin, the thunder of horses' hooves. And blood. So much blood.

Mother didn't experience dreams like mine, but she knew I had them. Their existence terrified her. Mother was a small woman of few words. When she saw me awake from the dreams, my head still fuzzy with half memories, her face paled and she looked away, helpless and afraid.

Her mother, my grandmother, had had the Sight. Mother both respected and feared its power. My grandmother saw her own death a week before it happened. She felt the hands as they tied her to a stake, smelled the smoke as the tinder beneath her bare feet caught fire, and heard the jeering of the crowd as they watched her burn as a witch.

Mother told me the story only once. That didn't mean it couldn't repeat itself.

Mother did the best she could. Many nights I awoke in her arms, not remembering her arrival, only knowing she came when my screams jolted her from sleep. She held me, rocked me, sang lullabies that ran through my body like blood. But her songs held no answers, offered no way to chase the images from my mind. She did what she could as my mother, but I faced the dreams on my own.

Except when I was with the boy no one could see. Sometimes he would brush against my thoughts like a feather falling from a passing bird. Sometimes we conversed without words. We could just *be*, and we understood.

As an infant, I lived with my mother and father and our decrepit horse. My sister Adelaide was born two years after I was. When I first saw her, wrapped like a pea in a faded gray pod, I stroked her little cheek with my finger and loved her without question. We were best friends before the newborn clouds faded from her eyes. Two years later, she moved out of her crib and my bed became ours.

Our brother was born that year. He died before he drew his first breath. We named him Reuben and buried him next to the barn.

Little Ruth arrived on a cloudless day in March when I was six. Ruth Mary Johnson. She was soft and fair and filled with light. Even my father, a man with little patience and less affection, gentled at the sight of her.

Neither one of my sisters had the Sight. Like my mother, they were slender and delicate, like fair-skinned deer. My mother's skin was always so pale, even under the baking sun, she looked almost transparent. The only way to bring colour to her cheeks was to make her laugh, and my sisters and I did our best to paint them pink. I took after my father, with his brown hair and plain face, though my hands weren't as quick to form fists as his. My arms and back were built for lifting.

By the time I turned seven, my dreams had become more vivid, and more useful to the family. I was able to catch Ruth before she tripped down a hill, able to find a scrap of cloth my mother sought. One winter I dreamed of a corn harvest, and my mother, daring to believe, planted a garden of it that spring. Her gardens never provided much food, because the ground around our home was either cracked by drought or flooded by heavy rains that stirred the dust to mud. That summer, though, the corn grew high.

Usually my dreams came when I slept, but sometimes they appeared when I sat quietly on my own. They weren't always clear. Most of the time they had faded into wisps of thought by the time I came back into focus, but they never fully disappeared.

My mother and I never talked about my dreams. Neither of us acknowledged them out loud.

Just like we never talked about my father's death.

It happened on the night of my seventeenth birthday.

I dreamed of a wheel from our wagon, its spokes blurred to a quick gray. Our ancient gelding pulled the bumping wagon over a moonlit ridge as my father returned from a late trip to town.

He slumped on the wagon bench, his weary body jiggling over every bump. I saw him lift his chin and glance toward the sky. Low-lying storm clouds glowed in the light of the full harvest moon. Everything around the wagon took on a strange orange tinge: the sparse patches of spring grass, the heaps of boulders casting pointed shadows in the dark. Tufts of salted brown hair peeked from under my father's hat, and he tugged the brim lower on his forehead. My father was not a patient man. He clucked to the horse and snapped the reins over the animal's back. In response, the gelding tossed his head and picked up speed just as they reached the peak of a long hill. My father should have known better. The pitch was too steep. Once the wagon started racing down the hill, the horse couldn't slow. The wheels spun out of control, bouncing off rocks and jolting my father so he barely stayed in his seat. He leaned back, lying almost flat as he strained against the reins, but couldn't slow the panicked horse.

The wagon clattered downhill, too fast to avoid a boulder in its path, and the front wheel smashed into splinters. Jerking in reaction, the wagon staves twisted from the horse's harness, ricocheted off a solitary oak, and hit the ground with a sickening crack. The horse screamed and ran faster still. My father struggled to loosen the reins tangled around his wrists, but couldn't do it fast enough. He was yanked from his seat and tossed into the air like a sack of flour. He hit the ground. Hard. His body crashed against rocks and shrubs as he struggled to free himself from the reins, tearing his clothes and scraping long gashes in his skin. The horse raced down the hill, eyes white with terror, chased by the screams and the body that thumped behind him like an anchor.

After a while, the screaming stopped. The horse checked its wild run and trotted to a stop, sides heaving, the insides of his back legs wet with white foam. His nostrils flared, and he bobbed his head nervously at the scent of fresh blood. But he sensed no imminent danger. He dropped his head to a patch of grass and began to graze. My father's lifeless body rolled to rest a few feet away.

The dream ended and I sat up, gasping, the neckline of my shift soaked with sweat. I twisted toward the window, but all was silent, silver under the moon. I threw back the covers and stood, shaking, on the cold floor.

I knew where to find my father's body. Not far—the horse had raced past a familiar oak my sisters and I often climbed.

I woke my mother and we ran without a word along the dimly lit path, faded nightgowns flapping around our ankles.

My father's body was little more than a heap of blood-stained rags. The horse stood nearby, chewing, glancing at us before dropping his head to the grass again. Scraps of cloth fluttered along the pathway the wagon had taken, bits of clothing caught on rocks. My father's tired gray hat lay at the top of the hill.

I stared at what was left of him and wasn't sure how I felt. He hadn't been a kind man. The only thing he had ever given us was beatings.

Still, I should have been lost in grief beside my mother, but my mind was on something else. My dreams had changed. For the first time, they had occurred simultaneously with the event. My dreams were no longer limited to vague messages forecasting the future.

Burying a man in hard ground is difficult work. It took two full days for Adelaide and me to manage a trench large enough for his mangled body. Even then, we had to bend his knees a bit so he fit into the hole. My mother read from her Bible, then nodded at me to shovel the earth onto his body.

Our father had never spent much time with us when he was alive. Even so, the house seemed eerily quiet after his death. It was strange not hearing his heavy footsteps, not hearing him gripe about the sorry state of his life. We mourned, but not terribly. When he left the living, my father took with him the stale reek of alcohol, a sullen expression, and a pair of overused fists.

My mother, my sisters, and I were forced to take on my father's duties, which included driving the wagon to town for buying and selling. The ride took over two hours each way, but once we arrived, we forgot every bump. My sisters and I never tired of the activity in town. The painted building fronts with fine glass windows, the people who walked the treeless street, kicking up dust as they visited the stores. Dirty children watched like sparrows on perches while fancy ladies strolled the boardwalks under parasols, protecting their faces from the sun, tucking their hands into the arms of stiff-backed men in suits and hats. Sometimes they were shadowed by people whose eyes gleamed white out of sullen black faces. My mother told us they were from Africa, brought to America as slaves.

The town of Saxe Gotha boasted more than two skin colours. Fierce tattoos and feathers enhanced the bronze skin and black hair of men who moved with the casual grace of cats. They avoided the plank walkways, preferring the dust of the road under their feet.

My father had told us stories about Indians and their blood-thirsty ways. We had stared open-mouthed as he regaled us with violent tales. So when I saw the Indians in town, they both frightened and intrigued me, but I never saw them attack anyone. They were in town for the same reason we were: to trade. An uneasy peace existed between them and the white men while business was conducted. They brought deerskins and beaded jewellery and left with weapons, tools, and rum. No one spoke to them on the street, and they offered no conversation. Business complete, they leaped onto the bare backs of their horses and disappeared into the shadows of the trees beyond the town.

I felt an odd connection to these men. When my mother led my sisters and me into the local shop to trade eggs or small hides for blankets or whatever else we needed, the other customers avoided us as if they were afraid our poverty might touch them. At the end of our day, we climbed onto our clumsily rebuilt wagon, pulled by the only horse we'd ever owned, and were gone.

We crossed paths with the Indians, but never came close enough to make contact. And yet their images began to appear in my dreams, to emerge from the trees and surround me with purpose, the tight skins of their drums resonating with the heartbeat of the earth.

CHAPTER 2

Battle Dream

There was so much blood. My senses reeled with the unfamiliar heat of it, the stench, the sticky weight of it.

It was more than a dream. It had to be. The images were real, but hadn't come from my own thoughts. It wasn't my bloodstained hand that gripped the slick hilt of a sword.

But I knew whose it was. He was perhaps twenty, a few years older than I, with deep brown eyes. I had seen him my entire life. We had grown together since I was a little girl, in dreams as clear as waking days.

Usually when I saw him, he was at peace. Not this time. His dark hair was pulled back from his sweat-streaked face, tied into a tail. His teeth were bared. He was weak with injuries and exhaustion, disheartened by the sight of an endless tide of red coats pushing toward him through a field of smoke. Muskets and cannons boomed in their wake.

Every one of his muscles ached. I rolled over in my bed, feeling the tension between my shoulders though I was cradled within my mattress. His head thrummed, echoing the drums in the field, the crack of guns, and his racing heartbeat.

I felt what he felt, but my body was miles away. My eyes burned with gritty tears. My limbs were heavy, weighted down by defeat. The stink of sulphur singed my nostrils, and my feet squelched through ice-cold muck while my body slept in my warm, safe bedroom, the air sweet with baking bread.

The sensations roaring through my veins were unlike anything I'd felt before. Fear forced the blood through my veins at an exhilarating speed, but I had to control the panic. He was in grave danger. He needed more than encouragement from me. He needed me to be a part of him. My senses were alive, my body untouched. I gave him all I had, despite the fact I couldn't touch him. Where he felt pain, I brought a healing touch. Where there was dizziness, I gave him strength.

A grunt alerted me to someone approaching from behind. In my mind I thrust out an arm, and the body I inhabited followed. He jumped, reacting to my unexpected presence, and I felt his sense of surprise. But of course I was there. I would never let him die. He took the strength I offered and turned it to rage. He roared, fighting for his life, twisting and moving with the violent grace of a wolf. His sword blocked a strike, although the smoke was so thick I almost didn't see it happen. Steel sliced through the air on his other side, and I turned to foil its attack, knowing he would turn with me. Again and again he blocked killing blows and struck out, cutting through the attacking soldiers. His strength was returning, his confidence back in place. I felt a surge of power as it filled his body and mind.

All the silent communication from our childhood had brought us to this point. I would never leave him. I would be wherever, whatever he needed me to be, if only in his thoughts. I would give him courage and strength and love. And he would give me the same whenever my mind called to him.

Close enough that our minds were like one, far enough that we never felt each other's touch. We were what we had always been.

HISTORICAL NOTE

A Little Back Story . . .

Somewhere to Dream is Adelaide's story, but a small part of my own family history is entwined with hers. I would like to thank my first cousin once removed, Patricia Hanson, for her diligence in passing along the family's stories. I am so pleased that I was able to incorporate this one into Adelaide's tale, thanks to Wah-Li.

As the story goes, in the early 1800s our ancestors, Greenberry and Elizabeth Taylor, came to northern Alabama from Washington County Tennessee (which was definitely Cherokee country), and they befriended the local Cherokees. At some point the daughter of the Cherokee chief fell quite ill, and the medicine men didn't seem able to do anything for her. Patricia's great-great-great-grandmother treated the girl with some "white man" medicine and managed to cure her. The chief was exceedingly grateful, and when the Cherokee scouts found out at the last minute about an impending attack by the Choctaws, the chief brought the Taylor family into their compound for protection. Supposedly the other white settlers in the area were massacred. Unfortunately, Patricia has never been able to confirm exactly where the Cherokees and Choctaws would have been in such close contact, nor that there were any actual massacres in this time frame (about 1810 or 1811), but that's the story. Anyway, the Taylors, obviously feeling beholden, asked the chief what they could do to thank him. His response? He wanted them to name their first daughter either Cherokee or Tennessee. Unfortunately, their first daughter had already been christened, but they promised to name the next one Cherokee. Priscilla Cherokee Taylor, born in April 1812, was Patricia's great-great-grandmother.

Rumour has it the Cherokees may have camped on land owned by Priscilla Cherokee's husband, Robert Jemison, Jr., when they passed through Tuscaloosa on the Trail of Tears. Patricia read that they were camped on Hargrove Creek (which runs through the Jemison plantation) when their chief gave an impassioned speech to the Alabama legislature.

The family name, "Cherokee," has since been passed down from mother to daughter for seven generations.